Emlyn Rees is twenty-eight and lives in London. He is the author of *The Book of Dead Authors*, and the co-author of *Come Together* with Josie Lloyd.

'Anyone who enjoyed Alex Garland's nightmare travel novel *The Beach* should get a kick out of *Undertow* ... an excellent modern thriller'   *Mirror*

'Brilliant'   *Mail on Sunday*

'Wonderfully black ... well plotted, spooky and in splendidly bad taste'   *Evening Standard*

'This dark, twisted tale of secrets, lies and the occasional dead body is an absolute must ... Emlyn has managed to create a world that sucks the reader in and leaves you tearing through the pages desperate to find out what happens next ...'   *Ipswich Evening Star*

undertow

EMLYN REES

review

First published in 1999
by HEADLINE BOOK PUBLISHING

First published in paperback in 1999
by Review

An imprint of Headline Book Publishing

10 9 8 7 6 5 4 3 2 1

ISBN 0 7472 5722 1

Printed and bound in Great Britain by
Clays Ltd, St Ives plc.

Headline Book Publishing
A division of the Hodder Headline Group
338 Euston Road
London NW1 3BH

www.reviewbooks.co.uk
www.hodderheadline.com

For my mother, Anne Rees, with all my love

ACKNOWLEDGEMENTS

Many thanks to Bill Massey, Paul Copperwaite and all at Headline.

Also thanks go to Jonny Geller and the Curtis Brown team, for top advice, support, and lunches . . .

Additional thanks to Patrick "Legal Eagle" Howarth for help with the technical stuff. And finally to Jo Lloyd, my erstwhile partner in crime, for continuity checks and fun.

CHAPTER ONE

kudos

When the LAPD, alerted by reports of a gun shot, broke down the door of Peter Headley's apartment at ten minutes before ten o'clock on the morning of Friday 14th August 1998, they discovered him slumped in an armchair, facing the television.

On the table to his left was a bottle of Jack Daniels, a glass containing ice which had not yet melted, a silver Zippo lighter engraved with his name, a crystal ashtray with the singed butt of a Marlboro cigarette rested on its rim, and a computer printout, three columns wide and thirteen rows deep, detailing names and dates and places.

His right hand lay on his lap, wrapped around an antique Luger pistol. An undried fresco of brain and blood and bone was behind his head. On top of the television, a video camera had been positioned, pointing at the chair. Its red record light was on.

James Sawday stopped typing, looked up from the screen of his laptop and checked his watch: twelve-fifteen. His hand squeaked against the cab window as he wiped the condensation away and gazed outside. The warehouses, hotels and carparks of Heathrow airport had been replaced now by the imposing facades of Knightsbridge department stores. The traffic was boot to bumper, but still a blessing compared to the gridlock he'd grown used to in L.A. The weather, though – he watched the rods of October rain pummelling the pavement and pedestrians – he would have traded for L.A. smog without a second thought. He rubbed his eyes, screen fatigue or flight fatigue – he wasn't sure which was affecting him worse – making him regret his decision to report into the office before going home.

Twenty minutes later, the cab pulled up in a street off Soho Square. James paid the driver, stashed his laptop back in his courier bag and dragged his battered suitcase with him. By the time he reached Hinton House, his white t-shirt had turned grey with rain. The wet soles of his trainers squeaked as he crossed the marbled reception to the lifts.

On the way up to the fifth floor, he checked his reflection in the mirrored wall. He look wasted, like he'd been out on a week-long bender. A crop of two day stubble patterned his jaw and dark pouches protruded beneath his eyes. His hair, darkened by the rain, so that it no longer matched his soft brown eyes, hung down over his forehead in long greasy curls. Even with a tan, his complexion, which normally led people to place him nearer twenty than thirty, was dull. He looked like he needed a hot bath, a hot meal and a good night's sleep. He looked like he needed someone to look after him.

He looked like the kind of man Peter Headley would have invited home and tended and cared for, propped up with a pillow and covered with a blanket, before picking up a baseball bat and beating their skull to a pulp.

James shook his head in an attempt to shake the thought, but it wasn't having any of it, stuck to him like a leech. Headley, although deceased, had been living in his head for the best part of two weeks now, since he'd gone over to L.A. to research the life that had led to his suicide two months previously. He'd taken up resident's rights and wasn't budging an inch, and the sooner James put the article to bed and evicted him, the better.

He stepped out of the lift, crossed the two yards of chequered carpet to the double glass doors and punched the code into the key pad. The lock buzzed and he pushed the door open with his foot and stepped inside.

'Hello, you're through to Kudos,' Marcus answered the reception phone, glancing up from his desk and waving at James, rolling his eyes as he finished reciting the company's official business greeting: 'The *only* men's magazine you'll ever need.'

James dumped his suitcase next to a rainforest of potted plants and put his courier bag on the reception desk, waited for Marcus to finish with the caller. He checked out the framed covers on the wall – ten editions in all, since *Kudos* had been launched back in January. He picked up a copy of the October edition from a display rack next to the desk, lingered over the cover shot of Winona Ryder for a couple of seconds, before flipping it open, leafing through, checking out what people had been up to since he'd been away.

'Yo, dude,' said Marcus, fixing a grin on James. 'Good time in Californ-I-A?'

'Spot on,' James said, rummaging through the papers in his bag. 'Even picked you up a souvenir . . .'

Marcus got to his feet and leant across the desk, peered down expectantly. 'Let me guess. A Raiders cap? A bag of crack? What was it you were doing out there? Oh, yeah, the Headley piece. Shit, if it's a dismembered hand or penis, you can keep it—'

'Not funny,' James said, locating the demo tape.

'Gross stuff, I take it?' Marcus asked, the mischievous sparks in his eyes doused.

'Gross doesn't come close. Even writing it up makes me want to puke.' James handed the tape over. 'But this has got nothing to do with that.'

Marcus read the label on the box and his smile returned. 'Nice one.'

'Album's released here in October, so keep it under your hat. Don't go bootlegging it.'

'Now what makes you think I'd do a thing like that?' James's raised eyebrows answered his question. 'So, where d'you get it?'

'Off the man himself. Met him at a club launch. He'd just come from the studio.'

3

Marcus rolled his eyes. 'Jesus, you lucky bastard. You get an interview off him?'

'Yeah, not long, though. I'll work it up into a profile. See what Jake reckons.'

'He'll love it. He packs you off Stateside to do some piece on that Headley nut and you come back with this, as well. He's gonna ask you to fucking marry him.'

James glanced at the clock on the wall. 'Is he in yet?'

'Is he ever out? Said he wanted to see you, soon as you got back. Got something for you.'

'Great,' James said, gathering up his bag and suitcase and heading down the corridor into the swarm of bodies and buzzing voices. 'More work. Just what I need.'

'Trouble with being good,' Marcus called after him. 'There's *always* more work.'

Jake was pacing up and down by the window in his office, taking in the view of Soho. At twenty-nine, only two years older than James, he was the youngest magazine editor in London. Dressed in creased Armani jeans, cowboy boots so beaten it was a wonder they hadn't pressed charges, and a t-shirt covered with a faded print of Jack Kerouac's face, he was talking – or, rather, shouting – hands-free into the speaker behind him on the desk, sucking on a cigarette like a straw.

'I need tits, tits and legs and butts. Ask round the photo agencies. She's bound to have done some skin flicks to kick-start her career. OK? That OK? Good. No, no one's gonna give a shit about her being into Zen Buddhism. Not unless you got an angle. You got an angle? She into that Tantric sex crap? Does she chime when she orgasms? No? Well fuck it, then. Dig up some dirt. I wanna know who she's fucked, who she's fucking now and who she's gonna fuck next. And I wanna know how much she enjoys it. I wanna know what she likes. D'you follow? Yeah? Well, sort it out. I've paid for you to go half-way round the world, so don't go telling me there's no story, OK? That's just P.R. bullshit. That's just what they want us to think. Believe me, with a body like that, she's gonna have a sex history as long as her fucking legs.' He laughed at his own joke, turned round and noticed James, nodded him towards the sofa, leant over the desk and stubbed out his cigarette in a Quaglino's ashtray. 'Yeah, yeah. Good. OK. You do that. Speak to you later.'

'Hollywood wives feature?' James asked as Jake stabbed his finger at the speaker and disconnected the line.

Jake nodded his head, slumped into the high-backed armchair behind his desk. 'Can't keep anything from you, can I, sleuth? Like having Miss fucking Marple on the staff.'

'Who've you got out there?'

'Lee Rickman. Calls himself a journalist. Bollocks. Way he's acting up at the moment, he couldn't find dirt up a tramp's arsehole.' Jake pulled his desk draw out. 'Shut the door and pull the blind down for us, will you?'

James did as requested and returned to the sofa, watched Jake cut a couple of lines of coke on his desk and snort them up.

'Want some?' he asked James. James shook his head. Jake rubbed at his nose, sniffed and closed his desk drawer. 'Course not. You don't, do you? Never did get round to asking you why.'

'Just because.'

'Yeah, but "just because" what?'

'Because I'm mad enough already?' James suggested. 'Because if I stuck anything more stimulating than my finger up my nose, I'd end up scrabbling round the floor of a nut-house, thinking I was a gerbil called Clive?'

Jake stared hard at James for a few seconds. 'Good point.' He continued to stare. 'You look shit, by the way.'

James studied Jake's own dishevelled appearance and decided to take this a compliment. 'Thanks.'

Jake walked over to the fridge and took out a bottle of beer, flipped the top on his teeth, spat it onto the floor and drank. He waggled another bottle at James, who shook his head, then replaced it in the fridge and returned to his chair.

James was thinking of the cool sheets and soft mattress waiting for him back at his flat. 'Marcus said you wanted to see me,' he said.

'Yeah?' Jake ran his hand back through his greasy mop of hair. 'Oh, yeah. How was L.A.?'

'L.A. was great. Pure Steve Martin. Insane people paying insane prices to indulge in insane activities.'

'And Peter Headley?'

'Peter Headley was too insane – even for L.A.'

'Uh-huh. Gonna make a good piece?'

'Gonna make a sick piece.'

'Sick is good. Sick I can live with. Sick's what our readers love. When can you have it on my desk?'

'End of the week.'

'Cool.'

James pulled a packet of cigarettes from his pocket, lit one. His bed was still beckoning. 'I take it you've got something for me.'

'Yeah? Any idea what?'

'Well,' James considered, 'It could be a rise —'

'Nope. Doesn't ring any bells.'

'An all expenses paid trip to Switzerland with next month's cover girl thrown in for good measure?'

'Nope. Not even getting a tinkle there.'

'An assignment, then?' James suggested. 'I know it's unlikely, you considering doing anything other than rewarding me after I've spent the last fortnight sifting through data and photos on dismembered bodies . . . but it's possible, I suppose.'

Jake clicked his fingers. 'Well deduced, Marple. It *is* an assignment.' He rifled through the spread of magazines and photos and newspapers on his desk. 'What d'you know about Grancombe?'

James hesitated for a moment, then said, 'Typical tourist town. Down on the coast. English Riviera. Surfers. Buckets and spades and sewage pipes emptying into the bay.'

'Yeah, that's the one. Only not so much typical. Not unless you fall for the Tourist Board line, anyhow. Some murders there back in 1989. Serial stuff. Sick stuff. Like Headley, only a lower body count. You remember?'

Nothing.

Nothing.

6

James remembered nothing.

His heart was pounding. He walked to the fridge and took a beer. He drank quickly, washed down the nausea that had suddenly risen in his throat. 'Yeah,' he said, crossing to the window, 'I remember.' He opened the window, flicked his cigarette out and turned to face Jake. 'Long time ago. Old news.'

Jake slid a tabloid paper off the desk, pushed it into James's hands. 'Not anymore, it isn't. This broke while you were away. Week or so back, now.'

James unfolded the paper. The front page headline read, *RETURN OF THE GRANCOMBE AXE KILLER*. But it wasn't the headline his eyes settled on. It was the eyes of the black and white photograph of the victim. It was the eyes of Daniel Thompson that bored into his own. His mouth opened involuntarily, his tongue sticking to the roof of his mouth, forming the word 'no'. He heaved breath into his lungs. The paper was shaking in his hand, the photograph sliding into animation. Daniel Thompson was moving. He was lifting off the page, inflating from two dimensions into three. His hand was reaching out for James.

James closed his eyes.

Nothing.

Nothing.

He remembered nothing.

'You all right?' Jake asked. 'For someone who doesn't do coke, you got the shakes pretty bad.'

Jake's words came at James like an alarm breaking into sleep. It took him whole seconds to open his eyes, realise where he was.

'Few too many comp drinks on the flight,' he mumbled, trying to steady his hand. He closed his eyes again, counted to ten. When he opened them, his hand had stopped moving. He looked down at the paper. Thompson had stopped moving, too. 'I'm fine,' he said, and read on:

Almost a decade after Kenneth Trader's body was discovered in the woods above Grancombe's South Beach, the Grancombe Axe Killer has struck again.

The body of Daniel Thompson, 27, was found yesterday morning by Tony Monckton, a tourist, while he was walking along the picturesque cliff top.

Thompson, who had been a known associate of Trader's before he was murdered, was lying less than fifty foot from where Trader had been found.

James's eyes swam out of focus. The print blurred. He felt his grip weakening on the paper, as if it was melting back into the pulp from which it had been dried, as if the past was jumping back into existence. He dropped it on Jake's desk.

'So?' Jake asked.

James drank again, concentrated on the taste of the beer.

'So, it's not old news,' he said. He paced across the room, lit another cigarette, stared at the door handle. He wanted to run. He wanted to run out of here now and not come back. But he couldn't. He wasn't a kid anymore. He had to deal with it. 'So what?' he asked. 'What's it got to do with me?'

Jake's eyes narrowed, scrutinised his face. 'Are you sure you're all right?'

No. No, he wasn't all right. His world had just split beneath him, sent him tumbling through space. Jesus. Why now? After all this time? How could this be happening? He closed his eyes. Bad dream. Make it go away. Daniel Thompson is nothing to me. So what if he's dead? It means nothing. It means – his eyes settled on the newspaper on Jake's desk – he doesn't even exist anymore . . .

'I told you,' he said, forcing the words from his mouth, telling himself, as much as Jake. 'I'm fine. Just fine.'

'Well, if you're just fine, how come you can't guess exactly what it's got to do with you? What's with the disingenuous crap?'

Jake was right. There wasn't any point in playing games. Better just to come out with it. So he did: 'I'm not doing it.'

'Not doing what?'

'Covering it,' he stated, looking Jake in the eyes. 'I'm not covering the story.'

Jake leant forward over his desk. 'Mind telling me why the fuck not?'

'I don't know.' James couldn't concentrate, needed out, needed out now. He groped around for a reason. 'The Headley thing. It's freaked me out. I need some time away from that sort of story. I want to do something fresh. I need to clean my head.'

'So get some fucking shampoo.'

James didn't laugh. 'I mean it.'

Jake looked down at his desk, as if it was somehow easier to discuss emotions with than James. 'Look, James, I can relate, yeah? We've all done shit stories. We've all been freaked before. But you get over it. You get over it and you get on with what comes next. You do your fucking job.'

'I'm not doing it,' James repeated.

'But it would be perfect,' Jake countered, looking up, his eyes bright, sensing a kill slipping from him, determined to run it down. Closure. James could feel him going for it. Don't take no for an answer. Pitch and close. 'Think about it,' Jake continued, 'We run the Headley piece alongside a piece on the Grancombe Axe Killer. American versus British psycho. It's fucking perfect.'

James felt his in-flight breakfast preparing for take-off.

'You make it sound like a sports fixture,' he said.

But the pitch kept on coming. 'It's an angle, James. Nothing more. It gets us a jump on the competition. It gives us edge. You get your arse down to Grancombe and hang out there for a week. You talk to the pigs and you talk to the locals and you talk to the tourists, and you find out what it's like living with the knowledge that there's a serial killer on the loose. You get into their heads and we print it. It's no big deal, not like I'm asking you to profile the killer like you did with Headley. They haven't even caught the killer, so there won't be any psych shit. There's nothing there that's going to go fucking with your head.'

'I'm not doing it, all right?' James snapped. 'No fucking way.'

Jake sighed and leant back in his chair, drummed his fingers on the desk. 'Listen, you're tired. I can see that,' – he jabbed a finger at James – 'even if you can't. You're not thinking straight. Why don't you get yourself home and get some sleep? And when you wake up, just think it over. That's all I'm asking. Think it over and we'll talk it through tomorrow morning, OK?' James didn't answer. 'I said OK?'

'OK,' James said.

'Good.'

James was back in his flat. If he'd had anything left in his stomach to vomit, he would have plastered it across his bedroom when he woke around eight that evening. But – since he'd left Jake's office and had locked himself in a cubicle in the gents, and had introduced a new kind of American fast food to Britain – he hadn't been able to hold anything down. So nothing but air came up now.

Forget.

Don't get drawn by the undertow.

Don't think about it.

Bury it again.

Deep.

But the image of Daniel's Thompson's face staring into his own after all these years wouldn't leave him, no matter how much he begged it to. Ghosts. Ghosts return to haunt the people who could have made a difference. Ghosts come back for the people who could have kept them alive. And only the guilty believe in them. Only the guilty can't make them go away.

James stumbled through to the bathroom, shut himself behind the glass door of the shower, and took a beating from the water. He scrubbed at his skin with soap and brush. But, even as he did it, he knew that nothing was going to be strong enough to disinfect his mind, leave him feeling clean again.

He dried off and dropped the towel onto the floor, walked naked from the bathroom back to the bedroom. He passed the windows overlooking the King's Road, careless of what other people might think if they saw him. This wasn't about him anymore. This was about who he once was. This was about an eighteen-year-old boy who'd left this flat seven years ago and moved to Grancombe for the summer. This was about a boy who'd seen too much and chosen to forget, a boy who hadn't believed in the power of ghosts.

Only now he did.

He rifled through the courier bag on the chair by the window and pulled out a bottle of Jack Daniels, snapped the cap and drank. The liquid yo-yoed in his throat for a few seconds, then settled, converting his stomach into a hot water bottle. His breathing slowed for the first time since he'd woken and he settled down by the radiator, rubbing his back against it. He drank again. And again. And then he rolled a spliff, closed his eyes and let the high carry him away.

Later, stoned, he found himself staring at the wardrobe. He got up and crossed the room and opened it, ripped the fallen clothes away from the base, uncovered a suitcase and jerked it out. It smelt musty when he flipped it in two. He stared for a twenty-four-hour minute at its contents.

He dug out the envelope of photos from beneath the papers. They weren't in any particular order: different films; different times. But all from that summer he'd spent in Grancombe. There was one of him lying on a bench on the sea front. It was a sunny day. He looked at peace, midsummer-dreamy, even dead. Next came a load from a party on South Beach. He checked the faces and remembered whose eighteenth it was. Then there was Daniel Thompson, a snap of him, knee-high in water, chucking up into the dusk-blooded sea, unrepentant Fosters can in hand. James quickly slid it to the bottom of the pack, looked instead at one of some girl Dan had been seeing at the time, posing like a catwalk model on the rock plateau outside Surfers' Turf. James hadn't seen her for years – he continued to flick through the deck of snapshots – hadn't seen any of them for years, not since he'd caught that dawn train back to London nearly a decade ago.

He flicked over another photo and froze. Suzie. There she was, sitting next to the fire, feet buried in sand, even more beautiful than he remembered her. She hadn't been looking at him, hadn't known he'd existed. He felt as if a sponge had expanded inside his throat, and he dropped the photograph onto the floor.

The next morning, the first thing James noticed was that his mouth and tongue felt furry. He peeled his lips off the floor and the rest of his body, muscles protesting at every inch, followed. He wiped some stray carpet fibres from his mouth and backed up to the bed, sat down and held his head in his hands. He looked round and couldn't believe what a tip his room was. Rogue Rizlas, record sleeves, CD cases and broken cigarettes lay strewn across the floor, like debris from a rock and roll air crash.

The other thing he couldn't believe was that he actually felt better. Spiritually, that is. Physically, things couldn't have been much worse. But spiritually, things were looking up. The ghost of Daniel Thompson, if not exorcised, had, at least for now, retreated back into the shadows. And with his departure, the ice had melted from James's spine.

He went to the bathroom and showered and shaved, studied himself in the mirror as he brushed his teeth and pronounced himself fit to re-enter the human race, all be it as a rank outsider in the runnings. He dressed, then collected up the photographs from where they lay scattered on his bedroom floor, and shut them back in the suitcase, returned it to the wardrobe and locked the door. He walked through to the kitchen and fixed himself breakfast, sat peering through the steam of his coffee at the wall.

Forget it all.

That's what had worked for him right up till Jake had thrust the newspaper containing the article detailing Dan's murder into his hands. And that's what would work for him now, as well. If the past was a foreign country, then he'd remain an unwavering xenophobe: he'd wear his Union Jack boxer shorts with pride, turn up his nose at the first whiff of garlic, and administer a good kicking to anyone who spoke a different language. If that was what it took to remain an island, to reassert control over his own destiny, then that's what he'd do.

That's what he'd told himself in the months following his departure from Grancombe back in 1989, when he'd moved from London to Edinburgh University and rented a flat in New Town, registered for his Fresher year in English Literature. And it had worked.

Sure, not at first. For most of that first northern winter, the nightmares had persisted, trailing him to the bathroom in the middle of the night, lurking in the shadows in the morning for whole minutes after he'd awoken, leaving him gripped by the possibility that the past had the power to infiltrate the present. They'd left him with sweat-soaked sheets and brow. And they'd left him wondering if he'd ever find peace.

But, with time, the morning hallucinations had ceased and, as winter had melted away with the snow, trickled down the gutters out of sight – as he'd increased his involvement in university and the here and now – even the nightmares had started to lose their solidity in his mind; turned watery too. He'd come to recognise them as memory, not reality. And finally, as he'd come to believe the lies he'd taken to telling others about how he'd spent the year sandwiched by his last year at school and his first year at university (staying with a relation and writing a novel that he'd never managed to find a publisher for), he hadn't recognised them at all.

He'd taught himself to forget.

This was his philosophy, his survival mantra: *Ignore something long enough and it will cease to exist.* It had restored his sanity, kept him going. And he wasn't about to go changing it just because Jake thought there was a good story to be found. Don't look back. Start doing that and you'll stop moving forward. Jake could go fuck himself. James wasn't going back to Grancombe. No way. Jake could find someone else to cover Daniel Thompson's murder, someone for whom it would just be another job and a break to the coast rolled into one. He could send some other investigative journalist down who wasn't going to find himself investigating his own past.

He got up and pulled on his coat, collected the bag containing his research on Headley and his laptop. Bury yourself in your work. Bury yourself so deep you can't see out anymore.

Concentrate on putting the Headley article to bed. Erase
Grancombe from your mind.

He walked down the corridor to the front door and noticed
the answerphone's red eye winking at him. He checked his
watch: plenty of time before he had to be in the office. (And,
after the way things had gone the previous morning, he
doubted if Jake was going to begrudge him a lie-in.) He
picked up a pen from the table, poised it over the note pad and
pressed play.

'Hi, gorgeous,' Lucy's voice crackled out of the speaker. 'If
you're there, pick up. Hello? Hell-o? I'm waiting . . .' There
was a five second pause, during which he could hear her
breathing. 'Guess I've missed you. Sorry. Didn't think you
were leaving for Heathrow till later. Must've been wrong.
Whatever. Shit.' Another pause. 'Oh, well, you'll be back when
you hear this, so I've probably missed you more than I should
by now. And I hope you had a good time and didn't get too
freaked out. And I hope you found time to have some fun, too.
And . . . and call me. Give me a call and let's fix up a time to
get together. Just give me a call . . .'

The machine clicked onto another message. His best friend
David this time: 'Hi, James. It's me. You're in L.A., so I
thought I'd call you in London. Logical, huh? It's about my
birthday. D'you pick me up a present in duty free? You better
have . . . Anyway, the birthday. The big two seven. I've hired
out T-Rooms. Friday after you get back. Bring the delightful
Miss Lucy Skinner. If that's still on, yeah? If she's still your
girl . . . ha, ha. Seriously, though. Do what you gotta do. She's
nice, really. I'm impressed. Too good for you, of course, but
who isn't? Only kidding. But if she's history, then bring
whoever. Even better, bring no one and have fun. Just make
sure you bring yourself. If you don't show, you die, my
friend . . . Oh, yeah, and enjoy L.A., you lucky fucker . . .'

James carried on scribbling names down on the pad as
other friends' messages wound by. Then came a voice he didn't
recognise.

'Hello. My name's Adam McCullock. This is a message for
Mr James Sawday. I apologise for calling you at home, but

I've had no reply to the two letters I've sent to you.' James looked away from the pad to the letterbox on the inside of the front door. He'd forgotten to check it. The whites and browns of envelopes were visible through the wire mesh. 'I'd be grateful if you could call me once you've had time to digest the contents of my first letter. I have something to tell you which will be to your advantage. And, if my letter has failed to reach you, then please telephone me on . . .'

James finished jotting down the number and stared at the name it lay next to on the paper. Adam McCullock. Never heard of him. And he didn't know James either, by the sounds of it. *Mr James Sawday*. No one called him *Mr* except for his bank manager. And, though James referred to his bank manager by a variety of colourful names, McCullock wasn't one of them.

James ripped through the mail: bills and junk. He got to two letters franked with the name of a London law firm last. The first he opened was from Adam McCullock, referring to a previous letter he'd failed to respond to. He opened the second and read what McCullock had written:

Dear Mr Sawday,
Re: Estate of Alan I'Anson deceased
Under the terms of a will made by the above individual, we were appointed executors to the Estate. We have completed an oath for executors and have obtained a Grant of Probate and are therefore entitled to administer the Estate of the deceased. Under the terms of the will, you are the sole beneficiary. In accordance with our obligations as executors, we were required to advertise for information of your whereabouts in a newspaper circulating in the area where you were last heard of. Following a response to our advert in the *London Evening Gazette*, a copy of which I enclose for your ease of reference, we were informed that you are currently residing at the above address.

The administration expenses and debts have now been settled, an account of which is available for inspection at our offices. We are now in a position to make distributions to you as sole beneficiary in respect of your entitlement under the will.

Your entitlement consists of the residue of the Estate, including title to the property of Alan I'Anson. In order for you to obtain title to all real and personal property, it will be necessary for you to attend these offices to complete the necessary paperwork and other formalities.

In this regard, I shall be grateful if you would contact me on the above telephone number to arrange an appointment.

Yours sincerely,

A McCullock

Adam McCullock
Partner

James heard nothing but the rush of his breathing as he read the letter again. He turned from the table and walked through to his bedroom, crawled onto the bed, the letter still in his hand. There were no tears. There was too much fear for tears.

He remembered now. How it had started. With darkness. How it had been that night in the summer of 1989. How the darkness had been there to greet him when the train had finally pulled into Grancombe station.

CHAPTER TWO

grancombe

It was already dark when the train finally pulled into Grancombe station. James looked up from the patch of worn carpet between his feet, pushed his fringe back away from his eyes and watched as the other passengers in the carriage shuffled along the aisle towards the exit. The concertina of bodies squashed to a halt by the doorway – a flesh-and-blood motorway pile-up – as a fat man in a *Guinness* t-shirt at the front simultaneously attempted to keep his three hyperactive children under control and wrestle a suitcase down from the luggage rack.

James pulled his sleeve over his palm and mimicked a windscreen wiper, rubbing a clear arc across the grime of the window. Out on the dimly lit platform, other passengers were already busily commandeering trolleys and studying the maps on the backs of their holiday brochures.

James remained in his seat. Keep it slow. Float downstream. Enjoy the scene. There wasn't any point in rushing. Even excluding the congestion in the aisle, the train wasn't going anywhere. The train tracks stopped here. Beyond them lay Grancombe. And beyond Grancombe, nothing but the sea. He checked his watch: just gone ten. The train had got here early. Alan wasn't due to meet him for another ten minutes. If he turned up at all, that was.

And there was no guarantee of that.

The phone conversation the previous afternoon between the two of them had left James feeling awkward.

17

Understatement. It had left James feeling paranoid, like he'd perpetrated the mental equivalent of breaking and entering, kicking the door down on Alan's personal space and walking dog shit all over his new carpet.

Prior to the call, though, making it had seemed like a good idea, and had continued to seem so, right up to the point when the stilted pleasantries had ended and he'd suggested to Alan that maybe it would be a good thing if he went down to visit him, and was that going to be cool . . .

'Why here?' Alan's voice, monotone and incommunicative, had eventually come back. 'Why would you want to stay here with me?'

'I just thought . . .' And it was here that James had begun to flounder. 'I'm sorry. If you're busy or something, forget it. If it's going to be a problem . . .'

'I didn't say that,' Alan answered. 'I just asked why.'

Why? James knew why. There was an army of becauses queuing up to answer that question. Because he wanted out of London. Because he couldn't stand staying in this flat on his own a minute longer, sensing its walls closing in around him like an iron maiden. Because it was his parents' flat and they'd died in a car crash two years back. Because Alan was a writer. Because James wanted to write, too. Because Alan was his uncle and his only living relative. Because he'd never really got to know him. Because he didn't have anyone else. In his mind, he had a million becauses, but what was the point of voicing them? Alan didn't care. Alan didn't give a damn.

'I'm sorry. Sorry to have bothered you.'

The silence had reasserted itself after James's words. He'd heard the flick of a lighter at the other end of the line and the inverted sigh of a cigarette being drawn on.

'What time does your train get in?' Alan had asked. 'I'll pick you up.'

James had lowered the phone slowly when the conversation had finished. Shit, shit, shit, had chanted inside his head. He'd continued to stare at the phone for a couple of seconds, waited for the paranoia to subside. It would be fine. Think calm, be calm. He'd stood up and paced round the living room of his flat, hopped from one foot to the other like he was queuing for a urinal after ten pints of lager. Maybe his friends had been right. Maybe he should have listened to them.

They thought he was crazy, hadn't exactly gone out of their way to hide the fact when he'd hit on the Grancombe idea. *You what? Do what? What for?* And he could see their point. There they all were, fresh out of school, most of them booting it and suiting it round London to save up enough money to go to Asia, or America, or just about anywhere with bigger horizons than the boarding school they'd been stuck in for the last five years. And there he was, already sorted in what had once been his parents' flat and was now his, mortgage paid off by the life insurance, rent free. He could understand their confusion. It would have taken him half the time they'd have to invest to save up the necessary cash to quit Britain for the summer and check out what the rest of the world had to offer. Even if he'd needed to work to get the money together.

But that was just it: he didn't. Money wasn't an issue, hadn't been since he'd turned eighteen six months before, since he'd got access to what his parents had left behind. Money was the least of his problems; only finding something to spend it on remained.

Sure, he could have booked a flight yesterday. He could have got his jabs and malaria pills and flown to Goa and told his friends he'd meet them there in a couple of months time. He could have gone and slobbed and surfed and tanned. He could have written stories till his pen ran dry and the ink on the paper dried in the sun. He could even have paid for them to quit their jobs and go with him. Or he could have stayed in London until they were ready to leave, undertaken an odyssey through everything the great city had to offer, trawled his way through the pubs and clubs, the arts and tarts. He could have selected any number of these options, as easy as plucking cards from a fanned deck.

Only he hadn't. After a few weeks in London, he'd reached burn-out. Enough of the traffic. Enough of the crowds. Enough of the packed pubs and crazy people. And, yeah, enough of his friends, too. Enough of a bunch of eighteen-year-old kids pretending they were adults, when that was the last thing he thought he was.

So he'd done it. He'd chucked the lot. He'd called Alan.

A glance down the corridor of the train carriage told him it was just about clear; the last passenger was filing through the door. He downed the remains of his Coke and crumpled the can up, first squeezing its centre in his fist, then resting it on the fold-down table on the back of the seat in front of him and pushing down on its top with his palm, crushing it flat. He remembered how he'd watched someone do that when he'd been a little kid and had then attempted to copy the action himself. He hadn't been able to do it. Too weak. But that was then. He'd grown stronger since. Mostly these last two years since his parents had died. He'd taken to working out like it had been an end in itself, had junked-out on the endorphins the exercise had released in his body. The grief counsellor had been right: it had helped occupy his mind, given him something to focus on.

Outside, leaning against the wall at the front of the station, waiting for Alan to arrive, depression descended. How many people had there been on that train? A hundred? More? It didn't matter. All that mattered was that they'd had something to come here for. Somewhere to go. Someone to go there with. Family. Just like the fat man who'd blocked the aisle with his kids and luggage. And a home to go back to after their holidays. Same as James's friends in London. Only playing at adventure and dislocation for kicks. Knowing that if things screwed up they'd always have some safe haven to return to. But not him. Not James. James was playing this game for real. Forget games. James had been doing this independence thing for the last two years. There wasn't anything fun or challenging about it. No one to lean on for support if his own legs gave way. Nowhere to run to when it got tough. Only him. Only here. Only wherever he was with himself.

The front of the station remained busy for about twenty minutes. James watched as, one by one, the other people who'd travelled down to the coast from London set off into Grancombe Town on foot, or climbed, laughing and chattering, into the backs of minibuses with camp site names stencilled on their sides. The string of taxis at the rank steadily reduced, until only a solitary vehicle remained. Its driver, sat hunched over his newspaper – basking in the glow of the car light like someone topping up their tan on a sun bed – was sipping from a polystyrene cup, occasionally glancing in his wing mirror at James with a vulture's knowing eyes.

James slipped his wrist from his cuff yet again and examined his watch. Alan was now half an hour late. Despite the earlier heat of the night, James was beginning to wish he'd worn a jacket. Five more minutes, then he'd prove the cab driver right and wander over and surrender Alan's address. He looked across the carpark and beyond, into Grancombe. From here, he could see straight down Grancombe High Street, all the way to where its hard black surface was replaced by the shifting, wind-blown sands of North Beach, the largest of Grancombe's two beaches, the one where the lazy majority of tourists would group together and stare out across the sea at the distant, craggy coast of Wales.

The High Street was manic with Saturday night activity. Sporadically, groups of people swayed across the road, exchanging one pub for another, heading towards the completion of the hedonistic crawl they'd set out upon earlier in the evening. The sounds of their intoxicated voices reached James's ears, leaving him feeling more isolated than ever. He turned his eyes away, examined the rest of the town. Other streets ran off on either side of the High Street, lit signs, hanging above every third door, advertising hotels or bed-and-breakfasts.

From where James was looking, it seemed as if the streets of the town might multiply away from the High Street forever, encircling the whole coast of Britain. But James had been here before. His current view was the result of an optical illusion. If he were to walk to the front of the carpark and look left and right, he'd see how the town ground to a halt after a five minute walk in either direction, petered out up the hill after five hundred yards. His stare consolidated on the High Street once more. Four people – two guys and two girls –

detached themselves from a larger group at the top of the street and started across the road towards the carpark. James looked at his watch, inwardly cursed; Alan wasn't going to show.

He got to his feet and slung his backpack over his shoulders and set off across the carpark towards the cab. The driver, noticing his progress, put his paper aside, started the engine and wound down the window. James reached him, rested his hands on the roof above the driver's window, and leant down to talk to him. Then he heard footsteps and looked up.

The four people he'd seen crossing the street were now standing on the other side of the cab. Up close, he could see that they were about the same age as him. One of the guys, about six foot two, a couple of inches taller than James, with cropped blond hair, wearing a ripped T-shirt with a faded surf logo on it, stared into James's eyes and slowly shook his head.

'Sorry, mate,' he said, his voice deep, its accent local. 'This one's ours.'

James checked out his three companions. The other guy was shorter, sinewy, like some actor out of a special forces movie. His hair was shoulder-length, black. He was wearing oval, mirrored shades and a shirt with its sleeves rolled up over his elbows. The tail end of a black tattoo showed at the bottom of his left bicep. On either side of him stood the two girls, both with fiercely bleached hair: surf chicks. They were drunk, or high, their retinas dilated. They reminded James of some women he'd once seen in an Andy Warhol film *Chelsea Girls*. One of them slipped her arm round the waist of the guy with the shades, whispered something into his ear and giggled. He didn't smile back. James slipped his backpack off his shoulders, walked to the back of the cab and opened the boot.

The stocky guy's face scrunched up. 'What d'you think you're doing?'

James threw his backpack into the boot and slammed it shut. 'I was here first,' he said, returning to the side of the cab and opening the passenger door.

'The fuck you were, tourist twat. I was born here. You just stepped off the fucking train.'

Both girls laughed and the stocky guy started off round the car. James released the car door and turned to face him. He wasn't backing down on this one. He'd learnt that a long time ago. Ground rule one: never back down to anyone. Do that and they're going to see you're weak and do you over anyway. When you don't have anyone to rely on, you learn to rely on yourself. He'd learnt that, too, these last few years. He checked on the sinewy guy. He hadn't moved, but a thin, anticipatory smile had spread across his lips. James turned back and watched as the stocky guy opened the boot and removed the backpack, held it up easily with one arm, as if it were packed with feathers. He stepped back, his calf muscles bulging bare beneath his long shorts.

'Will you kids just pack it in?' the cab driver implored half-heartedly out of the window.

'Who rattled your cage?' the stocky guy asked, before looking back at James.

James hadn't taken his eyes off him. 'Put it down,' he said. 'Now.'

The stocky guy just shook his head again and moved back a couple of paces. 'Come and get it,' he challenged with a sneer.

'Just get in,' James heard the other guy saying, and turned to see him holding open the back door of the cab and pushing the two girls inside. James span back to face the stocky guy, determined now to cut to the chase and make a lunge for the backpack.

He never got the chance. The backpack zoomed into close-up. It hit him full in the face before he could duck, smashed him back onto the ground. For a moment, he lay there, disoriented, conscious of the mess of clothes and possessions – *his* clothes and possessions. Then he threw the backpack aside and struggled to his feet.

The cab was already moving, the stocky guy nowhere to be seen. Instinctively, James chased the red glow of the tail lights for a few yards, then quit. He watched the cab reach the road and pull out. The guy in the shades was in profile, framed in the open back window. He looked across the carpark at James and slowly raised his arm, saluted him with his middle finger. Then the cab disappeared down the street, into the night.

James stood stationary for a moment, staring at the empty space where the cab had disappeared. He blinked. Here he was in Grancombe, already marked by the locals on sight as a tourist, no better than the families who'd filed off to their Bed & Breakfasts and campsites. He turned away from the road, stooped to the ground and began to collect his things up and stuff them back into his backpack.

'You done now?' a voice said.

Yeah, right, James thought. I'm done now. He reached for a pair of jeans, encrusted with dirt, and forced them down between the open zip of the backpack. I'm done now, like I even got a chance to do otherwise.

'Hurry up and get your stuff together. I haven't got all night.'

This time, James looked up. Ten feet away, its engine idle, its lights doused, was a Land Rover. In the front was the silhouette of a man, the face featureless in the shadows. James got to his feet. What was this, persecute a tourist week? He'd had enough. He'd been stitched up for a taxi and now some random passer-by was having a pop.

'What's your problem?' he asked, walking over to the car.

'My problem?' the driver in the car echoed, his voice shifting into familiarity along with his features as James drew near. 'My problem is that I've got a nephew who gets his arse kicked by a couple of local brats within an hour of getting into town.'

James stopped still. He peered through the darkness into the car. Then came the sound of a wheel spinning across a flint, and then there was light. The driver raised the flame to his face, torched the cigarette which protruded from his lips. He turned his bearded face towards James and then the flame disappeared, leaving his features cowled in darkness once more.

'Alan?' James asked. 'Uncle Alan? Is that you?'

'How many other uncles have you got?' the voice came back.

Then the ignition fired and the noise of the diesel engine dismissed any thought of a reply from James's mind. He stood motionless for a second, lost for an appropriate reaction. Then he turned, collected his backpack, tugged its zip tight and walked back to the Land Rover. He climbed into the passenger seat and slung the backpack into the back, watched a bony wrist slide out to the gear lever and shift it into position.

'Better put your belt on,' Alan warned, hunching forward and peering through the windscreen, as if there was a storm raging outside that only he could see, sticking his foot down on the accelerator.

James did as instructed. Then, listening to the grinding gears and roaring engine as the car swerved out onto the main road, he gripped the sides of his seat, an apprehensive kid on a fairground ride, and held tight. He watched the streets of the town flash by, and then they were in the country lanes, the car's headlights tunnelling a path through the dark.

He didn't want to think about what was going on. Not about the car's tyres carving out the dirt at the bottom of the hedges. Not about the brambles that shrieked across the paint work and scratched like cats' claws across the windows. Not about the speedometer's needle flickering further round the dial. And not about the blind bends they were reeling into, time and time again. He didn't want to think about any of these things. And nor did he want to address the question which kept popping into his head. He didn't want to address it, because he knew he didn't have an answer to why he was sitting in this car, in the middle of nowhere, in the middle of the night, being driven by a relative who, if the stink of alcohol on his breath was anything to go by, had completely lost his mind.

Blank it out. Make it disappear.

James concentrated on his hands, felt them digging further into the seat, grasping for support and security, locked in the dentist's chair, waiting for the drill to kick into its high-pitched whine and electrocute his nerves. Another blind bend flashed into view, and he closed his eyes against the fear of death.

But it was still death that his mind settled on.

25

❈ ❈ ❈

It had been a different Alan who'd met James when he'd stepped off the train at Grancombe in January that same year. Alan had been standing there on the platform, a bulky waterproof buttoned up tightly against the fierce coastal gale which whistled past the stationary train, insulated like a seasoned sea captain against the elements. His face had been clean-shaven, no sponge of beard there to soak up the rain. He'd spotted James labouring under the weight of his bags and hurried over to help him, taking one of them from him.

'Good journey, I hope,' he said.

James stared into his face, recognising the physical scars of grief that had characterised his own reflection for so long after his parents' death: the spider's web of red blood vessels woven across the whites of his eyes; the swollen sacks of grey below; and the deep furrows in the skin above that looked as though they'd been carved there with a knife. He tried to think of something to say, a phrase that would adequately convey the sympathy he felt for this man. But all he could think of was his own reaction to the hollow words his friends had attempted to salve him with after the accident which had stolen his parents from him for good. Words meant nothing at times like these. Only the look. Only the look of shared pain in another person's eyes.

'I'm sorry,' he heard himself saying. 'I'm sorry. There's nothing else.'

Alan nodded slowly. He swallowed hard. 'I know.' He looked up into the sky. Rain ran down his cheeks and fell from his chin, like tears. 'Come on,' he said, turning away. 'Let's get to the car. If we stay here any longer, we'll drow—'

It was too late. The last letter of the sentence hadn't even left his mouth, but it was still too late.

Drowned.

Alan ground to a halt. The bag fell from his hand. His eyes closed and he stood immobilised, as if someone had pulled his plug, drained him of all his energy.

Alan's wife, Monique, had drowned. It had happened the week before, on New Year's Day. Sucked by the undertow off

South Beach. Dragged beneath the waves, out of Alan's present, into his past. Into another world. From the phone conversation which had brought him from the friend's house he'd been staying at for the Christmas holidays to here, James already knew all about that.

She'd left Alan in their bed, dressed in her swimming costume and wrapped up warm in a track suit and jacket, taken her towel and walked – as she'd walked each New Year's day of the fifteen years she'd lived here with Alan – across the fields, through the woods and down the cliffside path which led to South Beach. And then she'd placed her towel and clothes on the beach and walked across the sand into the sea.

Her body had been found two hours later, bobbing against the rocks at the foot of the cliff. She'd been spotted by a tourist out walking, clambering over the rock pools that the tide had left exposed, trying to work off the alcoholic excesses of the night before with a dose of fresh sea air. In his befuddled state, he'd mistaken the rhythm of the waves for signs of animation in Monique's corpse and had jumped into the sea to save her.

Alan had been out walking South Beach himself by this time. He'd already found her towel and clothes there on the sand, unattended and crumpled, blown over themselves by the wind. He'd followed her footsteps to where they'd disappeared and the wet sea-stained sand had begun. And then he'd heard the mournful wail of the siren coming from the carpark on the cliff at the far side of the beach and turned towards it and run. By the time he'd reached the warren of rock pools below, exhausted, terrified, fighting the urge to retch, Monique's towel still gripped in his fist, the tourist was being stretchered away, wrapped in a shiny, metallic blanket. Two policemen had been standing over Monique's body, staring down, lost for what to do next.

They'd had no words of comfort to give.

Now, on the platform, wiping the rain from his face, Alan opened his eyes and stared into James's. 'She was still beautiful, you know. Even after she died. She was still more beautiful than anyone I've ever met.' His face spasmed and his voice began to crack. Tears blended with the rain running down his face. 'I should have died, not her. She was mine. She shouldn't have been allowed to go first.'

He wrapped his arms around himself and began to sob.

The screech of tortured rubber pierced James's ears. Alan swung the wheel hard to the right, like he was caught in a storm at sea, desperately changing tack. The black concrete of the road disappeared from view and the car tilted heavily, throwing James against the car door, the fairground ride gone horribly wrong. The plastic seat belt burnt across James's throat and his body reacted, froze into a block of clenched muscle. He waited for the inevitable: the sound of rendered metal, broken glass and bones.

It never came.

Instead, out of the blackness, came light. A lit window. The silhouette of a house. He followed the sweep of the headlights. They were on a driveway. The noise of gravel being spat up by the wheels, clattering against the floor of the car like hail, lessened as the vehicle slowed. James heard his breath come out in a heavy sigh. And again, its sudden volume making him wonder if he'd been holding his breath for the whole journey.

'Scare you, did I?' Alan sneered, glancing across, before switching back to the driveway, the car ploughing on. 'Too drunk to drive. That what you're thinking?'

James stared straight ahead. He didn't want to get into this. He was sober. Alan was wrecked. Keep quiet. That was the best option. Wait till the morning. See what Alan was like then. He focused on the land thrown up by the headlights: the stream on the left, running parallel with the drive; the out-buildings on the right; and there, ahead of them, the house itself.

A memory burst like a firework out of the darkness. That cold January day when they'd all returned from Monique's funeral to the house. James remembered how he'd stood on the terrace at the rear of the building and stared out across the fields to the woods which led to the sea. So much beauty.

Alan's gift to Monique on their wedding day. Meaningless and cold and ugly without her.

The car crunched to a halt beside the pond at the front of the house and Alan, muttering something incomprehensible under his breath, got out and stumbled off towards the house. James reached over and turned the engine off, killed the lights and slipped the keys into his pocket. Silence blanketed him. He watched Alan reach the gate which led to the terrace at the front of the house and slump across it as he fumbled with the latch. Eventually it swung forward and Alan with it. Then he doubled up further, as if in some failed attempt to vault it, and the sound of vomit spattering across stone slabs pierced the silence.

James pulled his backpack out from behind the seat and got out, walked round the car and locked the doors. He waited for his uncle to finish. But the noise kept coming like a drain in a storm. James turned and walked to the pond, crouched down and stared into the still surface. He slid his hand into the cool water, watched the moon and stars ripple into a shimmering blur.

When he got to his feet and turned round, Alan was nowhere to be seen. He walked to the open gate and stepped over the puddle of puke. Its scent, mixed with the heavy odour of the wisteria which had colonised the whitewashed wall of the front of the house, rose to his nostrils and filtered down his throat, inviting his stomach to make a contribution of its own. He moved quickly on. The wooden door to the house was open, the light in the hall on.

Inside, there were signs of neglect. Scattered beside the wood-burning stove in the hall was a collection of crumpled beer tins, high-alcohol lagers – the kind of liver-pickling vinegar James had got drunk on when he'd been in his early teens and hadn't known any better. On the extravagantly patterned Indian rug which lay in the centre of the flagstoned floor, was a heavy stain, approximately the same shape as Australia, as if some bored kid had spent hours making it that way. It might have been spilt soup, though judging by Alan's recent display outside, it was probably something less palatable. Dust drifted like television interference in the air below the antique lamp which hung from the thick wooden beam in the centre of the ceiling. As he was looking at it, the lamp shook, and footsteps clumped across the floor above, faded away into silence.

James walked through to the living room and deposited his backpack on the sofa. It was a mess in here, too. Clothes – boots, socks, a shirt and trousers – had been cast carelessly across the floor. A stranger would have been forgiven for mistaking these for evidence of some passionate sexual encounter. They wouldn't have known that sex would have been the last thing on Alan's mind when he'd clawed his clothes from his body and stumbled drunkenly towards his bed.

The kitchen was in a similar state of disarray. Unwashed crockery was stacked in teetering piles near the sink. The sink itself was full of brackish water. Plates and saucepans pro-truded like scuppered ships through its rank, greasy surface, forgotten and left to rot. On the coffee-stained work surfaces were food wrappers and sodden tea bags. And in and around the bin were food tins, some empty, most half-full, and more beer tins; more beer tins than James could count. James thought about opening the fridge, searching for something to eat, then thought better of it. He knew what he'd find: curdled milk, rotting vegetables, rotting meat. He knew this just like he now knew instinctively that his uncle had been rotting towards this state, a process of rapid degeneration triggered by Monique's death. Half a year. Half a year without her. On his own. Left to his own devices. Resorting to his own vices. Left to twist his sorrow and pain in on himself.

James switched out the light, returned to the sitting room and sat down next to his backpack. Who was he kidding? All he was doing was projecting his own experience onto Alan. It meant nothing. How could he know what had been going through Alan's mind over the preceding months, what silent screams lay cemented inside his skull? He didn't know the first thing about him. Never had. His only true memories of Alan were memories of funerals. Recently, that of Monique. And before, that of his parents, conducted in the Putney church on the bank of the Thames. The same church – as someone in the year above him at school had casually pointed out – where the scene in *The Omen*, in which the spire had tumbled from the sky and pinned the priest to the turf, had been filmed.

There, in the graveyard after the service, James remembered, was the first time he'd ever spoken to his mother's brother. His other memories of Alan were emotionally fraudulent, culled from the photo albums of early childhood visits to Grancombe, animated through the lens of his mind's eye into events he sometimes imagined he'd actively participated in. In reality, though, that wasn't possible. In those distant summer days before his parents had fallen out irretrievably with his uncle and aunt, James had barely mastered the art of standing on his own two feet, let alone standing side by side with the adults.

He stood and walked to the window, stared through the purple darkness of the paddock behind the house and into the impenetrable shadow of woodland beyond. He still didn't really understand what had caused the rift between his parents and Alan and Monique. Something to do with money, his father had once told him. Something to do with the division of the inheritance left by James's grandmother after she'd whispered her last goodbye, back around the same time that James had gurgled his first hello. At the time James had heard his father's unexpansive explanation – some five years back now – he hadn't questioned it. Just like he'd never really questioned anything his father had said. He'd been too young to be too curious. He'd respected and trusted his father too much to doubt. It was only recently, now that he'd become older, legally a man himself, that he'd reached the point of maturity where he had questions to ask, answers to seek.

Only there was no one left to ask. No one, but Alan.

He heard footsteps coming down the stairs, a muffled curse. He turned to face the door to the living room. He needed his father. Needed him now. He needed to ask him if the animosity between his uncle and his parents had crossed the generation like some hereditary disease. He needed to know if he'd been

31

left infected. He wanted someone to tell him whether he should stay here, or return to London on the first available train.

Alan, wearing only urine-stained underpants, his belly slopping like an overflow of dough over their elastic waistband, lurched through the doorway and slumped against the wall. For a few seconds, his dark, unwashed hair hung in greasy streaks across his face, concealing his eyes, and then he looked up and slowly pushed his hand back across his brow, smoothing his hair down into a slick. Gradually, his back straightened, bringing him to the same height as James. He swayed uncertainly, a hanged man, as if an invisible noose led from his neck to the ceiling, preventing him from crashing like a packed sack to the ground. They stared at one another for a moment, then Alan raised a hand to his face and scratched roughly at his beard.

'You look like shit, boy,' he said. 'Better get some sleep. Got to get up early. Things to do.'

James didn't move. 'What things?'

'Search party.'

'What?'

'Search party.' Alan's eyes closed for a moment and his brow furrowed. Then he shook his head and started across the room towards the kitchen. 'South Beach,' he muttered. 'Six-thirty. Said I'd be there. Told them I'd bring you.'

'What search party?' James asked, but Alan was already on the move.

James followed him through to the kitchen. Alan was standing before the open fridge, peering inside, his pale skin ghostly in the shaft of weak light cast by the fridge. James observed him in silence for a moment, watched him remove a tin of beer, crack it open and drink.

'Medicinal,' Alan explained, without looking at James, crumpling the drained tin up in his fist and dropping it on the floor. He belched loudly. 'Helps me sleep.'

'What search party?' James repeated.

Alan continued to stare into the fridge, belched again and slapped his hands on his belly. 'Dawes. Jack Dawes. Six-thirty. We'll leave here at six.' He pushed the fridge door shut, dropped the room into dusk, and squeezed past James into the living room. 'You can sleep in the room at the back,' he said as he walked towards the door which led to the stairs. 'You'll find clean sheets in the . . . I don't know.' The volume was dropping in his voice. 'Somewhere, I suppose.'

And then he was gone.

James found the room, but not the sheets. He undressed and briefly entertained the idea of going to the bathroom for a wash. But immediately, a vision of a blocked toilet and a grime-encrusted basin assaulted his mind. He closed the door, deciding it was probably wiser to risk his own germs for a night instead. Shivering, he pulled the dusty duvet from the floor and climbed onto the bare mattress, wrapped the duvet round him and switched off the light. He gazed out of the window. Stars sparked in the black sky like silver studs on a leather jacket. The moon hung low on the horizon, cold and distant.

Gradually, as his night vision increased, certain of the room's features became defined from the murky uniformity that had previously claimed them, made the shift from two dimensions into three. Prone on the soft mattress, his brain buzzing, his muscles tight with tension, observing these forms looming towards him from the dark, he felt like he was drifting on the sea bed. He waited, let the images come. The antique writing bureau in the corner of the room and the simple wooden chair before it. The leather armchair and its attendant footstool next to the window. And the bookcase, rising from the carpeted floor to the papered ceiling. Stacked with books. A regiment of paper spines. All of them Alan's. All of them written by him. Ten published books in all. Every edition of each. Hardback. Paperback. Large print. Braille. And the babel of translations, covering the major languages of the globe.

James closed his eyes, letting imaginary ocean currents wash over him. Ten novels. Hundreds and thousands of sales. Hundreds and thousands of fans around the world. He conjured the book spines before him, watched the lettering of Alan's name which adorned them flickering like the dials of a fruit machine, rearranging themselves into the letters which made up his own name. One day. One day when Alan was sober. One day Alan would teach and James would learn.

CHAPTER THREE

assignment

'How did he die?' James asked, staring across the desk at Adam McCullock. McCullock had avoided telling him over the phone when he'd called him after reading the letter that morning. 'I need to know.'

McCullock couldn't have been more than thirty, and now the conversation had swung to this, it showed. He avoided James's stare and looked through the window, took up the offer of the view across Green Park for a few seconds, adjusted his tie. It was the first time during the meeting that he'd showed signs of discomfort. Up until now, he'd explained the terms of the will to James with professional ease, discussed it as innocuously as the weather. He'd kept things impersonal, consistently referred to Alan as the deceased, relayed the facts of the case, outlined the various paperwork that needed to be done. He'd dealt with the records of life and death, not life and death itself. He continued to stare outside, apparently wishing he was there rather than here.

'Mr McCullock?' James prompted.

McCullock turned back to him. He removed his glasses and rubbed at the bridge of his nose. His hand stayed there, hovering over his mouth as he spoke. 'He committed suicide. I don't know any other way to tell you. I'm sorry. People normally know before they come to me. I'm terribly sorry.'

James breathed deep. It was what he'd dreaded hearing from the moment he'd read the letter. But it was obvious. How else would Alan have bid the world goodbye?

'When?'

McCullock named a date. It was a few weeks before Dan had been killed. James remembered the adage: bad luck comes in threes. He hoped it was just bullshit. Two was enough. He pulled a pack of cigarettes from his pocket, scanned the desk's surface. There was no ashtray.

'Do you mind?' he asked McCullock. Do you mind? Do I care? He slotted a cigarette between his lips, lit it before McCullock had a chance to object.

McCullock opened a draw and produced an ashtray, pushed it across the desk. His nostrils flared as the smoke drifted towards them, making James immediately mark him down as an ex-smoker. 'No, please go ahead.'

James smoked for a while without speaking. McCullock made no attempt to break the silence, reverted to looking out of the window. Finally, James asked, 'What happened? How did he do it?'

McCullock replaced his glasses and shuffled through the papers on his desk. 'I have a copy of the Coroner's report. I can Xerox it for you, if you want.'

'No,' James said, 'just tell me what happened.'

McCullock selected a clutch of stapled papers. He read as if he were reading the news on television, as if the words weren't his and he had no responsibility for the information they conveyed: 'He shot himself. With a twelve-bore shot gun.' He looked into James's eyes. 'Death would have been instantaneous.'

'How long was he there?'

'I'm sorry?'

'How long was it after he shot himself before he was found?'

McCullock licked his forefinger and leafed over a couple of pages. His eyes continued to traverse the print as he spoke, then his cheeks reddened. 'The estimated time before discovery is two weeks.'

This came as no surprise either. Alan had followed the script he'd written for himself even after he'd died. Kept himself to himself, even denied the world this final intimacy.

'Who discovered him?'

McCullock continued to examine the document. 'Two young boys from Grancombe. It appears that they thought the farm was deserted.' He looked up for a moment. 'As I said, the property is in an extremely dilapidated condition. And,' he continued to read, 'they broke into one of the barns adjacent to the main property. They saw him there, sitting in an old armchair and started to run, thinking that he'd charge them with trespassing. It was dark in there. But when he didn't shout out or chase after them, they went up to him and had a closer look. They called the police from the museum further down the lane.'

'What museum?'

McCullock consulted the paper again. 'The Jack Dawes Museum.' He looked up. 'The artist, I believe.'

'There's a museum named after him?'

McCullock checked the paper again. 'It would appear so.'

'What about the kids?'

'I'm not sure I follow,' McCullock said.

'The boys who found him. Are they all right?'

'Well, yes, I think so.' He read over the remains of the document. 'There's no further mention of them.' He rubbed at his nose again. 'There's no question of them having been responsible for the death, if that's what you're thinking. The report makes it quite clear that—'

'No, that wasn't what I meant.' James stubbed out his cigarette. 'I just wanted to know they were OK. It can't have been good for them. Discoveries like that aren't good for anyone. Especially kids.'

McCullock checked the report again, before concluding, 'I'm afraid I can't be much help on that, Mr Sawday. I could give you the telephone number of the police officer who dealt with the matter.'

'No,' James said, 'that won't be necessary.'

Standing on the landing, waiting for the lift to arrive, James shook McCullock's hand and said, 'Thanks for all this.'

McCullock nodded. 'I'll let you know, then – when all the paperwork's sorted out. I'll need you back for some signatures.'

'Fine.'

'Have you decided what you're going to do with the property? It shouldn't take long to get it transferred to your name.'

'No,' James admitted, 'I haven't thought about it yet.'

'No, of course not. All in good time, eh?'

'Yes, all in good time.'

The lift door opened and James nodded at McCullock and stepped inside.

Outside the building, he stood stationary for a moment, breathed in the cold air, watched it leave his mouth in clouds, drift towards the sky. McCullock had a point. What *was* he going to do with Alan's house? The options were limited. He wasn't going to live there. And he didn't want to keep it on as a holiday home. (He'd rather go sightseeing in Baghdad.) So that left two choices: either flog it off or rent it out. And unless McCullock was given to wild fantasy (a possibility contradicted by his sober grey suit and polished brogues), neither option was going to be simple to carry out.

The house was a dump. The outbuildings, too. Even the kids who'd found Alan had concluded that. Hardly the ideal pad for a tourist family to rent for a break, then. That left flogging it off. He couldn't exactly see an estate agent begging for the opportunity, but at the same time, he couldn't see them turning it down either. It would be a hassle, but they'd shift it in time. The right upwardly mobile family or opportunistic builder would come along and see its potential, just as Alan and Monique had done all those years before. And James wasn't in a rush. He hadn't given a damn about either it or Alan when he'd woken up this morning, before he'd opened the post, so why should he let it bother him now?

Hadn't given a damn about Alan.

That would be nice. Get rid of him, just like the house. Hand his memory over to some wide-boy estate agent and tell him to sort it out. Then things could go back to how they'd been the day before. That would be nice, all right, to disassociate himself from what had happened, to think about Alan and not give a damn, not to think about Alan at all. But 'nice' didn't work that way. 'Nice' was what you got when you'd fulfilled your responsibilities to someone. It was what you got in bucket-loads when you knew you'd done your bit and weren't to blame.

But James *was* to blame. Same as with Dan. OK, so he hadn't squeezed the trigger on Alan, hadn't wielded the axe on Dan, but he could have prevented these things from happening. He pictured Alan in his final moments, peering through the gloom of the barn. No James there. No one. Just Alan and the gun. Just him and the cold metal solution to his depression. No one there to tell him that things didn't have to end this way, that things never had to end this way. Then he pictured Dan, on top of the cliff, the psycho pounding after him, hounding him down, splashing his blood up into the winds.

James could have changed that, too. He could have altered history in a million ways, said something to Dan back in eighty-nine that might have sent him on a different path, kept him clear of the one running along the cliff. If he'd stayed in touch, maybe Dan would have chosen that weekend to leave Grancombe for a stopover in L.A. If they'd been friends in ninety-eight, maybe Dan might have seen that there were other horizons to explore than the one seen from Grancombe's South Beach and left it behind, moved to London.

Maybe. There were a million maybes. Maybe even more. There were maybe millions of ways James could have made a difference. But he'd ignored them all. He'd taken the easy route, done the coward's shuffle, shifted into reverse and backed off, kept on shuffling till Alan and Dan had disappeared from sight. He'd done it because things had been easier that way. Easier for him. Only easy – he started the walk down Piccadilly towards Soho – wasn't always as easy as it sounded. Sometimes easy turned difficult. Sometimes easy turned out to be the hardest thing in the world.

Jake wasn't in when James got to the office, just after four. Still out at lunch, according to Marcus. Still on the piss, in other words. James fixed himself a coffee out of habit more than the need for stimulation (he'd had more than enough of

39

that already today), then sat at his desk and checked his e-mail, sorting out the junk and the jokes from the messages from various contacts and sources. Tomorrow. He'd deal with them then. Complications and leads were the last thing he needed right now. He flipped open his laptop and booted it up, accessed the Headley file, read through what he'd done and checked it against his notes. Then, keen to fill the time between now and Jake's return in any way other than thinking about Alan and Dan, he started to type:

When he committed suicide, Peter Ian Johnson Headley was a short, thin man. (He had recently been diagnosed as suffering from AIDS.) Standing five foot-seven and weighing just under nine stone, he appeared, if not athletic, then at least healthy. He wouldn't have looked out of place jogging slow and methodical circuits in a local park.

Photographs from his high school year book show that his facial characteristics had altered little in the twenty-three years since he'd graduated in 1975. His thin, blond hair remained long, with his fringe falling down to his eyebrows, drawing the casual observer into the trap of his eyes. They were, as his mother described them, 'Blue. Incredibly blue. Like looking into the sea on a sunny day. The kind of blue that made you want to smile.'

In his late teens and early twenties, there were no external signs of the path his life would take later. His high school friends described him as popular, his teachers as intelligent. During these years, his homosexuality was invisible to those around him. He had a string of hetero-sexual relationships at both high school and college.

Pattie Estrada, who dated him for six months in 1974, finds it impossible to relate the man who appeared in the newspapers following his suicide in 1998 to the seventeen-year-old boy she knew. 'He was fun,' she said. 'Rebellious, but not stupid rebellious. Not like most other kids his age, just doing it for the kicks. He thought about things too much for that. He wanted to go places most other people would never go, do things most other people would never do. He loved talking about foreign countries and crazy things that other people had done. The way he saw it, you only landed on earth once and you had to get out of it what you could. You had to live, you know? I mean, really live. Try everything. You had to check out the whole deal.'

Kids, James thought. Always categorising danger signs as cool. Never bothering to think about what direction they're really pointing in. But maybe that's the beauty of being young and naive. Not knowing what danger is. Not knowing when to be afraid. And maybe that was what growing up was about: the knowing. The sense you develop for danger. The ability to chicken out of something and not feel you've missed out. The knowledge that being cool can get you burnt.

'Oi, Marple. Get your arse in here.'

James looked over his shoulder to see Jake leering at him, propped up against the doorframe, a cigarette hanging from his lower lip.

'I'm in the middle of something,' James called back.

'So put it on the backburner.' Jake withdrew the cigarette from his mouth and grinned, beckoning James with his hand. 'Come on, we need to talk.'

James noticed that the paper with the story about Dan in it was still on Jake's desk. He sat on the sofa and caught the pack of cigarettes that Jake threw him. He lit one and tossed it back.

'Cheers.'

'So where were you this morning? Oversleep?'

James couldn't be bothered with this. Jake always got officious after a few lunch time beers, started acting like he ran the place, rather than just getting on and doing it.

'No, my uncle died while I was away. Killed himself. Had to go and see a solicitor, clear some stuff up.'

The information had its desired effect. Jake even stopped smoking for a couple of seconds. 'Fuck, man,' he finally said.

41

'That sucks. I'm sorry.' He peered at James. 'You OK and all that?'

'I'm fine.' James felt the need to justify the statement. 'We weren't close. Hadn't seen him for years.'

Jake exhaled, relieved by James's lack of awkwardness, returned to his usual banter. 'Best way with relatives, I think. Keep the fuckers at bay.'

'Yes.'

'Suicide, though,' he reflected. 'That's a tough one.' His expression altered as a thought hit him. 'You mind me asking how he —'

'How he did it?' James interrupted. 'Yes, I do.'

'Only Tim Lee and Mark Lane are doing a piece on weird ways to go and —'

'You know what, Jake? You can be a real sick bastard sometimes.'

Jake shrugged. 'Sorry, mate. Just doing my job, you know.'

'Forget about it. Let's just change the subject.'

'OK,' Jake considered. 'How about what we were talking about yesterday? The Grancombe thing. Axe killer job. You given it any thought?'

'I've been kind of busy.'

'OK, so d'you wanna think about it now?'

'Nope.'

'Well, I think maybe you should. Keep your mind off what's happened, if nothing else, right?'

'You're a real Samaritan, Jake.'

Jake waved his hand dismissively. 'Hey, just trying to help . . .'

'. . . yourself.'

Jake smiled. 'Whatever. So, what's your answer? You gonna do it?'

James had lied when he'd said that he hadn't thought about it. He'd thought about little else. On the walk over from McCullock's office and before that, too. Before he'd even met McCullock, the possibility of Alan's house being his responsibility had weighed on his mind as heavily as if every ounce of its bricks and mortar had been strapped to his back. If Alan hadn't died and it had been just a matter of Jake asking, then it would have been a matter of just saying *no*. Or if *no* hadn't worked, then *fuck off*. Or if *fuck off* hadn't worked either, then *I quit*. But the choice wasn't clear-cut anymore. Other issues had swept into focus, blurred the original picture.

He was going to have to return to Grancombe to sort things out. An estate agent would have to be appointed with the task of converting the property into cash. And then there were Alan's belongings. Someone was going to have to go through them, throw stuff out, keep stuff back, wipe Alan's existence from the place, put his ghost to sleep. And the only someone who could do that was James.

And if he was going to have to return to Grancombe, then he might as well keep Jake sweet by doing the article on the psycho while he was down there. It didn't need to be detailed. He knew enough about the place and its history already for him to keep his investigations down there to a minimum. He could stick pretty much to himself, didn't need to risk getting sucked back into Grancombe. A word with the local rag's editor should do it. Nothing more involved. Only not now, not *get your arse down there Monday*, as Jake would no doubt suggest. There was the issue of the legal paperwork to be resolved before the house was put in his name and the keys in his hand. If James was going back to Grancombe, it was only going to be once. Not for Jake and then for the house. Two birds, one stone. One shot. Clean and quick. Then back to London. Back to the future.

So how much did he tell Jake? Forget telling him his uncle's name. Jake had started out writing book reviews for one of the nationals. He'd probably be able to list Alan's backlist of titles without pause. He might even be able to recite a few plotlines, quote a couple of lines. And he'd definitely have read about Alan's death in the papers. There were sure to have been obituaries printed while James had been away. Telling Jake the truth would be fatal. He could see him now, jaw-dropped, pinned back in his chair, hallucinating headlines, plucking them from the air. James wouldn't put it past him to somehow try and tie Alan up with the Grancombe Axe Killer, hypothesise that the killer had upgraded their chosen tool of slaughter from an axe to a shotgun, changed their target pattern from randoms to icons, pulled the trigger on Alan, popped a local celebrity, fed their own fame with Alan's. A real nineties angle. Keep the information caged: a.k.a. *lie*.

'All right,' James said, 'I'll do it.'

Jake frowned. He knew James too well to just buy this submission on sight.

'How come?' he probed.

'Just because.'

'It's always just because with you. Yesterday no yes. Today no no. What's changed your mind?'

'Dunno.' James felt Jake's curiosity focus tighter on him, like he was on stage. He looked round the room, as if waiting for a prompt to fill him in on his lines. 'Maybe you were right yesterday and I was tired. And maybe you were right about not letting something like the Headley piece get to me. Doesn't really matter, though, does it? You've got your result. You should be pleased.'

Jake grunted. 'I am.'

James got to his feet. 'So everything's cool. I'll polish off Headley and then I'll get my arse down to Grancombe.' He stopped by the door. 'One thing, though. Because of my uncle and all that, I'll need some time off. Stuff to tidy up, you know?'

Jake folded his hands behind his neck. 'Sure. No problem.'

James turned to go.

'One other thing,' Jake said.

James faced him. 'Hit me.'

'That photographer. Freelancer. Did the shoot for your boy band exposé.'

'Lucy?'

'Yeah, that's the one. You still fucking her?'

'If that's your sophisticated way of asking if I'm seeing her, then the answer's yes.'

'It's what bits of her you're seeing that I'm asking about,' Jake said, all grin.

'What's your point?'

44

Jake lit a cigarette. 'We-ell, way I remember – and correct me if I'm wrong – she did a good job last one we pushed her way.'

'Yes, she's good. So what?'

'So you've scratched my back, seeing sense about this Grancombe piece and agreeing to do it, so now, being how what comes around goes around, I'll see what I can do about scratching yours.'

'Meaning what exactly?'

'Meaning I'll keep her in mind for jobs in the future, see if I can chuck anything her way.'

'She'll appreciate that.'

Jake laughed. 'I couldn't give a fuck if she appreciates it. Just so long as she shows her appreciation by appreciating you, yeah? That's what matters.'

James shook his head. 'Thanks, Jake. Very noble-minded of you.' Then he relented, 'Seriously, though. I appreciate it.'

'Good. Consider it done.'

Friday came and David's birthday with it. James hung round work till seven, getting the first draft of the Headley piece finished. The rush for final copy had been negated now that he'd agreed to do the Grancombe Axe Killer piece. He'd polish it off later, probably cut and paste it with whatever he managed to churn out in Grancombe between sorting Alan's house out and getting it on the market. He'd use the former article's strength to disguise what he already suspected would be the latter's weakness. For investigative journalism to work, it required an objective journalist, and James had no illusions on that score. When it came to Grancombe, he was already in it up to his neck.

It was tipping down outside, so he chucked the idea of tubing it over to T-Rooms, opting for a cab instead. In the back, he checked his bag. Inside, amongst all the other clutter, were two boxes, one wrapped in a Waitrose bag, the other given the full Disney Christmas treatment, with gold wrapping paper, ribbon and gift tag. David and Lucy's presents, respectively pragmatic and adorned, real boy/girl. He pulled a card from its plastic sheath and smiled again at the crude cartoon, then opened it up and scrawled a quick, barely legible, 'Happy Birthday, Shithead,' to David.

He weighed the pen in his hand as he flipped over the gift tag and stared at its blank surface. Lucy was less easy to define. He still hadn't quite worked out what she was to him. The tentative reference made to her by David on the answerphone still rang true. Was it still on, the boyfriend/girlfriend thing? Or had it melted into nothing, snuffed out, gone the same way as all of James's previous relationships?

The trip to L.A. hadn't helped. Separate from someone for a while and you either miss them or forget them, right? That was the way things were meant to be, anyway. Only it hadn't happened like that. While he'd been Stateside, the a/b options had been ceremoniously ignored and, instead, his mind had conjured up and settled (or, rather, fluctuated over) option c. Miss her some days, roll over and breathe in the pillow and wish it was her some nights; forget she'd ever existed others. How were you meant to make a decision with that kind of inconclusive data?

He'd met her two months before he'd left for America. It had been in a Camden café that one of the boy bands' P.R. pimps had considered cool and street enough for them to be interviewed and, more importantly, photographed in. He'd got there early to hook up with Lucy and brief her. He hadn't dealt with her before, had needed to make it clear that this was a hatchet job and that the dopier she made the teen-throbs look, the better. He could play the meeting in his head like a segment from a favourite movie. Christ, he could even remember the colour and cut of the clothes she'd been wearing, the sound of her voice and the flash of her smile which had stunned him like a camera.

A couple of days later, they'd met up again, at the office, to run through the photos. She hadn't been in the game long, had only got the gig because Jake's preferred usuals had been tied up (literally, in one case, as a Polaroid on Jake's office wall now testified to the world). Afterwards, they'd gone out for a drink to celebrate and the first drink had flowed into another, and another, finally washing them up exhausted on the bed in her flat the following morning. As he'd lain there, staring through the gap in the curtains at the brooding sky, he'd kept his fingers interlocked with hers, let her continue to cradle him, drifted back into sleep. And, after that, he'd tried to make a go of things, and now, things were going OK.

He listed:

She was beautiful.

She was intelligent.

She even made him laugh.

She was everything he could want, so how come this dithering do know/don't know/not sure? What was the thinking behind *that*? Why was it that every time he started something with someone he reached the point where he doubted he could finish it. Habit. That was a possibility. So many failed relationships over the last few years. Maybe the attitude had settled into his DNA and he wasn't ever going to be capable of settling down.

An electronic bleeping popped his thought bubble and he exchanged Lucy's present for his phone, lifted it to his ear and said, 'Yes?'

'Hi.' It was Lucy. 'I just called the office. You on your way over?'

James checked the scenery outside. 'Yes, should be there in twenty minutes. You?'

'I'm at home. Just got back. I'm going to have a shower, get dressed. It's not smart, is it?'

'A party thrown by David? You've got to be kidding.'

She laughed. 'Forget I asked.' Static crackled along the line. 'You still there?'

'Yes.'

'Don't drink too much before I get there.'

'Why not?'

'I haven't see you in ages.'

'And?'

'And I want you fully functional.'

'In what way?'

'In every way.'

The connection cut and he sat for a moment, staring down

47

at the phone. He *was* looking forward to seeing her, and not just because of the end of the evening his imagination had just projected for him. He hadn't seen her since he'd got back. She'd been off on a job in Manchester for some music mag. He'd called her, but the scratchy mobile chitter-chatter hadn't been enough. He'd wanted to see her. He'd wanted her close. Conclusion: he did care about her. All he had to do was relax, follow his feelings for a change and maybe this time the relationship wouldn't suddenly switch into half-life and disintegrate before his uncaring eyes.

All he had to do was change, have faith in the fact that he was capable of falling in love, remind himself that it wasn't like it had never happened to him before.

He slipped the phone into his jacket pocket and picked the gift tag up again, settled for writing, *A gift from the States. Enjoy*, signed his first name and *xxx*'d it. Then he added, *I've missed you* and attached the tag to the present. He stared out of the window, following the delta of raindrops on the glass.

Wasn't like it had never happened to him before . . .

CHAPTER FOUR

search

'So, are you going to tell me what this is all about?' James asked as the Land Rover pulled to a halt at the front of the carpark on Eagle's Point, the section of cliff which at high tide bisected South Beach from North Beach and the town. 'You said Jack Dawes. What about him?'

Alan shut off the engine and stared across the flat sea and the stonewashed horizon. 'He's a friend.'

James pinched the bridge of his nose with his forefinger and thumb, clawed the scabs of sleep from the corners of his eyes with his nails. Finally, his mind, still moving slowly, an engine on a cold morning, turned over and made a connection. 'Your neighbour?'

Alan turned to face him and eyed him strangely. 'You know him?'

'Yes. The guy from the farm on the other side of the woods, right? The artist. Made a speech at Monique's funeral . . .'

Alan lit a cigarette, commenting, 'You've got a good memory.'

'So what's happened to him?'

'If we knew that,' Alan said, reaching for the door handle, 'we wouldn't be searching for him, would we?' Alan hesitated, stared across the sea again. His expression altered. 'No one's seen him. Three days. Maybe four.'

'But why the search party?'

Alan exhaled loudly, remained hunched forward. 'Why do you think? To find him, of course.'

'But he might have gone on holiday. Anything.'

'What are you,' Alan snapped, twisting violently in his seat to face him, 'a fucking detective? He's missing, OK? Hasn't been on holiday since the day he was born here. Why should he start now?'

James looked away. 'I'm sorry. I didn't —'

'No,' Alan interrupted, his tone suddenly apologetic, 'I'm sorry. I shouldn't be going off at you like that.' He pointed at his head. His hand was shaking. 'Feels like it's going to explode. Feels like my brain's turned to porridge.' His fingers shook as he took a drag on his cigarette. Ash collapsed onto his lap. He ignored it, either not noticing or simply not caring. 'He was meant to be doing a photo shoot at his house three days ago for some magazine. And yesterday, some interview for the exhibition he's got lined up for his new collection. Didn't answer the door for either. Not like him. Murphy – he's the head copper round here – went round and broke in.'

'What did he find?'

'Cooker still on. Bottom of a pan burnt out. Some solid black muck that he reckoned might once have been stew all up the sides. Said it had probably been on for days. Said it was a miracle the place hadn't burnt down. Not that Murphy's word's worth shit. Fucking animal.'

'And Jack?'

'Nowhere. There was the dog, too. Zack. In a complete state. No water. No food. Murphy said he didn't even have enough energy to wag his tail.' He shook his head. 'That's what turned it. The search party, I mean. Jack loved that dog. His only companion. There's no way he would've just left him there like that.'

'So what do you reckon?'

'I don't know,' Alan said, taking another long pull on the cigarette, opening the door and sending the butt spiralling out of the window with a flick of his fingers. Morning sunlight swept across his legs. A light breeze dislodged the ash on his lap, rolled it like tumbleweed across the denim of his jeans onto the floor. 'Come on,' he said, climbing out. 'Time we got going.'

Despite the bright sun and cloudless sky, it was cold outside. Alan walked to the wooden fence at the front of the carpark and leant over it, gazed down. James hooked the small rucksack, which he'd convinced Alan to stock up with bottled water and chocolate bars from a garage on the drive in, over his shoulder and joined him. To the left stretched South Beach, and to the right Grancombe harbour, North Beach and the town itself. Dawn fishermen stood along the shore of North Beach, rods as thin as insect legs pointing at the sky.

James wrapped his jacket closer around him and followed Alan across the carpark to where it cut to emptiness, the drop of the cliff. His eyes traced the zig-zag of steps cut into the rock, polished as smooth as marble over the years by tourists' feet, bouncing the sunlight back towards the sky like mirrors. A gull scythed through the air, then caught a thermal and rapidly rose into the blue, until its body vanished and only the twin arcs of its wings remained. It hung there, seemingly stationary, a cliché from a child's painting of summer. Then, as the sun began to bleed raw onto his retinas, and he lowered his stare, James spotted other signs of life, down on South Beach, this time human. There, some two hundred feet or so below, were people being drawn across the beach like iron filings being dragged towards a magnet, converging at the front of a long, single-storeyed building on a high plateau of rock at the back of the beach. James squinted against the sunlight, tried to read the bright red lettering of the sign above the door.

'Surfers' Turf,' Alan said, as if reading James's mind, setting off down the steps to the beach. 'Let's hope Suzie's got some coffee on. I'm not searching for shit until I've got some caffeine in my belly.'

James drew level with him and they continued their descent side by side. He kept his hand on the metal rail cemented into the rock as he walked. Alan was moving quickly. Certainly quicker than James, on the evidence of the state of his metabolism during the events of last night, would have thought him capable of. Alcoholics. They could defy the laws of biology. That's what James's father had said. Same as amphetamine

51

freaks. Same as the headcases James's father had commanded during the Falklands. Give some of them enough of what they craved and they'd be wired until they killed or got killed. Give them a big enough buzz on life and they'd snatch someone else's without thinking twice about it. James glanced at his uncle. Sweat slid down his brow like melting ice. Stepping down. Stepping down. Resolute. Surfers' Turf. Focused. Caffeine up. Right now, Alan would probably have killed if he'd been denied this one thing he craved.

'Who's Suzie?' James asked, his eyes scanning the steps before him, his fingers still trailing on the rail, confident of his stride now, but wary that one slip would more than likely result in a compound fracture and a screech from his lungs that would rival that of the wheeling gulls above.

Alan was panting when he spoke, but his pace didn't slack. 'You've got a lot of questions.'

'The only route to knowledge, isn't it?'

Alan jumped two steps. 'You've been reading too many books, boy. Life's not that simple. Some questions it's best not to know the answers to.'

James lengthened his stride, caught up with him again. 'How can you say that? You're a writer. How can you say I've read too many books?'

'Some things you don't want to know. Some things it's best you never find out.'

'But—'

'But nothing.' Alan came to a halt. They were now maybe fifteen steps from the bottom, from where the rocks slid into the sand, disappeared to unfathomable depths like roots in soil. He faced James. 'You still want to write, don't you? Just like you were banging on about when you were at Monique's funeral. That's why you're here, isn't it? Because you want to learn how it's done.'

James felt the skin on his face begin to tingle, like he'd been out in the sun too long. He'd cornered Alan after the funeral, at his house, after most people had left. James had been drunk. But Alan had been beyond. He couldn't believe the conversation they'd had had primed itself on Alan's tongue, been left till now to be launched into attack.

'You remember that?'

'Drunks remember everything. That's why everyone hates them. They're the people who sit there till dawn with you and then remind you what an arsehole you've been when you come round six hours later.'

'I'm sorry.'

Alan sneered. 'You can forget apologies. You're too old for them. Anything you do, anything you say – you've got to live with it. Get used to the fact; it's there until you die.'

'And writing. I suppose I should forget that, too?'

'If you can forget that,' Alan said, turning front and walking on, 'then you shouldn't have ever thought about doing it in the first place.'

'So, you going to tell me—'

'About Suzie?' Alan asked, stumbling down the last few steps then sinking his feet into the sand. 'She's young. Like you. Why don't you ask her yourself?'

And then, before James could answer, they were amongst the bodies gravitating towards Surfers' Turf, like supporters swept forwards by a sports crowd. Alan exchanged a few grunted greetings with the people nearby, didn't bother introducing James to any of those who looked him curiously up and down.

They reached the wide concrete steps leading up to the rock plateau. The bodies grew thicker here, the chatter louder. Alan shouldered his way unceremoniously through the crowd, ignoring the mild complaints which came in reaction. James stuck close, trailing in the older man's wake, suddenly self-conscious in the face of this intimate gathering where everyone so apparently knew everyone else. Eventually, they reached the open doors of the beach bar and moved inside.

The rush hour of people jammed into the place reminded James of the London pub that, until recently, had been his local. Squashed flesh. Jabbing elbows. A sauna of other people's breath. Cigarette and pipe smoke drifted across the room, like dry ice in a night club. But the similarity between the two locations quit there. This place was way too weird to

be confused with anything James had encountered before.
Surf boards hung from the rafters in the ceiling, their waxed
surfaces painted with erratic, psychedelic patterns. Photographs of tanned kids against two-tone backdrops of sand and
sea, surf boards standing to attention by their sides, were
scattered across the bright pink sections of wall not obscured
by the current crowd. To the right, tables and chairs lay
stacked on a raised section of floor, next to a couple of
amplifiers. James turned away, followed Alan across the room
to the bar and squeezed in next to him. A fog of steam hung in
the doorway to the kitchen behind. The contrasting aromas of
brewing coffee and frying bacon drifted temptingly through,
clogging the air. Behind the counter, a burly man in an apron
was rapidly logging a serial breakfast order down on a pad.
He finished and looked up, caught Alan's eye.

'Good to see you, Al,' he said.

'You too, Jimmy.'

'Shame about the circumstances . . .'

Alan nodded. 'Yes.'

'Still, bet it'll turn out to be a load of fuss over nothing . . .'

'Yes,' Alan repeated.

James turned his attention from them to the laminated menu
on the counter. The scent of food in the air had acted like a
catalyst on his previously inert stomach, sent it into a series of
spasms and groans. He scanned the available options, searching for a remedy: full English, continental, burgers, fries, bacon
rolls; pretty much what he'd expected.

'Everything's off except the rolls,' a woman's voice said.
'Sorry, but there's been kind of a rush.'

He looked up and she was there.

As his eyes locked with hers, the movie of his life was put
on pause. His sight became predominant, as if the nerve
endings comprising his other senses had been singed, left dull
to stimulation. The sounds of the people around him – his
uncle's grunted conversation and the livelier chatter behind –
cut to a vacuum. The smell of food evaporated. His fingers
clung numbly to the menu. Only her image remained, frozen
there like a still on a screen.

Then, as quickly as it had occurred, the moment vanished into memory. He watched her blink, long eyelashes snapping down, momentarily stealing her mahogany eyes away from him, taking him with them, swallowing him whole. She brushed a hand across her glistening brow, smiled, obviously amused.

She was stunning.

'You look like you've just seen a ghost,' she said.

He shook his head, felt the skin across his cheeks prickle and burn. 'Sorry,' he said, glancing down at the menu. He looked up again, avoiding the time-trap of her eyes, and took in her slender figure, the short black hair tucked behind her ears, the two silver studs in her right ear, the silver star in her left. 'I'm tired. Haven't quite managed to get my brain into gear.'

The smile broke on her face again, more open this time, emphasising her high cheekbones. 'You're tired? You should try serving this lot.'

His stare consolidated on her glossed lips, the crenellations of bright teeth between. Jesus. Just looking at her made him feel like a miniature acrobat was using his stomach lining as a trampoline. 'Tough start to the day?' he managed to say. 'I take it things aren't usually this busy?'

'If only. I'd be able to retire by the end of the summer.'

'You're too young.'

She laughed. 'You're never too young to quit work.'

'No, I suppose not.'

She took a good look at him. 'You're not from round here, are you?'

'No.'

'Well, if it was a quiet breakfast you were after, you picked a bad day. Are you down here on holiday?'

'Sort of,' James said, nodding towards Alan. 'I'm with him.'

She looked at Alan, then back. 'Al I'Anson?'

'Yes, he's my uncle. I'm staying with him for a while.' He offered his hand across the counter. 'I'm James.'

She raised a tanned arm from her side and pushed her hand towards him, before hesitating, lifting her palm towards her face and examining it. 'Cooking oil,' she commented, wiping it across her apron, then shaking his hand. Her grip was strong and he had to readjust his own to prevent his fingers from collapsing inside hers like a child's. 'Firm grip,' she said, releasing him. 'You a windsurfer?'

He shook his head. 'You?'

'Always. That and surfing.'

'Fun?'

'The best. You should give it a go while you're here.'

'When you two are done chatting,' Alan said, leaning across James, 'how about fixing us up a couple of coffees and bacon rolls?'

'Sure, Al,' she said. 'Take away?' She glanced at the luminous hands of her diver's watch. 'I think they're planning on setting off in about five minutes.'

Alan nodded his head and she wrote down the order. She looked at James, said, 'I work Wednesdays at the Surf School on North Beach. Maybe I'll see you there,' and then she turned away.

James watched her walk back into the kitchen, bronzed calf muscles disappearing into the steam. His heart was pounding. Was she flirting? Was that an invitation to meet up? It was only then that he realised she hadn't told him her name. It had to be Suzie. He stayed at the counter, waiting for her to reappear. She didn't. A couple of minutes later, Jimmy emerged with their coffees and rolls and James followed Alan outside.

An injection of order had entered the anarchy of people outside in the form of three uniformed policemen. The eldest, early-forties, with premature splashes of grey on his black hair, tall and paunched like a boxer gone to seed, was standing at the top of the steps with a clip-board in his hand. Must be Murphy. *Fucking animal.* That's how Alan had described him.

'Right, people,' he barked, 'let's get this show on the road. Let's have you all at the bottom of the steps. Good. Quick. Let's get to it.'

Down on the sand, James chewed on his roll, washed it down with coffee, and listened to Murphy explaining what was going on. They were to be divided up into groups and allocated areas to search, the idea being to cover the surrounding shoreline and countryside.

'What happens if we find something?' someone called out.

'Any of you find anything,' Murphy answered, 'whether it's an item of clothing or something else, I don't want you to touch it. Let's all be very clear about this. Just leave it be and send one of your party back here.' He nodded at the other two policemen. 'One of us will be here, so just tell us and we'll take over from there. Everyone got that?' A murmur of agreement ran like dominoes through the crowd 'Good. Now let's get down to business.' He pointed to the far left of the assembled people, the opposite side to where James stood. 'Right. You, Lok Waterstone, Chris Matthews, Simon Crook and Cyrus Mower. I want you to head across to North beach and check out the caves. The tide's going out, so it should give you a good few hours. You next, Hetherington. Take Biff, Helen, Ross and Emma . . .'

As Murphy continued to dissect the body of people before him, James finished his coffee and looked around for somewhere to ditch the polystyrene cup. There was a roll bin towards the back of the left side of Surfers' Turf. He checked out Murphy's progress. Three-quarters of the crowd still remained, standing disinterested or rocking on the balls of their feet with apprehension, like overgrown school kids waiting to be picked for a team. He checked Alan out: cigarette cemented to his dry lips, staring over the roof of Surfers' Turf into some imaginary vanishing point in the heart of the black cliff beyond.

'Back in a minute,' James muttered, removing Alan's cup from his fist.

As he approached the bin, he crumpled the two cups up into a spongy ball at the centre of his fist, drew back his arm and let fly. Aerodynamic, it wasn't. It got maybe half-way to the goal represented by the bin, before it disintegrated like some ill-designed prototype missile, and drifted lazily towards the ground. Half-hearted applause came from somewhere to his right and he turned to the source. The girl from behind the counter – the one he was assumed was Suzie – was standing there, smoking a cigarette.

'There are laws against littering, you know,' she said, moving forward and bending down to pick up the debris.

James walked over and crouched down next to her, collected the remaining pieces and placed them into the cup of her hand. 'You didn't tell me your name. Are you Suzie?'

'Yes,' she said, pushing her fringe back away from her face.

He nodded with comprehension, tilted his head towards the building. 'This is your place, then.'

'Every atom.'

They stared into one another's eyes for a second. He felt his gut lurch, like he'd just driven over a speed bump at sixty miles-an-hour. She was beautiful. Just looking at her, he could see the years multiplying before him, carrying him from first kiss to love. He slammed on the brakes, concentrated on keeping his voice calm, and said, 'Pretty impressive.' He looked across the plateau. 'What is this place? It doesn't look natural.'

'It's not. They used explosives to flatten it out during the war. Stuck a couple of guns here. Invasion fears, you know. I used to come here when I was a kid, just sit and stare out to sea.'

He nodded. 'It's beautiful.'

'So when I grew up, I borrowed money from the bank and got this place built.'

'To let other people share the view ...'

'Something like that.' She got to her feet. 'It's only been up and running a few months.'

'Going well?'

'It's fun, if that's what you mean. I don't think it's ever going to make me a millionaire.'

'Well,' he said with a shrug, 'if you're having fun, you don't need to be a millionaire.'

She rolled her eyes. 'You try telling the bank that.'

He checked her face, saw that the concern there was genuine. 'Tough, is it?'

Her expression shifted, hardened, then relaxed again. 'No, it's OK. Summer's here. Lots of tourists. Things are fine at the moment.'

'Just dreading the winter?'

'Yes. Probably have to shut it down for a while. Go back to working at Dad's pub.'

'In Grancombe?'

'He runs the Moonraker. Down on the High Street.' She looked over his shoulder. 'You'd better get going, you know.'

He nodded, turned round and looked back at the beach. The crowd had been culled to a small group in his absence. 'Always was the last to get picked,' he said.

She looked down at the polystyrene petals in her hand, then grinned at him. 'With a throw like that, it's not surprising.'

'Well,' he said, taking a couple of paces back, 'I'll see you around . . .' It was meant to be a question, but it came out as a statement. But that was cool, wasn't it?

'Could be,' she said.

He waved his hand and hurried back to the beach. He reached the top of the steps and his heart, still racing after speaking to her, ran into a brick wall. The dregs of the drained crowd stood there on the beach. Only two of them remained, standing in front of Murphy and the other policemen. Only two out of that whole company of strangers. Two faces he recognised from the carpark the night before. The black-haired guy with the tattoo, and his sidekick, the one who'd scattered James's belongings like seed across the barren car park. James considered turning his back, playing the tourist and walking carelessly to the edge of the plateau, then lowering himself onto the beach and leaving this whole scene behind. But it was too late. One of them, the stocky guy, glanced up and saw him. He slowly shook his head.

'Well, well, well,' he said, 'look what we've got here.'

Before James could reply, Murphy turned and spotted him. 'You Al 'Anson's nephew?'

'Yes,' James said, watching the guy with the tattoo incline his head towards the stocky guy and mouth something.

'He said you were round here somewhere,' Murphy continued. 'You've missed going with him. He's taken a group in his car. Be back here along with everyone else at noon. Jim, isn't it?'

'James.'

'Well, get over here. I'm Cal Murphy and these' – his mouth pinched in distaste – '*boys* are Alex Howley and Daniel Thompson. You can go with them and check out the woods at the top of the cliffs between your uncle's place and Jack's. We had a scout round there on the day we found out he was missing, but it's probably best to check it out again. D'you know your way round up there?'

James walked down the steps and stood next to Murphy, concentrated on keeping his poise intact in front of Alex and Daniel. No Fear. Just like the logo on Daniel's T-shirt.

'No, never been there in my life.'

Daniel stared at James like he wanted to punch him. Eventually, he said, 'What use is he gonna be? Me and Alex will get on better without him.'

Murphy spun round to face him. 'Button it, all right? You keep your bleating to yourself.' His stance shifted and his chest reared out over his gut. 'Either that or I'll take the pair of you off the search party and it'll be last night all over again.' He took a step forward, glared right into their faces. 'That what you want, you little shits?'

Alex's shades sparked in the sun as, apparently unfazed, he turned and gazed across the beach. Daniel stared back at the policeman for a few seconds then finally grunted, 'No.'

'Good.' Murphy looked James over, assessing him like a collector might a bug, his nicotine stained teeth protruding in a crooked smile. 'Don't mind him; his bark's worse than his bite. Anyhow,' he added, slipping Daniel a sideways glance, 'if these two give you any trouble, you tell me, and I'll sort them out. In spades.' He clamped his hands together and his knuckles cracked. 'It wouldn't be the first time someone's had to knock some sense into them.'

James looked into Murphy's eyes – amusement, or maybe something more malevolent danced inside them – then turned to face Alex and Daniel. Daniel was – what? – a stone, maybe two stones heavier than him. Fit in a genetic sort of way. But not honed, not worked-out. Muscle through nature, not nurture. Visual muscle, nothing more. He didn't look the colossus he'd done the night before. The t-shirt and shorts were the same, but the aura had drained away, presumably along with the alcohol in his bloodstream, left him exposed without his shell. If it came down to it, James reckoned he could take him.

And then there was Alex. Lighter. But of the two, he was still the danger. Even without seeing his eyes – those shades might as well have been surgically attached – James could guess what secrets they held. He could imagine the violence residing at the core of Alex's retinas. It was there in his lazy stance. It shouted through his silence. He was the danger, all right. The one who wouldn't speak until he was prepared to commit. The knife carrier in the night club who you wouldn't even notice until he was clinically spearing your kidney on the end of its blade. James didn't need to see his eyes to comprehend this; it was written all over his face.

'Don't worry,' he said, addressing the reply to Alex and Daniel, not Murphy, staring into the heart of his reflection which bounced back at him off Alex's shades, 'I can look after myself.'

Alex's only reaction was to turn and trudge away across the beach. Daniel spat on the sand between his and James's feet, then followed his friend's lead.

'I find you two slacking,' Murphy called after them, 'you know what you'll get.' He frowned at James. 'Little cunts,' he said, before warning James: 'Like I said, you get pissed off with them, you let me know . . .'

James forced a smile and walked away. He trailed behind Alex and Daniel as they crossed the beach, sand lodging in the grips of his boots with every step he took, inducing fatigue, sapping the kick of the caffeine from his system. Ahead of him, neither Alex nor Daniel was speaking. He wasn't sure whether it was Murphy or him who'd made them this way. He shook his head, cursing the pang of environmental conscience over the coffee cups that had cost him going with his uncle, and left him stuck with these two instead.

CHAPTER FIVE

partner

'Who's that?' Justin asked, staring through the London crowd towards the entrance to T-Rooms.

David looked up and laughed. 'Put the shark back in the tank,' he told him. 'She's with James.'

James twisted round in his seat and followed Justin's stare, caught a glimpse of Lucy, standing in the doorway, pushing her short blond hair back from her rain-splashed face.

'That's Lucy?' Justin asked.

'Lucy,' David bellowed across the room, confirming Justin's deduction. 'Over here.'

She didn't look over, the buzz of the people's voices around the bar consuming David's words before they reached her. She peered around and, still not seeing them, despite the fact that David was now standing and waving his arms like he was guiding a plane in to land on an aircraft carrier, slipped off her coat and hung it on a peg by the door. Then a scrum of bodies shifted between them and she slipped from view.

'Glasses,' James explained. 'She's blind without them.'

'Take it she wasn't wearing any when she met you, then,' Justin said, winking at David.

'Piss off,' James said, getting to his feet. 'At least she's not like the women you hang out with who have to use a magnifying glass to get a good look.' He patted Justin on the shoulder. 'And I'm not talking about your face. No one, no matter how curious, would want a close-up of that mess.'

'Yeah, maggot-meat,' David joined in. 'Shut the fuck up

and behave. You're talking about the woman James loves.'

Justin's eyebrows darted up so high in reaction to this that they threatened to disappear into his cropped black hair. 'Love? Get real. I doubt he even knows how to spell it.'

James flicked him the finger and got to his feet, threaded his way through the crowd towards where he'd last seen Lucy. He found her at the bar, ordering a glass of wine. She hadn't noticed his approach and so he slid in behind her and, affecting a gruff Cockney accent, slipped his arms around her waist and said, 'All right, darlin'? Fancy a bit?'

'Get your fucking hands—' she snapped, spinning round to face him. She shook her head, a wide smile wiping the consternation from her face. 'You bastard,' she said, leaning forward and kissing him. 'You're lucky I didn't knee you in the bollocks.' She squinted through the crowd. 'Where are David and the others?'

'At the back. We've got a couple of tables.'

'Who's there?'

'Well, there's David, obviously, and Becky and Justin and Spence – they were there at Crossroads, yes – and a bunch more people from Uni and David's work. You'll like them. There are a couple of tossers, but I'll make sure you don't end up sitting with them.'

'I'm nervous.'

'Don't be. They'll love you. Justin's already fallen in lust with you and he hasn't even met you.'

'I don't mean about meeting them.'

He noticed a blob of congealed mascara where the rain had splashed in the corner of her eye, wiped it clear with his fingertip. 'What, then?'

'You. It's been a long time.' She squeezed his hand. 'Too long.'

'I've missed you, too . . . if that's what you mean.'

She smiled, kissed him again. 'Good. That's all I needed to hear.'

'So, you ready to make an entrance?'

'Yes.'

The barman pushed a glass of wine across the counter and

James reached over Lucy's shoulder and picked it up.

'Tab it, all right? Thanks. Table six,' he told him, walking away from the bar, feeling Lucy's fingers interlocking with his own.

'Oh, Christ,' Lucy exclaimed, suddenly tugging him to a standstill.

'What?'

'I forgot to tell you.'

'What?'

'Your editor. Jake, right?'

'Yes. What about him?'

'He called me.'

James remembered his conversation with him after he'd agreed to the Grancombe job. 'Oh, right. He said he might. Has he fixed you up with some work? What?' he asked, her smile infecting him, so that he couldn't help but smile back. 'What's so funny?'

'You'll never guess,' she teased.

'No, you're right. I won't. Tell me.'

'Just call me partner.'

'What?'

She stretched up and whispered in his ear, 'Grancombe.'

He pushed her back, said, 'What?'

'Grancombe. The story you're doing in Grancombe on the psycho. He's asked me to join you down there for a couple of days, photograph the murder sites, sort out a couple of establishing shots of the town. You know, snaps of the graveyard where the victims are buried. Relatives – if I can get them. That sort of thing.' Her smile wouldn't fade, her voice kept coming fast, her tongue tripping over itself in excitement. 'Isn't that incredible? Just me and you down there on our own . . .' She waved her hand around the bar. 'Out of London. Away from all this smoke and noise. Just you and me and the sea.'

That bastard. That stupid, interfering bastard. If Jake was here right now James would wring his neck. Dumb son-of-a-bitch. James closed his eyes for a second, still couldn't believe it. Anger was racing through him like a current, charging him up, threatening to explode. Don't lose it, his sanity was shouting. This is nothing to do with Lucy. Don't go balling her out. It's not her fault.

He took in her expression. The grin was still there, like her lips had been glued to her gums. What the hell was he going to tell her? How about, *no*? No, you're not going to Grancombe. Not with me and not with anyone else. Not ever. Yeah, *no* was good. *No* would avoid a lot of questions he didn't feel like answering right now. Like how come he hadn't told her that his uncle had just died? Like how come he'd never even mentioned he had an uncle? Like how he'd also failed to tell her that he'd lived with this *slipped-my-mind* uncle for a long, hot summer when he was eighteen.

And that was just to begin with. Lucy wasn't stupid. Her questions wouldn't quit there. Inevitably, they'd progress. How long did you live there? Are there people still living there you used to know? Why don't you want me to meet them? And biggest of all, the question he most dreaded having to answer: Just what was it that happened there that's left you so fucked up?

But at the same time, he knew that *no* was no good either. Just saying 'no' to her would be like red-flagging a bull at spitting distance. She wasn't the kind of person you told what to do without having a damn good reason. The questions would come the same as before, only this time barbed with indignation. She'd trample him into the dust.

So don't say shit. Deal with it tomorrow. Tell Jake to pull the offer from under her feet. Again, though, he knew this was another dumb bet. She'd know. She'd know it was down to him that Jake had changed his mind. And once she knew that, she'd know that he was hiding something from her. And once she knew that then trust and friendship and everything she'd talked to him about would mean nothing. And once their talk meant nothing, she'd walk. He felt it in his gut. She was in this with him for real. If she even suspected that he was messing her about, then he'd lose her. And he didn't want that. No matter how unsure he was about where their relationship might lead, he was sure it might lead somewhere.

And he was equally sure that he didn't want to quit on it just yet.

One thought comforted him. A consolation prize. At least he'd be able to keep an eye on her when she was in Grancombe. At least he'd be able to keep her eyes closed to the things he didn't want her to see. He breathed deep and when he breathed out his words came calm.

'That's great, Lucy,' he said. 'Really great.'

'I knew you'd love it.' She squeezed at his hand. 'Come on. Let's get drunk and celebrate.'

'Bar chat,' David slurred into James's ear a couple of hours later.

James turned to check on Lucy, but there wasn't any need. She was wrapped in conversation with Rick and Becky, smiling, relaxed and having fun. He had to admit it gave him a buzz, the way things were working out. Maybe Lucy was more than just potential now. Maybe she was already there as part of his life, part of him.

Rick was a pushover for a pretty face, so the fact that he was doing the nodding dog, lapping up everything she said like a teenager at his first job interview, wasn't a big deal. But Becky... Becky was choosey. She'd only met Lucy once before and it had been in a club where conversation hadn't really graduated further than exaggerated facial expressions and bellowed comments. Here was different. Here she'd be examining Lucy and the way James was with her. Here she'd be drawing conclusions. It was she and David, not Rick and the others, whose opinions James trusted.

Like David, Becky – who James and David had shared a flat with in Edinburgh – wouldn't hold off telling James if she thought Lucy wasn't right for him. Come to think of it, she wouldn't hold off from telling Lucy the same thing to her face. She'd done it before, acted the guardian angel, kept an eye on her boys and been responsible for more girlfriends getting the flick than Henry VIII. David had discussed her tendency to police their love lives with James. He'd put it down to her just being one of the boys, cited her drinking prowess, football lust and shockingly blue vocabulary as evidence to back up this theory. And James had agreed, not because he'd believed that David had been right, but because one night up in Edinburgh, laced with whiskey and beer, Becky had confessed through tears and snot and sheer bloody pain that she'd been in love with David from the moment she'd met him. And James had promised her that he wouldn't interfere, that he'd let her deal with it in her own way and that he'd never mention a word of that conversation to David. But if Becky had taken a dislike to Lucy, it wasn't obvious. She'd been charmed. Same as Justin. And, yes, same as James. He stood up and Lucy sensed the motion beside her and turned round.

'Just going for a pint with David at the bar,' James said.

'Sad tradition,' Becky explained. 'Every birthday, every year, same two pissed dickheads slumped over some bar talking bollocks.'

'How d'you know we talk bollocks?' David protested. 'For all you know, we might be discussing ways to make the world a better place – world peace, you know, all kinds of shit . . .'

Becky shook her head, her fair hair sweeping across her brow. 'I can believe the last part.'

David tutted. 'Just because you're a girl and you're not allowed to come with us . . .'

Becky's lip curled sarcastically. 'Consider me gutted at not being invited.' She turned to Lucy. 'What say you and me get all sad and girly and go to the loos with our handbags and swap lipstick and talk boys and other sad stuff?'

'Sure,' Lucy said, playing along, 'let's go be secretive.'

'What about me?' Rick asked.

'Well,' Becky said, 'either you can be sociable and talk to the others, or you can just sit there and enjoy your own company . . .' She ran her tongue across her teeth. 'Something I'm sure you do most nights, anyway.'

Rick shook his head, dismissed her with a wave of his hand, and shuffled up the bench to talk to Spence. James and David ploughed through to the corner of the bar and established some elbow room, ordering two pints of lager and four shots of tequila.

'Cheers,' David said, chewing the lemon, licking the salt off the back of his thick fist, dropping the shot and wincing like he'd swallowed a wasp. He watched James follow suit, then repeated the sequence with the second shot.

'Good catch,' he commented.

'What?'

'Lucy.'

'In case you hadn't noticed,' James pointed out, 'she's not a fish.'

'Indeed,' David admitted, 'but if she were, it's my opinion that she'd be a salmon. And not one of those farmed ones, either. Oh, no. She'd be from a Scottish river. An exclusive Scottish river owned by gentry, where not even chartered accountancy firms have bought rights. She'd be the kind of salmon you'd want stuffed on your mantelpiece.' He grinned. 'Well, stuffed somewhere, anyway.'

'OK,' James said with a groan, 'let's cut the line on the fish metaphor.'

'Oh, ha-ha. What, doesn't it tickle you anymore?'

James shook his head as he thought. 'No, just leaves me feeling gutted.'

'Oh, ha-ha, again. Really, though, you going to stick with her? Assuming she wants to stick with you, that is . . .'

James threw the question back at him. 'I don't know. What do you think?'

'I think you two look good together. I think you make each other smile and I think that can't be bad. But—'

James stubbed out his cigarette. 'With you, there's always a but. What is it this time?'

'Same as it was on your birthday last year when you were seeing that Zen chick, Naomi. Same as it'll probably be when your birthday swings round this year, whether it's Lucy you're with . . . or someone else. I mean, Naomi was all right. It wasn't like—'

'Apart from the fact she used to get me to meditate with her before sex.'

'Apart from that,' David acknowledged. 'But she was OK, you know. You've got to admit that. And it's the same with

Lucy now. She's fun. She suits you. I think even Becky's warming to her and that's, like, almost unheard of. But end-of-line, yeah, the big but is it's nothing to do with them why your relationships never work out. It's you. You can't settle. Sure, you blame it on them. You fixate on stuff like the meditation crap and you use that as your excuse to bail. But it's deeper than that.'

James rolled his eyes. He'd heard it all before. 'Is that a fact?'

'Reckon so. On the surface, sure, you're just like me: moving on all the time, not prepared to settle and give up on the game.' David swirled his drink for a moment, before adding, 'Only motive-wise, I think it's different with you. I think you really *do* want to settle down with someone. That's what's with all these short-lived relationships. Otherwise, you'd do what I do: you'd get the one-night stands in and move on the next morning, not look back. But you try. You try and make it work with all of them. And then, when you suss they're not perfect – and by now, you should've cottoned on to the fact that no one is – you chuck them, convinced it's not going to work out anyway. Am I right, or am I right?' David nodded his head and raised his glass. 'Profound, huh?'

James didn't speak for a few seconds, waited until he was sure that David had finished, then said, 'Becky's right, you know. We do talk a lot of shit.'

David laughed. 'Becky's right about a lot of things.' He raised his glass. 'To Becky, the best woman I know. Our guardian angel.'

'Becky,' James concurred, toasting her with his own glass and drinking. He waited till David's eyes met his. 'So,' he said, 'since we're being so honest with each other . . . if you reckon Becky's the best woman in the world, how come you've never . . .'

'How come I've never what?' David asked, looking at him amusedly. The suggestion hit home. 'What – *that*? With *her*? You serious?'

'Sure I'm serious.'

David frowned. 'Well, I dunno. The situation's never arisen.'

'OK, but hypothetically —'

'Hypothetically . . . Christ, I dunno. It's like asking me if I've ever thought about banging my sister. It's not something I've thought about.'

James wasn't being put off. Becky would castrate him if she could hear him going on like this. But it was only hypothetical, right? No big deal. Just a game. 'So think about it now,' he said.

'OK,' David said, doing just that for a moment, pulling all kinds of troubled faces. 'Well, she's attractive, yes. I mean, if you like that kind of thing.'

'And do you?'

David considered this a while longer. 'Suppose. But you know me,' he added quickly. 'Not like I'm fussy at the best of times . . .'

'Point taken. But you're great mates with her, and you *do* find her attractive. Attractive-*ish*, anyway . . .'

'I'll run with that,' David said, his expression serious now. If Becky had looked across now and seen him, she might have withdrawn her earlier comment: it really did look like it might be a route to world peace that was on his mind.

'So back on the hypothetical, say the situation did arise where you *could* – question is, *would* you?'

'But we're mates . . .'

'Which means you wouldn't have to go through all the crap of getting to know her and finding out it's a waste of time.'

'The James Sawday Speciality, you mean.'

'Call it what you want,' James said, overlooking the dig, keeping on his case. 'Just answer the question.'

'OK, OK, so yeah – *if the situation arose* – I might have a crack.'

James lit another cigarette. He was riding the tequila now, holding nothing back. 'So maybe – instead of spending the rest of your love life shagging nameless bodies you've met in clubs – you should.'

'Fine,' David said, though his belligerent expression showed that it was far from it. 'So switch it.'

'What?'

'What about *you*? Hypo-bloody-thetically, what about you? You know her as well as I do. *If the situation arose* with you, what would you do?'

'It wouldn't.'

'Uh, uh.' David wagged his finger at him. 'You're not getting out of it that easily. It's as likely it happening to you as to me.'

'It's not.'

'How's that?'

'Because it's not me she's interested in.'

'What's that meant to mean?'

'Work it out.'

'She said something to you? That what all this is about?' It was thrown out, almost with anger.

'No, she's said nothing. It's just a hunch.'

David stared into his eyes and neither of them spoke. Then he looked away.

'What's with the long faces, boys?'

James turned his head. Becky was standing between them with her hands on her hips. Lucy was standing beside her. James's eyes briefly engaged with David's and the antipathy between them dissolved as they cracked up laughing.

'What's so funny?' Becky asked, eyeing them both suspiciously. 'Should my ears be burning?'

David rested a hand on her shoulder. 'No, we've just been talking bollocks, just like you said we would.'

'That's what I love about you, David: you're so fucking predictable.'

James finished his drink and said to the others, 'We'd better get back to the table.' He nodded at David. 'Can't form a splinter group on your own birthday.'

David checked his watch. 'Good point, and if everyone's still up for moving on to a club, we'd better sort it out sharpish.'

James stepped forward only to walk into Becky's out-stretched hand. 'Not so fast,' she said.

A dart of panic passed through him. For an instant he thought that maybe she'd overheard what he and David had been discussing, and was about to conclude the hypothetical argument with a very real torrent of vitriol. He calmed; she wouldn't have waited this long.

'What?' he asked.

'We got us a plan,' Becky said.

'We sure have,' Lucy agreed.

David asked, 'And?'

'What do you say to getting out of London for a few days, birthday boy?'

David looked puzzled, shrugged. 'Bad plan. Hangover's going to nail me to my bed all day tomorrow. Reckon it's claimed my arse for Sunday, as well.'

'Not now,' Becky told him.

'So when?'

Becky pointed a finger at Lucy, said, 'Fill him in.'

'You know James is going down to Grancombe for *Kudos*, yeah?'

'News to me. He never tells me shit. First I hear about what he's been up to is when I buy the damn rag.'

'No work conversations,' James explained to Lucy. 'Unless it's quitting or getting fired. Instigated it the moment he decided to become an accountant.'

'That's the way he tells it,' David interrupted, shoving James playfully against the bar. 'The truth is his brain simply isn't up to comprehending what I do for a living.'

'Now, now,' Becky said. 'Back to the point, which is James is going to Grancombe to write an article and Lucy's going with him to do the photos to go with it. And Lucy said, let's make it a happy foursome – so to speak.'

David and James's eyes linked for a second.

'When?' David asked.

Lucy waited for James to speak, but when he didn't, she answered, 'James's editor wasn't sure. James has got his L.A. thing to finish off first. Some time in the next fortnight, though.' She grinned at James. 'That's right, isn't it?'

A sound rather than a word left James's mouth. His head nodded.

'Cool,' David said uncertainly, looking to James for confirmation. 'Always up for a bit of fresh air. Air quality up here sucks.' He took a long pull on his cigarette to drive this point home. 'So long as that's OK with Mr Sawday, you can count me in.'

For James, what happened next was like an out-of-body experience. It was like he was floating, buoyed up by a solution of alcohol and helplessness. He listened to himself. It was his voice, all right, but not the words he wanted to be speaking. He heard himself agreeing to the idea, watched the others smiling and laughing and hatching plans about what they'd get up to. And all the while, he was powerless to intervene, to speak his mind. How could he have let this happen? Smart-arsed bastard thinking he could deal with Alan's estate and the article simultaneously. Yeah, so how smart did he feel now? First Lucy and now David and Becky. The three people he cared more about than anybody else were now going to the one place he feared more than anywhere else. The situation had ballooned out of his control. Everything was fucked.

Fucked up bad.

He got back to his flat with Lucy around one-thirty a.m. They'd left the others at a club, grabbed a cab back instead. James had switched to Red Bull and vodka round midnight, which had had the dual effect of keeping him peaked and leaving him too wired to contemplate sleep. Lucy, on the other hand, was drunk.

'Come here, babe,' she said, dropping her coat onto the arm of the sofa.

He walked up to her and she pushed him back onto the sofa. He took her hands and pulled her towards him, so that she ended up sitting astride his waist. For a moment, he just stared into her eyes. Then she closed them and leant forward and they kissed. His eyes remained open, watching her face as their tongues intertwined and his hands instinctively stroked over her thighs and slid beneath her skirt.

He knew what he should be thinking. That she was beauti-ful. That he was lucky she'd chosen to come home with him and not someone else. He should have been grateful that she'd waited for him while he'd been away, hadn't jumped lazily onto the first easy offer going.

But her facial features were becoming blurred. It wasn't her he was thinking about at all, even though he'd been thinking about having sex with her from the moment he'd seen her walk into T-Rooms earlier that night. Fantasy was taking over. Another time in another place with another person was filling his vision. A situation that should have been, but never was.

Lucy's thighs locked onto his and her tongue pushed deeper into his mouth. He reacted, started to unfasten her shirt. Then she was on her feet, walking through to the bedroom, threading her arms free from her shirt, letting it slide to the floor. Now crooking her arms behind her back, unfastening her bra, dropping that as well, halting briefly to kick her shoes free from her feet. He followed, stripping down himself, adding his own clothes to the trail she'd left behind her.

She was naked by the time he reached the bed, lying on her back, her eyes closed, breathing deep, waiting for him. He pulled his shorts off, stood staring for a few seconds, then climbed onto the bed and pulled her up towards him.

'I've missed you,' he told her.

Again, they kissed. And this time, he shut his eyes.

Suzie.

So long ago now. So far away. Might not even be alive. Maybe not even living in Grancombe anymore. Perhaps did what she said she one day would: left and travelled. Maybe Sufers' Turf went bust, left her with nothing to come back to.

He was inside Lucy now, moving with her, wrapping themselves up like a parcel between the sheets. But it was Suzie he wanted. Here with him now. Now. Another chance.

I've missed you. I've missed you, Suzie. I've missed you so much . . .

He shivered, starting to come.

Later, in the dark, he could hear Lucy breathing beside him. He glanced at the bedside clock and dread crawled across him before he remembered that tomorrow was the weekend. He rolled across the mattress and waved the red eye of the cigarette he'd been smoking over the bedside table until its reflection winked back from the glass ashtray. He stubbed it out and stayed there, propped up on his side.

'Are you OK?' Lucy whispered.

'Yes.'

'Are *we* OK?'

'Yes.'

She placed her hand on his shoulder, pulled him over, then held his jaw in her hand, gently turned it so that he faced her. A weak shaft of moonlight stretched from the gap in the curtains across her face. She kissed him, kept her nose pressed to his and whispered, 'You would tell me if we weren't, wouldn't you? You would let me know?'

'Yes.'

'Good,' she said, rolling over and shuffling her back up against his chest. 'Because I'd want to know. I'd want to know so that I could make things right.'

James stayed there, staring through the curtains at the moon. He was legion. All these voices in his head. All these crazy, mixed-up thoughts, stopping him from sleeping. Calm it, he commanded himself. Block them out. Just like his ex, Naomi, had taught him. Replace them with nothing. Dwell on the nothing until nothing else matters.

David had slagged off Naomi and all her Buddhist baggage, but James had stuck with the meditation techniques she'd taught him in the brief interval that their relationship had turned out to be. Just on a chill-out level. He hadn't bought into any of the spiritual path to enlightenment crap. But he'd meditated most days since they'd split, just as stress control, just to block out the multitude of worries that were prone to rattle round his mind. He didn't bother with any of the positional stuff either. Not the full lotus, the half-lotus, the quarter-lotus, or even the Japanese slackers' version of adopting a kneeling posture and wedging a cushion under your bum to stop your ankles from aching. James just went for the lying on his back, breathing through his nose, counting the exhalations: in – two, in – four, in – six, in – eight, in – ten, in – two, and so on.

Until he forgot.

Just like now.

Lucy twisted and mumbled in her sleep.

Keep the thoughts out. Just concentrate on the breathing. No Grancombe. No *Kudos*. No grief. Just the numbers. No Lucy. No Alex and Dan. No David and Becky. No Alan. No responsibilities. Just being. Two, four, six, eight . . . No Suzie. No thoughts of whether she'll still be there. Two, four, six, eight . . .

CHAPTER SIX

stoned

James looked across South Beach, beyond the figures of Alex Howley and Daniel Thompson, as they headed towards the cliffs. It was maybe a half a mile across, no more. In the far corner that they were heading for, he could already make out the black scar of the steps in the cliff, the same steps Monique had walked down for the last time on New Year's Day. Hidden from view at the top were the woods that sheltered Alan's house from the scything sweep of the coastal winds.

When they reached the low slope of barnacle and mussel-studded rocks which formed the foot of the cliff, Daniel stopped and sat down. 'Smoke break,' he muttered, digging into his shorts for a cigarette.

'No,' Alex said, standing over him. 'When we get to the top. I stop now, I'll never get going again. Anyhow,' he said, glancing back across the beach, 'I wouldn't put it past Murphy to be watching us with binoculars.'

'Fuck him,' Daniel said, threading a cigarette into his mouth.

Alex clicked his tongue and moved on. Daniel replaced the cigarette in the packet and got to his feet.

'What you looking at, posh-boy?' he challenged, catching James staring.

'Nothing,' James said with a shrug, brushing past him and starting up the steps after Alex.

'Watch your step,' Daniel called after him. 'You could have a nasty fall round here.'

James, having overtaken Alex about half-way up, was the

first to reach the top of the steps. He stood for a moment with his hands on his rib-cage and waited for its heaving to subside. He felt good, away from the other two, up here at the top of the world. He turned and surveyed South Beach. His eyes settled on the distant block of Surfers' Turf.

He pictured Suzie as he'd left her, imagined what it would be like to press his lips against hers, imagined the scent of her breath mixing with his. He shook his head at the thought in a futile attempt to dismiss it. Dream on. He had about as much chance with someone who looked like her as he did of ending up mates with Alex and Daniel. No point in wondering about what isn't on the cards. He walked a few paces across the uneven, springy turf, dropped the rucksack and lay down on his back. With his hands cradled behind his neck, he stared up into the vast blue sky.

'You're a healthy bastard, aren't you?' Alex said, collapsing next to him. His heavy breathing competed with the breeze. 'What's the deal? You some sort of sports freak?'

James rolled onto his side, faced him. The sarcastic expression he'd expected to be lodged on Alex's face was absent. 'It wasn't that bad,' he said, his tone neutral, still uncertain whether Alex was being friendly or trying to rile him.

Alex struggled into a sitting position, crossed his legs and sat like a guru, looked towards the top of the steps. 'Like hell it wasn't. I'm knackered. Feel like I've swum the Bristol Channel.'

Daniel's body slid slowly into view as he covered the last few steps, like a swimmer walking out of the sea. 'That's it,' he gasped. 'I'm telling you, that's *it*.' He stumbled over to where they sat and sank to his knees. He wiped the sweat from his eyes, and shuddered into a coughing fit. 'That tosser Murphy,' he wheezed. 'He can kiss my hairy arse, if he thinks I'm walking one step further.'

Alex snorted laughter and lit a cigarette, 'Shit,' he exhaled, his mouth a chimney with the wind whipping smoke from it. 'My throat's as dry as a desert.'

James reached for the rucksack. 'Here,' he said, tossing it over. 'Water.'

Alex rummaged inside and pulled a bottle out, held it up to the sun so that diamonds of sunlight exploded inside. He smiled at the effect. 'Perfect,' he said, unscrewing the cap and drinking deep. Bubbles of air soared vertically through the liquid. He lowered it and passed it back to James. 'Cheers.'

James watched Daniel watching him out of the corner of his eye, then drank himself. 'Hits the spot, doesn't it?'

Alex nodded and lay down. 'As good as beer, right now.'

Daniel wiped the sticky patches of spit from the corners of his mouth. 'Give it here,' he said.

James ignored him, checked Alex for a reaction. There wasn't any. He looked back at Daniel. He was leering at him like a drunk whose drink he'd knocked over, whose girlfriend he'd glanced at. So this was it. Back down now and forever hold your peace. Back down now and take a mortgage out in losers' corner. Or call his bluff, follow it through if it wasn't a bluff to begin with.

'You deaf or something?' Daniel said. 'I told you to give it here.'

James raised the bottle to his lips and slowly sipped. He put the bottle on the ground, twisted the top tight and stared into Daniel's eyes. 'Fuck you,' he said.

Disbelief clouded Daniel's eyes for a moment, then blackened into a storm. 'You what?'

'Who's deaf now?' James said. 'I said, fuck you. You want me to repeat it, fine: fuck you.' He checked Alex again. Motionless. As he lay there with his shades on, his chest slowly rising and falling beneath his shirt, he could even have been asleep. 'That too complicated for you?' James went on, concentrating on keeping his voice clinical, aware that this war of words might well be as far as this went, knowing that if that was the case then he'd win by keeping his cool, using his brain to run circles round this jerk. 'You want me to explain it? That's fine. Fuck you, because last night you chucked my clothes all over the carpark. Fuck you, because you've treated me like a piece of shit all morning. And fuck you, because if you want a drink you're going to have to get past me to get it.'

'Right,' Daniel barked. He got to his feet, his prior

exhaustion suddenly swept away like a cork by the torrent of adrenaline pumping through his veins. His face was the colour of an open wound, like someone had peeled its skin free. 'You're fucking going down.'

James was already standing. Their eyes locked, the bottle between them, two dogs about to run for the same scrap of meat. James heard his breath coming shallow. He wanted this. He spread his feet, stabilised himself against the inevitable assault. This son of a bitch had it coming.

'Sit the fuck down.'

Neither of them moved.

'Sit the fuck down,' Alex repeated, 'and chill the fuck out.'

Daniel's head swivelled round to face him. 'What the fuck are you talking about? You hear what this twat just said?'

Alex was still flat on his back. 'Just can it, will you? Both of you.' He craned his neck over in James's direction. 'You too.' He sat up and dug into his pocket, produced a beaten tobacco tin. 'We were out of line last night, but who gives a shit, right?' He opened the tin and peeled a couple of cigarette papers off the packet inside, set about constructing the beginnings of a spliff. 'We were legless, so it doesn't mean anything,' he continued, sprinkling the contents of a cigarette and a thick pinch of grass onto the papers. He looked down, lifted the packed papers to his mouth and ran his tongue along their glue-stained borders, proceeded to roll. 'So, Dan,' he said, looking round for his lighter, 'you say sorry about chucking his bag at him. I'll say sorry about taking his cab. And you,' he concluded, threading the spliff between his lips, and looking at James, 'give Dan the water and come and have a smoke.'

'I don't believe this,' Dan began. 'You can't—'

'I can and I have. Now apologise to him and then can it.'

Dan shook his head, his eyes darting in confusion from Alex to James and then back to Alex again. 'But—'

'But nothing,' Alex said, lighting the spliff. 'Just do it.'

Dan said nothing for a few seconds, then shot James a foul look and muttered something under his breath.

Alex lowered the spliff from his mouth and exhaled smoke

through a wide grin. 'I think that was your sorry,' he told James, holding out the spliff towards him. 'Now give him the water and let's all relax.'

'Here,' James said and sent the bottle spinning towards Dan.

Dan snatched it from the air, unscrewed the top and took a drink. He nodded at James, but said nothing more. He could have meant anything from *thanks* to *the moment you turn your back on me, I'm going to drive an ice-pick through your brain*. Dan took another drink and walked over to Alex, slumped down next to him, eyed the spliff still snip-gripped between Alex's fingers, still pointed at James.

'You want it, or not?' Alex asked James.

James stood where he was. 'I don't smoke.'

'Why not?' Alex asked, handing it over to Dan.

Dan settled back on the ground and commented, 'Hash virgin. That's all we need.'

'That true?' Alex asked.

'What?'

'You never smoked gear before?'

James considered lying. But what was the point? Alex would guess straight away. Same as Dan just had. These people knew their drugs. It had been apparent from the first moment he'd seen them. Dan there with his disconnected look until he was riled. And now, here, what time was it? Not even eight, and they were already getting stoned. Alex, dazed by the daylight, a vampire with his shades protecting him from bursting into flames and crumbling into ash. Sitting here now, cross-legged, the Sultan of Smoke, the Maharaja of Marijuana. No, there wasn't any point in lying. They'd see straight through him like he was made of glass. And whatever respect he'd just earned would be smashed just as quick.

'No.'

'Told you,' Dan said, returning the spliff to Alex, who accepted it like communion, lifted it to his mouth.

Alex smoked for a minute in silence, then asked, 'Why not? Lack of opportunity or lack of desire?'

James knew he didn't have to justify himself to these two.

At the same time, though, there was something compulsive in Alex's voice.

'Bit of both, I suppose,' he admitted. 'I did a lot of sport at school, so I didn't smoke cigarettes. Same went for dope. Didn't want to wreck my lungs.'

'What about now?' Alex asked. 'I take it you're not at school anymore.'

'No, just finished.'

Alex handed the spliff over to Dan. 'Same as us, then. What about the sport? What did you do?'

'Rugby. Football. Cricket. The usual stuff.'

'Team sports,' Dan grumbled. 'Load of crap.'

'You still playing them?' Alex asked, ignoring Dan's comment.

'No. Probably when I get to university.'

'Yeah? Where you going?'

'Don't know yet. Depends on my results. What about you? You going somewhere?'

Alex nodded. 'I got some offers. Dunno, though. The thought of another institution doesn't appeal too much right now. I'm putting off going for a year, anyhow.'

'What about you?' James asked, addressing Dan for the first time since they'd faced each other off.

'He's too thick for university, aren't you, Dan?' Alex teased, slapping his hand down on his friend's shoulder.

Dan rubbed at his eyes, gave the spliff back to Alex. 'Load of shit. More teachers. More of their bullshit. They can stick it.' He turned his attention to James. 'We're going travelling. Me and Alex. Off to Thailand and that. End of the summer. Getting the fuck out of this stupid town. Ain't that right, Alex?'

'Yeah, Dan. We're getting out.' Alex smiled at James, held the spliff up before him. 'Forget your lungs. It won't hurt. Give it a go.'

As James took the remains of the spliff from him and held it to his lips, he was aware of Alex and Dan scrutinising him. Laboratory rat. Throw in the stimulus. Watch it squeak. He hesitated before inhaling, remembered what his father had told him about drugs, about how soft led to hard, about how someone who was happy in himself didn't need artificial stimuli to make them feel good. Then he sucked in, listened to the spliff softly crackle, felt the smoke burning down his throat. What did it matter? He wasn't happy in himself. Hadn't been for as long as he could remember. He held his breath, kept the smoke in his lungs the same way he'd watched them doing, concentrated on not coughing. Then he exhaled, watched the smoke funnel from his mouth into the air, savoured the herby scent in his nostrils, the dryness in his throat. So what if soft led to hard? Life's hard. Toughen up and get with the programme. He inhaled again.

'Not so bad, is it?' Alex said a minute later, grinning.

'Not so bad at all,' James agreed, suddenly aware that his lips were twitching of their own accord into a smile.

Alex began to roll another spliff. 'So you're Al I'Anson's nephew, huh?'

'Yes,' James said, his voice dropping, sounding deeper than usual. He took another pull on the spliff and leant unsteadily forward, giving it to Dan. 'The one and only.'

Dan sniggered, rolled onto his front, and adopted a BBC news announcer's clipped tones: 'Grancombe's natural beauty has provided inspiration for many people over the years. Current residents include the writer Alan I'Anson and the painter Jack Dawes.'

'What's that?' James asked.

'Tourist brochure,' Dan explained. 'Your uncle always gets a mention.'

'So how long you staying here?' Alex asked.

'Don't know. It was going to be for the summer, but I'm not sure now.'

'Why's that?'

'Alan, I suppose. He seems pretty fucked up at the moment. I get the feeling he'd be happier on his own.'

Alex lit the second spliff as Dan finished the first. The smile had faded from his face. 'Hardly surprising, considering what happened to his wife.'

'You knew her?' James asked.

83

'Sure. Everyone knows everyone round here. Ain't that right, Dan?'

Dan accepted the spliff. 'Yeah. She was nice. Got on well with my old dear. Mum reckoned it would screw your uncle up, her going like that. Screw anyone up, I reckon.'

Alex nodded his head. 'Yeah. Shit way to lose someone. Poor bastard. What about you? You close to her?'

'No, I only met her a couple of times.' A wave of sensation tingled through James's body and he stifled a giggle. 'Jesus,' he said, embarrassed. 'This isn't funny. I shouldn't be laughing.'

'Great thing about drugs,' Alex said, his grin grown wide again. 'Kill manners cold.'

'I need a piss,' Dan announced, standing quickly and handing the spliff to Alex like a relay baton, before running over to the edge of the cliff. He stood there, fumbling with his flies and swaying in the breeze. 'Hey, Murphy,' he called out across South Beach, releasing a high arc of urine. 'Drink this.'

Alex sat up, passed the spliff to James. 'Be careful, you dozy bastard,' he shouted at Dan. 'Get back here before you get blown off.'

'Nah,' Dan shouted back, 'he's too far away.'

'What?' Alex asked.

'Murphy,' Dan cackled, turning round with his penis exposed, still urinating. 'He's way too far away to blow me off.' He cackled again and asked, 'Get it?'

Alex shook his head slowly. 'Yeah, Dan. Crap joke. But get this . . .'

'What?'

'You ever heard of the expression pissing into the wind?'

'Of course I—' Dan suddenly realised what Alex was talking about and looked down. 'Shit,' he shrieked, spotting the dark, urine-drenched patches on his jeans and spinning round to face the beach again. 'That's your fault an' all, Murphy,' he yelled. 'You wait, you fucker. I'll get you. Just you fucking wait.'

'Some people never learn,' Alex told James.

'Tell me about Murphy,' James said. 'What's the problem between you guys?'

'He's a fucking prick,' Dan answered, squatting down next to Alex.

Alex pushed him playfully away. 'Look at you,' he said, holding his nose. 'Worse than a hobo, you piss-ridden scumbag. You carry on like that, and we'll have to get you a colostomy bag.'

'Suck my dick,' Dan muttered, lying down and spreading his legs. 'Sun'll soon dry it out.'

'Murphy,' James repeated. 'What was he on about last night for?'

Alex pointed at the joint in James's hand. 'Nothing. Just caught us spliffing on the beach. That's where we'd just been when we bumped into you in the carpark. I swear, we were so wrecked we didn't even see him till he was standing over us.'

'He didn't bust you, then?'

'Nah, not worth it. Searched us, but we didn't have much on us. Not enough to nick us. Left it with the girls in the pub. Lucky, considering. Didn't stop Murphy threatening to bang us up for the night and telling us to fuck off home, though. Giving us a hard time for the sake of it, you know?'

Dan nodded in agreement, then said with relish, 'Fucking hates us, he does.'

'How come?'

'He hates everyone, miserable piece of shit. But there's the raves we've done up on Eagle's Point,' Alex explained. 'In the carpark. Gets right on Murphy's tits. Seeing us making money and having a good time.'

'Why?' James asked 'Illegal?'

'Nah, it's fine,' Alex said. 'No laws stopping you partying outside. Not yet, anyhow. They reckon the government's on the case, so it's probably just a matter of time. Safe as houses now, though. Anyhow, the car park up there's owned by Arnie Oldfield. Private land. So there's piss all Murphy can do about it.'

'What's Murphy's problem, then? Drugs?'

'Yeah, that's what he tells everyone, anyhow. Usual shit.

Bangs on about the people who've started coming here. People down from London for weekend kicks. Corrupting the local kids. All that shit. And people listen to him. Lot of people round here who'd rather things went back to how they were. Family holidays. Buckets and spades and ice-creams. Pretty postcards.' Alex smirked. 'That's what he tells them, but it's not what he thinks.' He shook his head. 'Murphy's so full of shit he should have a public health warning on him. His brother runs a club down on the front. Dixie's. Biggest in the town. All the business him and his brother have been losing to the raves is what really cranks Murphy up.'

'What about Oldfield? How come he doesn't mind you using his land?'

Dan laughed. ''Cos he's as mad as a fish.'

'Yeah,' Alex agreed, 'Murphy's tried having words with him about it, but Arnie doesn't give a shit. We slip him some cash, let him hang around and watch. Besides,' he added, 'Arnie hates Murphy. Maybe even as much as Dan here.'

'How come?' James asked

'Murphy tried to bust him for some assault on a tourist a couple of years ago. This bloke got his face smacked in up on Eagle's Point one night when he was getting into his car. Smacked in bad. Whoever did it had a balaclava on. Robbed him. Left him totally fucked him up. Murphy reckons it was Arnie who did it.'

'And did he?'

'Who knows? Maybe. Maybe not. Comes from a right screwed up family. Short of cash, too. His old man ended up in the nut house for rape. Used to run the farm next to the car park. Went bankrupt round the same time he got put away. Left Arnie skint, so he lives off what he gets from the car park and casual work. Mowing people's lawns, that sort of thing. But he's not the only nutter round here up for doing something like that.' He spat into the air, readjusted his head and caught the blob of spittle in his mouth. 'Anyhow, they couldn't stick it on him, so he walked. Wouldn't put it past Murphy to have done the guy over himself, either. Violent son-of-a-bitch. Kicked the shit out of Dan here a few months ago 'cos he reckoned he'd been joyriding.'

'Christ,' James said. 'Did you report him?'

Alex snorted derisively. 'Who to? Round here, he's Judge Dredd. The fucking law. Nearest town with a cop more senior than him is forty miles away. He can do what he fucking well likes. Besides, who's gonna take our word against his?'

'So that's why you're here today?' James asked. 'Because of Murphy catching you with the spliff?'

Alex rolled onto his front, spread his legs like a frog. 'Guess so. No way you'd find us up at this time otherwise. Murphy said he'd bust us if we didn't show. Don't reckon he would have, though. Not worth it. But still, makes for a quiet life, us being here. Shows willing. Community spirit and all that. We toe the line today, then maybe he'll get off our cases for a while.'

'What about Jack Dawes?' James asked. 'Don't you want to know what's happened to him? How come you're not worried when everyone else is?'

'Dunno.' Alex's voice sounded sleepy. 'The way I see it, he's old enough to look after himself. He'll turn up.'

'But something must be wrong, him going missing like that. Why else would the police bother with all this?'

Dan picked up a stone and threw it over the cliff. 'Because they've got fuck all else to do. Makes Murphy and his buddies feel like they've got a life.'

'Exactly,' Alex concurred. 'If you're looking for drama, James, forget it. This is Grancombe, not London or New York. The only thrills you get round here are the ones you sort out yourself. He's probably just done a bunk. Artists, you know. Weirdos, the lot of them. Jack Dawes. Jackdaws.' He slowly flapped his arms to emphasise the point. 'Maybe he's made like a bird and flown.'

James rubbed at his eyes. The sunlight was starting to sting. He lay down and stared up at the tree above his head, tried to count the leaves on a branch, then stared at a leaf, navigated the junctions of its veins. It felt good, just lying here, wrecked, imagined the crawling sap. He could stay here all day, no worries. He smiled at the thought of himself lying here stoned, tried to picture looking down at himself from the top of the tree; wanted to see if he looked as totally content as he felt. He checked out the colours of the leaves, wished he had a pen and paper here to record them with. There were words in his head he wanted to get down, whole books he wanted to write. Feeling this relaxed, this released from pressure, they'd come easy, regular, like the slow, unhurried beat of his heart. He shifted his focus to the sky and watched the dead cells, or 'floaters' as his mother had called them, rise and fall across his eyes as he tried to track them and hold them still.

'Munchies,' Alex called and James felt something land on his chest.

'Cheers,' he said, his hand roaming across his body and locating the chocolate bar that Alex had taken from the rucksack. He slipped a piece into his mouth, closed his eyes and gently chewed, savouring the sugary sensation.

Later, his saliva thick across his teeth, he woke and looked up. Alex was leaning over him, smiling.

'Come on,' he said. 'Let's go check out the woods, like the good copper said.'

James slowly got to his feet. He massaged his neck. 'Have I been asleep?' he asked, collecting the water bottle and draining it, picking up the rucksack and stashing the empty bottle inside.

'Yeah, about an hour.'

Alex's voice was distant and James turned and saw that he was already ten yards away, fading into the sun-starved gloom of the woods, the colours of his clothes being subsumed by the patchwork of green and brown. His body faded like a ghostly vision, leaving James alone for a few seconds, scratching his head, staring down at the impression he had left on the ground where he'd slept. He looked around for Dan, but he was nowhere to be seen, and so he set off in the direction Alex had gone, following him out of the sunlight and into the woods.

For the first few steps, the debris of fallen leaves and twigs crackled beneath his feet, and then, the canopy of foliage thickening above his head as he trod deeper into the false twilight, the sound of his steps softened as the ground slowly slid into rotting mulch. He felt the drop in temperature, drew his arms around his body and rubbed at the cold. Sunlight filtered down in sporadic shafts from the sky above, leaving dappled patterns on the patches of ground that it reached. There was no sign of Alex, but he walked on regardless for a few minutes, quickening his pace, ducking under branches and navigating brambles and pools of black, unruffled water, assuming each time that the next obstacle he overcame would bring him in sight of the others.

Eventually, though, he stopped and listened, heard nothing but the sound of his lungs churning out the humid air. He turned a full circle, attempted to get his bearings. But no matter which way he looked, the woods left no clues for him to move either back to the cliff, or forward towards Alan or Jack's homes. He stood there, motionless in a vertical shaft of weak light, a member of the Starship Enterprise crew waiting to be beamed up from an alien and potentially hostile planet.

'Alex,' he shouted. 'Dan. Where the hell are you guys?'

A faint echo, then the same suffocating silence as before.

'Hey,' he called out again, unable to eradicate the hint of hysteria from his voice. 'If you guys can hear me, shout.'

Nothing. He stared around again, at a loss for what to do next.

'Aaaaaargh!'

The scream came like an explosion, sending James diving into the mud. He looked up, spotted a flurry of motion out of the corner of his eye. He spun on his heels to face it. A swirling blur. Then definition. Arms, flailing like windmill sails in a hurricane, flashing towards him out of the undergrowth. Dan's face warped, grotesque, a Halloween mask, his mouth wide open, the scream still coming.

'Gotcha,' Dan shouted in triumph, leering over him, his dark eyes sparkling like wet pebbles. 'Man, you looked like you were gonna squit your pants.'

Before words found their way to James's tongue, another noise trapped his mind. Purposeful this time. Behind them. James stood and turned, and there was Alex, walking towards them, holding a stick before him like a fencing sword, menacingly swishing it through the air. Speared on its end was a rabbit, half decomposed, half-eaten. Its dirt-encrusted bowels lay exposed, like someone or something had tried to turn it inside out.

'You wait till you smell it,' Alex sniggered, only a couple of feet away now. He thrust the stick forward, causing James to leap back like he'd been confronted with a flaming torch.

'Keep that the fuck away from me,' Dan warned, his voice wavering awkwardly between appreciation and disgust.

'Run rabbit, run rabbit, run, run, run,' Alex began to chant softly, turning from James and striding towards Dan. Still advancing, he glanced at James. 'Ever been hunting?' he asked. James just stared back, confused. 'Make a change to see a rabbit hunting a human, I reckon,' he commented, running his tongue with slow deliberation across his lips. 'What d'you reckon, Dan?'

'Yeah, I suppose,' Dan's face twitched with apprehension, a combination of intuition and experience suggesting to him what might be coming next. 'It would be pretty weird.'

'So, run,' Alex screeched at him, lunging the stick forward, and shaking it before Dan's face, leaving him staring at it like some primitive hypnotised by a voodoo totem.

'Shit,' Dan bellowed, suddenly twisting round and breaking into a run, crashing into the undergrowth.

'C'mon,' Alex laughed at James, starting to sprint down the channel Dan's bulk had carved through the woodland landscape. 'Let's get this rabbit its first kill.'

James gave chase. As his speed increased, the brambles and bracken and trees and flowers on either side of him slid into a brown blur, rushing past like a muddy stream, or the view from a train. He monitored Alex's progress ahead of him from the corner of his eyes, using his ears as much as his eyes to track him, concentrating the majority of his sight on the erratic obstacle course of roots and rocks and ruts on the ground.

'C'mon, rabbit,' Alex was shouting. 'Smell the blood.'

And then there was a yelp. Bestial. Like a dog bounced off

a car bonnet, a fox disappearing under a pack of baying hounds. James's pace slackened instinctively in the face of the sound. He looked up, everything suddenly coming in slow motion. Alex was motionless, maybe ten yards ahead, standing at the top of a mud bank, looking down, the stick raised at his side, his silhouette that of a Zulu warrior. Alex's arms dropped to his side. The stick fell to the ground, jolting the rabbit's cadaver free, so that it rolled down the slope and slumped in an unidentifiable ball at the bottom.

'What?' James was saying, his feet on autopilot, dragging him forward with them, a lemming towards a cliff, in spite of the fact that something in his mind was telling him to turn, to leave this place.

Alex slowly turned to face him. His lips made shapes, but no words came. He pulled his shades from his face and for the first time James saw his sky blue eyes. James reached him now and, together, they turned and looked down.

Dan was there, huddled up like a foetus in the womb, his knees jammed up against his open jaw. But it wasn't Dan that James's eyes focused on. It was what lay next to him. It was what the blizzard of angry flies were descending on as he watched, buzzing like a distant motorbike. It was the clear picture of the man lying there, his body impossibly collapsed beneath his filthy clothes. It was the maggots crawling across the ragged flesh, the flies squatting to add to their numbers.

It was the corpse of Jack Dawes, the man they'd come here to find. Despite the fact that flies massed along the long, deep gash which split the face in two, James knew that this was so.

Alex was the first to react. James watched him step forward, half-slide, half-stumble like a novice skier down the mud bank towards his friend. Alex hesitated when he drew level with Jack Dawes' body, then knelt down beside it, waved his arm across Dawes' face. The swarm of flies that had masked it, soared as a unit, wheeled, and then disbanded, scattering into an aerial battle of swirling black. Alex turned to James and drew his finger in a symbolic line across his neck. Slowly, he turned and rose, stepped over the body, and James watched the frenzied flies descend once more, settle like frog spawn.

Then, in a failed attempt to look away, James found himself examining Dawes' body, taking in his mud-smeared shirt, following the stripes down the sleeves. For a moment, his brain refused to translate what he saw. Something was wrong. Something didn't fit. The sleeves ended, squared off in neat stitching. Pearls of buttons wrapped tightly around Jack's wrists. Only – his brain flashed the message up – the hands weren't there.

The hands weren't there.

Oh, Christ.

The hands weren't there.

He didn't even get the chance to feel sick. It just came. Up in a jet. Busting through his teeth with the pressure of a fire hose, forcing his jaw open. His eyes streamed water. But he couldn't blink. He couldn't look away. He felt the vomit, warm and heavy, running down his chest, gluing his shirt to his skin like sweat. The message flashed up again. Insistent, challenging him to continue denying what he saw with his own eyes. No hands. Just stumps, bloody and raw, protruding from Dawes' sleeves like joints of meat in a butcher's window.

James lifted his hands to his face and shielded his eyes. The world plunged into blackness. The smell of vomit. And beneath that, baser, pungent as goat's cheese, another smell. Foreign. Beyond his experience. The smell of death and degeneration.

When he uncovered his eyes, Alex was crouched beside Dan. How could he do that? How could he stay so calm? Alex slapped Dan hard across the face: nothing. He repeated the action and, this time, Dan flinched and raised his hand to protect himself.

'Get a fucking grip,' Alex snapped. 'Stand up,' he instructed, but Dan just stared dumbly back. 'Now,' Alex shouted, grabbing him by the arms and yanking him to his feet. He held him upright, shaking him violently. James watched Dan's eyes roll loosely in their sockets. 'Say something,' Alex was shouting. 'Say something, you stupid prick.'

'I—'

'You what, you dumb shit?'

'Ph-phh-phhhhh—'

'What?'

Dan tore free of Alex's grip, stumbled back a pace, collapsed onto his knees as if in prayer. His head lolled forward and his hand hovered over his knees. Something maroon and sticky was smeared across the skin where his shorts tapered off.

'Phhh . . .' he groaned, screwing his eyes up. 'I phh-phhh-I fucking fell . . .' His eyes opened and flickered towards Jack Dawes' body, before flicking forward again, registering only what was before him, only Alex. 'On him. He's all over me,' he mumbled. 'That dead fucker's all over me.'

Alex took a step forward. 'Get up. Now. Get on your feet. We've got to get you out of here. This shit's gonna screw your head up. You've got to move.'

Dan was crying now. He looked to James for support, wailing, 'I can't. I can't move my legs.' He stared at his knees again. 'Look at me,' he sobbed. 'All over me . . . all over my fucking legs . . .'

'So what?' Alex grunted, kicking his foot into the earth between them, sending a shower into Dan's face. 'He's dead. So what if you fell on him? Get up. Get a fucking grip. You scared of him? That it? You scared of Jack Dawes?' A hiss of derision burst from his lips. 'He's dead. You get that? Dead. He can't do shit to you.'

Dan made no move to rise. His eyelids were clenched tight again. His lips shivered as he muttered some incomprehensible mantra over and over again. Alex glanced over at James, his blue eyes resolute, solid as blocks of ice. Then he walked past Dan, over to the body.

'Watch this,' he called over at Dan, standing beside the body until Dan's head slowly twisted towards him.

Then – James couldn't believe what he was seeing – after the smallest hesitation, Alex dropped onto one knee and pushed his hand firmly through the swarm of flies and pressed his palm onto Jack Dawes' face. When he withdrew it, he raised his arm into the air. The same muck on Dan's knees now lay in a thin film across Alex's palm. He stood up and walked back to Dan.

'Now get the fuck up,' he told him, waving his hand before

Dan's face. 'This stuff doesn't mean anything. Flesh and blood. Fly crap.' He held out his clean hand and Dan took it, still mesmerised by the other one, allowed himself to be hauled to his feet. 'Good,' Alex said, ducking down and wiping his palm on the earth, keeping his grip on Dan's hand. He then turned and Dan turned with him. 'Come on,' he said, leading Dan round the body and up the bank. 'I need a cigarette.'

They were sitting on the other side of the bank. No one had spoken for ten minutes. Dan was sprawled on a patch of grass, tearing clump after clump of turf free from the ground and rubbing furiously at his legs.

'It won't come off,' he kept muttering. 'It won't fucking come off.'

Alex reached a hand out and firmly wrapped his fingers around Dan's wrist. 'It's gone,' he reassured him. 'You're clean.'

Dan didn't reply for a moment, then slowly nodded, dropped the clump of turf he was holding. Alex wedged a cigarette between Dan's fingers, but Dan made no move to smoke it.

'One of us should go,' James said. 'One of us should go and get help.'

'In a minute,' Alex said, his shades back on, his voice soft, soothing, like it had been when he'd been stoned. 'Finish the cigarette first. Get our heads together. Back to normality. It's probably the last breather we're gonna get today. Savour it.'

James's heart was doing the hundred meter sprint. 'Savour *what*? There's a fucking dead man, the other side of that bank.'

Alex laughed. 'What d'you think?' he said, lighting another cigarette, despite the fact that the first one lay loosely between Dan's fingers, slowly burning down, unattended, as Dan stared into the middle distance, apparently registering nothing.

'I don't know,' James said.

'You ever seen a dead man before?' Alex demanded. ''Cos I haven't.' He lay on his back, launched a spinning smoke ring through the still air towards the branches above. 'Never touched one either,' he added.

James suddenly wished Alex wasn't wearing shades again.

Looking over at him now, he couldn't read anything into his face, had no option but to rely on the even projection of his voice and take his words at face value. Still, though, he couldn't credit himself with fully understanding what Alex had just said or the way he'd said it. The smile that had accompanied the words had to be some sort of reaction to the horror they'd just encountered. Hysteria. Shell-shock. He remembered the flies closing over Alex's hand like quicksand. Then he continued to stare at Alex. Lying here, the cigarette hanging limply from his mouth, his hands cushioning his head, he could have been in bed, post-coital. He could have – should have – been anywhere but here, after what they'd just found, after what he'd just done.

'I know why you did it,' James said quietly.

'Did what?'

'You know what I mean. I know you did it to calm me and Dan down, to let us know that we shouldn't be scared.'

Alex removed the cigarette from his mouth, expelled smoke from his lungs in a heavy, exaggerated sigh. 'That's why, is it?'

'Why else? There's no other reason why you—'

'Sometimes you've got to find out where your limits are, James. Sometimes you've got to explore, stick your hands into the dark and see what's there.' He sat up and faced James. 'You never wondered what you're capable of? You never wondered where your guts ran out?'

James felt faint. The trees were closing in on him. 'You make it sound like you enjoyed it.'

'It's progress. Evolution. You've got to open the door to see what's in the next room.'

'I can't deal with this. Stop it, all right? This isn't a fucking game.'

Alex stood up, crushed the cigarette butt under his boot. 'Well,' he decided, 'if it was a game, it's over now.' He glanced at his watch and scanned the woods. 'One of us should stay here. Might not be able to find our way back otherwise.'

'I don't think we should move Dan,' James said. 'And I don't think we should leave him here on his own. Besides, I doubt he'd answer someone's call if they came back to try and find him anyway.' He stood up. 'I'll go. You wait here with Dan. I'll run. It'll be quicker.'

'There's no rush,' Alex said, inclining his head towards the mud bank. 'Don't reckon he's going anywhere.'

'That's not funny.'

Alex shrugged. 'Whatever.'

'The sooner we get Murphy, the better. Then we can get Dan out of here.'

Alex nodded, got his tobacco tin out, pulled out a Rizla and flattened it on his thigh. 'OK, I'll stay put. You go call the cavalry.'

'You reckon that's a good idea?'

'Makes sense. I mean, you're right: we shouldn't leave Dan here on his own.'

'I mean the grass,' James said. 'What about the pol—'

Alex clicked his tongue. 'Forget the pigs. You think they're gonna give a toss if I'm wrecked when they get here? You think they're gonna even notice?'

'I don't understand,' James said. 'How can you just sit here like nothing's happened?'

Alex shrugged. 'We've all got our way of coping with shit, James. This is mine.' He looked up. 'You know the way back to the cliff?'

James looked around and shook his head.

Alex pointed behind him. 'That way. Keep going straight. When the ground runs out, you'll know you're there.' He lowered his head and concentrated on the spliff. 'See you in a while, crocodile.'

Some sort of delirium had swamped James's mind by the time he stumbled down the last few steps to the bottom of the cliff. He felt drunk, didn't know if it was some after-effect of the grass he'd smoked, or plain exhaustion. A kaleidoscope of images span through his mind: the crazy patterns of the leaves in the forest; the glitter of the sea; the sun exploding across the sky. And Alex, Alex's hand, always there, pushing through the leaves, rising from the waves, blocking out the sun and casting a shadow across the land. He slipped across a mop of seaweed, fell, heard his knee crack on the rock, but couldn't feel the pain. His limbs protested as he rose up and moved on, the lactic acid they'd produced over the last fifteen minutes turning sour, finally threatening to burn through his muscles and send him sprawling face-first onto the sand his feet had now reached. Couldn't stop now. Wouldn't ever start again. Close. Close enough to make it. One final effort. His breathing howled through his throbbing ears and he hesitated for a moment, set his sights across the beach at Surfers' Turf. Then he forced himself into motion again, tried to distract his mind by estimating how many paces it would take him to hit his target. He counted them off: one, two, three, four . . .

Someone must have spotted his erratic progress across the beach, watched him weaving left and right, a shell-shocked soldier running towards the enemy over mine-strewn territory, as his legs buckled and prevented him from moving in a straight line, because by the time he reached Surfers' Turf, Murphy and the other two policemen were standing on the plateau, staring at him through narrow, bemused eyes.

'The others get too much for you?' Murphy asked as James stumbled up the last few steps onto the rock plateau.

Crumpling onto the ground, James ignored Murphy and the other policemen, distracted by movement in the doorway behind them: a woman, moving forward. Suzie? He tried to focus his eyes, but the land lurched sideways. Just like it had when he'd been with his father. Just like when his father had used to pick him up when he was a kid and spin him round, then set him back down on the ground, watch him lurch round like a drunk. The woman slid from his view. He sank his knuckles into his eye sockets, twisted them violently.

'James?' a voice came. He felt a hand laid on his shoulder. 'James? Are you all right?'

When he opened his eyes, his vision was still blurred. Disembodied facial features floated before him for a moment, rogue jigsaw pieces, then finally settled into a face. Suzie's. He looked into her eyes and held them steady.

'Water,' he mouthed, no sound coming from his mouth, and she stood and turned, walked away. He dropped his head.

'Fancy yourself as a bit of a runner, do you?' he heard

Murphy asking. James looked up, saw him nudging one of the younger policemen and glancing in the direction Suzie had gone. 'Trying to impress the girls, is it?' He frowned. 'Well, I reckon you overdid it this time, son.' Murphy peered at James's front, then reared back, covering his nose and mouth with his hand. 'Look at the state of you,' he said once he'd retreated a safe distance. 'Caked in vomit from bloody head to foot. You been on the piss?'

James couldn't believe what he was hearing. Was Murphy blind? Couldn't he see how James's brow was drowned in sweat, or how his eyes were popping, threatening to plop onto his cheeks? Or the cocoons of sticky phlegm lodged in the corners of his dry lips? None of this? James tried to speak, felt a string of gob stretch and snap like a rubber band between his teeth. His words came out jumbled, an asthmatic rattle of wheezes, overriding their vowels and consonants. Murphy smiled. Actually smiled. One of the other policemen sniggered. Anger detonated inside James, exploded from his lungs and drove through his throat, over his tongue.

'Dawes,' he growled, then the explosion subsided, leaving him breathless again as his lungs attempted to reinflate.

'What's that, son?' Murphy asked, lowering himself so that his head was level with James's. 'You say "Dawes"?' His voice had switched. Intensity had driven the earlier flippancy from his face. 'Jack Dawes? That what you're trying to say?' He reached forward and shook James roughly. 'You telling me you found something?'

James shook his head. 'No.'

Murphy shook him again, anger flashing in his eyes. 'Then what? What are you talking about?'

Suzie reappeared, crouched beside James and draped an arm across his shoulders. She raised a glass to his lips. 'Slowly,' she whispered, gently tipping the glass towards him, so that the water glossed his lips, sank into the sponge of his tongue. 'A little at a time.'

He did as he was instructed for a moment. The water seemed to sting, the flesh in his mouth and throat contracting greedily as the liquid penetrated its cells. Then the pain subsided and he took the glass in both hands, threw his head back and felt it cascading down into his stomach. Cramps twisted his guts. He glared up at Murphy, a voice chattering bitterly in his head. Fancy myself at running, yeah? Like to impress the girls, hey? Stupid bastard. Dan had been right: this man was a fucking prick. Not smiling now, though. Not nudging his mates over his bullshit comments anymore.

'Come on,' Murphy demanded. 'Tell me now. Did you find something?'

'Not something,' James spat out. His voice came loud, resuscitated by the water, his words running fluidly into sentences once more. 'Him. We found him. Up in the woods. Jack Dawes. Dead. We found him dead.'

CHAPTER SEVEN

angel

As James read the sign – WELCOME TO GRANCOMBE –
it wasn't so much butterflies flapping in his stomach as
pterodactyls. Their clawed wings were shredding his guts up.
He'd done his best to prepare for this inevitable freak-out
during the drive down. He'd visualised all the changes that
would have occurred over the past decade: new shops, new
faces, new buildings and infrastructure. And he'd prepared
himself for how his eyes had changed, how it would probably
seem smaller than it had done when he was eighteen. But
maybe – he was approaching the High Street now – he hadn't
prepared enough.

The journey had been quick, too quick. It was mid-week,
winter. No caravans acting like blood clots on the road,
clogging up the flow of traffic. Hardly any traffic at all, in fact,
since he'd left the motorway and tunnelled into the country
lanes. And especially the last fifty miles, as he'd closed in on
the coast. Even the traffic lights in the series of prettified
towns he'd passed through had been in his favour, the roads
clear, starved of their summer rations of tourists. Dread had
done that creeping thing, starting as vague queasiness and
growing towards panic the closer he'd got to his destination.
He hadn't experienced anything like this for years, not since
those days his parents had driven him back to boarding school
for the start of terms. Those were the only other times he
could remember journeys as being more desirable than
arrivals.

He checked out the world the other side of the windscreen. There was no doubt about it: Grancombe *had* changed. His mind's eye view had been of blazing sun above, grey shadows below. The flick-flack of the windscreen wipers, as he hit the High Street and strained to see out, repetitively pointed out how wrong he'd been. Unfamiliar shops and pubs, parking zones. Grancombe seemed to have grown in his absence. He continued past the cinema, absurdly expecting the same films that had been showing last time he'd been here to still be on. They weren't, of course. Just the same stuff that had been premiered in Leicester Square a month back.

He reached the bottom of the High Street and pulled into the car park off North Beach. Then he got out of the car, collected his jacket from the back seat and sealed himself against the fierce wind. The sky was a thick vortex of swirling grey, like some backdrop from a Biblical epic. Still, at least the rain was easing off. He looked around, and immediately his eyes were trapped by a building across the road. Some new club, windowless and black from gutter to foundation. Its name, CURRENT, was strung across the door in unlit neon bulbs, beneath a vast sign with a picture of a lightning strike hitting the ocean. A memory flashed into James's mind. Dixie's. That had used to be Dixie's, Grancombe's biggest club. He shook his head. Yeah, things definitely had changed.

He looked across North Beach to where the cliffs reared up towards the sky. Not a person in sight. So different from the last time he'd been here. And the lack of human sound, too. It might as well have been half a century ago when they'd evacuated the town for a week following an invasion scare. He locked the car and activated the alarm, walked up the High Street and stepped into the first estate agent he reached. The quicker he appointed someone to flog Alan's place the better.

By the time he'd finished in there and agreed that they could come round and evaluate the house at the end of the week, once he'd had a chance to sort out Alan's belongings and (though he didn't mention this to the estate agent) make a start on cleaning up what he suspected would be a total pit, his stomach was loudly reminding him that it was lunch time and that he hadn't eaten anything apart from a microwaved doner kebab, courtesy of a motorway service station, since he'd left Lucy snoozing in his bed early that morning.

He glanced up and down the street. The Moonraker was out. He wasn't risking his old local just yet. He wanted to stay incognito for as long as possible. Not that he thought he'd get away with it for his whole stay. Once – if – he started asking questions, people were sure to repay his curiosity with their own. He hadn't changed enough in the intervening years. No scars or massive gain in weight, nothing to kid anyone who'd once known him that he was anyone but himself. So keep hidden for now. Stick to the lonely places until you feel at ease.

He grabbed a couple of pasties from a newsagent and stood under its striped awnings, eating and watching the people walk by. Then, gazing across the roof tops, he saw the tower of St Donal's Church, and decided that there were some people he should visit after all. He walked back into the shop.

It was only when he reached the church, lifted the latch of the wooden gate and entered the graveyard, that he realised he had no idea where to look. The rain had stopped and he stood still for a moment, pushed his hand roughly across his head, squeezed the rain out, flinching when it trickled down his neck.

He remembered the day he'd stood in this graveyard with Alan and Dan on the day of Jack Dawes' funeral. Them and so many others. Would it have been that way with Alan? James doubted it. If even his own flesh and blood hadn't bothered to turn up, who else would have? Still, there'd be a gravestone. Alan's will had made sure of that. Then there was Dan. His funeral would have been a different matter. Much loved son. Much loved brother. Child of Grancombe. People would have come. And it would have been here. James was sure of that. Not cremated, stuck in a pot in a mantelpiece. He would have been buried here, with his grandfather before him. Dust to dust.

James scanned the gravestones as he walked, looking for fresh cut stone among the crumbling slabs. Flowers, plastic and fresh, stood in jam jars and vases. Dates from the seventies and eighties. Will Not Be Forgotten . . . Mother of . . . Son of . . . Sister of . . . Testaments to existence. Comfort for those left behind that they too wouldn't be forgotten, that their lives too wouldn't have been lived in vain.

He found Alan's first. The old parish priest, Mark Gale, must have taken pity, turned a blind eye. Polished granite, his uncle's name chiselled across its middle. The date of his first breath and the date of his last. No plot outside the graveyard reserved for the mortal sin expedited by the shot-gun Alan had nursed in his last moments. Beneath the name was an inscription, culled from the Bible, just as McCullock had said Alan had specified in his will. James read:

Set me as a seal upon thine heart, as a seal upon thine arm: for love is strong as death; jealously is cruel as the grave.

It wasn't the morbid nature of the choice that surprised James, more the source. Alan hadn't been religious, at least not while James had known him. More God-hater than God-fearer. God, the murderer of Monique. God, the black beast who'd stolen her from him. God, whose arms had turned into waves and dragged Monique to be at his side. The jealous God who'd taken her for himself.

James heard a sound like the flickering of a fire and looked down to see the wind flattening the plastic-sheathed flowers he held in his hand against his chest. He knelt down and placed one of the bunches on the ground before the grave. Colour burst against the grey stone, like flames in a hearth. He reached to his left and pulled a rock from the mud, weighed the flowers down with it to stop them being swept away by the wind. There were no vases here. There were no other flowers. He walked backwards onto the path, as if Alan's grave was an altar from which he'd just received communion. But there was no sense of communion here. Nothing had been shared. Everything refused, left to take its own course, leaving Alan to pick up that gun and pull the trigger. Everything left to rot.

'Why?'

The word came from his mouth in a wheeze, unthought, a breath of wind soon swallowed by the gale. Why? James had no answer to give. He turned from the grave and, still clutching the second bunch of flowers to his chest, continued to walk among the dead, continued to search for an answer.

He found Dan's grave on the other side of the churchyard. Fresh flowers – hundreds of them – lay about the rectangular gravestone. James's eyes wouldn't settle on the epitaph, only Dan's name and age – the same as his own. They'd been born within a month of each other. Anger stung him. Didn't deserve to die. Murdered. Murdered by a sick-head. Maybe Alan was right. Maybe there was no good. Only evil, coming to get you every time. Peter Headley's face hovered like an apparition before James's eyes. The morgue shots he'd seen in L.A. Animal. Better off dead. He pictured himself shooting Headley. Shooting him in the face. Blowing him away time and time again. But Headley kept rearing back up, shot away like a gun target on a range. He was laughing at him. *Kill me again. Do it*, James heard him screaming. *Be like me. Become like me . . .*

He crouched down and propped the flowers up against the gravestone, traced Dan's name with his finger. The stone was cold. An impulse brought James's hand retreating to his side, like he'd been stung. Too late. Only reach out to the living. Nothing else counts. He ignored the tears running down his face and the flow of sweat beneath his shirt. The wind felt warm. He wiped a clammy hand across his clammy brow. He had no right to cry. Sentimental crap. Can't nurse the dead.

He stood up. His legs felt weak. He shouldn't have come here. No point. He shouldn't have come to the graveyard and he shouldn't have come to Grancombe. There was only death for him here. The gravestone moved before him and he tried to steady himself by reading the engraving. Letters slid into new words, a language he couldn't translate. The heat was eating him. He pulled at his collar, dragged air into his lungs. Then the gravestone slipped sideways and the tower of the church fell crashing across the darkening sky.

✳ ✳ ✳

He felt himself moving, being lifted up. Rain slapped down on his face. Feeling cold, so cold. He opened his eyes, saw a hand closing round his jaw, slowly moving it from side to side. Lightning cracked across the dark sky. The wind howled.

'What?' he managed to say.

'Try not to speak,' someone said. 'You've fallen. Your head's bleeding.' The hand moved from his jaw and under his armpit. 'Help me to get you sitting.'

He nodded his head and leant forward towards his knees. 'Uh.'

'This might hurt a little. I'm sorry.'

He felt a hand fingering through his hair. He hissed through his teeth and flinched as the pain came.

'It's OK,' the voice said. 'Just a cut. You're lucky.'

'What—'

'You've had a fall. You're soaked.'

James looked at the gravestone in front of him. 'Dan,' he whispered, remembering where he was.

'You knew him?' the voice asked.

'Yes.' James stared at the flowers he'd left there. 'He was my friend. You?'

'Yes.'

James twisted round and looked into the face of the owner of the voice. Black hair. Then inwards, to the eyes. And across. And then he knew. Sparkle. The silver star in her left ear.

One word came to him. 'Suzie?'

Her mouth was open now. Slowly, her head shook and her arms withdrew, leaving him propped up in the mud on his elbow. She blinked. And again. Confusion. She reached out her hand, as if to touch his face, then stopped, leaving it frozen between them. This couldn't be, he thought. Just a statue. An angel. Guardian of the graveyard. Stone hand. Stone face. Stone heart.

'Suzie?' he asked again.

'Yes,' she said, standing up and looking down. 'Yes, James. It's me.'

And now he believed his eyes. Then came the jolt – as if

105

he'd just touched a live wire – hitting him the same as when he'd first seen her in Surfers' Turf the morning of the search. He remained crouched, as much stunned by her as by the ache in his head. Had she changed? He couldn't be sure. Winter was here and heavy clothing screened everything apart from her head. Her hair was longer, down past her shoulders. It lay in thick, wet streaks across her face, black as a crow's feathers. Her face wasn't lined, but still older. Something had changed in her eyes. Their mahogany colour had matured, hardened. Still beautiful, though. As beautiful now as when he'd seen her in his dreams. He reached out to her.

'Can you help me up?' he asked.

She ignored him for a few seconds, continued to examine him in silence.

'Please,' he said.

This time, she nodded her head and closed her fingers round his and pulled him smoothly to his feet.

'OK, now?' she asked.

'Better.'

'OK to walk?'

He rocked his weight from one foot to the other. 'Yes.'

'Good.' She released his hand and pulled his arm around her. He felt the weight of water in his clothes. 'Where are you staying?'

'Nowhere. I mean Alan's. Only I haven't gone there yet. Only just arrived. My car's parked down by North Beach.'

'Come on,' she said, walking him back onto the path. 'There's a fire in the 'Raker. I'll fix you up with some clothes till yours dry out. Check that cut out, as well.'

Later, in the Moonraker, he blinked, his eyes beginning to sting from staring into the fire for too long. He looked down at the clothes he was wearing: tatty denim shirt, thick jumper and jeans. He'd changed in the bathroom in the flat above the bar. They were Dan's clothes. Suzie hadn't needed to tell him that when she'd handed them over. Her hands had given her away, holding the ragged bundle so gently, reluctantly surrendering it.

He looked across the room to the bar where Suzie was

fixing them both a drink. So little had changed. He'd swear the same punters were still conversing in hushed tones at the bar. He felt like he'd never left, like the years between had been nothing more than a dream. Suzie's Dad, Johno, as if reading his thoughts, nodded at him from behind the bar and smiled. It had been the same when Suzie had brought him in out of the storm. Not even a flash of surprise to mark the passage of time, just acceptance and that nod and that smile. He'd remembered James's name, had greeted him like he'd last been in the night before. So much for trying to fox your past. Suzie came round the bar and walked towards him. He busied himself with lighting a cigarette.

'Here,' she said, handing him a pint. 'Dad said that'll soon warm you up.'

'Thanks.' He took a swig. It was bitter and strong. 'He wasn't kidding. Make it himself?'

'Yes, he's got it down for his Christmas Ale.'

'Well, he should have a few satisfied customers.'

'Sure should.'

He felt awkward, like this was a blind date. There was so much to say to her. How many times had he imagined this reunion? He'd lost count way back. All those bitter nights in Edinburgh the year after he'd left Grancombe when it had been her face that had accompanied him to sleep. And sporadically since, as he'd moved from girlfriend to girlfriend. Even lately, while he'd been in the States, a sea away from Lucy, left alone with his dreams once more. But now that it was for real – her here, him here, reality – what was there left to say? That she looked incredible? Forget it. Adults now. Not infatuated with her. Too old. And too wise.

'What?' he asked, noticing her staring at him.

'How does your head feel?'

'Still stings, but better. Thanks again.'

She rolled her eyes. 'Anyone would think I've saved your life.'

He looked down. 'So here we are, then.'

'Yeah, here we are.' Her mouth pinched in a reluctant smile. 'And the last time I saw you must have been . . .'

'A few years back now.'

'Yeah. A few years back.' A look of exaggerated puzzlement crossed her face. 'And what were the circumstances? Was it? No, I can't quite seem to remember. How strange.' She raised her eyebrows, suggested, 'Maybe your memory's better than mine ...'

OK, he thought, here goes. 'On the door step. Outside of here. Hot summer night, 1989.'

She clicked her tongue, sat back in her chair. 'Well, that's something, at least. You do remember.'

'I do.'

Her face scrunched up. 'And then you kissed me goodnight and told me you'd call me.'

'I did.'

'Right, only you didn't.'

'I know. I left town.'

'And?'

'And I guess I owe you an apology.'

'I guess you do.'

He caught the trace of a smile on her face. 'Are you enjoying this?'

'Might be.'

'You are, aren't you?'

She wagged her finger at him. 'Ah-ah. Don't try and switch this round on me.'

'I'm not.'

'Yeah, you are. It's you who's in court, not me. And you're meant to be apologising.' Her eyes narrowed. 'So ...'

'All right. Fine. I'm sorry. I mean it. It's just ...' A sigh came out instead of words. 'I don't know. Something came up. I had to leave. I —'

'Whoah.' She was grinning now. 'Enough. Punishment over.' She raised her glass to him. 'We were kids. Apology accepted.'

'That's it?' he checked. 'You're not angry?'

'I'm twenty-nine years old, James. I think I've kind of grown out of hating people for not calling me when they said they would.'

He clinked his glass against hers. 'OK, then. Cheers.'

They both drank. 'It seems a long time ago now,' she said, returning her glass to the table. Pain suddenly crossed her face like a cloud. The light in her eyes faded. 'So much stuff's gone down since then.' She closed her eyes and he heard her drawing breath into her lungs. 'So much bad fucking stuff.'

Say it, he told himself. Don't duck it. And so he spoke. 'About Dan . . . I'm sorry, Suzie. I'm so fucking sorry.' Her eyes stayed closed. 'I just . . . You must be . . .' Her lips had rolled in on themselves. He could almost feel her teeth biting down on them. 'It's OK,' he told her. 'You don't have to keep it in.'

Her head was shaking. 'No, not here. I mustn't talk about him here. Not now.' Her eyes opened and she looked over her shoulder at her father. 'Not with Dad here.' She faced James again, sat upright, as if leaning forward would tip the tears from her eyes and onto her face. 'Come on,' she said, 'let's talk about something else. Let's . . . Oh, Jesus, let's just have another drink.'

James watched her walk over to the bar and disappear behind it. He should have stayed. He knew it for real now. He could have changed things. All things. His life. Hers. And, most important of all, Dan's. He shouldn't have run. It had got him nowhere, just back to where he'd started from.

A noise came, high and insistent, and the heads at the bar turned to face him. He stared along the squad of faces, confused.

'You gonna answer that, or what?' Johno asked.

'What?'

One of the locals laughed. 'That bump on his head must be worse than we thought. Your phone, kid. Your bloody phone.'

Another one of the locals pointed at a sign on the wall. 'That's a quid you owe.'

James read the sign: *MOBILE PHONE PENALTY – £1.* He shook his head, managed a smile and picked his mobile off the table. 'Yeah, Jake,' he said, seeing his name flashing on the display, 'how you doing?'

'Good, Marple. Real good. Where you at?'

James turned away from the staring faces, embarrassed, twisted his chair round towards the fire again, kept his voice low. 'Grancombe. Just got in.'

'Had yourself an ice cream yet? Seen any nice titties on the beach?'

James wasn't in the mood for this. 'In case you hadn't noticed, Jake, it's mid-winter. And in case you'd forgotten, the only women who sunbathe topless on British beaches are the models you plant there for your smutty articles.'

Jake cackled down the line at him. 'Hey, hey, hey, just providing a service, you know. Just giving the readers what they want.'

'Just giving the readers what you want them to want, Jake. There is a difference.' James crushed his cigarette into the ashtray. 'Anyway, what can I do for you?'

'Nada. Just checking your mobile's working. Never can tell with the provinces.'

'Civilisation does exist outside the M25.'

'Yeah, yeah. Still, better give me your hotel number. Assuming the hotels down there have telephones, that is.'

'I already told you, I only just got here. Haven't found anywhere to stay yet.'

'OK, but let me know as soon as you're sorted.' Jake sniffed loudly. 'What about your woman? She down there with you?'

'No, Friday.'

'Yeah, well no honeymoon suite, OK? You're there to work, right?'

'Sure.'

'Good. So what are your plans?'

'How so?'

'For digging me up some dirt. What's on the cards?'

'I dunno. There's a local paper down here. Suppose I'll start there, check up on the history of the murders and all that. Should be able to get enough background to get the article up and running. Then have a chat with the cops. Usual leads . . .'

'Yeah, well you be careful.'

'What for?'

'What, you never seen *The Wicker Man*? Guy goes to some poxy country place and asks the wrong questions, next thing they're trying to waste him.'

'Yeah, Jake. Meanwhile back in reality . . .'

'OK, you're probably right. You should check it out anyway, though. Great shag scene in it with Edward Woodward and some blonde bird. Name slips me . . .' There was silence for a couple of seconds, Jake obviously savouring this screen memory. 'Anyway, later, my man. Speak soon. Let me know how it's coming on.'

And the phone went dead.

He turned the chair back round and saw Suzie standing by her chair, two drinks in her hands. Her face ran red before him.

'Get out,' she said.

'What?'

'Get the fuck out of my pub now, you piece of shit.'

'Now hang on a minute. What are you —'

She put the glasses on the table, leant forward, so that her face was inches from him. 'What am I talking about?' she asked, her voice shaking. 'You've got the fucking nerve to ask me what I'm talking about, when you've just been talking to some wanker on the phone about some article you're writing on my brother's death.' The flattened palm of her right hand shrunk into a fist. 'You go. You go now.'

James stood on the doorstep of the Moonraker, holding a plastic bag containing his wet clothes, and stared down the street. The wind stung his cheek. This was fucked. He couldn't believe how fucked this was. She'd been there, back in his sight. And he'd lost her again. Worse than when he'd left and run away. There'd been no confrontation then. But now . . . now she had a solid reason to hate him. Not just confusion over why he'd left. But loathing, loathing for him and who he was.

He checked himself. It was just a row. Just a row between two people who used to be friends. I've grown up. Moved on. What did I expect? That I'd fall in love with her all over again? That she'd want me back? What kind of crap is that?

I've got another life now. She's not part of it. I don't need her back. I've got Lucy. I've got a job. I've got friends. I've got a flat in London and a future. I don't need Grancombe and all its small-town shit.

But he felt sick, sick to the core.

He folded his arms across Suzie's dead brother's clothes and set off into the town to find a hotel.

CHAPTER EIGHT

funeral

Alan stood there, held upright like a shop dummy by the pressed contours of his black suit, his face as grey as the stones of the church wall behind him. His shoes were polished, his beard gone. He was immaculate. Above him shone the sun, burning relentlessly down on him, casting his distorted shadow across the open grave. He was visibly shaking, his eyes raised to the sky, as if he was talking directly to God.

'I know what I'm meant to tell you,' he was saying to the crowd of mourners. 'That Jack was a good man. That Jack didn't deserve this. That no one deserves this. That's not what I feel. That's not what anyone who knew Jack feels. Any of us. His friends.' His arms collapsed to his sides, hands curled into fists. 'And so I'm not going to calm you with clichés.'

'We're not here to celebrate Jack's life,' he said. 'His life was stolen. We're here to demand justice – to demand that the scum who hacked him down in the woods is caught. No matter what it takes. Is caught and punished.'

James watched the elderly parish vicar, Mark Gale, bow his head, exaggerating his stooped body even further. His lips moved in silent prayer and then, as Alan had done before, he looked to the sky. Was that where the answer lay? Up there in that great blue mirror? Was what had happened to Jack Dawes on the Wednesday night – they'd pinned the time of death down now, to a matter of hours – locked there like a negative, waiting to be developed?

James looked around the assembled people. St Donal's

graveyard was packed. Young and old. People had formed lines behind one another between the ancient gravestones, as if waiting in orderly queues for buses to arrive. Hundreds of them, those who'd arrived late standing in the road outside the low stone walls. The whole spectrum of the local population was represented. Faces matching that of Jack Dawes in age. People who'd attended Grancombe's primary school with him, watched him pick up his first paint brush, splash colour across a white sheet for the first time. Then those older, men and women who'd known Jack's parents, babysat for him, carried him home after he'd scuffed his knees on the rocks off Eagle's point, given him a tissue to dry his tears. And those younger. Teenagers like Alex and Daniel. People who'd read his names in the tourist brochures, made a joke of the national fame placed on the shoulders of a man they were used to seeing walking the streets of the town and talking to their parents since birth. And then there were Murphy's sidekicks, in uniform, standing next to the TV crew and reporters who'd come here, ensuring that they recorded their tributes from a distance, didn't interfere. And Murphy himself, also glancing occasionally up into the sky, studying it like a fisherman searching for omens, then turning his gaze back to the crowd, watching, watching and waiting, knowing, as everyone knew, that it was possible that Jack Dawes' killer was amongst them now.

'After my wife, Monique, died, Jack was there for me. Just the same as he'd been there for Monique and I every day we'd lived here. Friendship isn't a strong enough word. Nor loyalty. Nor trust. Jack epitomised all these qualities.' Alan's voice started to crack. 'He helped me so much when she went. He helped me to carry on living. And now he's dead and I'll never have the chance to repay him.' Alan reached into his pocket and withdrew a bunch of keys. He stepped forward and dropped them into the grave. They landed with a clatter on the coffin lid. 'The keys to your home,' he said to the ground. 'Your trust. Returned to you now.'

James looked across the grave at Alex. He was standing next to his mother, his arm around her waist, the domestic

stance somehow making him look older, removed from the
teenager who'd sat on the cliff top and passed James the
spliff. His shades were missing, his eyes downcast. Behind
him, to his left, back in the crowd, was Dan, his blond head
raised above the crowd. James hadn't seen either of them
since he'd left them in the woods. Dan's mouth was sealed,
silent, not how Jack remembered him, not how Jack remembered him at all.

James looked up. Alan had finished speaking. He'd stepped
back from the grave and now stood with his head bowed,
scrutinising his shoes. Mark Gale had taken over the proceed-
ings. He was sermonising, interspersing his theme of grief and
mourning with appropriate quotes from the Bible. The camera
crew were packing up, the outside broadcast over, preparing
to move onto the next tragedy in the next town. Next to Alan's
earlier passion, Gale's words sounded rehearsed, meaningless:
background noise. Gale must have sensed this. He raised his
fragile voice, a shepherd whose flock had deserted him as he'd
slept. The change in voice, though, failed to snag James's
attention. James had spotted Alex moving, edging slowly
sideways through the crowd, until he'd successfully detached
himself from it entirely. He was now leaning against a gravestone, staring at James, his shades back in place. He raised
his hand, pointed to the entrance of the graveyard, then turned
and walked.

'What kept you?' he asked, when James joined him in the
street a few minutes later.

'I don't know.' James glanced back at the church. Some of
the people gathered there were staring at them. 'I didn't feel
right about leaving like that.'

'Bullshit. Your uncle said what needed to be said. Gale's
senile. He'll be there for hours, giving it the religious thing.
Biggest congregation he's had for years.' He cocked his left
eyebrow over the frame of his shades. 'Suits you.'

'What does?'

Alex stretched out his arm, pinched the lapel of James's
jacket. 'The suit.'

'It's Alan's,' James explained, taking in Alex's faded jeans and white t-shirt. 'Said I should wear it.'

Alex looked at his watch. 'Come on,' he said, setting off down the street, the sun casting an elongated shadow on the concrete surface before him. 'It's opening time. Reckon we should get a drink. Reckon we deserve it for sticking that out.'

'What about Dan?' James asked, walking next to him. 'Is he coming?'

'Nah.'

'How is he?'

'Dunno. Haven't spoken to him since we were in the cop shop with Murphy. I tell you, man, the way he put us in separate rooms to question us about how we'd found the body and what state it had been in and all that, you would've thought it was us that had killed the bastard. I tell you, he was loving it. Getting a buzz. Bored cop. Big murder. Must've made his year.' Alex lit a cigarette. 'He ask you if you'd touched anything?'

'Yeah.'

'What d'you say?'

'I told him no.'

'What about me? Me and Dan? He ask you if we touched it?'

'Yeah.'

'And?'

'I told him Dan had fallen on the body.' James stared ahead. They were rounding the bend of the road, walking past the train station. He knew what Alex was really asking him, knew it wasn't about Dan's fall at all. 'I didn't tell him anything else.'

Alex placed his hand on James's shoulder for a second, squeezed. 'Good. I knew you'd keep your gob shut. Not that it would have mattered,' he added quickly. 'Didn't mean anything anyhow, right?'

'Sure,' James said. 'Didn't mean a thing.'

'Still, it's good you didn't tell him. Never can tell with someone like Murphy. He's got a sick mind. Can't tell how he'd interpret something like that, how he'd try and use it to his advantage.'

James didn't want to talk about this any more. It made him uncomfortable. Forget how Murphy would interpret what Alex had done. James wasn't even sure how to interpret it himself. It was still there in his mind. What Alex had done. What he'd said about it afterwards. All that stuff about sticking your hands into the dark, seeing where your guts ran out. It had sounded like preparation, as if it had been some test Alex had needed to put himself through. But why? That's what really bothered James. No one volunteered to take tests unless they thought they were going to get them somewhere, open themselves up to opportunities previously denied.

'He warn you off speaking to the journalists?' Alex asked, maybe sensing James's discomfort. 'Feed you the line about not making matters worse by giving them more to write about?'

'Yeah, like they haven't got enough to fill the front pages for the rest of the week.'

'Makes sense, though. My old girl was telling me that the train out of here the night the news broke was packed with families getting the fuck out. Only thing I reckon Murphy's been right about in his life: soon as it's out of the papers the better for everyone. Act like nothing's happened, that's what Dan's dad says. Business as normal till the business comes back.'

'Do you know how he is?' James asked.

'Who?'

'Dan. I heard that Mark Gale guy saying he was in a bit of a state.'

'Medicated up to his eyeballs, the way I heard it,' Alex said. 'He looked well spaced-out in the graveyard. Like a zombie.'

'Poor sod.'

Alex laughed. 'Poor sod nothing. Free drugs. Pop down the doctor's and get doped up. Lucky sod, more like.' He looked sideways at James. 'Don't sweat it. Dan'll be fine. Just give him a few days.'

They turned into the High Street. James scanned the shop fronts. Closed signs hung in their doorways. Tourists stood in confused huddles outside on the pavement, empty shopping baskets in their hands.

'Morons,' Alex commented, as they approached a particularly confused looking couple. 'Looks like no one's told them that Grancombe ain't opening till the funeral's over.'

'So where are we heading?' James asked.

'The Cove. Down on the sea front.'

'Why will that be open if everywhere else is shut?'

Alex grinned at him. 'Your uncle gave a good speech, yeah, but not everything he said was true.'

'Like what?'

'Like all that stuff about loyalty and trust. Not everyone thought of Dawes that way.'

'I don't get you. All those people at St Donal's. All those people crying.'

'Women,' Alex corrected, brushing past a group of middle-aged tourists. 'Just the women.'

'Whatever. They wouldn't have cried unless they cared.'

'I'm not saying they didn't. A lot of women did care about Dawes. If rumours are right, a fuck of a lot of women cared.'

'What are you saying?'

'That a rich and famous artist in a small town like this is a pretty desirable proposition, especially when he's single. That there are a lot of bored women round here married to boring men. Work it out, man. Work it out.'

James nodded. 'Just rumours, though, you say?'

'Some, yeah. Some, no.' Alex turned right at the bottom of the High Street. The beach was studded with tourists, the tide out. 'I can think of at least one confirmed kill chalked up by Casanova Dawes.'

'Who?'

'Josie Tawnside. Will Tawnside's wife. Actually caught her in the sack with Dawes. A couple of years back.'

'What happened?'

'The usual, I guess. Slapped his wife. Punched Dawes. Divorced his wife. Never spoke to Dawes again.'

Alex slowed to a halt outside a thick-stoned, thatched building overlooking the beach. A sign hung from the black beam over its front door: a weather-beaten painting of the sea dashing against the rocks, the words *THE COVE* beneath.

'This is Tawnside's place,' Alex said, pushing the gate to the beer garden open and heading for the door. 'Strictly tourist. Wouldn't normally be seen dead here.'

James followed Alex, ducking through the small doorway into the pub. He stopped for a moment, the internal gloom suddenly eclipsing the sun, leaving him dazed. He watched Alex stride across the uneven, flagstoned floor towards the bar, then gradually the room came into focus. It was tacky, to say the least. Alex had been right: strictly tourist. Clichéd paintings of Grancombe (kites being flown on the beach, raging storms, kids licking ice creams) straddled the walls, probably the produce of local artists, though equally probably not the works of the late Jack Dawes. A large chest freezer, stacked with ice-creams stood wedged up against the wall in one corner. Next to it was a wooden stand, displaying box upon box of home-made fudge. At the centre of each of the tables was a glass jar with zebra-striped sticks of rock protruding from its rim. James knew without taking a closer look that the word *Grancombe* would be printed through their stems. The ceilings, like the door, were low, and James had to stoop to avoid knocking his head against the beams as he crossed the room.

It was fairly quiet. Still it was early. Not even noon. And recent circumstances were probably just as much to blame. A family of four, whom James recognised from the train, sat at one table, slopping fried breakfasts into their mouths. One of the kids looked up at James and opened his mouth, showing off some half-chewed bacon and egg, before collapsing into a fit of giggles and starting to choke. Two teenage girls at another table watched James idly over the top of their drinks as he walked the last few paces to the bar. Alex was sitting on a bar stool and James drew another one up beside him and sat down. The acrid odour of spilt beer and stale cigarette smoke weighed heavy in the air. James looked at the varnished flagstones beneath his feet. In the yellow light caused by the sun straining at the drawn curtains, they looked wet, like some drunk had relieved himself at the bar.

'Service in here sucks, huh?' Alex reflected, leaning forward over the empty bar and craning his neck in the direction of the door which led to the back of the building. 'Will,' he shouted, banging his fist on the bar counter. 'D'you want us to serve ourselves, or what?'

'All right,' a deep voice came back. 'Hold your bloody horses. I'm coming.'

Alex winked at James. 'Warning: Will's one big fucked up bastard.'

A form stumbled through the doorway behind the bar. Alex hadn't been kidding. Will was big, maybe six foot five. Fat with it. A girth like a pregnant whale. Breasts that a stripper would have killed for. A thick red beard covered his jaw and throat. His momentum carried him half-way over the bar, where he finally slumped to a halt. He fixed Alex with scrunched-up, piggy eyes.

'Young Mr Howley,' he said. 'Haven't seen you in a while. Didn't think my pub was your kind of place.'

Alex smiled tolerantly. 'Fancied a change.'

Will snorted. 'Did you fuck. Only place that's open, more like.'

'Whatever.'

'D'you go to the funeral, then?'

'Yeah.'

'Good, was it?' He grinned broadly. 'Good entertainment had by all?'

Alex humoured him: 'Yeah, Will, laugh a minute.'

'Yeah? Maybe I should've gone after all. Livened things up a bit more. Been laughing since I heard what happened to him, me . . . Better off dead, that one. Got the coffin lid on him. Best news I've heard in ages.' He nodded in agreement with himself, then his eyes narrowed and he asked, 'Many people there?'

'Most of the town.'

'Stupid bastards.' He looked bitterly round the sparsely populated room. 'Dawes is probably laughing at them all from the grave. Turned the town into a ghost town, hasn't he? Scared half the tourists off.'

'Yeah, yeah,' Alex said, losing his patience. 'Now, how about a drink?'

'What are you having?'

'Dunno,' Alex said, scrutinising the beer taps on show. 'None of the crap you sell the tourists, that's for sure . . .'

'Saying my home brew's bollocks, are you?'

Alex ignored the question. 'Give me a Stella.'

Will turned on James. 'You?' he asked, his breath almost flammable with alcohol fumes.

'The same.'

Will pulled a couple of pint glasses down from the shelf above the bar and slid one under the Stella tap, flicked the handle. 'Any news on who done the good deed?' he asked, tilting the glass as it filled.

Alex shook his head. 'No.'

'Shame,' Will said, his grin returning, switching the empty glass under the stream of lager. He finished pouring, put the two pints before Alex and James. 'You find out who done it, you send 'em here. I'd like to buy whoever it was a drink. Congratulate them on a job well done.'

Alex handed over some cash, didn't wait for the change. 'Come on,' he said to James, 'let's grab a pew.'

'Howley,' Will shouted after them.

Alex stopped and turned. 'What?'

Will was holding a full shot glass to his lips. 'Cut his hands off, didn't they?'

'Yeah.'

Will downed the shot, gasped. 'Someone should've done that years back. Might have stopped him putting them places they didn't belong.'

Alex tapped his finger against the side of his head. 'Seek medical help,' he muttered, turning round and walking to a table in the corner.

James joined him, sat down.

'Not bitter, then,' he commented.

'Psycho,' Alex agreed. 'Used to be a nice guy, before all that

121

stuff with Dawes and his wife. Kind of tipped him over the edge. Almost understandable, you know.'

'Suppose so.'

'Yeah, and he's doubly pissed off, 'cos Murphy had him in for questioning. Had him down as a suspect.'

James sipped at his beer. 'Not surprising, if he's been going on like he did just now.' He watched Will for a few moments. He was refilling his glass, staring down at the bar counter, the animation of the previous few minutes totally evacuated from his stance. 'You reckon he might have done it?'

'Who knows?' Alex said. 'It could have been anyone.'

'Even you,' James said.

Alex slowly shook his head. 'Me and Dan are just about the only people who couldn't have done it.'

'Yeah? Says who?'

'We weren't here, were we?' Alex pointed out. 'Only got back from holiday the day you got here. And Dawes was wasted two days before we found him. Half-rotted by then. Reckon that puts us totally in the clear.'

James's stomach rolled at the image. 'Guess that puts me in the clear as well, then.'

Alex smiled. 'Guess it does.'

'So, where did you go on holiday?'

'Majorca.' Alex surveyed his forearm, rolled his wrist to emphasise its contrast with the milky skin on his underarm. 'It's hot here, sure, but you don't get a golden brown like this in Britain. No matter how much time you spend squatting on the beach.'

'Did you go with your folks?'

He sneered. 'Nah, you wouldn't get my mum out of Grancombe when it's high season. Not if you used a cattle-prod. Too much money to be made. Runs a B&B in Clarnton Street,' he explained.

'What about your dad?'

'Dead.' James was about to speak, when Alex continued, 'Might as well be, anyhow. Sorry son-of-a-bitch. The old girl left him when I was eight. Used to beat her. Me too, she says. When he was drunk, which was any day with a Y in it, the way she tells it. Only I don't remember it too good any more. Don't remember what he looked like, even.' Alex fell silent for a few seconds, unwrapped a piece of chewing gum and stuck it in his mouth. 'What about you?' he asked, then smiled. 'Let me guess. Nice middle-class mum and dad. A brother or a sister. Nuclear family. Patio and barbecue in the back garden. Volvo estate and a dog called Rover. Getting warm?'

'No.'

'Not even close?'

'Not even on the same continent.' Alex was waiting for him to speak, so James told him. 'They died in Cyprus. My parents. Two years ago. Road accident. No brothers and sisters.'

'Fuck.'

James held up his hand. 'It's OK.'

'On your own, then?'

'Yeah, apart from Alan.'

Alex's brow furrowed. 'I'm sorry, man. I didn't know.'

'Look,' James said, 'if it's OK with you, let's just leave it. Talk about something else, you know. It's not something I'm good with.'

'OK, whatever you—'

''Scuse me.'

They looked up. One of the two teenage girls was standing over them. She was medium height, more scrawny than slim. Her long fawn hair hung unkempt, streaked unevenly with bleach. Up-close, her face was pasty, her eyes tired.

'What?' Alex said.

The girl shifted her weight awkwardly from one foot to the other. 'I don't want to go butting in . . .'

'You already have,' Alex said.

'Sorry. It's just I heard the barman calling after you. You're Alex Howley, aren't you?'

'Maybe.'

The girl looked confused for a second, then collected herself, smiled. 'You know a friend of mine. Christine.'

Alex shook his head, lit a cigarette and looked the girl up and down.

'She met you at Bar Tab a couple of nights ago,' the girl
went on. 'Said you sorted her out.'

Alex sipped at his beer. 'Did she now?'

The girl giggled insecurely, glanced over at her friend, then
back at Alex. 'Said you might be able to sort us out, as well.'

'That a fact?' Alex asked, craning his neck forward and
checking the other girl out.

'I don't know. Is it?'

'What's your name?'

'Hazel.'

'You got money?'

'Yeah. Some.'

Alex nodded. 'OK. What d'you need?'

'What's going?'

'The range. Pills, powders, grass.' He examined her body
again, settled on her face. 'How old are you?'

She glanced at Will, watching them from behind the bar.
'Nineteen,' she hazarded.

Alex raised his eyebrows. 'Crap.'

She leant in closer. James could smell her perfume now. He
tried not to stare too obviously at the dark line of her cleavage.
'OK,' she said quietly, 'seventeen, but it doesn't matter, does it?'

'Maybe,' Alex said. 'What about your mate? Same age?'

The girl was getting nervous. She nodded. 'Yeah, but so
what?'

'Depends.'

'On what?'

'On who you're down here with. I'm not fixing you up if
you're with your parents. Too much grief. I don't want your
father going squealing to the pigs.'

She rolled her eyes. 'Do I look like I'm into family holidays?'
He didn't answer, so she did. 'Well, I'm not, OK? There's just
the two of us.'

'OK, I'll take your word for it.' He drew pensively on his
cigarette. 'Tell you what,' he said. 'Why don't you tell me
where you're staying and I'll come round in a bit?'

'OK,' she agreed after a second's hesitation. 'We're up at
Brock Wood Caravan Site. Number sixteen.' She raised a

studded eyebrow. 'See you there – when? – about an hour?'

'Sure,' Alex said. 'About an hour. Maybe sooner. Depends.'

'OK, later,' the girl said and walked back to her table.

'You up for it?' Alex asked once she was out of earshot.

'What, pills?' James frowned. 'No.'

'Nah, not pills. Christ, you only tried your first smoke a few days back. Give me some credit. What, d'you think I'm planning to have you on crack by the end of the week?'

James smiled, as if the idea was as crazy as Alex made it sound. 'What, then?'

'Them.'

'The girls?' James asked.

'Yeah. You on?'

James took a drink, surreptitiously checked the girls out over the top of his glass. Hazel's friend was staring at him. Enough make-up for a drag queen. Face round and flat, like she'd run into a wall. They looked into one another's eyes for a second, and then he broke the connection, lowered his glass and turned back to Alex.

'They're pretty grim,' he said.

'Grim, pretty, makes no difference. Passes the time, doesn't it? They're all right. Enough to make your dick go north and your balls go boom. What more d'you want?'

'You reckon they're interested?'

'Doesn't matter either way.'

'How's that?'

'Doesn't matter whether they're after our minds or our bodies. Doesn't matter if they're not after either. We've still got something they want.'

'Drugs,' James deduced.

'Drugs,' Alex concurred, flicking his glass with his fingernail, making it chime. 'Better pull than muscle power and brain power put together.'

'I don't know, Alex. It doesn't really feel right doing things that way.'

'See you in a bit,' Hazel said, as she walked past on their way to the door.

'Bye,' her friend said to James.

James watched her walk out of the door, then heard Alex laugh. When he looked at him, he was nodding, his cigarette clamped between his teeth. He removed it, revealed the extent of his smile.

'You're up for it, all right,' he said 'If your eyes were teeth, they would've bitten her arse clean off.'

James didn't reply for a couple of seconds, then admitted, 'Her body's all right.'

'Come on,' Alex scoffed. 'Where's the harm in it? What's the problem?'

'I told you.' James said. 'It doesn't feel right, using the drugs to get to them like that.'

'Don't give me that. Drugs are just bait. Same as turning on the charm, same as having a fast car, smooth clothes. Jesus, no worse than aftershave. Where's the difference? It's not like we're pinning them down and force-feeding them. Remember, it was them that came to us, not the other way round. Not my fault it's a sellers' market, is it?'

'No.'

'So what's your problem with this?' He flipped his shades onto his brow. 'You got a girlfriend back home? That it?'

'No.'

'Didn't think so.'

James felt himself flush. 'What's that meant to mean?'

'Well, no offence, mate, but you hadn't smoked before you came down here, so who's to say there aren't a few other things you haven't tried as well?' Alex held his hands up. 'Look,' he said, 'you don't have to do anything, do you? Just come along and see how things pan out. Let nature take its course and all that. Can't object to that, can you?'

James felt his resolve weakening, like it was a pill being dissolved in the flow of Alex's words. Everything seemed clear when Alex spoke. Answers to all questions. Explanations for all doubts. He was a born salesman. Drugs. Ideas. It didn't matter. His approach was the same: if you had a problem, he had the cure. But still something nagged at James.

'What about the others?' James asked. Alex frowned, so James went on, 'The people from the funeral.'

'Let them find their own girls,' Alex said, his eyes sparking.

James smiled, despite himself. 'I don't mean that.'

'Just as well. I'm not well into sharing. That kind of stuff's for perverts.'

'Alan said they were all heading for the Moonraker afterwards for a drink.'

'So let them. They're hardly gonna miss us, are they? You saw how many people were there. Don't reckon half of them will squeeze into the 'Raker.'

'Suppose not.'

James remembered Suzie, how she'd said her parents ran the Moonraker. He'd looked for her at St Donal's, hadn't managed to pluck her face from the crowd. He'd thought about her the night before, as he'd been lying there in bed, unable to sleep, unable to look out of the window into the woods without thinking that somewhere out there, breathing in the shadows, was someone who'd done that sick stuff to Dawes. And today, at the funeral, even though he'd failed to locate her, the thought that she might have been there, similarly scanning the crowd for him, maybe even watching him, had kept his mind clear, distracted him from imagining the contents of the coffin.

'All the same,' he said, 'we really should go.'

Alex finished his drink, ran the back of his hand across his mouth, belched. 'I don't do should. Only want.' He leant on the table and pushed himself to his feet. 'You coming, or what?'

He didn't wait for James to answer, just turned and walked to the door. James sat alone for a few seconds, watching the family at the table nearby. They'd finished eating now. The father and mother were engrossed in newspapers, the little boy rolling a stick of rock back and forth across the table's surface, making engine noises. His sister's head was resting on her hands, her back rising and falling regularly in the motions of sleep. James finished his drink and left.

'Wait up,' he shouted after Alex, running down the street to catch him up.

Alex walked on a while, then sat on the thick concrete seawall that severed the street from North Beach. He slipped his t-shirt from his back, tucking it beneath his belt so that it hung down across his thigh.

'What's that all about, then?' James asked, sitting down next to him and nodding at the tattoo of a black cockerel on his arm. 'Black magic, huh? Voodoo?' he joked.

'Something like that,' Alex said without smiling. 'Got it done last summer.'

James looked across North Beach. There were maybe a hundred people scattered across the sand, like huddled desert outposts, segregated from one another by parasols and wind-breaks, sweating it out against the sun. A caravan of donkeys, saddled with toddlers and escorted by camera-snapping parents, plodded wearily along the shore, tails swishing, hooves kicking up the sand. To the left, below the hill on which St Donal's stood, was Grancombe Harbour. Thirty or so yachts and powerboats were berthed there, bobbing against the rubber tyres which girdled the concrete quays. Even from here, James could hear their masts tinkling in the breeze. Further out at sea, where the waves chopped each other into angry white, a group of windsurfers cut past one another like jousting knights.

'So?' Alex asked. 'What's it to be?'

James slid off the wall. 'Let's do it,' he said.

Alex dropped his shades back down onto the bridge of his nose. 'Nice one,' he said. 'You won't be disappointed.'

They walked along the street, past the junction with the High Street. James felt liberated at having made the decision to duck Dawes's funeral wake, like he was back at school, ducking a class. He slid the knot of his tie down, removed his jacket and folded it over his forearm. He undid the top button of his shirt, rolled his sleeves up and felt the warm breath of the sun envelop his skin. Hot summer days. Perfect in every way. All that was missing was the touch of another person's hand in his.

'The Moonraker's run by Suzie's parents, isn't it?' he asked. 'The girl who owns Surfers' Turf?'

'Suzie's parents. Dan's parents. Johno and Lil. Call them what you want. Yeah, they run it.'

James slowed to a halt. 'Suzie's Dan's sister? You're kidding.'

'What you stopping for?'

James moved on again. 'Nothing. I just didn't have those two down as being related, that's all.'

'Yeah. Elder sister. How come you know her, anyhow?'

'I don't really. Had a quick chat with her before the search. And she was there when I went back to get Murphy.' He checked himself. 'She was nice. Stayed with me till Alan got back.'

'Nice? What the fuck does nice mean?' Alex enquired with a laugh. 'Nice as in she visits pensioners in her free time and makes them cups of tea and listens to them waffling on about rationing in the war? Or nice as in she's got the prettiest little tits in Grancombe and you wouldn't mind getting your hands on them and giving them a good squeeze?' He monitored James's face for a reaction, got the one he was looking for. 'Jesus,' he said, laughing, 'that's it. You fancy her. You got a hard-on with her name all over it.'

'No,' James said, flustered. 'Well, not now that I know she's Dan's sister.'

'But before, yeah? Before you knew. Before that you were up for her, right? Got her in your head?'

'Yeah,' James admitted, 'maybe I've been thinking about her. Just a bit, though, you know? No big deal.'

Alex cut the joking, switched to analysis. 'Don't blame you. Good-looking girl.' He hawked and spat. 'Wouldn't touch her with a barge pole myself.'

'Why? Because of Dan?'

'Nah, Dan wouldn't give a toss. They're not exactly close.'

'Why, then? Is she seeing someone?'

'Nah, just not my type. Too – I don't know – too fucking adult. Too square. No fun. It's like having your granny in the room when she's there. Disapproving looks. All that crap. Can't just be yourself. And she's only a year older than us. Not like she's got an excuse.'

Alex turned off the road into the car park next to the harbour. James followed him as he wove between the bonnets and boots. They stopped between a clapped out VW and a red Spitfire, its roof down, its tiny steering wheel glinting in the sun. James walked round to the other side of the VW.

'Wrong,' Alex said, pulling a jangle of keys from his pocket and climbing into the Spitfire's driving seat.

James walked slowly round. He hesitated by the passenger door. 'This *is* yours, isn't it?'

Alex laughed and slid a key into the ignition. 'Chill out,' he said, his grin being far from reassuring. 'I haven't been joyriding for months.'

James remembered the conversation they'd had with Dan on the cliff top. 'So, Murphy was right, then? About Dan when he beat him up?'

'Right about suspecting him, sure. Nothing right about what he went on and did as a result.'

'How bad was it?'

'Bad enough for Dan to have to tell his parents he'd been mugged.'

'I still say you should've grassed Murphy,' James said, climbing into the passenger seat. 'Told Dan's parents. Let them sort it out.'

Alex ran his hand through his hair. 'Someone tried that once. A few years back. A guy a couple of years older than us called Paddy Hayworth.'

'Paddy who?'

'Hayworth. Dealer. I kind of took my cue from him, took over when he stopped. Used to buy off him. Good guy. Anyhow, he tried to get Murphy busted.'

'What's the story?'

'The story? Someone burgled Murphy's house when he was on holiday, vandalised the place a treat. Sprayed all kinds of stuff about Murphy and his wife over the walls. Even laid a turd on the kitchen table.

'Murphy reckoned it was Paddy,' Alex continued. 'Probably right, too. From what Paddy told me, he had reason enough. Murphy had bust in on his flat a few months before. Class As all over the place. Hadn't nicked him, though. Murphy's too sharp for that. Went for the cash option instead.'

'What, blackmail? You're kidding.'

'More like taxation. Regular payment each week. Made Paddy's life hell. Same as he would with me, he ever caught me with anything more than grass.' Alex reached behind the seat and pulled out a bottle of Jack Daniels, took a slug and passed it to James. 'So Murphy grabbed him on suspicion of the burglary, took him down the cop-shop and gave him a good shoeing, tried to get him to confess.'

James drank from the bottle, wheezed, 'And did he?'

'Nah. Kept his gob shut. And as soon as Murphy let him out he went and got himself a lawyer.'

James sat back, half-closed his eyes against the glare of the sun bouncing off the car bonnet. 'So what happened? How come Murphy's still here and not in prison?'

Alex sighed. 'Because Paddy ain't.'

'Where is he?'

'That's the million dollar question. Disappeared the day after he'd seen the lawyer. Hasn't been seen since.'

'What are you saying?' James scoffed. 'That Murphy knocked him off? Come on, it's a bit of paranoid, isn't it?'

'Bit of a coincidence, as well, him vanishing like that.'

'Still—'

'Still, nothing. Whether it was actually down to Murphy or not ain't the point. Point is there's a lot of flooded slate mines round here where a body wouldn't ever be discovered, and me and Dan don't want to find out first-hand if Murphy specialises in watery graves.'

Alex snatched the bottle back and stowed it behind the seat. He fired the ignition.

'Jesus,' James said, listening to the threatening growl of the engine. 'Nice bit of machinery.'

'Fucking should be,' Alex said, slipping into gear and navigating his way round a tour bus. 'Cost me enough.' They reached the street and Alex leant across and opened the glove compartment. He rummaged around for a few seconds, the engine idling. 'Here,' he said, producing a pair of shades and dropping them onto James's lap. 'Put them on. No point being in a car like this and not looking the part.'

The car pulled away and James slid the shades into place. Day slipped into dusk in an instant. They cruised back down along the sea front.

'So how fast can this thing go?' he asked.

The car slowed as they reached the junction and turned into the High Street. 'You really wanna know?'

An edge in Alex's voice told James that maybe he didn't. But what was the problem? He checked the speedometer as the High Street slid past. Twenty miles an hour. It was daytime. People on the pavement. Murphy up at St. Donal's. As far as he knew, Alex hadn't ingested anything more dangerous than a pint of lager and a thimbleful of J.D. all day. They turned right out of the High Street, headed for the bend in the road that would lead them past St Donal's.

'Yeah,' James said, 'I wouldn't have asked otherwise.'

'Yeah? Well, I hope you've had an enema recently.'

'What?'

''Cos if you haven't, you're gonna end up shitting your pants.'

No sooner had Alex finished his sentence, than James felt the acceleration kick in. Air powered against the windscreen, dipping down over its top into his face, ventilating his scalp like a hairdryer. Eye of the storm. The noise of the engine rose and fell like a siren as Alex shifted busily through the gears. The Spitfire squealed into the bend and James felt the G-force wedging him sideways. And then, maybe two hundred yards up the hill, he saw the faces outside St Donal's begin to turn and stare. Alex released his hand from the gear stick.

'Sounds,' he shouted, flicking the stereo on.

House music burst out of speakers in the doors. The vibrations wracked James' body, threatening to shudder his teeth from his gums.

'Shit,' he yelled, impulsively ducking down in the bucket seat as they drew level with St Donal's, narrowly missing a woman crossing the road.

He covered his face with his hands, didn't want to be spotted doing this with the funeral still going on. But alongside the fear of exposure, was something more powerful. A release, a feeling that this was something he'd been born to, something he'd been denying himself for years. He lowered his hands and twisted his head round. The road flowed away behind them. White water rafting. The people outside St Donal's were left stranded in their wake.

'You're a fucking madman,' he shouted over the music.

'So, welcome to the asylum,' Alex said, cutting the volume of the music. He slowed down as they left the town behind and they followed the gully of the lane like bobsleighers, the hedges rearing up on either side, keeping them channelled.

'How far's this caravan site?' James asked.

'This far,' Alex replied, yanking on the handbrake and slewing into a driveway. He released the brake again and steadied the vehicle, slowed.

James felt the flow of his adrenaline begin to taper off. Flat fields spread left and right, uneven with sheep-trimmed grass. Up ahead was a plain farmhouse, its slated roof dull against the sky. From here, a jumble of outbuildings, ranging from concrete shower units to corrugated iron animal shelters, radiated outwards. Caravans lay like sleeping cows in a random pattern across the field to the right of the house. As they covered the last few yards of driveway before they reached the parking area, they passed a small swimming pool and play area, complete with swings, a roundabout, a slide and attendant kids.

'There's a wash bag in the boot,' Alex said. 'Dig it out and don't go leaving it anywhere.'

Alex slapped his hand down on his shoulder as they walked towards the small concrete bunker with a reception sign bolted to its door. Blood smeared across his skin. 'Horsefly,' he commented, scratching at the skin. 'Bastards. Worse than wasps. Been a bad summer for them.' He pushed the door open and moved inside. 'All right, Marge,' he said to the middle-aged woman sitting smoking behind the counter, reading a tabloid paper.

'Alex,' she said with a nod, not moving.

James noticed her fingers, crooked and tanned with tar.

133

The room was hot and stank of stale cigarette ash. He picked up a tourist brochure from the scratched glass surface of the table in the corner of the room and idly leafed through its glossy pages.

'Business good?' Alex asked.

'So, so.'

'Great.' Alex sounded bored. 'Number sixteen,' he said, cutting to the chase. 'Where is it? We're meeting some people.'

James looked up. Marge stood up and leant over the counter, studied a list on a clipboard. Her breasts clinched together like an arse hanging out of a fat builder's jeans. 'Hazel and Georgie,' she read aloud.

'That's them. Where's their caravan?'

'Out the door and right. Tenth one up. Blue door. Friends of yours, are they?'

But Alex had already turned his back on her and was halfway through the door. James watched her sit back down and cloak her face with the newspaper once more. He replaced the brochure and followed in Alex's footsteps.

Hazel waved at them as they approached. She was sitting in the doorway of a decrepit yellow caravan. Her legs swung gently back and forth, a child on a swing. The soles of her bare feet brushed against the lush grass, making it hiss.

'Hi,' she said as they reached her. She stood up and ducked inside. 'Come on in.'

The doorway led into the caravan's main room. It was cluttered with clothes and crumpled cigarette packs. The smell of takeaway food clogged the air. Georgie was lying down on one of the bench seats, smoking a joint. Her bra strap lay exposed on her shoulder, white against the tan of her skin.

'All right, there,' Alex said, crossing over to the brown formica table and sitting down.

'All right,' she echoed, taking another drag of her joint.

James sat next to Alex. 'Nice place you got here,' he said.

Georgie giggled. 'Yeah, right.'

Alex pulled the tartan wash bag from James's grip, put it on the table before him and unzipped it. 'Down to business,' he said. 'Let's see what Uncle Alex has got in his bag o' tricks.'

The sound of the zip and Alex's accompanying words acted like a catalyst on Georgie, shook her from her dazed state. She shifted smoothly to her feet and came and sat opposite James at the table. Hazel slid along the bench next to her and leant forward. Her hair fell across her face as she peered into the bag. Then she tossed her head back and stared into Alex's eyes.

'What's your buzz?' Alex asked.

The girls looked at each other. Georgie's lips stretched back over her uneven teeth as she mouthed the letter 'E'.

'What're they like?' Hazel asked.

'Good. Reliable. Quick up. Long stay. No aggro.'

'How much?' Alex named a price. 'OK,' she said quickly. 'We'll take ten.'

Alex counted out ten pills and pushed them across the table's surface. 'That it?'

Hazel picked up one of the pills and rolled it between her forefinger and thumb, examining the design on it. 'You got coke?' she asked.

'Course. You want some now?'

Hazel nodded and Alex took a wrap from the bag and opened it on the table. He shook a proportion of the coke it contained onto the table and got his wallet out, withdrew a credit card, proceeded to cut the coke into four lines.

'I'll give it a miss,' James said. He saw Hazel switch her stare to him. 'Too early,' he excused himself.

Alex said nothing, his only reaction being to cut the now obsolete line into the other three. Hazel pulled a handbag off the shelf behind her and rummaged through it until she found her purse. She produced a ten pound note from it and rolled it into a tight, nostril-sized pipe. Alex was finished now and she leant forward, holding the note to one nostril, blocking the other with her finger.

'No,' Alex said, resting his hand on her forearm.

She pulled back, surprised. 'What?'

Alex took a thick bundle of notes from his pocket, peeled off a fifty and rolled it up. He passed it to Hazel. 'If you're gonna do something, might as well do it properly.'

Hazel smirked and took the note from him and vacuumed one of the lines up. Her head reared back, eyes closed. Her nose twitched and she sniffed over and over again, a rabbit in a lab experiment.

'Ooooph,' she exhaled, leaning down and inhaling the stray left from the original line.

'Good?' Alex asked.

'Good,' she confirmed, pulling the note from her nostril and wiping her nose, starting the sniffing routine once more.

Alex reached over and took her hand in his. Nothing was said, and they couldn't have touched for more than a second, but James, just like them, understood that the connection made between their eyes had gone further. Then Alex's hand withdrew, the fifty safe in his grasp. He did a line and passed the fifty onto Georgie.

They did another line each. James had retired to the bench seat by now. Light broke through the half-closed slats of the blind, casting his suit trousers into pinstripe. The coke had vocalised itself now. Jabber, jabber. The others were talking quickly, too quickly for James to track. Binning one topic for another, forgetting this and getting into that. Over the preceding twenty minutes he'd felt his ego shrink, listened to his voice fade to static that they didn't have the patience to strain to hear, like a weak radio signal in the mountains. He looked at the others. Hazel had moved round and was now sitting next to Alex. Her arm was draped territorially across his shoulder as he fixed them another line. James closed his eyes, studied his eyelids, the colour of blood as they filtered the sunlight. Soon he couldn't hear the laughter and voices at all.

His eyes flipped open like shutters.

'Hello, sleepy-head,' she said.

'Georgie,' he said, still half-asleep, recognising her from the pub. Then waking fully, craning his neck around her seated body, seeing the table empty, 'Where's Alex?'

'Next door.'

'Wh—'

'With Hazel,' she explained. 'Fucking.' She shrugged. 'I suppose. They've been in there for ages. Said she wanted to

show him a book. That's what she always says back home
when she wants someone.' She smiled. 'Never seen her read
anything the whole time I've known her.' She leant down and
brushed her nose over his forearm, inhaled. He felt the hairs
on his arm shift. He went to sit up, but she gently pushed him
back down. 'Sorry,' she said, lifting her head. 'The smell the
sun makes on skin – I'm addicted.' She placed the palm of her
hand on his brow. Sweat leaked from his pores into hers.
Then she combed her fingers up through his hair, leaving it
glistening, gelled. 'Stay where you are,' she said softly. 'Go
back to sleep. I didn't mean to wake you.'

'It's OK,' he said, meaning it. Her fingers continued to run
through his hair. 'That feels good,' he said, closing his eyes.

'D'you like me?' she asked.

'I don't really know you.'

'Yeah, but d'you like me?'

'Yes.'

He felt the scent of her breath funnel up his nostrils: vodka
blended with cigarette smoke. He lifted his head and found
her lips. They parted and his tongue brushed against hers.
The saliva between them was thick and warm, like sweat. Her
hand stroked down from his hair, over his neck and onto his
shoulder. She squeezed at the bow of muscle there and her
tongue probed deeper between his teeth, forcing his tongue
back onto the roof of his mouth. Then she pulled back and he
heard himself gasp.

'Nice,' she said, looking down his body, her hand caressing
his erection through his trousers.

He felt his trouser zip slide down more than he heard it.
But the sound was part of it, too. The sound of the zip and the
music. The taste of the smoke in the air. The smell of her
perfume cutting through it like a flower shop on a London
roadside. Her face. Still. A painting in a gallery. Able to absorb
his scrutiny. He could feel the tingle of intense apprehension
in his groin, spreading its feelers across his body, twisting his
stomach inside out, familiar from moments alone with magazines, from nights alone in the flat in London. His penis
twitched and this time she gripped it hard, twisted it through

the flies of his boxer shorts. He felt it spring, free now from the confines of his trousers.

And still she continued to stare into his eyes, watching, waiting for a reaction. But he wasn't going to give one. He knew how some people could read the thoughts crossing other people's eyes, as sure as if they were watching credits rolling down a cinema screen. His father had been like that. Impossible to lie to. Always watching for the rapid series of blinks, the unwillingness to sustain eye-contact, the flash of panic. He wasn't going to give this girl that. Coked up. Toying with him. He wasn't going to let her know that this had never happened to him before, that no one had ever touched him like this. But it felt good. So good. Maybe the coke didn't matter. Maybe it was like the hash: good once you'd tried it, a path to another place. A key. Open the door to another room. Step inside. Take the ride. He stared back at her, returned the challenge, and finally her own stare wavered and her head ducked out of sight towards his lap.

Her mouth felt warm on his penis. He flinched and a groan escaped from his lips. He didn't care any longer. Beyond care. Beyond anything he'd known before. Her head was moving. He tried to work out which area her mouth was operating around, which point of bare skin her tongue now caressed. But he couldn't pin it down. He'd become liquid. He could feel his breath coming strong now, the same as that day on South Beach as he'd run towards Surfers' Turf and Murphy. Towards Suzie . . .

He watched her hair shake across his stomach as her head bobbed. It moved like seaweed beneath the waves. She was panting now, her elbow shunting back and forth. He gave up fumbling with her bra strap, clawed at her back. His thigh muscles contracted as he tried to fight the inevitable spread of orgasm, plug the rush of ejaculate. He didn't want this to end. Just go on. On. Jesus, this is it. Oblivion. Oh, Christ. He gripped his head with his hands. His teeth ground tightly together, and the groan came again, louder, sustained.

An hysterical shout came from the bedroom: 'Fuck.'

James's body snapped into an L shape. Georgie, her hand

still gripped around the base of his penis, followed his stare to the bedroom door. It was shaking visibly, choreographed, moving in time to the sound of falling objects that came from inside the bedroom. Other noises: grunts; breaking glass. Another shout, the word, or words, incomprehensible this time.

'Sounds like someone else is having fu—,' Georgie started to say.

Then the bedroom door burst open. Alex stood there, his shades perched at an absurd, uneven angle on his nose, his hair tousled. His t-shirt was missing, his jeans unbuckled. His belt fell across his thigh like an exhausted tongue.

Georgie's voice was sharp with surprise: 'What the fuck—'

Hazel appeared at Alex's side, her breasts half-covered by a towel she was clumsily attempting to wrap herself in.

'Pigs,' she squealed. 'Fucking pigs. Outside.'

Alex slid into motion, an athlete released from the starting blocks, his bare feet crossing the floor to the table like he was performing the triple jump. The bag was there, open. A wrap lay on the table beside it. James saw Georgie move out of the corner of his eye, felt his penis spring like a jolted compass arm to one side, then right itself; point upright once more. He stayed there for a second, confused, then caught sight of Hazel staring at him. A shiver of self-consciousness swept through him, and the blood rushed from his penis into his face, leaving the one spineless as a slug, the other red as a cut. He quickly tucked his penis out of view, stood up and jerked at his trouser zip.

'Lock the fucking door,' Alex was shouting as he packed the bag and zipped it tight. 'And get rid of the fucking pills.'

Georgie ran for the door and flicked the catch, dragged a chair across the floor and jammed it under the door handle. A fist pounded on the outside.

'Where?' Hazel was screaming, staring in panic at the pills on the table.

Alex turned round, a look of disbelief on his face. 'I don't fucking know. In your mouth. Up your arse. Just get them out of fucking sight.'

'Open up,' a shout came from outside. 'Police. Open the door, or we'll break it down.'

Hazel, suddenly spurred into action by the immediacy of the threat, cupped one hand beneath the edge of the table and swept the pills into it with her other hand, looking absurdly domesticated for a second, like she was sweeping crumbs away, clearing the table at the end of a family meal. Then she spun round and ran towards the bedroom. The towel fell as she disappeared through the doorway, and James watched her bare arse disappear from sight.

'Right,' Alex shouted at him, striding past, the bag now in his hand. He tugged at the blind on the window at the back of the caravan, creating a peep hole, and checked outside. 'All clear. That dumb shit, Murphy, hasn't even got the brains to surround the Indians before he opens fire.' He looked sideways at James. 'Time to get your Nikes on, mate.'

James stared at him, blinked once, twice, tried to view him with rationality, but couldn't. What was he on about? Doing a runner? He'd seen the window when Alex had checked through the blind. It was constructed of two panes of glass divided by a thin, unvarnished wooden strut. The only part of it that opened was at the top, a gap maybe wide enough for a cat to contort itself through. Not a human, though. Not someone with a wide skull and bones that wouldn't bend like rubber.

Something harder was thumping against the door now. James turned and watched the thin wood bow inwards, again and again, like it was preparing to give birth.

Alex shouted at the door: 'All right, I'm coming. I'm fucking coming, all right.' He turned back to James, held the bag out towards him. 'Now or never,' he said. 'Them or me. Make your fucking choice.' The pounding kept coming at the door. More shouting. Alex thrust the bag at James, wedged it against his chest. 'I'm caught with this, I'm fucking going down. You understand?' He pushed the bag harder at James. 'You with me, or what?'

James gripped the bag. This was wrong. Jesus in the desert. Taking the temptation. Accepting the devil's gift. Was this who

he'd become? He shook his head at Alex, but his voice contradicted the action. He'd climbed too high to come down now.

'OK,' he said, 'let's do it.'

'Nice one.'

Alex scanned the room, moved swiftly to the kitchen area
and grabbed a scum-encrusted aluminium saucepan out of the
sink, weighed it in his hand, then discarded it, sent it clattering
to the floor, picked up a heavy frying pan instead.

Back by James, he said, 'Soon as I do this, you get the fuck
through there and you run. You get your shirt over your head
and you run and you don't look back. This ain't a movie. No
one's gonna shoot you. You run and you don't look back and
you get the fuck out of here.'

'What about you?'

Alex ignored the question, pulled the string which hung
down along the window frame and raised the blind fully,
exposed the world outside like a stage.

'Count of three, OK?' he instructed.

James nodded, looked through the window. It backed onto
another caravan. A gap of maybe four foot lay between the
two structures. Once he landed, he'd have to break right,
duck round the other caravan. Head for the back of the
property. The woods lay that way. Into the wilderness. Safety.
Somewhere so safe that a corpse could remain undiscovered
there for days. He could make it. Murphy was overweight.
He'd be slow.

He could leave those fuckers for dead.

'One,' Alex began, 'two . . .'

And as Alex hit three, he brought the frying pan crashing
down against the glass. The window split in two, disintegrating
like a dropped ice sculpture. Claws of glass hung stubbornly
to the frame and Alex attacked them with rapid movements,
snapping them off from the wood.

'Do it,' he roared.

And James did. And as he did – as he vaulted through the
window and landed in a crouch on the ground, the bag
clutched to his chest with one hand, the other hand already
dragging his shirt up over the lower part of his face in a

defensive mask – adrenaline burnt like electricity through the circuit of his veins.

He was alive.

He got to his feet and ran.

CHAPTER NINE

pirate

James kicked himself out of the hotel bed early on Thursday morning and took advantage of the free breakfast thrown in with the price of the hotel room. He slopped the bacon, eggs and toast down into his fizzing stomach. After the incident with Suzie the day before, he'd resorted to an evening of satellite TV and half a bottle of Jack Daniels. And now he was paying for it. He looked across the dining room. Two waiters were chatting in the corner, but otherwise it was empty. A rectangle of grey sky filled the window. Fresh, cold air. Just what the head-doctor ordered.

He picked up his car and called in at a garage at the top of the High Street, stocked up on petrol and cigarettes, then headed round past St Donal's and onto the road to Alan's place.

If the town had changed, the countryside had stayed the same. As the car cut through the lanes, James anticipated the turns and straights, as familiar with his route as a Grand Prix driver on his penultimate lap. Maybe more so. His memories of the route were close up, the kind of detail you only got from walking. When he'd lived here, his main form of transport had been his feet. He hadn't passed his test. Hadn't had any choice but to walk, unless Alex or Dan had given him a lift.

He pulled into Alan's drive and stopped the car, stubbed out the cigarette he'd been smoking and replaced it with another, switched off the engine and closed his eyes. He smoked in silence for a minute in a futile attempt to calm his nerves down, then slowly opened his eyes. *You can deal with this. You can cope.*

But still, the further he looked up the drive, the more he felt like retching. Too much shit had gone down here. Too many memories he'd tried too hard to forget. And yet, now he was back, he understood that he'd never really killed them off. Everything was how he'd left it. The outbuildings still stood in need of repair. Alan's house, with its shabby windows staring back at him like blind eyes, left him feeling hollow and depressed. Forget the fact that Jack Dawes' place had been turned into a museum. This place was as much of a museum as Jack's place would ever be.

Somewhere here, the kid James had once been was waiting for him. And James was going to have to face him. He was going to have to face up to what he'd done.

He restarted the engine and drove up into the yard at the front of the house, parked alongside Alan's Land Rover. Jesus. He couldn't believe he'd kept it on. Its engine had been spluttering like an asthmatic back in eighty-nine, so Christ knows how wrecked it was now. He'd guessed right about Alan. Things obviously hadn't picked up for him after James had done a bunk. He stared through the windscreen at the front door of the house, his earlier nausea returning as he imagined what kind of state it would be in inside.

He unbuckled his seatbelt and happened to glance in the rear view mirror. There was a white van parked next to one of the barns – the same barn, he guessed, that those kids had found Alan's body in. The barn door was ajar. Then he saw a flash of motion inside. Then a body, a man in work clothes, stepping out through the door and freezing, clocking James clocking him. James got out of the car and watched the man disappear back into the barn. He felt a stab of panic. No one should be here. Then he calmed. It was probably nothing. Just some farmer that Alan had had some sort of arrangement with. Maybe using the barn to store hay in or something. He walked towards the barn, but when he was still ten yards away, he saw the man reappear in the doorway. He was holding a crowbar and strode purposefully towards James.

Another man came out of the barn and ran along its front, stopping at the drive and looking down.

The first man stopped a foot away from James. He was big, maybe six-four. Shaved head. Fortysomething. Thick neck and bulbous gut. He was swinging the crowbar in and out of his palm, making a smacking sound.

'What you got?' he shouted at the other man, not turning to face him, his eyes running over James like a laser on a barcode, summing him up. Accent wasn't local. More Cockney.

'Fuck all,' his companion shouted back.

'Yeah, well stay put and make sure it stays that way,' the man with the crowbar called out, before addressing James: 'This is private property, pal. You must be lost. Ain't nothing here you want.'

'You're right,' James said, monitoring the crowbar which the man was still slapping against his palm. 'It is private property. But I'm the owner, not you.'

The man's face scrunched up in confusion. 'You what?'

'This house and that barn and everything here belongs to me.'

'Bollocks,' the man said with a sneer. 'This place used to be owned by—'

'Alan I'Anson,' James said. 'I'm his nephew. He left it to me in his will.'

The man stared at him, his expression now blank. 'In that case,' he finally said, 'we've got ourselves a bit of a fucking problem.' He shouted to his mate again. 'Get your arse over here with the phone.'

'Look,' James said, as the other man ran over, 'I don't know what—'

'Unless you want some of this,' crowbar man interrupted, 'Shut it.'

'What's going on?' the other man, beefy, early-twenties, asked.

Crowbar man ignored the question. 'Gimme the phone.'

James stood motionless, transfixed by the crowbar, which was now resting casually on the man's shoulder as his thumb punched a number into the phone pad. 'That you?' the man asked. 'Yeah, 'course. No, we got us a problem. No, that's sorted. Some geezer just turned up. Says he owns the place. Inherited it.' He fixed James with a stare. 'Nah, everything's under control. Yeah, now. Make it quick, all right?' He cut the call and slipped the phone into his back pocket. 'Right, mate,' he told James. 'Now I don't know who the fuck you are and I don't know if you're talking shit or not. And right now, I couldn't give a fuck either way.'

James glanced at the car. Twenty yards. In spite of the thousands of cigarettes that had scalded his lungs over the past few years, he had enough adrenaline racing through him right now to make it. But getting in the car, getting it started and getting the hell out . . . he wasn't sure.

'Forget it,' crowbar man said, as if James had been thinking out loud. 'You be good and we'll treat you good. I got nothing against you right now, so let's just keep it that way, OK? I said OK?'

'OK,' James said.

'Good. Now move it,' he said, circling James and nudging him in the back with the crowbar towards the barn. 'I'm freezing my tits off out here. There'll be someone here soon who's gonna sort this out.'

James started walking.

It was maybe twenty minutes later that James heard the sound of a car pulling up outside the barn. Crowbar man stuck to the policy of silence he'd instigated the moment they'd entered the barn. He nodded at the younger guy, who got up off the crate he'd been sitting smoking on and went outside, slid the barn door shut behind him. There was the sound of a car door opening and closing and a muffled conversation. Then the barn door opened and the younger guy stepped back into the barn. Another figure ducked through the door behind him. James couldn't make out his face too good in the dim light. He was wearing a heavy, expensive-looking overcoat. A tie was visible against a white shirt underneath. His eyes were hidden by a pair of black shades. He stared at James for a while and still no one spoke. Then he stepped forward a couple of paces.

'Hello, James,' he said, removing his shades. A grin cracked across his face. 'Long time, no see.'

The eyes, even in this gloom, were unmistakable. They were the colour of the summer skies James had walked beneath when he'd lived here. And the body of the man who stood before him now belonged to the man who'd walked beside him then. Alex. No longer kitted out like a beach bum. Serious. Clean-shaven. The tattoo out of sight. Suited and booted and managing events. His face had changed, too. A straight line of white scar tissue ran from just beneath his earringless earlobe to the bottom of his chin. Knife-slash. Either that or careless shaving . . . But nothing about Alex had ever been careless.

'You know this guy?' crowbar man asked.

Alex continued to stare at James. 'You could say that. You could say we're old friends.' His teeth showed in a passing smile. 'Isn't that right, James?'

James didn't answer.

'A hello would be nice,' Alex continued, lighting a cigarette and tossing the match onto the dry barn floor. His accent slid from local to Home Counties in a half-hearted attempt at impersonation. 'Hello, Alex. How the devil are you? Looking good. Looking fine. What say you and me go for a drink and chat over old times? Crumbs, Alex, it's just so good to see you.' Then his accent cut back to natural. 'Well? How about it? You gonna say hello?'

Alex's attempt at intimidation had the opposite effect to the one intended. All it did was remind James of the banter they'd once shared. It restored equality to the situation. The suit and thugs slipped from James's mind and there were just him and Alex, aged eighteen, sizing one another up on South Beach on the morning of the search party. Kissing butt wouldn't have won Alex's respect then and the same rule applied now. James got to his feet and approached Alex. He held his stare.

'Hello,' he said. 'How the devil are you?'

Alex laughed. 'That's better.'

'Good. Now do you mind telling me what the fuck's going on?'

'Gee, James,' Alex said, blowing smoke into James's face, 'I always remembered you having better manners.'

'Yeah, well they kind of deserted me when your crew grabbed me and locked me in here.'

Alex snorted. 'My crew? You make me sound like a pirate.' He held his hands up and examined them. 'Nope, didn't think so.'

James found himself staring at Alex's hands, too. 'What?'

'No hook,' Alex observed, causing crowbar man to snigger. Alex looked up towards the rafters. 'And no skull and cross-bones. Guess you're just being paranoid, eh?'

James's cool switched to boiling. 'Paranoid? Yeah, fucking right. What have I got to be paranoid about? I drive up and catch Tweedle Dum and Tweedle-fucking-Dee here stashing Christ-knows-what in my barn. And when I ask them what the fuck's going on, they get heavy on me and tell me to wait till Mr Big shows up. And then – get this – when he does finally fucking show, guess what? He's some fucking psycho I used to hang out with when I was a kid. And you think I'm being paranoid?'

'Good point,' Alex said, nodding his head, 'and, yes, well-presented.'

'So how about getting moron and moron here to pack their boxes of shit back into their van and get the fuck out of my life?'

Crowbar man stepped forward. 'Who the fuck are you calling a moron, moron?'

James kept on staring at Alex. No fear. They're Alex's people, won't do a thing without his say-so. Show fear and the show's over. Alex will have you cold. Ultimatum the bastard. Only language he understands.

'Well?' he asked. 'You going, or am I calling the pigs?'

Alex darted his cigarette onto the floor and ground it out with the heel of his shoe. 'Neither. Sorry, James, but that's just the way it is.' He turned to crowbar man. 'Everything unloaded?'

Crowbar man was still scowling at James. 'Yeah,' he grunted.

'OK. You two wait outside. I'll sort this out.'

Crowbar man wasn't convinced. 'You sure you don't want—'

'Just leave, OK?'

Alex studied the ground between his feet until the others had left.

'We've got us a problem here, James,' he finally said, looking up and pulling a packet of cigarettes from his pocket. He held the pack towards James. 'Smoke?'

'No.'

He looked at James, curious, almost friendly. 'What? You quit?'

'No.'

'Just don't fancy one now, huh?'

'Something like that.'

Alex shrugged and lit a cigarette, inhaled and exhaled in silence. 'Thing is,' he said, 'the stuff in those crates. I'll need to keep them here a few days, till I sort somewhere else out.'

'What's in them?'

'That's not your problem. The point is—'

James lost it. 'No,' he snapped, 'fuck you. The point is you're not keeping shit here unless I say so. You want me to call the pigs? You want me to fucking call them?'

Alex's voice came calm, a teacher to a child. 'You don't get it, do you?'

'Don't get what?'

'This.' Alex's expression hardened. 'You're not in charge. I am. What I say, you do. Right now, there are two head-cases outside who want to smack your face in, and the only thing that's stopping them from doing just that is yours truly. So, right now, you owe me. And because you owe me, you're gonna behave. And because you're gonna behave, you're gonna hear me out. OK?'

James was on the verge of snapping back a reply, when he stopped himself. Alex was right. For the moment. Till they disappeared down the drive. Till then, just play along. Say whatever it takes. Then call the pigs.

'Doesn't look like I've got much of a choice, does it?' he said.

149

Alex studied him closely, then his face relaxed. His voice, this time, was softer. 'No. Now, I didn't bring this situation on you. You did. You're the one who rocked up here out of the blue. Inheritance, huh? That mad old fucker leave you the house?'

'Alan left it to me in his will, if that's what you mean.'

'OK. So things are starting to make sense. And you're down here to flog it, yeah?' His smile was back. 'Not planning to move back to Grancombe and hang out with your old mates?'

James felt his skin prickle. 'What do you think?'

'I think no. But I want to be sure. So?'

'So, you're right.'

'Right. So you're here and the crates are here. Now, for me, this isn't a problem. For you, on the other hand, this is a major fucking problem. You don't like me. You don't like me telling you what to do. And I can understand that. I wouldn't like it either.' Alex drew deep on his cigarette. 'Reverse psychology, I think they call it. And following on down that route, if I were you, what I'd be thinking right now is: *Fuck him. The moment he's outta here, I'm gonna call the police. Let them bust open those crates and then let them bust him for whatever's inside 'em.* 'Cos that's the other thing you're thinking, right? What's in those crates ain't legal . . .'

'You sound like you've got it all worked out,' James said.

'I *have* got it all worked out. That's my job.' He stabbed a finger towards James. 'Now, some advice. You call the pigs, or so much as touch one of those crates, and either me or one of my friends out there is going to bust your head open.' His eyes fixed on James's, unwavering. 'You and me have history, James. You know me. You know what I'm capable of. I warn you now: fuck with me on this, and you'll regret it.'

'You've got no power over me anymore,' James told him. 'Nothing. I left this place. That was the end of us.'

'D'you remember the last person who fucked with me, James? That was the end of him, as well, wasn't it?'

'I don't know what—'

'Yeah, you do,' Alex interrupted. 'Every second. Every second of every minute of what happened down on the beach that night. Every second of every minute of what happened up on the cliff-top. Every fucking second.' Alex smiled as the colour drained from James's face. ''Course you do. You remember it all.'

James's mouth had turned dry. He forced the words out: 'Nothing. I don't . . .'

'That a fact?' Alex sneered.

'Nothing . . .'

'You heard the news about Dan? About him being found gutted?'

James wanted to curl up in a ball. The light in here: too dim. The walls were shifting. He felt weak. 'Yes,' he whispered.

'Know what that means?'

'It means he's dead.'

'It means the killer's still here, James. And if the killer's still here, then what you me and Dan did down the beach that night can happen again.' He paused for breath, gave James's brain time to soak the information up. 'Time's moved on, but nothing's changed. Nothing. There's enough in those crates to put me and number of other people away for life. There's nothing I won't do to stop that from happening. Nothing,' he said with finality. 'You understand that?'

'You wouldn't,' James said, but even as he spoke, he knew he was wrong.

Alex walked across to the crates and rested his hand on one of them. 'Maybe you're right. But I don't reckon it's a maybe you're gonna bet on. Not just because you don't want me keeping a few boxes in your barn for a couple of days. Could prove to be a pretty fucking dumb move, you ask me . . .' Alex sneered. 'Reckon I got you stitched up, mate.' He ran his finger from his navel to his throat. 'From here to here.' He cocked his head to one side, placed his hand back on the crate, spat on the floor and looked across at James. 'So what d'you say? You gonna babysit these boxes, or what?'

James stood beside his car, watching the van and Alex's BMW turning out from the bottom of the drive and into the lane.

Alex had waved at him as he'd pulled away. The piece of shit had actually *waved*. Like they were still mates. Like James was just doing him a favour, for Christ's sake.

Then James was sinking. Down to his knees. But deeper than that. Into the past. To a time, several weeks after that day when the police had raided Hazel and Georgie's caravan. To the end of that summer. To when Alex and he had no longer been friends. To South Beach. To the night Alex had just spoken about. To the night James had made his decision to leave this place for good.

The gravel of the yard softened beneath his shoes.

Then it was sand.

It was sand and he was eighteen once more.

campfire

He was stepping onto the sand at the bottom of the steps which led onto South Beach, then on past Surfers' Turf. In the distance, at the far side of the beach, he saw flames, a campfire. Alex. His favourite spot. It could only be him. James surveyed the fire's position, remembered sitting there himself. It was thirty yards along the rocks from the steps which led up to the woods at the top of the cliff. He could pass, a shadow, and they'd be none the wiser. Then he'd be home, away from them. He walked on.

And then the shouting stopped him dead.

For a moment, he couldn't work out what was going on. He heard a voice – Dan's voice – bellowing something. Then a figure burst out of the darkness of the cliff, pounding across the sand towards him.

Dan's voice again, an earthquake: 'You fucker.'

The running figure was closing on James now. A man, tall and thin. Features broke out of his face, features James didn't recognise. The man saw him, too, slowed. Then Dan's unmistakable silhouette appeared behind him, closing him down. Another figure rushed up behind. Alex. It had to be Alex. The thin man turned and clocked them, started running at James again.

'Drop the fucker,' Dan shouted at James. 'Don't let him—'

Instinct tensed James's body, sprung it like a snare. He was back on the rugby field. Focused. Just you and him. Last line of defence. Take him out. Bring him down. He found himself moving across for the interception. The thin man kept coming. Going to try and run through, try for a try. James side-stepped, then switched back as the man drew level with him. He piled into his gut, knocked him sideways and dumped him flat on his back on the sand.

'Cunt,' the thin man cursed, already on his feet. He checked over his shoulder, his hand sliding into his back pocket. And then he was dropping down into a crouch, moving swiftly towards James.

James didn't see the blade until it swiped across him, sliced through his shirt. Warmth spread across his chest. Then pain. Then heat. He felt like he was bleeding lava. He stared into the thin man's eyes, couldn't believe what was happening. He felt himself staggering back, unable to stop the momentum. He pressed his hand against the wound, felt his shirt slip across his skin. The thin man was grinning now, maniacal, coming on again. His arm swung back. The knife blade trapped the moonlight, shone.

And then Dan hit him.

James stood there as they crashed to the ground and rolled across the sand. All he was aware of was that he was bleeding. He hugged himself tightly, convincing himself that it would staunch the flow. Then Alex was there. On top of the other two. They were twisting across the sand. A flurry of motion, too fast to track. Then Dan was pinning the thin man, flattening his weight across his shoulders and head. And Alex was rearing up, the knife in his grip. His arm snapped up and down, a piston.

Again.

And again.

And again.

There was a gargling noise, like a bath being emptied. It got weaker and weaker, running dry.

And then it stopped.

'What the fuck have you done?' Dan groaned. 'What the fuck have you done?'

Alex said nothing, slumped back in the sand.

'Check his pulse.' Dan was frantically rolling the thin man

over, pulling Alex's hand towards his throat. 'Check his fucking pulse. He can't be. Fucking tell me he's not. Check him.'

James stumbled towards them. 'Wha . . .'

Dan stared up, jerked his hands off the thin man like he was on fire. His fingers clawed at James's jeans.

'What the fuck has he done?' He spun round on Alex, seized him by the shoulders and shook him. 'What the fuck have *you* done?'

Alex threw him off and knelt over the thin man. The knife handle was sticking vertically up out of his chest. He took it in his hand and pulled. The blade made a squelching sound as the flesh gave it up.

'You saw,' Dan was shouting at James. 'It wasn't our fault. He was gonna kill you. You saw it. You're our fucking witness. It was an accident. It was self-defence. He was gonna kill us. Alex had to stop him. He had to fucking stop him.'

But he hadn't just stopped him, he'd stabbed him. And he hadn't just stabbed him, he'd stabbed him until he was dead.

'Be quiet,' Alex said. His voice was steady, but to James, it sounded distant, like it was coming from another room. 'Stay there.' Alex got to his feet and walked up to James, reached out his hand and told him, 'Move your hands. Let me see.'

James's arms fell limply to his sides. 'Is . . .'

'He's dead.'

Alex was unbuttoning his shirt. When he'd finished, he pulled it open and examined James's chest. 'You're OK,' he said. 'It's not deep. Just skin. You don't need a doctor or anything. You'll be fine.'

He helped James out of his shirt, yanked it tight around his torso, tied it there. James was numb. He felt nothing.

'I'm scared, Alex,' Dan was mumbling. 'This is real. This is too fucking real. He's dead. He's fucking dead.'

'Shut up,' Alex said, moving a few paces away from them and staring at the sand. 'Let me think. I need to think.'

'But—'

'Forget but,' Alex snapped. 'He ripped us off. He got what was coming. His knife. Not ours.' He glared at the still body,

155

'He did it to himself,' he said, before sitting down on the sand with his back to them.

The sound of Dan's heavy breathing and the waves hissing across the sand filled James's ears.

'I'm going,' he said. 'Murphy. I'm going.'

Alex stood, walked over to him. 'You're going nowhere.'

James wrapped his arms round his body again, backed away. 'I'm not a killer.'

'And now?' Alex asked, gripping James's face with his sodden hands, pushing his fingers back through James's hair, running them down over his shoulders, smearing the thin man's blood across his skin. 'What are you now?'

James felt his stomach begin to twist.

'I'll fucking tell you,' Alex went on, 'you're whatever I want you to be. You're blooded, same as us. Unless you want to spend the rest of your fucking life behind bars, you're gonna stay put till I tell you to go.' He released James and turned to Dan. 'Pick that fucker up and follow me.'

James didn't think as he followed them across the beach to the camp fire. He was past thinking. All he could do was move; float on the shock wave. There were no decisions left to make. His power had been drained. He watched Dan dumping the thin man's body on the rocks near the fire and it meant nothing. It was a video. Nothing more. It wasn't fucking real.

'What we gonna do?' Dan asked quietly, taking a pinch of coke, staring into the flames. 'Burn the fucker? Barbecue the fucking evidence?'

'You're gonna do as you're told,' Alex said, rummaging through the thin man's pockets. 'And I'm gonna sort it. I'm gonna sort it out, so no one knows shit.' His hand pulled free, grasping a thick wedge of notes and a sealed parcel. 'Thieving fuck,' he muttered, stuffing them into his own pockets.

He reached across to the stack of chopped branches next to the fire, picked up the axe.

'Give him a hand,' he told James, setting off towards the steps, 'we're taking him up.'

Alex left them to collect their breath at the top of the steps, disappearing into the woods. When he returned, he was carrying a flat boulder. He placed it on the ground next to the body, knelt down and gripped the axe handle.

'What the fuck are you doing?' Dan asked, sliding back across the grass.

'Question,' Alex said, looking from James to Dan. 'What's the best way to get away with something?' Neither of them spoke, just stared at the axe, transfixed. 'Answer: put yourself out of the picture and put the blame on someone else.'

'I don't . . .' Dan started.

Alex ignored him. 'Jack Dawes,' he said, pulling at the thin man's arm, positioning the wrist on the boulder. 'Cut up in the woods.' He raised the axe above his head with both hands. 'Multiple wounds.' He brought the axe sweeping down. He repeated the movement and this time the stone sparked. He put the axe down next to the body and showed them the severed hand. 'Hands cut off. Never found again.' He dropped the hand on the grass and lifted the boulder, hefted it round to the other side of the body. He reached for the axe and raised it again. 'Only a psycho could do something like that. Not a kid. Not a kid like me or you.'

The axe came flashing down.

Alex was sitting back now, staring at them, panting. James couldn't move his head, couldn't look away.

He couldn't even blink.

Alex lit a cigarette, blew smoke into the night. 'And it could be anyone who's done these two murders. Anyone at all. But not us. Can you guess why, Dan? Your thinking cap working well enough to suss that one out?'

Dan's head shook rapidly.

'Because we weren't here when Dawes got his. 'We were on holiday.' And James wasn't here either. Hear that, James? I've saved your fucking arse again.'

James couldn't move his mouth.

Alex clicked his tongue, tossed his cigarette away, took a wrap from his pocket and licked it clean of coke. 'Makes you wonder what you've got to do to get a "thank you" from some people.'

'What about Ken?' Dan asked, his eyes flicking to the thin

man and back again. 'He must've told someone he was coming to meet us, must've told someone how much we were buying off him.'

'So what if he did? If they talk – which they won't – we just say he never showed. No one's seen us since he met us by the fire. No one's gonna know any different.'

James couldn't move his mouth.

Alex leant forward, then stood up. 'We've got some clearing up to do,' he said, walking up to James. 'You know, axes to hide, sand to kick over on the beach in case the tide doesn't come in on time, camp fires to put out . . . That sort of thing. But I'll tell you what. Just in case you're thinking of doing anything stupid . . .' He suddenly yanked James's hand forward and slapped something soft into his palm. 'Shake on it, buddy. And when you've done that, bury it. And then . . .' He hawked and spat on the ground by James's feet. '. . . keep the fuck out of my way and forget.'

But James never did forget the touch of that hand in his.

He never forgot the walk back through the woods to Alan's house. He never forgot stripping off his blood-stained clothes and burying the bin liner in the undergrowth behind Alan's house. And he never forgot standing on the platform the following morning, waiting for the dawn train to arrive, watching the sun stain the sky like an open wound.

Instead, he buried it. Just like he'd buried the hand. Just like Alex had told him to.

CHAPTER ELEVEN

hacks

James looked down at his hands. They were red. The blood was back, like he'd never washed it away. Then he understood. The rain: it was chucking it down. Mud. Mud, not blood. He lifted himself up from the ground and looked up at Alan's house, remembering where he was, remembering Alex and the men in the barn. His clothes were filthy. How long had he been sitting here?

Get a grip.

The house no longer scared him. Anything was preferable to what his mind had just dredged up. He got his bag out of the car and hurried through the rain to the front door. He fumbled for the keys. Fuck the past. You can deal with it. You've dealt with it up till now. You can deal with it again.

He turned the key in the lock.

Opening the door for the first time since he'd been a teenager made James feel like an astronaut. For a whole minute, he just stood there, letting the rain pelt down on his head, staring at the flagstoned floor and the frayed Indian rug, wary about venturing forth, wondering if the surface would sustain his weight. Then he remembered that this was no longer Alan's home, but his. (Despite what Alex and his thug mates might think to the contrary.) He stepped inside and, as he did, he claimed it as his own.

It was cold; colder than outside, if that were possible. The smell of damp was overpowering. He reached for the light switch and flicked it on: nothing. Hardly surprising; no one left to pay the bills. He chucked his bag, that he'd brought on the off-chance he might stay the night, on the floor, apprehensive about exploring the house further. Instead, he busied himself stocking up the wood-burning stove with faded magazines and cobwebbed logs. He lit a cigarette and then the fire and sat cross-legged before it, stabbing at the flames with a rusted poker. Taking out his mobile, he spent twenty minutes talking to the electricity people, explaining the circumstances and asking for an emergency call-out. They said they could make it the next day. Heat spread through him and he stripped out of his wet clothes, wrung them out and hung them on the back of a chair before the stove. Then he got some fresh clothes from his bag and dressed.

'OK,' he said aloud, 'let's get this show on the road.'

Speaking was a mistake. His words got sucked into the walls as soon as they'd left his mouth, leaving only the crackle of the fire. Thank God he had the hotel to return to. There was no way he could spend a night here. Not even a day. He thought of his car, parked in the drive. The temptation was there to run, drive back to Grancombe, hand the keys over to the estate agent and get the hell out. Leave the clean-up to him. But, at the same time, he knew he couldn't do that. Respect for the dead. His mother's brother. Even if not for Alan, then for her. He had till the end of the week to sort Alan's possessions out. It shouldn't take too long. Just the personal stuff. Leave the rest to be flogged off with the house, or contract in some local firm to organise a house sale.

He still hadn't moved.

Now. Do it now.

He picked up the poker, weighed it in his hand, looked at the doorway through to the sitting room. Then he let the poker clatter onto the flagstones. What was the point? Ghosts had no bodies. Ghosts felt no pain. Pain was what they'd left behind. And, anyway, there were no ghosts. He'd found that much out in the graveyard when he'd woken in Suzie's arms. Only the living. He saw her face as she'd told him to leave the Moonraker. Only the living remembered him now.

He dug out a note book and pen. Might as well keep a

record of what he was planning to keep. Then he set off into the rest of the house. Quickly. The sooner this was over, the better. Then work. Back to work. Back to what Jake had sent him down here for in the first place.

An hour later, he was huddled once more in front of the fire. He stared at the notebook between his legs, flipped through the pages. He hadn't written much down: Alan's computer, papers and books, his photographs and several paintings. He'd checked the paintings, but surprisingly, none of them had been by Dawes. The rest – the furniture, crockery, clothes and other possessions – he'd leave for the estate agent to deal with. They meant nothing to him. Or, rather, they meant too much. They were reminders of a time he just wanted to forget. The estate agent could burn them for all he cared.

He'd been surprised at how orderly the house had been. Each room he'd entered had been tidy, meticulously so. Right down to the beds being made, the sheets turned neatly back over the blankets. Since he couldn't imagine anyone else who would have acted the Good Samaritan following Alan's death, James had to assume it was Alan himself who'd been responsible. His final act of cleansing. Even the kitchen and bathroom had been spotless, sanitary products lined along their shelves. All new. All bought for this one purpose. It had been the same all over the house.

Apart from the basement. That had been locked. The one room James had been denied access to whilst he'd lived here with Alan was still off-limits. During his inventory tour, it had been the one door James had actively homed in on. As he'd approached, he'd heard the noises of Alan's nocturnal pilgrimages playing on an endless loop through his mind. The sound of the study door opening. Footsteps in the corridor. The key being slipped into the door which led to the cellar. The opening of the door and its bolt being rammed home on the inside. Then silence. Silence once more. Standing there, now an adult, James had wanted to break it down, had even gone so far as to shove his shoulder against it to test this possibility. But it had been solid. Without the key, it might as well have been made of concrete.

James picked up his mobile again, called McCullock. A receptionist and then a secretary patched him through.

'Hello, Mr Sawday,' McCullock said. 'How can I help?'

'I'm down in Grancombe,' James said. 'Alan's place.'

'Oh. Is everything in order?'

'Yes, very much. There's just one thing. The keys you gave me. That was all there were?'

'Yes, the two sets of house and car keys. All on separate key rings.'

'You're sure of that?'

'Positive.'

James thanked him and cut the line. The basement key would be here somewhere. Probably in Alan's room. A bedside table, or something, maybe a kitchen drawer. He considered checking these locations out, then rationality got the better of his curiosity. It could wait. He had the rest of the week. Might as well have a positive reason to return here. For now, though, it was time to leave. Back to the hotel. Hot shower. Get the smell of this place off his skin. And sleep. Sleep off the exhaustion of seeing Alex and this house.

Alex. That situation wasn't over yet. Not by a long way. Not until he was out of here, safe in London again.

He closed the vents on the fire, but stayed kneeling there for a while, gazing round the gloomy room. Suddenly, a surge of nostalgia ran through him. He thought of Monique and Alan, how they must have sat here on other winter days, warming themselves by the fire. Then, after her death, Alan, alone. He wondered what Lucy would make of this place, what it would be like to sit here with her beside him. And then he thought of Suzie, and the pain he'd felt outside the Moonraker stung him once more. Just memory, he told himself. Just wanting to be a kid again, wanting to feel what it was like before you grew up. Natural. Nothing more. Just wanting that happiness back.

He stood up and pulled his dried clothes from the chair and stuffed them into his bag, heading for the door.

* * *

Later, James shuffled his chair round and put his feet up on the hotel bed.

'*Grancombe Gazette*,' a woman's voice chimed.

'Oh, hi. My name's James Sawday. I'm a journalist with *Kudos*, the men's magazine. I'd like a word with the editor, please.'

'I'll just see if he's there, Mr Sawday. And – sorry – who did you say you work for?'

'*Kudos*. The men's magazine.'

'Right, hang on a second.'

A pan-pipes version of The Beatles' *Lucy in the Sky with Diamonds* came on, doing nothing to improve James's mood. He rubbed his hair, still wet from the bath, with the hotel towel and flicked through the copy of the *Grancombe Gazette* he'd bought on the way back from Alan's. It was a weekly. Twenty pages long. There was a photo of some councillor on the front, the headline reading, 'Grancombe Sails Past European Beach Standards'. The rest was petty news, interspersed with feature advertisements for various restaurants in the local area. A half-page ad for CURRENT caught his eye, promoting a rave to be held there at the weekend. He was surprised by the names of the DJs who'd be playing, recognising two of them from London. He knew the fees they charged, couldn't help being impressed that anywhere in off-season Grancombe could afford them. Might even check it out with Lucy and co. when they got down.

'Hello. Neville Forster speaking.'

'Hello, Mr Forster. This is James Sawday. I work for *Kudos*. The men's—'

'Yes,' Forster said, 'I've heard of it.'

'Right, well I'm down here to write an article on—'

'The Grancombe Axe Killer—'

'Yes,' James said. 'How did you—'

Forster laughed. 'Call it an educated guess. And here's another one: you want some help with the background.'

'Right again. I take it I'm not the first person who's called you up?'

'The first *this* week. I was under the impression that the press had had enough of the story for now. Till the next death, anyhow.'

'It's a feature article I'm doing. An overview. And I'd appreciate the opportunity to run a few things past you. I've got a lot of stuff from the articles already written, but there are a few gaps I wouldn't mind filling.'

'Rather like the police.'

'Quite.'

'Do you drink, Mr Sawday?'

'I'm sorry?'

'Do you drink?' Forster repeated.

'Yes.'

'Good. Meet me in The Cove. It's down on the front.'

'Will Tawnside's place. I know it.' James rolled his eyes as soon as the words had left his mouth.

'You're extremely well-informed, Mr Sawday . . .'

'It's my job.'

Forster grunted. 'Only your information's a little out of date. Tawnside's dead. Heart attack. Two years ago. They found him slumped behind the bar, bottle of whiskey still in his hand. Tragic.'

'Oh.'

'No matter, though. The Cove's still running. If anything, the beer's improved. Half an hour suit you?'

'That's fine. Thank you.'

'No, Mr Sawday. Thank *you*.'

'What for?'

'The drinks you're about to buy me, of course.'

It wasn't hard to spot Neville Forster. Not because he fulfilled the stereotype James held of a regional editor: overweight, balding, mid-fifties, smoking and drinking his way towards retirement. (He didn't. He was round the same age as James, athletic, with thick black hair.) But because Neville Forster was the only person, aside from a surly-looking woman behind the bar, in The Cove. Forster nodded at him, James obviously embodying whatever stereotype Forster held of a London magazine hack.

'Mr Sawday, I presume,' he said, standing up and shaking James's hand.

'James, please.'

Forster smiled and drained the remains of his pint. 'OK, James.' He passed James his empty glass. 'Pint, please.'

'Cheers,' James said, a few minutes later, clinking his pint of Bass against Neville's.

Forster drank deep. 'Rugby season,' he commented. 'Got to keep my weight up.'

James lit a cigarette. 'Winter,' he said. 'Got to keep my lungs warm. Who d'you play for? Grancombe?'

Forster nodded his head. 'Second fifteen. Nothing too serious.'

'In it for the social life, yeah?'

'Partly. Do you play?'

'Not since school.'

'Where was that?'

James named his old school.

'Public school, huh?'

'Yes. What about you? You a local boy?'

'Yep.' Forster took another drink. 'I hope you don't mind my asking, but how old are you?'

'Twenty-seven. Why?'

'Just curious. Like you, I'm sure, it comes with the job.' He smiled, scrutinised James's face. 'I swear I almost recognise you. You been down here on holiday before?'

James felt uncomfortable, like he was playing poker and Forster reckoned he had him beat. Forget it. He'd never met him before. Just being friendly, that's all. 'No,' James said, 'this is my first visit.'

Forster snorted. 'Well, James, without wanting to make you look like a total arse, do you mind telling me how you know Will Tawnside used to run this place?'

James bluffed, 'I remembered his name from one of the articles. The police had him in for questioning after Jack Dawes was killed.'

'No, you didn't.'

'What?'

'You didn't remember his name from any article, because his name wasn't mentioned in any article. Believe me, I know; I've read them all.'

James didn't reply for a few seconds. He wasn't sure what the appropriate adult response was to someone who'd just called him a liar and had then gone on to prove that this was the case. His only frame of reference was school and he could hardly break down in tears and beg Forster not to put him in detention. In the end, he held up his hands in surrender. Honesty was probably the best policy. Either that or tell Forster to go fuck himself and walk. But he needed Forster, so that wasn't an option. Besides, aside from what had just happened, he liked Forster. He spoke his mind. No bullshit. He looked like someone he could trust.

'You got me,' he said.

Forster raised his glass, grinned. 'I know it. So, you going to tell me the truth? You don't have to, but I am intrigued.'

'OK, but I'll start my answer with a question.'

'Shoot.'

'How old are you?'

'Twenty-nine.'

'Well, that might explain why you recognise me. I spent some time down here when I was a kid. Back in 1989. Haven't been back since.'

Forster nodded slowly. 'The year the killer came. No wonder you know so much. How long were you down here?'

'The whole summer. I was staying with my uncle.' Forster waited for him to expand. 'Alan I'Anson.'

For the first time, Forster looked surprised. 'Jesus, you really were in the thick of it.' His expression softened. 'And I'm sorry, by the way. About your uncle. Not nice. I wrote his obituary. I can give you a copy, if you want.'

'Thanks.'

'I didn't see you at the funeral.'

'You went?'

'Yes. Just about the only bastard who bothered, though.

His profile round here kind of faded once he stopped writing and coming into town.'

'I take it it was quiet, then.'

'As the . . .' Forster's sentence collapsed into a wince.

'Grave,' James said, filling in the blank.

'Sorry.'

'It's OK. At least you went. I was abroad,' James excused himself. 'I didn't hear till it was too late. Thanks, though. Thanks for going.'

'I used to like him. And his books.' Forster nodded, then frowned. 'Hang on a minute. I'Anson's nephew. You were there when they found Jack Dawes' body, weren't you?'

'Yes.'

'Fuck me.' Forster scratched at his jaw, shot James a look of pity. 'You and Alex Howley and Dan Thompson.' His expression saddened. 'Poor Dan. Finds that body and ten years on the killer finds him. Did you stay in touch with him?'

'No. We kind of fell out.'

'Yeah, well don't feel bad about it; you weren't the only one. Junked out big time the last couple of years. Still, he didn't deserve to die like that.' Forster stared across the room. 'I was at school with him, you know. Couple of years above. Same year as his sister, Suzie. You know her?'

'Used to. She used to be a friend.'

'Lovely girl. Taken his death pretty bad. Shit, if anyone should have got it, it should have been Howley. Nasty piece of work. I tell you, that's one murder I wouldn't mind writing up.'

'What's he doing now?'

Forster whistled, sat back in his chair and relaxed. 'What *isn't* he doing is probably a better question. Officially, right, he runs a club down on South Beach. Called "Current". Used to be called "Dixie's", owned by Murphy's brother. A right shit-hole. Alex bought him out a couple of years ago, did it up. And, officially, that's where he gets his money from.'

'And unofficially?'

'That's what I'd like to know. Or, rather, that's what I'd like to prove. Smart car. Smart house. Smart clothes. *Current*'s popular, all right, but only because of the names he gets down here to play. No way the gate money can cover the lifestyle he leads, though, so he must be getting his money from somewhere else. The place is a front. It's obvious. Trouble is,' Forster reflected, 'nothing sticks to him. The proverbial "Teflon man". Murphy tried to nail his arse for years and got nowhere.'

'Why the past tense? Has he given up?'

'Jesus, you haven't heard, have you?' Forster asked, consternation spreading across his face. 'No reason why you should have, I suppose,' he reflected. 'Didn't make the nationals or anything.' James stared at him blankly. 'He disappeared,' Forster said. 'Vanished. Three years ago.'

'What do you mean, disappeared?'

'Just what I say. He left the station one night to walk home and that was the last anyone ever saw of him. Everyone thought it was the killer again to begin with. There were search parties and everything, but they never found him.'

James could barely believe what he was hearing. Murphy gone, just like that. That self-assured giant from his childhood having vanished like one of Alex's smoke rings in the wind didn't seem possible. He looked down at the table and noticed that his hand was shaking.

'What do you think happened?' he finally managed to ask.

'Anything's possible with a bastard like that,' Forster considered with a nonchalant shrug. 'Could have had a breakdown, done a bunk – anything. Down under missing persons now. And three years is a long time to stay missing. My guess is he'll stay that way. Did you know him?'

'Yes, we didn't get on.'

'Hardly surprising if you were hanging out with Howley . . .'

'No.'

'Yeah, so there you go. Murphy disappeared and Howley's had it easy since.' Forster growled, actually growled. 'I tell you, nothing would give me greater pleasure than getting that little prick locked up. Ever since he started running those raves back in the Eighties and that kid OD'd . . . He doesn't give a shit about anyone but himself.'

'So dig up some dirt on him,' James suggested.

'Easier said than done. The people who work for him are loyal. Totally. Like fucking dogs. If I started snooping around, they'd be more likely to give me a smack in the mouth than some information. If you don't believe me, try it out for yourself.'

'On that recommendation, I think I might give it a miss.'

'Very wise. So,' Forster continued, 'unless someone gives me a lead, I'm pretty stuck on where to start.' He gazed down at his glass, shook his head, then looked back at James. 'Well, I've got to admit, I wasn't planning on giving you much help. We've got a bit of a pact running down here, me and the powers that be. I write up the news for the *Gazette*, but I don't sensationalise it. And I don't give anything to hacks. Nothing they don't know already, anyhow. Fucks with business. Not good for the town.' He finished his drink. 'But this is different, I suppose. You're not going to go demonising the town, are you?'

'No,' James said, meaning it.

'In that case, I'll have another drink.' Forster's smile returned. 'And think yourself lucky: you're probably the first journalist I've spoken to who might actually get something for his money.'

James went to get the beers in.

'Suspects,' James prompted when he settled back in his seat. 'Tell me about the suspects.'

Forster grimaced. 'Well, James, the thing is, there aren't any.'

'Oh, come on,' James encouraged. 'There must be someone . . .'

'I'm serious. The police have come up with . . .' He made an 'O' with his finger and thumb. '. . . zilch. They've had people in for questioning, of course. Like they did with Will Tawnside here. And there've been others since, but they've drawn a blank.'

'That's insane,' James said. 'There've been three murders now: Jack Dawes and Kenneth Trader in 1989 and now Dan. The police must have an idea.' James stared into Forster's eyes. '*You* must have an idea. I know what this place is like for rumours. People must be whispering someone's name.'

'People are always going to whisper names, James. People down here are afraid. You can see it in their eyes. All of them. Most of the parents won't let their kids out after dark. Most of the parents won't go out themselves. They've all got names they whisper, faces they point their fingers at. But that's not the same as knowing. And knowing's all you can publish. You know that as well as I do.'

'But you *do* think it's a local who's doing it?'

Forster pulled a face, exasperated. 'I can't even be sure of that. I mean, look at the facts. Three murders. Dawes and Dan were locals, but Trader wasn't. Trader and Dan had apparently had drug dealings before – Dan and Alex got grilled by Murphy after Trader was murdered – but had nothing in common with the respectable Mr Dawes. And why the gap? Two in eighty-nine. One this year. That's nearly a decade. Could be a drifter. Could be someone who's been in prison in the years in between, or been abroad, or whatever. Could be some freak who's set off by the fucking position of the stars, for all I know.' Forster traced his finger thoughtfully round the rim of his glass. 'The only certainty, if you ask me, is that whoever's responsible is a Grade A whacko. There's no motive connecting the murders. Not sex. Not money. Nothing.' He drank from his glass, wiped his lips. 'And the one certainty about whackos is they don't stop till they're caught.' He eyes burrowed into James's. 'Or until they're killed.'

They stayed in The Cove for another drink, which Forster actually paid for, and continued to hypothesise. Between them, though, they came up with the same as the police: zilch. Finally, Forster said he had to get going, had to check the copy for Saturday's edition. James walked back with him to the *Gazette's* offices on the High Street and Forster photocopied the editions that had covered Trader's and Dan's deaths. He also gave him a copy of the edition with Alan's obituary in it. As they walked to the door, he told James to give him a call if he needed to run anything else past him, or needed any introductions. They stood in the doorway, Forster holding it open, James clutching the papers in his hand.

'Thanks, Neville. Thanks for everything.' He took out a business card from his wallet, handed it to Forster, commenting, 'Next time you're up in the Smoke, give me a call and we'll go for another beer. My mobile's on there, in case you think of anything I might find useful.'

'Must be weird for you,' Forster said, 'being back here again, having to sift through your own past.'

'Tell me about it.'

'Bet your editor loves it, though – having a man on the inside.'

'He doesn't know I used to live here.'

'How come?'

'I don't know. When he gave me the job, I kind of freaked. Too many bad memories down here. And I know what he'd want: the gory stuff. Me finding Dawes's corpse. Sensational, you know. Personalised. Big banner line over the article: *MY DEALINGS WITH DEATH*. Some crap like that.'

'But it's not going to be like that, right?'

'No, I just want the truth.'

'That's what we all want, James. That's what we all want.' Forster smiled. 'Sometimes, though, maybe it's easier to believe the crap.'

Later, back at the hotel, James stared at the stubble left in the basin after the water had run out. He ripped some toilet paper off the roll, dabbed at a cut on his jaw, and stared into the mirror. He looked better. No doubt about that.

He turned at the sound of his phone, went through to the bedroom and dug it out of his jacket.

'James speaking.'

'Hi, babe.'

'Lucy. Jesus, it's good to hear your voice.' He meant it.

'Hey, come on,' she said with a laugh. 'It's only been two days.'

'Yeah, but this place, I tell you, it feels like the end of the earth.'

'Well, it's not. And, anyway, we're down tomorrow. David and Becky have got it all cleared with work, so we're driving down together. Should reach you round lunch time.'

James pulled back the curtain, looked across the grey sea. 'Make sure you bring loads of jumpers. It's freezing.'

'I'm so excited. You done any groundwork for me yet?'

'What?'

'Locations. For the article photos. The way I see it, the sooner we can get that out of the way, the sooner we can have some fun. How's the piece going? You finished it yet?'

James looked across at his laptop on the desk. He'd put a few hours in since getting back from meeting Forster. 'No. About half-way, though.'

'Well, hurry up. There's so much I want to do. Cliff-side walks. Fishing. *Everything*. I want to *do* Grancombe.'

He laughed, her enthusiasm hooking him. 'Well, don't get too excited. It's only a small town.'

'And the hotel? What's it like?'

'Nothing special,' he said honestly. 'Quiet. I think I'm the only guest here. I've booked rooms for David and Becky.'

'What about us?' she asked. 'You got a double bed?'

'Sure.'

'Well, keep one half free for me.'

'Don't worry. I will.'

She blew him a kiss, then asked, 'What are you doing tonight?'

'I'll take your advice, see if I can finish the article off.'

'Right answer.' He heard someone calling her name in the background. 'Gotta dash. Jane's just called round. Cinema. You take care all right. And keep your hands off the local girls,' she joked. 'You're mine and don't you forget it.'

'I won't,' he said, turning the phone off and walking over to the desk and switching the laptop on.

He sat down and continued to type:

Despite the fact that at this juncture there was no firm evidence of foul play, many of the townspeople joined in the search party for Jack Dawes. 'He was a popular man,' a local landlord said. 'And an artist as well. A tourist attraction in his own right. We were worried, felt we should do our bit to help find out what had happened to him. We just wanted to know he was OK.'

The search party, under the guidance of the town's police, convened at a cafe on South Beach near dawn and set out shortly afterwards to search the surrounding countryside. Three local teenagers, Alex Howley, Tim Sunday and Daniel Thompson set out to scour the woods lying between Dawes' property and the cliffs above South Beach. It was only a matter of hours before they found what they were looking for.

They discovered Dawes' mutilated body at the heart of the woods, some seven hundred yards back from the cliff. Its hands were missing, nothing left but bloody stumps at the end of its arms. The rest of the body was in an advanced state of decomposition, leading to one of the teenagers, Daniel Thompson, having to be treated for severe shock.

Of the three young men party to this discovery, the first, Tim Sunday, left Grancombe later that summer, never to return. The second, Alex Howley, can still be found there, now the proprietor of a local night club. Daniel Thompson, however, was not so lucky. Nearly a decade later, his own body was to be found, similarly mutilated, a victim of the killer's return to the woods after almost a decade's absence.

James pulled his hands back from the keyboard, stood up and walked to the window, watching the rivulets of rain snake down the glass. Maybe Forster was right. Maybe sometimes it was easier to believe the crap.

CHAPTER TWELVE

pigs

It was mid-August, just gone noon. It was long before the killing of Kenneth Trader on the beach. James was sitting on an old wicker chair on the terrace at the back of Alan's house. He looked along the back wall of the building, following the uneven stone surface to where it broke at the window of Alan's ground floor study. The curtains were drawn tight, as they had been since Jack Dawes' funeral. James glanced at the sky. No barrage balloons. No dark smudges of flak patterning the even blue. No bomber formations raining death on the landscape below. Nothing external to excuse the blackout that Alan had imposed on himself.

And while Alan sat inside, insulated in a private universe like some latter day Nero, outside, the property was going to pieces. Anorexic fingers of grass clawed upwards from the moss between the paving slabs. The garden beyond was lush with weeds, becoming wilder by the day, blending into the untended wilderness of the paddock which led to the woods.

James sped up the passage of time in his mind, projecting a model of how this place would look in a few years time if nature was left to its own devices: shattered roof slates lay buried beneath a jungle of brambles and nettles across what had once been the terrace; ivy and wisteria wrapped itself like a green fist around the house, threatening to crush it into dust; and still, the curtains of Alan's study remained drawn, the irregular sound of fingers clattering across a keyboard being the only remaining sign of human habitation.

The mental image faded. Alan might not even be here in a few months time, let alone still be garretted in his study. He might not even be alive by then. James waved his notebook across his face, chilled the sweat on his brow. Might not be alive *then*. Christ, there wasn't much evidence that he was alive *now*. James saw him maybe once or twice a day. Came across him in the kitchen, slopping cold soup from a tin into a bowl, or collecting beer from the fridge. Once a week, he'd see him walking to the Land Rover and disappearing in search of provisions, returning later with more beer, more soup and more cigarettes. Or he'd hear him flushing the toilet, then listen to the padding of his bare feet down the corridor, followed by the slamming of his study door. And other noises, too. Always later at night. Always the same: the noise of Alan entering the cellar.

But even though Alan was physically here, as far as company went, he might as well have been dead. When they crossed paths during the daytime, it wasn't so bad. At least then, Alan would speak to him, reply to his questions in monosyllables. But at night, when the drink flowed through him, it was hopeless.

At first, it had worried James. More: it had scared him. It had made him remember the way he'd once been himself. Watching Alan stumbling through the shadowed recesses of the house had dredged up the horrors that James had hoped were buried for good. The old images had returned: the hours spent looking at the newspaper articles that had detailed his parents' death, the obituary listing his father's achievements for Queen and country, the single sentence given over to his mother's fifty years; the view of the city his eyes had glazed over as he'd sat on the ledge at the top of the Clock Tower at school, hating himself for not having the guts to let go of the stone, slide forward and tumble silently through the dark.

'Why don't you just leave me alone?'

That's how Alan had replied when James had encountered him in the kitchen a couple of weeks back and tried to speak to him. The booze had already done its work. Alan's facial muscles had been slack, immune to stimulation. When he'd spoken, there'd been no anger in his words, no inner voice trapped inside, crying out for help.

There'd been no emotion at all.

'I know you don't want to,' James had said, 'but we've got to talk. I can't just stand by and watch you doing this to yourself.'

Alan's eyes had slowly opened, like someone waking from sleep. He'd stared at the tin of beer in his hand. 'I'm fine,' he'd said. 'Nothing's wrong. Everything's fine. Everything's going to be all right.'

James had stepped forward. He'd reached out, rested his hand on Alan's shoulder. Even his body had felt cold. 'You need to see someone. Talk to someone. There are people that can help. I know it's not what you want, but please, Alan, it's what you need.'

Alan had raised his hand, pinched at his brow, as if he'd been attempting to coax a response out of his brain. 'It's done now,' he'd said, his hand draped across his eyes and mouth. 'No one can bring them back. No one can change what's gone.'

'Please, Alan. Just give it a go. You've got to. I know someone, someone who helped me.'

Alan had shaken himself free of James's grip. His muck-clogged teeth had glowed yellow. 'The only people who could've helped me are dead.'

James had heard his own voice cracking. In pity for Alan's tragedy, or in frustration at his inability to help? Both. He'd tried again, even though he'd known that the conversation had already burnt out. 'Look at yourself,' he'd pleaded. 'Just look at yourself in the mirror. You can't not see what's happening to you.'

'There's no point,' Alan had said. 'I already know what I'll see. I already know what I am.' He'd opened the beer, taken a drink. Beer had trickled from his lip onto his shirt, his mouth feeling nothing, like he'd been anaesthetised by a dentist. His face had reverted to neutrality. His eyes had registered nothing, as if James had suddenly ceased to exist, disappeared from his view. 'I'm sorry,' he'd said, pushing past James. 'I've got to go now. I've got things to do. My work. I got to get back to my work.'

And he'd left James there, invisible; a ghost he'd chosen not to believe in any longer.

James brushed a wasp away from his thigh, returned his attention to the notebook. He read over what he'd written. It was the beginning of a short story, set in Grancombe, like all his writing had been over the past month or so. He'd given the first story he'd written to Alan, slipped it under the study door, with a note attached, saying that he'd appreciate Alan's opinion. That had been three weeks ago now. He'd heard nothing. For all he knew, Alan hadn't even picked it up from the floor.

The lack of a response had angered James to begin with. It was the first time he'd shown his work to anyone. But it hadn't lasted. Getting feedback from Alan about his work had only been part of the reason he'd handed over the story to begin with. Just as important had been the hope that the story would act like a fishing fly on Alan, lure him out of his dank study into the daylight. A sober conversation. That's all James had really wanted. The only one he'd really had with Alan since the funeral hadn't exactly been in ideal circumstances. And Murphy hadn't exactly gone out of his way to aid the restoration of familial relations between them, either.

It was maybe a month since the episode with Hazel and Georgie at Marge's caravan site. James couldn't be exact. Time didn't seem to mean much anymore. Not like when he'd been at school, when the days had been severed into distinct slices by the clanging of bells and the switching on and switching off of lights. Not like London either, with the chattering of its radio DJs, its rush hours and weekend evacuations. Here in Grancombe, one day slid into the next, as imperceptibly as waves lapping over one another as they rolled onto the beach, cancelling one another out.

❊ ❊ ❊

As he'd sprinted away from the caravan and headed for the woods, cursing the way the cigarettes he'd been smoking had affected his fitness, he'd heard his name called. Distinct. A single syllable, familiar and aggressive, like an owner calling their dog to heel. For an instant, he thought it was Alex, assumed that there'd been some change of plan, that it wasn't the police who'd been banging down the door, that some whacked-out mates of Alex, even Dan, had been winding them up. He slowed, and the shirt slid from his face. He turned his head, and there was Murphy, stationary at the side of Hazel and Georgie's caravan, his arm outstretched, like it had some crazy cartoon capacity to extend, become telescopic, reach out and clamp James by the collar.

His name came again, in synch with the movement of Murphy's lips. This time, fear dropped like a net over him. Another policeman appeared at Murphy's side and for a second nobody moved. Then Murphy's face warped, slid into a mask of anger and the other policeman darted forward towards James. Over, James thought. It's over. Cold. Caught cold. Dead. Dead meat.

'Do it.'

James's face panned across like a camera to the caravan. There in the window was Alex, holding onto the frame. An octopus of uniformed limbs engulfed him, dragged him backwards, out of sight.

James ran.

Faster, faster. Rollercoaster.

Murphy's sidekick who gave chase didn't get close. With the amount of adrenaline that had been released in James's metabolism over the preceding few minutes, he didn't stand a chance. It was like a clean athlete trying to catch a fellow competitor reared on steroids since birth. James was gone, past the first caravan in what felt like a stride, past the next and the one after that. Then ducking between two, providing himself with cover, he completed his escape. He checked behind him after he'd cleared the last of the caravans and broken out into the open fields. The policeman wasn't even in sight, let alone closing him down. James slowed his pace, got his bearings. He headed for the woods.

Murphy had already arrived at Alan's house by the time James got there an hour or so later. James saw the police car from the bottom of the drive. His first instinct was to run. But a policeman was standing by the car and, from this distance, James wasn't able to tell whether he'd been spotted or not. Besides, his legs were slaughtered. He stayed still for a second or two, then remembered the bag in his hand. In that instant, it transformed from something he'd forgotten about to something impossibly heavy, a weight that could take him down with it, sink him, just like it could have done to Alex before.

Still, the policeman didn't move, failed to betray any sign that he'd seen James or not. The compulsion to throw the bag away was becoming unbearable now. *Don't panic. If he hasn't seen you, you can hide it in the long grass further up the drive, drop it by the bush there in the shade, out of sight, and no one's going to be any the wiser. But if you throw it now, or try and stash it, or run, and he has seen you, then it's finished. Game over. No credits left to spend. Murphy's going to get his man. You're going to be all washed up, flotsam on the shore.*

James started to walk slowly forward, staring intently at the policeman, keeping the bag by his side. Worst case scenario: if the policeman saw him before he dropped the bag by the bush, he could run again. His legs ached, his throat was dry enough to splinter, but he could still manage it. As far as the woods again. As far as safety. He drew level with the bush and released the bag. The noise of it landing on the grass crashed as loud in his ears as if he'd dropped a cymbal backstage during a mime act, but the policeman didn't so much as flinch.

As he drew near to the outbuildings and the policeman's face came into focus (it was the same one who Murphy had sent after him at the caravan park), James went through new things with Murphy would play out. Murphy hadn't only seen him before he'd run, he'd called him by his name, so there wasn't going to be any point in denying he'd been there to begin with. That left him with the problem of explaining why he'd chosen to run. Drugs. He'd been carrying the drugs.

Murphy had probably already guessed that much. But without proof, he wasn't going to have a thing on James. So admit to the runner. Don't explain why. Deny the drugs. Deny the drugs no matter what.

He had about fifteen yards to cover now, before he'd reach the police car. Murphy was nowhere to be seen. With Alan? Probably. Already speaking to him, telling him what had happened, telling him his suspicions, detailing the exact nature of the grief his nephew had just brought crashing down on himself. And Alan's reaction? That was less simple to predict. What Alan's reaction was going to be was anyone's guess.

James stopped where he was. The policeman was smoking a cigarette, gazing at the ground. James was close enough to see the dried chewing gum of acne scars on his face. A couple more paces forward and he'd be able to reach out and tap him on the shoulder. Instead, though, he waited, something holding him back. What was he meant to do now, just walk on up and hold his wrists out. Or wait here till the policeman noticed him and collared him in whatever way he saw fit?

He glanced around the rest of the yard. Something wasn't right. Then he realised what: Alan's Land Rover was missing. The funeral. Of course. He looked at his watch. But it would have finished by now. So where was Alan? At the Moonraker with the others? Maybe. Or still in the churchyard, unable to motivate himself into motion. Paralysed by grief. Or worse – regret swept through James – sickened at his nephew's delinquent behaviour, driving past St Donal's like that, not giving a damn for the dead.

'Stay put, you little shit.'

'I'm not going anywhere,' James replied as the policeman flicked his cigarette away and strode up to him.

'You're right there, son,' the policeman snapped, grabbing James by the shirt and dragging him towards the car.

James pulled against him. 'Take it easy, all right?' His voice sounded weak, ineffectual. The was no equality here and he knew it.

The policeman jerked the door open and shoved James

inside. 'If I were you, I'd keep my trap shut; you're in enough shit as it is.'

'What?' James asked. 'What have I—'

But the policeman wasn't listening. The door thudded shut and he jogged up to the house. Then James's attention was diverted. Murphy stepped out of the front door, closed it and fiddled busily with the lock. Nausea hit James, leaving him punch-drunk, reeling. Where was Alan? What was Murphy doing in the house with Alan away? Jesus, he didn't want this without Alan here. A red smudge of fly lay impacted on the windscreen, left Murphy's face bathed in infra-red as James watched him listening to the policeman's busy chatter. Then Murphy nodded, suddenly animated, and headed quickly for the car. The policeman fell into step behind him, a dog at heel.

'Make a habit of walking into the lion's den, do you, you dozy bastard?' Murphy asked, his fat neck fighting to escape his collar as he twisted round in the passenger seat.

The other policeman sat in the driver's seat and stared straight ahead.

'That was a question,' Murphy pointed out, then his voice pitched up, 'So give me a fucking answer: tell me where the drugs are.'

'I don't know.' James coughed, frightened now, trying to keep his voice steady. 'I don't do drugs.'

The words sounded weak as soon as they left his mouth, watered down, insincere. Murphy fired out an arm, gripped James's neck and wrenched him forward.

'You playing games with me?' Spit flew from his mouth, landed on James's face. It burnt like acid. His yellow teeth zoomed in closer. 'That what your mate told you to do? Fuck me around?'

James's bowels began to churn. 'Please don't. I swear to God, I haven't got—'

'Don't talk to me about God, you piece of shit. You don't give a fuck about God any more than me. I saw you driving past St Donal's.' He started to shake James violently. 'That's why I came for you. Thought that was funny, eh? Bit of a fucking laugh?'

James was whimpering now. 'No. No. I didn't. I—'

Murphy threw him back against the seat. 'I'm going to ask you again and this time you're going to tell me. You're going to tell me, because you're not stupid. You're going to tell me exactly where they are, because your little bitch friends told me that Howley gave them to you before you ran off. And you're going to tell me, because if you don't, I'm going bury you.'

Tears broke from James's eyes. Shame drilled down. He put his arm across his face in a futile attempt to conceal them. 'You've got to believe me. I don't know.'

'You don't owe Howley shit,' Murphy told him. 'That why you're shutting me out? You think he gives a fuck about you? Think he'd give a flying fuck if I'd caught you with the gear?'

'I don't know.' James was wailing now. He wanted this to go away. He wished he'd never set eyes on Alex. Jesus, if only he could turn back time, make things different. 'Please stop.'

'You're pathetic,' Murphy spat. 'Look at you. Least your mate Howley's got balls. Not you, though, eh? Sitting there blubbing like a queer.' Murphy paused, sniffed. 'Probably runs in the family.'

James lowered his arm, stared at Murphy. Cracked voice: 'What?'

Murphy grinned, wiped his hand across his hooked nose, leaving it quivering for a second or two. 'I've been in there, haven't I? Pest-hole. Wouldn't keep a pig in there. Scum. That's you, boy. And your uncle. Filth. Should be put down like dogs. Put out of your misery.' The grin vanished. 'Now tell me where you've put the stuff.'

James's guts were melting now. He opened his mouth to speak, then clamped it tight again. Deny everything. Deny everything and everything will be OK. He covered his eyes, mumbled, 'I told you . . . I don't know anything . . .'

Rapid movement in the front of the car, the door opening, slamming. He looked out of the window, but it was already pulling away from him. Faintness hit him and he recoiled across the seat. Murphy reached inside and hauled him out.

He felt himself free falling, plummeting from an aircraft towards a concrete sea.

'This isn't the end of this,' Murphy growled, holding him upright outside the car. Then he dropped him, watched him sink to his knees. 'You remember that next time you see Howley. You take a good look at the bruises on his face and you remember me.'

James stayed where he was as Murphy got back into the car. The engine started and the wheels squealed back across the yard. James whimpered as the urine drenched his pants and trickled onto the ground.

Alan returned about an hour after Murphy had left. James was on the sofa in the sitting room, his eyes fixated on the television screen.

'Proud of yourself, are you?' Alan asked.

James sat up and pulled the dressing gown he'd put on after he'd showered tighter round his waist.

'Murphy told me it was you in that car that went past with the music on.'

James didn't reply.

'You make me sick.'

James's voice came back, hollowed of emotion: 'I'm sorry.'

Alan turned his back on him, walked towards the door. 'You've got nothing to say that I want to hear.'

But James wasn't listening to him either.

Murphy.

Animal.

Pig.

Filth.

Only Alex remained for him. Not perfect. But better than Murphy, better than Alan, too. Alex would still be there for him. His friend.

He hauled himself up off the sofa and walked down the drive, scrabbled around in the dirt until he found the bag, then picked it up and returned to his room.

James watched a housemartin dart across the blue sky and duck out of sight beneath the guttering on the house. With an effort of will, he could make the day of the funeral lie dormant in his mind, blot it out. He didn't want it coming back to haunt him. He was over it. *Get that*, he told himself, *you're over it. Things have changed. Or rather, you've changed. And the catalyst for the metamorphosis? Alex. It all comes down to Alex. Be sure of that. Where Alan drove you away that night, the next morning when you returned Alex's bag of drugs to him, Alex accepted you. Where Alan reflected nothing but death, Alex launched you into life.*

James stretched, tilted back in the chair, enjoying the sensation of sun on his face. Then commitment clawed its way into his conscience. He looked at his wrist instinctively, before remembering that he'd lost his watch somewhere on the beach the week before. Already, the white scar where his watch had sheltered his skin from the sun had turned to the colour of copper. He closed the note book and got to his feet. The temptation to go inside and pick up the phone would have been irresistible, if it wasn't for the fact that the phone had been disconnected the week before. (James had found the final payment demand screwed up on the floor next to the bin in the kitchen.) Just as well. It was going to be a bigger kick making the calls together. Him, Alex and Dan. He could see it now. The three of them, squatting at their usual table in the Moonraker, passing Alex's mobile phone round and ringing their schools, finding out if their A-level results had cut them free or caged them in.

James was sitting in one of the cool stone alcoves of the Moonraker, waiting for Alex and Dan to arrive. He felt the sweat on his brow, generated on the walk here from Alan's house, begin to cool. He wiped the condensation from the full pint of lager on the table before him and transferred it to his face, then pulled a packet of Marlboro from his pocket and lit one.

It was the first of the day. Even though he'd been smoking – what? – ten to twenty a day for the past few weeks, his lungs still couldn't deal with inhaling heated tar in the morning. Sure, he'd done it from time to time, smoked dope through till dawn with Alex, Dan and assorted groupies down on the rocks on South Beach after some party or another, watched the embers of the fire fade to grey in the growing light, but most days his lungs just didn't want to know. Like some remnant of his past, they kept on trying to keep his new lifestyle at bay. He swigged at the pint, lubricated his throat and inhaled again. This time the smoke curled down smoothly, settled like a velvet lining on his throat. His mind buzzed gently as the nicotine kicked in.

He looked down at the tanned skin of his forearms, and that of his knees where they protruded from the long surf shorts. The brush of hairs, customarily brown, now lay blonde, bleached by the sun, fine and wispy as dandelion down. He studied his reflection in a mirror on the wall. His fringe, uncut and uncombed since the day of Jack Dawes' funeral, now hung low, tucked behind his ears, streaked like straw where he'd repeatedly applied the lemon juice while he'd baked his body on the beach day in day out. He looked good, like he'd been born to this, like he belonged.

He glanced across at the clock above the bar. The others were late. Hardly surprising, really. They'd had some business to do this morning, a few loose ends to knot up for the rave tonight. Logistics. The generator that would power the sounds and lights up at Eagle's Point had been playing up the day before. Alex had had to drive over and pick up a mechanic today to sort the problem out. Then there was the council with all their bye-laws and safety regulations to satisfy (shouldn't be a problem, Alex reckoned, since he'd done everything legal for once in his life). And Dan was on another mission: charging round the nearby villages and towns with a bunch of mates, slapping flyers up on every available wall, informing the world that, for tonight at least, Grancombe was definitely where it was at.

James smiled. It was going to be good. The party of the summer, Alex reckoned. Like putting all the other raves they'd run out at the same time. Full-scale. For real. The climax of the season. Two bands were booked to play. No one major, but a couple of possible next-big-things. And then the DJs, the real reason people were coming. The stage was already constructed, the amps in place. They were expecting over a thousand punters to show. A couple of hundred from Grancombe and the surrounding area, the rest from beyond, from London, from Bristol, from Manchester, from anywhere where the word slipped round easily. And at a five-quid gate charge, money matters were shaping up nicely. Even less the money Alex would declare to the tax man ('Doing it by the book's gonna bust Murphy's balls . . .'), him and Dan would be set up for their end-of-summer Thailand binge with cash to spare.

Grancombe wasn't going to know what had hit it.

The light reflected on the table changed subtly and James looked up to see the pub door opening. Someone came in, buried in shadow against the bright daylight for a moment. Then the door swung shut and he saw that it was Suzie. She walked to the bar and sat on a stool with her back to him. Johno, who'd been serving a baggy-trousered guy with a heavy Mancunian accent (one of the pilgrims, no doubt, who'd journeyed down for tonight's festivities), wandered over to talk to her, fixed her a pint of Coke.

James hadn't seen much of her since she'd acted nurse for him on the day they'd found Dawes' corpse. This hadn't really been down to him, more circumstances. When Alex had said that Dan and his sister weren't exactly close, he hadn't been kidding. Most of the time, Dan wasn't really aware of her existence. They'd been to a party down at Surfers' Turf a few days before and Dan hadn't even spoken to her. 'Too straight,' had been his only comment as he'd looked around the room. 'Bunch of boring bastards. Drug-free, fun-free fuck-wits.'

The one time James had spoken to her had been when he'd gone round with Alex to visit Dan in his room in the flat above the Moonraker. The visit had been wired with bad vibes as it was, what with Dan still being wiped-out after his way-too-close encounter with Dawes up in the woods.

It had been Suzie who'd answered the door. 'Oh,' she'd said the moment she'd seen Alex, 'It's you.'

'Good to see you, too,' Alex had replied.

'What do you want?'

'Came to see Dan, check he's all right.'

She'd noticed James, lurking on the stairs below Alex. 'Is that you, James?' she'd asked.

'Yeah, hi,' he'd said, then, noticing the look of disappointment on her face, 'How you doing?'

'You gonna let us in now?' Alex had interrupted. 'Or we gonna stand here talking all night?'

'He's resting. Doctor said he shouldn't be disturbed.'

'Your mum said it was OK.'

'Since when was my mother a doctor?'

Alex had pushed forward. 'Just let us in, will you?'

She'd stepped back. 'He's in his room.'

'Thanks,' James had said as he'd followed Alex past her into the flat.

'Hanging out with Alex and my brother now, are you?' she'd asked him once Alex had dropped out of earshot.

'Yeah, they're all right.'

She'd shaken her head and muttered, 'Thought you'd have had more sense,' before disappearing off into the living room without giving him a chance to reply.

Hardly what you'd call a dream date. But the evening hadn't been a total waste. At least they'd left Dan in good spirits. They'd stayed there with him for a couple of hours, wired into Nintendo, zapped the bad guys and saved the day, smoked a couple of spliffs. Dan had even smiled from time to time.

'Here,' Alex had said, as they'd made to go. He'd placed a pill next to the glass of water on Dan's bedside table. 'This'll sort you out for tonight. We'll be round to pick you up tomorrow. Back to life. Back to reality. Business as usual.'

Dan had picked the pill up, slipped it onto his tongue and swilled it down with a gulp of water. 'Yeah,' he'd said, lying back and closing his eyes, 'sweet dreams.'

James wasn't sure what the pill had been. Probably Ecstasy. More likely an upper than a downer. He still wasn't clued in on what was what as far as pills went. He had resisted the temptation to join Alex and the others on their narcotic-fuelled transcendental explorations, and had stuck to the devils he knew; alcohol, and now grass. Whatever it had been, though, the trip had done the trick. By taking him out of his mind for a night, it had brought Dan back down to earth. They'd done as they'd said the next morning, and Dan had been there waiting for them. Subdued to begin with, sure. But by the end of the week, he'd been back, resurrected, as loud and as leery as the first time James had encountered him.

His attention reverted to Suzie. Even now, with her back to him, unaware of his presence, she still had the ability to flip him out – boom-boom his heart like a drum machine. He knew he had things to tell her, things she'd tell him back, things he'd want to listen to. He played a psychological drama out in his mind, just like his grief counsellor had taught him. Imagine the alternatives. Pitch yourself into the ideal and discover what you really want. He closed his eyes and saw palm trees, their trunks rearing up towards the sun-fired sky. Then down from the horizon, close now: him and Suzie. Miles from anyone. No Alex. No Dan. No past. Just him and her. Air crash survivors, stuck together on an uninhabited tropical island. He'd chuck all this – the money in his pocket, his new friends, his whole life – to be on that island, to pull her out of the wrecked plane, carry her through the waves onto the shore, lay her on the sand, knowing that his face would be the first thing she'd see when she awoke.

He opened his eyes. She wasn't looking at him at all. Back to him as before. He exhaled heavily, drank from his pint. Sentimental crap. Not kidding anyone. Love at first sight's for suckers. Crap you drilled into your head after watching too many happy-ever-after endings in movies. Not backed-up by what happened in reality. Not backed-up by what he saw before him now. He lit another cigarette and willed her from his mind.

Dan was the first to arrive, bike helmet under his arm, his face wet with exertion. He spotted James immediately and made a pint-tipping motion with his hand on his way to the bar.

'What you having?' he shouted.

'Stella.'

'Reassuringly brain-scrambling,' Dan said, lifting the hatch and going behind the bar. 'All right, Dad. Suzie . . .'

he said, pouring out a couple of pints.

Suzie swivelled in her chair to see who her brother had been talking to. She nodded with recognition when she discovered it was James, then turned back to the bar and continued her conversation with her father.

'Good day's work?' James asked as Dan joined him in the alcove.

'Fifteen villages. Donbury and Rothton, too. I tell you, man, I see another fucking poster and I'm gonna spew.' He drank deeply from his pint and gasped. 'Thirsty work,' he said appreciatively. 'Talk about earning your drink . . . Alex showed yet?'

'No, probably still up at Eagle's Point.'

'Nah, I called there on the way back. He'd left an hour ago. Must be down the council. Fucking pen-pushing pains in the arses.'

'How's it looking up the Point?'

'Massive. Marquee's up. Bar's stacked. Danny Peel sorted the JCB out – dug a trench at the back.'

'What for?'

'Toilets. Gotta piss somewhere, haven't you? Good drainage. It'll run straight down the cliff onto the beach. Right onto some tourist's ice cream with a bit of luck.' He lit two cigarettes, passed one to James. 'And the stage looks sorted. Generator's up and running. Mechanic even got that wartime search light sussed. It's gonna work a storm. Fire it up at the sky tonight. Be able to see it for fucking miles. Wouldn't surprise me if Batman put in an appearance.'

'Just so long as Gotham City's finest don't make it their business to gatecrash, too,' Alex added, appearing behind Dan and sitting down.

James examined his face. The bruises donated by Murphy had faded into his tan completely now.

'Where've you been?' Dan asked.

'Supplies,' Alex said.

'Everything sorted?'

'Yeah, enough chemical treats on board to open a laboratory.'

'Usual source?'

Alex shook his head. 'Didn't have enough. Had to go to somewhere.'

'Dodgy?'

'Chance you take .' He smiled. 'Don't worry, they're just for punters. I got them off Trader. I've got some left from the old batch for us.'

Dan's face relaxed. 'Push the shit on, hold the gold back. Good. So long as it's not me who ends up dead in casualty like that kid in the papers. How about the council? All sussed?'

'Yeah. Got them eating out of my hand.'

Dan stood up and addressed Alex: 'What you drinking?'

'Right,' Alex said once Dan had returned. He placed his mobile phone on the table. 'We gonna do this shit, or what?'

They each lit a cigarette.

'So, who's first?' Alex challenged.

James stared at the phone. 'Not me. No way.'

'Dan?' Alex asked.

'What's the point? Already know I've failed.'

Alex clicked his tongue. 'Well, someone's got to do it.' He drew pensively on his cigarette. 'Tell you what, we'll spin for it.'

'Spin what?' James asked.

'This,' Alex said, resting his hand on the phone and setting it spinning.

James watched it slow, past Dan, past Alex. It came to a rest, the aerial pointing directly at his chest.

'Typical,' he said and picked it up.

Two hours later, James was slumped numbly in his chair, staring at the carnage on the table before him. A sculpture of empty pint glasses obscured his view of Alex and Dan. He jammed his cigarette down into the ashtray and missed, ended up grinding it into the table's surface instead.

'Watch the fucking Chippendale,' Dan cried out, reaching across the table and knocking a stack of glasses onto the floor. He turned round and saw his father slowly shaking his head as he polished a glass. 'Sorry, Dad.'

'Oxford,' James said to Alex for what must have been the

fiftieth time. 'I still can't believe you never said you had an offer. Jesus.' He slumped across the table and slapped Alex on the back. 'Who'd have fucking guessed? And now you're in. You're going.'

'Yeah,' Alex said, 'whatever.'

James looked at him in amazement. 'Well, you've got to be pleased. Christ, I'm going to Edinburgh and I'm over the moon. So you . . . I can't even begin to imagine how wired you must be.'

'Yeah, you miserable bastard,' Dan agreed. 'Here's me with just enough to scrape into Tech, and I'm smiling. What's your problem? Enjoy it.'

Alex pulled his shades off, rubbed them on his t-shirt. 'Anyhow, I never even said I was gonna go.'

James leant forward. 'What? You can't not. Opportunity of a lifetime, isn't it? You can't just trash it. I mean, you two are still having a break for a year, going to Thailand. It's not like you're having to sacrifice anything.'

'Matter of priorities,' Alex said, getting to his feet. 'That's all that matters at the end of the day: what's going to get you where you want the quickest.'

'Where you going?' Dan demanded.

'Home, man. I gotta crash.' He wagged his finger at both of them. 'You guys should, too. Get some zeds. We've got a big night ahead of us. James,' he added, 'I'll pick you up round five at your uncle's. You all right for getting home?'

'Yeah,' James said, nursing his half-finished pint in his hand, 'I'll walk, get going in a minute.'

Alex laughed. 'You walk, it'll be five by the time you get there, the state you're in. You get there at all . . .' He pulled his wallet from his pocket. 'Here,' he said, handing over a twenty. 'Get a cab. I'll call one for you now.' He held up his left hand, fanned his fingers. 'Five. Don't forget.'

CHAPTER THIRTEEN

valentine

James woke on the Friday morning to the sound of a storm. The white blind which covered the window of his hotel room momentarily lit up like a projection screen. He listened to the screech of the gale and counted: *one, two, three . . .*

Then, *crash*; thunder rocked the town.

He twisted his neck and looked at the clock on the headboard of the bed: six-thirty. Habit told him to close his eyes, ignore the day for another hour, but his body wasn't having any of it. He'd gone to bed before ten the night before, blacking out seconds after the bulb of the bedside lamp. Too much sleep. And too deep. No chorus of car horns lullabying him through the night. Nothing but the soothing sound of the sea. Lightning flashed against the blind again. *One. Two.* And *crash*. No doubt about it: the storm was closing in.

He lay there for while, trying not to think. *Meditate,* he told himself. *Breath in. Breath out. Count the breaths.* But this morning, his technique failed him. His mind kept plunging down black tunnels.

Alex was back in his head. As bad as Headley on the way from the airport to the office. The crates in the barn nagged. Alex's attitude, too – the fuck-you confidence he'd exuded. James replayed the confrontation in his mind, wondered if he could have handled it better. Smacked Alex one? Once his minders had left the barn? Decked the bastard, laid him out? Would that have solved anything? Probably not. He'd probably just have laughed. Alex had him in his pocket. He knew James's weaknesses, just like he knew his own strength. The murder on the beach had bound them like Siamese twins. They breathed the same air, shared the same lungs. Until one of them died, that was how it would stay. While Alex still lived, James would never have full control of his life.

His train of thought switched track, burrowed into another dark tunnel. Lucy. Coming down today. And David. And Becky. People he cared about. They'd be leaving London in a few hours, packed bags in the boot of David's car, jumpers and jackets and boots, happy holiday music pumping out of the stereo, mentally flipping London off and homing in on the countryside, equating it with peace, relaxation and rest. None of them knew what awaited them here. And he couldn't exactly warn them. He couldn't exactly say, 'Hey, guys, I killed someone. Well, not personally, yeah? But I was there. I watched a man shudder in the sand and die. I carried his body. I buried his hand. But it was a long time ago, right? You can forgive me, right? We can still be friends.' Yeah, right. His instinct to protect himself was greater than his instinct to protect them.

But greater than even that was his fear that they'd find out anyway. He feared himself. He feared them discovering who he really was. His luck was fucked. Of that, he was convinced. There were too many coincidences racking up against him. Alex at the house. Suzie in the graveyard. Hatred everywhere. He could sense it rushing through the grass towards him, stretching out to coil around him like a snake; wring the breath from his body.

And it could get worse. It *would* get worse. He just knew it. So he had to prepare. For the worst case scenario. Like some crazed Vietnam vet on his final tour. For what he knew was coming. For the end. So he thought. Ops Scan. Today was Friday. Lucy and co. would be staying till Sunday. Three days. Three whole days when someone might recognise him, might come up with a handshake, a 'Hi', or – more likely, on current from – a punch. So reaction . . . He'd have to be on his guard; shepherd them through the weekend; keep them safe from the wolves. He'd have to plant eyes in their backs as well as his own.

He showered, shaved and dressed, went downstairs and ordered breakfast. His appetite was shot, his stomach full-to bursting with butterflies. He pushed his food around his plate and tried to distract himself by planning out his day. The morning was his. He was up to scratch on the article, which meant he could get down to dealing with Alan's house. Hopefully get most of the stuff packed up by lunch time. But stash it where? Not in the car. Lucy and co. would only ask. Besides, there probably wasn't enough room. So rent a lock-up, ditch the gear there and think about moving it on Monday once the others had gone back to London. Then back to the hotel to wait for David's car to pitch up outside, put on a disingenuous smile and greet them, just like nothing was wrong. Happy James. Carefree James. The James they knew and loved.

As he walked through the hotel's small reception area, the manageress called him over to the desk.

'I've got a letter for you,' she said, sifting through the mail.

James looked sceptical. 'For me? Are you sure?'

'James Sawday,' she said, reading his name off the back of the unstamped envelope and handing it over.

He took a seat and opened the envelope, pulled the letter out and read:

Dear James,
We need to talk. I'll be in Surfers' Turf all morning.
Please come. This is real.
Suzie.

James stared at the piece of paper, reading the words over and over again. Finally, though, he quit. It was pointless. He willed his racing pulse to slow. Grow up. You're acting like it's your first Valentine card. There's no love here, no hidden meaning: just statements. So what the hell was she playing at? Hadn't she said enough already? Maybe she wanted to give him more grief. He'd walk in and she'd lay into him. What did she take him for – a fool?

He crumpled the piece of paper up in his fist and dropped it in the bin on the way to the door. Forget it. There was nothing to talk about. He was a piece of shit and she knew it. There was no point in even wishing it were otherwise. He got in his car and headed up the High Street. But, before he'd even reached St Donal's, he was regretting throwing the paper away. *Dream chaser*, his pride snapped back. Then stoicism. Dream chaser. That's what he'd always been.

And there was a lot of hope. Too much hope to be killed off by a single row – no matter how hideous. There was still a maybe. Maybe she could forgive. Maybe they could talk. Maybe he could say the things he'd said to her so many times when she hadn't even been there to listen. Dream talk. And – fuck it – what else was there but dreams? *Decision: make one, just one. For once in your life, let your instinct point the way.*

He turned the car and headed for the cliffs.

He hesitated at the top of the steps leading down to South Beach. How was it possible that he could still have such internal GBH feelings for this woman? A decade had passed. Other women had entered and exited his life – *Don't call us, we'll call you*. But they'd never got past the audition stage. He'd moved on. So Suzie had been his first – so what? Everyone had a first. But they didn't care about them. They were history, pub stories at best. Not fixations. Not like this.

He shivered. It might not even be her. She might just be the focal point. This view and the memories of the search it evoked, this whole town . . . Everything here was unresolved. Perhaps that was why these feelings for her wouldn't dissipate. Because he'd run from her, as he'd run from this town, and as he'd run from himself. Because claiming her back would mean claiming back the part of him he'd left behind. Because only then would he be complete again.

He turned his jacket collar up against the wind and began the descent.

A hand-written sign on the door of Surfers' Turf read 'CLOSED FOR BUSINESS'. It was unnecessary. James had been able to tell from a hundred yards off that business wasn't exactly booming. Forget the lack of welcoming lights glowing through the morning gloom, the blistered paintwork of the sign said it all. The original colour, red – the one that James remembered from when he'd first walked up these steps in pursuit of a caffeine cure for Alan's hangover – showed beneath a tramp's coat of green that must have been applied in the intervening years. A crack, like a fork of lightning, ran across the glass door. He tossed his cigarette away and opened the door.

'Hello,' he called, standing inside, the door swinging closed behind him like a seal. There was no reply and, for a moment, he felt like a trespasser. He stared around. Footprints covered the floor, hallmarks stamped on the dust. It was like the beach was creeping up, claiming it back as its own once more. He remembered what Suzie had said back then, about business being slow in the winter. But this wasn't slow, it was stationary. He wandered over towards the serving counter. The fridges behind it were unplugged. And then the weirdest thing: he smelt cooking. Same as the day of the search. The scent of bacon trailing through the air. He shook his head, beat the ghost back down, and called again, 'Suzie. It's James. Are you here?'

This time, there was noise. Footsteps coming from the kitchen towards him. He leant across the counter, tried to look relaxed and in control. He tried to be everything he wasn't. Then he saw her, and his act faltered. She stopped in the doorway, and stared. He stared back. Now was a time for silence. He knew this technique from his job. Sometimes silence was the most effective way of getting people to talk. So let her. She asked you here. The onus is on her. Let her speak and then reply. Or leave. You don't need to say anything at all.

Instead, though, he heard himself saying, 'I'm sorry.'

She exhaled through her nose. At first, he mistook it for derision, but her words showed it for what it was: relief. 'Don't be. I was wrong yesterday. It was all too quick. Seeing you. Finding you there in the churchyard. I shouldn't have gone off at you like that. I had no right.'

'It's understandable,' he said. 'I just wish you'd given me a chance to explain. Will you now?'

'There's no need.'

'Of course—'

She cut him off with a sharp shake of her head. 'No. Neville called. Neville Forster. He called in at the 'Raker last night, said you two had been out for drink. He said you'd mentioned me.'

'And?'

'And he's a good friend. He said you weren't in this for the same reason as the other hacks, said your editor didn't even know you used to live here.' Her brow knitted. 'You've done well for yourself. I shouldn't have resented you for coming here to do your job. He said he trusted you.' She glanced back down at the floor before addressing him again. 'I should have trusted you as well. I was crap, crap judging you. It was stupid.'

He didn't know what to say. Their row was over now. He was forgiven. 'Smells good,' he commented, at a loss for anything else to say. He nodded over her shoulder. 'I've already eaten, but I won't say no.'

She told him to go and sit down while she got some bacon sandwiches together. Same as the morning of the search. Back in time. Just the two of them. The moment frozen, stored in his mind. He chose a table near the window overlooking the beach, watched the distant waves breaking on the shore. It would be so easy, he thought, to just be here and relax. That's how it must be for others. There was peace in this place. He felt it like nostalgia; an ache. He wished things could be different, that he could just relax and enjoy, that this view could just be sand and sky and sea. Not death. Not the memory of fear. How it was. Her and him. And the future poised between them. Nothing else.

'Tuck in,' she said, joining him and biting into her sandwich, washing the mouthful down with a swig of coffee from a stained mug.

He looked over the room, unable to hide the pity from his face. 'It's over, then,' he said.

'What?'

'Your dream. This place. Everything it was going to be.'

She shrugged, her face stoical. 'You can't have everything.'

'I'm sorry.'

'Life moves on,' she said dismissively. 'It doesn't mean what it used to. Not so important.'

'How so?'

'Independence. Freedom. This place was all those things when I was young.'

'You *are* young,' he interrupted. His hand moved, an impulse hitting him, telling him to take her hand. But he cut it cold, reached for his coffee instead, held the hot mug tight.

'OK, younger, then. But you grow up, you know. You look older, you act older.'

'Is that a good thing?'

She studied his face for a few seconds, settling on his eyes. 'You've turned out all right.'

'Good,' he said, meaning it. He held her stare, even though he knew that this was wrong, even though he had a girlfriend who he cared for, and who cared for him. But risk. It was here. Now. A branch. Take the main road to the life he already knew. Or choose something else. And face it: he still wanted her. So go back. Remember her. Remember you. Remember that that's all life was then: choice. There, at least, he was the person he wished he still was. He watched her turn from him, and look out of the window, away. *Turn back. Turn back to face me. Turn the pages back and let me find you again.*

'You were saying,' he prompted. 'About it not meaning as much.'

'Oh, yeah,' she said, pulling back from her reverie. 'It went well for the first few years after you left. I made some good money, kept the mortgage payments going. The last couple of years – last summer in particular – though, and, I don't know, the tide turned. Alex set the club up on North beach and the scene moved with it. People kept coming here day time, but nights, they were his.' She lit a cigarette. Smoke curled through the dust. 'Times changed and I didn't change with them.'

'But you don't mind?'

'No. Not since Dan died.'

'Nothing matters compared to something like that.'

'No.' She sighed. 'I spend a lot of time at the 'Raker now. Dad wants me to take it over after Christmas. They're going to move. Mum doesn't want to be round here. Hardly leaves the flat any more. Just prowls round up there, packing the boxes over and over again. She just wants out.'

'Where they going to go?'

'I don't think she cares. Just away. Dad's got some idea about going North. Away.'

'And what about you?'

Her eyes fixed on his, resolute. 'This is my home. No one's driving me out. Not the killer. Not Alex. Not anybody.'

'Alex?'

Her bottom lip rolled inwards, thinning to a line. 'I don't know how much Neville told you yesterday.'

'He said Alex was scum, that he was up to his neck in all sorts of bad shit. He said he wanted the bastard banged up.'

'So he didn't tell you about Dan? About what Alex did to him?'

'No. Just that Dan was a mess towards the end, just what a fucking shame it was.'

'There's more to it than that. A lot more.'

'You going to tell me about it?' he asked, then watched her face scrunch up. Again, the impulse was there to touch her, to hold her – anything to let her know that he cared, cared for her more than he was allowed to say.

'You got out,' she said. 'You did the right thing. You got away from Alex.' She twisted her cigarette out violently. 'Dan never did. Alex just drew him closer and closer, sucked him in till there was nothing left. Then – a couple of weeks before Dan died – he just spat him out.'

'I don't—'

'Dan worked for Alex,' Suzie explained. 'Always did from when they left school. Sure, he had plans. Same as Alex. They both said they were going to go away, maybe go to college, maybe leave Grancombe behind.'

'They were going to go travelling,' James said, remembering. 'And then university and college.'

'Well, they never did. They just stayed, carried on dealing, making more money. And Dan . . . Dan just carried on taking what Alex dealt, moving on, sinking deeper and deeper.' She lit another cigarette and stared at its glowing tip, as if the solution to her anxst was written there. 'They made a lot of money. They got the cars. They got the girls. They ended up spending half their time in London, half down here. Dan never talked about it.' She blinked heavily. 'We sort of stopped talking altogether. And then there was the club. They opened that the year before last. Only it was Alex's name on every-thing. He owned it. Dan was too messed up. Said he was joint manager. But he wasn't anything. Just another one of Alex's thugs.' James saw hatred in her eyes for the first time. 'Then Alex fired him and he wasn't anything any more.'

He waited for her to continue, but she didn't. 'Go on,' he finally nudged.

'He was so wrecked all the time.' The colour was draining from her face. 'Even after that, Alex cutting him loose like he didn't mean a thing . . . even then Dan couldn't see the situation for what it was. Right up to the end, he was out there – in the pubs, in *Current*, getting wasted. He just didn't get it.' Her eyes were waterlogged. When she rubbed them, James saw her knuckle glisten with tears. 'I saw him the day before he was killed. Christ, James . . . Even then, all he could go on about was that he had it made, that Alex was going to sort him out, that Alex owed him big time. The stupid sod thought he was going to get out, move abroad, get straight. He didn't realise how Alex had used him. Not once. Not once before he went for that walk and didn't come back . . .'

Dan must have been wasted, James thought, to walk those woods alone at night. James could never do it. No matter how wasted. Not unless there was a gun at the back of his head.

'I'm sorry,' he said and, this time, he did take her hand. He gripped it tight, like he was stopping her from falling from a cliff. He watched as her shoulders trembled and the tears flowed, and he wished he really could pull her back up onto solid ground. He wished it was within his power to save her.

All he could say, though, was sorry. He repeated the word over and over, as if it had the ability to wear her sorrow down to nothing.

'Eat,' he finally said, nudging her plate towards her, 'before it gets cold.'

She wiped her nose on her sleeve and lifted the sandwich to her mouth and held it there, her lips parted. She watched him over it and the tears slowed. Sore streaks scarred her cheeks. Then she ate. He lit a cigarette, watched her. They stared at one another in silence for a minute or so. Finally, she mumbled something, her mouth full, then did the strangest thing. She laughed. It started as a smile, so thin that James mistook it for pain. Then came the glint in the eyes, the sparkle he remembered so well, as if the good parts of that summer had lain trapped there till now.

'What?' he asked, confused.

'Nothing.' She rolled her eyes. 'I was just looking at you, remembering . . .'

He was smiling now, too. 'Remembering what?'

'How nervous you used to be of me.'

'I was a kid.'

'I know. But you never realised how nervous I was of you.'

'I didn't understand women then.' He laughed. 'Christ, I still don't.'

Their hands were still linked. She lifted his and examined it. 'No ring,' she observed. 'So either you're not married, or you don't like jewellery . . . Which is it?'

'Both.'

'Girlfriend?'

It was a difficult question, sitting here with Suzie's hand in his. He thought of Lucy, tried to imagine himself greeting her within a few hours, taking her in his arms and feeling emotion, warmth, the desire to return her kiss. But she remained abstract, distant, dreamt. All he felt was what he held now. This was all he wanted to touch. This was the only warmth he needed to sustain him now.

'Yes,' he said, but added, because he now knew that it was true, 'She's fun, but it's nothing serious. It's only been going on a couple of months.' As soon as he'd finished speaking, he knew how lame this sounded, what a typical guy thing it was to say. It would hardly be difficult for her to read between the lines: *She means nothing to me, Suzie. I'm telling you this, because you do. I'm telling you this, because you've cancelled her out. Because of you, she no longer exists* . . . He felt himself flush, asked, 'What about you? Are you married?'

'No. And no boyfriend, either.' She let go of his hand, withdrawing her own across the table. 'There was someone. Mick. I went out with him for over three years. Moved in. The works.

'But . . . I've never really sussed out what went wrong. More that things didn't go right, I suppose. More that we just ended up comfortable and we would have carried on comfortable and next thing I would have been married and bringing up the kids of someone I didn't really love. So I moved out. I moved out and I moved back home and then he moved away. We haven't spoken for over a year. I don't even know where he is now. And I don't really care.' She lifted her mug and drank. 'Yuk,' she said, wincing. 'All cold.'

He stared at her, suddenly nervous. He wanted to make a move on her. He wanted it so bad that he couldn't risk it. He didn't know if he could handle it, her saying no. He didn't want to face the possibility.

'Yeah,' he said, 'I should get going.'

'Article to write?'

'That and my friends. They're coming down from London for a couple of days.'

'Your girlfriend?'

'Yeah. She's coming with them. She's a photographer, doing some snaps for the article,' he qualified, before moving quickly on. 'And Alan's place. I've got to pack his stuff up. I'm putting it on the market.'

'I thought you probably would. I'll ask around, see if there's anyone who might be interested.'

'Thanks.' He looked at her, heard his breath coming strong. This was right. Her. Here. He didn't want to leave. He should never have left in the first place.

'What about his stuff – the stuff you're packing up. Are you taking it back to London?'

He nodded his head. 'Yeah, I'll need somewhere to keep it, till I get it together to get it sent up there. There won't be enough room in the car. Do you know anywhere?'

'I'll give Dad a call. You can dump it in the garage until you're ready to move it. He'll be fine about it.' She pulled a set of keys from her pocket, slid one off the ring and handed it to him. 'Here, it's round the back of the 'Raker. Number eight.'

'Thanks again.'

'So . . .'

'So . . . I guess I should be going.'

She got to her feet and he followed suit. She stood there for a moment, her hands dug deep in her pockets. Beautiful. Her mouth opened, as if she was about to speak, then clamped closed again. He followed her to the door.

'What about this place?' he asked. 'You going to sell it?'

'I'll try. Can't see anyone being stupid enough to buy it, though. Hardly an ongoing business . . . I suppose I'll just have to watch it rot.'

Then it happened. As he'd dreamt it would. As he'd always wanted it to be. She lifted her face to his and they kissed. He felt her tongue move against his and then her body pressed tight. And then she was gone, stepping back away from him.

'I'm sorry,' she said, smiling. He cheeks burnt, embarrased. She cradled her head in her hands, her mouth forming an 'O' – consternation, pleasure, he couldn't tell which.

'Don't be,' he said. 'It was—'

She shook her head. 'It was stupid.' But her smile contradicted her words. 'Go,' she instructed, opening the door. 'Go and meet your girlfriend.'

He stepped outside and turned back to face her. 'This isn't goodbye. You know that, don't you?'

'Right now, I don't know what I know.'

And she closed the door on him, left him to the winds, not knowing, as he now knew, that it was only a matter of time before they blew him straight back to her.

The electricty guy was already there when James reached

Alan's house. Apparently there was some sort of problem, a short circuit. It might take an hour or so. James left him to it, headed upstairs and dug out some boxes and began to pack. He felt more at ease with someone else in the house and he worked quickly, running through the list he'd made the day before. He had the first load packed in the car by the time the lights came on and the radio in Alan's room crackled into life. He paid the electricty man off and drove back into Grancombe, unloaded the boxes in the garage at the back of the 'Raker. He didn't bump into either of Suzie's parents. This was good. He wasn't in the mood for explanations, for more discussions of death. Just the here and the now. That's all he wanted to deal with. And, time-wise, he was doing fine. Lucy and the others wouldn't be down for another couple of hours. There was time to do another load. Then that was it. He'd never have to set foot in that house again.

When he'd finished packing the second load, he scouted the house a final time. There was nothing left he wanted. The main items of interest – Alan's papers and computer files – he could study at his leisure. Everything else here held no meaning for him. Only the basement nagged. Only the lack of a key to fit its lock. He went through the various drawers in the house again: nothing. OK, so he'd have to come back. One last time. Once the others had returned to London. He checked the basement door. A crowbar and a bit of sweat would see to it. Then out, his mind at rest. Probably nothing down there, anyway. Then away. Back to London. Back to London for good.

But even as he was thinking this, he was thinking of Suzie. She'd never leave this place. She'd said as much. So leaving here meant leaving her. Another sacrifice. But that was the way it was. He couldn't stay here. Not with Alex on his case. Not with the killings still going on. He'd never find peace inside this tent of fear. Maybe he could persuade Suzie to leave. Anything was possible, wasn't it?

He walked out to the car and stared down at the barn. He didn't even have the courage to walk over and see if the crates were still stashed there, let alone disobey Alex's command and break into one and discover what was inside. Not that it took much to guess what it was. Drugs. Crates that size, it had to be hash. And what was a shipment of hash to him? It wasn't like he didn't indulge himself. It wasn't like he had a moral objection. Just Alex. Alex was all he objected to. Just Alex telling him to jump and him being too weak to do anything other than ask, 'How high?'

He got in the car and set off to Grancombe to meet the woman he now knew for sure that he didn't love.

CHAPTER FOURTEEN

orgasm

The radio alarm in James's room in Alan's house burst into song at four-thirty. James opened his eyes and the ceiling span, blurring above him like a helicopter blade. He remembered the 'Raker with Alex and Dan, only hours before, their A-level results, the booze . . .

He tipped onto his side as what felt like a bucketful of vomit cascaded from his mouth onto the carpet by the side of the bed. He lay there for a few agonised seconds, staring at the technicolor porridge, clawing at his stomach, willing the cramps away. He wiped the dripping drool from his chin on the pillow case and risked sitting upright. The room was steadier now, still lurching occasionally, sure, but no longer rapidly revolving like it had been flung from the epicentre of a passing typhoon. Things were definitely looking up.

Or maybe not.

'Jesus,' he said aloud, as the stench of the spew reached his nostrils.

He puked again, into the cup of his hand this time. Vomit begets vomit. He held his full palm to his face, waiting for the inevitable third intestinal blast. Then calm. He lowered his hand a few inches. The moment – or movement – had passed. He shuffled along the edge of the bed, his feet hovering above the mess on the floor; a reluctant kid on the edge of a freezing swimming pool. Only once he was past the viscous landmine did he risk standing. Felt the same as he had when he'd been concussed in a rugby match at school. He stumbled to the door, reached the bathroom without any further stomach-tantrums, and emptied the contents of his hand into the toilet. Then he stripped down and showered.

'Look at the state of you,' Alex said, examining James with evident amusement as he collapsed into the Spitfire ten minutes later and fastened his seat belt. 'You'd be better off in a hearse. Didn't your mother ever tell you you'd catch cold if you went out with your hair wet?'

'My brain feels like it's been chewed up by someone and shat out the other end,' James groaned. 'You got any para-cetamol?'

'Got something better than that.'

He turned the car round and headed down the drive, pulled into the shade provided by one of the outbuildings, cut the engine. He reached beneath James's seat and pulled out the wash bag, unzipped it on his lap and produced a wrap.

'I don't know,' James said.

Alex ignored him, pulled a copy of the *Face* out of the glove compartment, laid it on his lap tipped a portion of the cocaine onto it.

'Here,' he said, passing James the rolled-up note once he'd done a couple of lines himself. 'Indulge yourself a little. It's no big deal. Think of it as caffeine with a feel-good factor. Like sticking your brain in a washing machine. Leave you feeling squeaky clean. Bright and white. Up for fun.'

James stared at the two remaining lines. It was going to happen sooner or later. Only a matter of time, right? So why not sooner? See what all the fuss was about. Experience. That was what this summer was here for. He turned round and looked at the house, school-boy guilt momentarily slapping him, half-expecting to see Alan walking down the drive towards them, wagging his finger in disapproval. No chance. Locked in his room as usual. Doing his own writing. Teaching James squat. He turned back, accepting the note. If the teacher's on strike, better learn to teach yourself. Discover what's out there. He inserted the note into his nostril and mentally recoiled at its damp touch; he couldn't help thinking of Alex's snot bonding with his own. Then he bent over Alex and down. He stifled a nervous giggle, suddenly wondering what some passerby would make of it, seeing his head disappearing behind the dashboard onto Alex's lap.

Fizzzzzzz . . .

Space dust.

Sherbet.

Toot.

His nose and his eyes watered and he gritted his teeth to neutralise the impulse to sneeze. He finished the first line, polished off the second, sat bolt upright and unrolled the note, placing it in Alex's outstretched palm.

'Welcome to the Pleasure Dome,' Alex said with a grin, licking his finger and dabbing up what was left on the magazine, rubbing his finger along his gums like a toothbrush. He chucked the magazine onto the floor by James's feet, adjusted his shades. 'Looking good, feeling good?'

'Feeling better,' James said. And he was. Already. His vision was clearing. The TV aerial was being retuned. Cataract extraction. Everything was becoming spectacularly clear. Headache fading, too. Focused on the good life. Adios Shitsville. He leant over the door, examined his face in the wing mirror. 'But still looking like I've just slipped the morgue.'

Alex started the engine, raised his voice over the noise. 'The looks will come,' he assured him, 'Phase two of the wondrous metamorphosis from dead-head to coke-head: five minutes from now and no mirror's gonna be big enough for you. You're in for an ego explosion of nuclear proportions. Total destruction of the world as you've known it up till now. You're gonna be the wittiest, sexiest, smartest bastard on the face of the earth. Film star. Philosopher. Call it what you want. You're gonna need an agent by the time the night's out, just to field the fucking calls.'

James leant back in his seat, stared straight into the sun. 'That a fact?'

'Trust me,' Alex said, adjusting his shades and slipping the car into gear. 'Right now, that's the only fact that matters.'

James shook his head in wonder. He felt good. Better than

good. Better than best, too, for that matter. 'Excellent,' was all he could think of to say.

The car pulled out into the lane.

'Lift-off,' Alex shouted, stepping down on the accelerator. 'Up, up, up and away.'

Time, and the car, flew. They hit Eagle's Point with a screeching of tyres. A fence of local farmers' sons, baseball-capped and black t-shirted, drafted in by Alex and Dan for security with the promise of free beer and easy cash, surrounded the perimeter of the site. And there, parked at the entrance, was a police car and van. Murphy, leaning on the bonnet of the car, turned his head, followed the unhindered progress of Alex's Spitfire through the main gate like a security camera.

'Fuck 'em,' Alex shouted, noticing James staring at them. 'Nothing they can do.' He pointed at his shoulder. 'The legal eagle's perched here for now. They lay a finger on us in public and it'll crap all over them.'

Alex parked the car between a burger van and the marquee that housed the bar. They got out and he retrieved the wash bag, opened the boot and set about separating its contents into his pockets. When he'd finished, he locked the bag in the boot and patted the tops of his thighs.

'Tried and tested on the right,' he muttered to himself. 'Potential garbage on the left.'

James noticed a man walking towards them, though walking was maybe too regular a word to use to encompass his movements. He stumbled a couple of paces, paused and moved on. His upper body was twisted at an obtuse angle from his legs, as if he couldn't make up his mind which way he wanted to go. He kept on grinning at them apologetically, letting them know that he'd get there in the end. He was tall, taller than Dan, but scrawny, undernourished. Between forty and fifty years old, though the uneven stubble on his jaw and the farmer's cap covering his scalp made it impossible to be certain. His clothes – mismatching suit jacket and trousers – hung loosely on his limbs. His shoulders, elbows and knees looked sharp beneath the material, as if they might puncture it any second, leave his bones protruding like a battlefield corpse.

'Who the fuck—' James started to ask.

'Arnie Oldfield,' Alex said quietly. 'The owner. Been at the cider. Leave the talking to me.'

Arnie finally reached them. ' 'Ello, Alex,' he said, his voice husky.

'All right, Arnie.' Alex looked him up and down, any intimation of distaste buried beneath his shades. 'Like the suit. Dressed to kill. Ladies better watch out tonight with a Romeo like you on site.'

Arnie cackled, accepted a cigarette off Alex, eyed it for a second, saying, 'Not one of your funny cigarettes this, eh?'

'Nah, nothing worse than tar and nicotine in that.'

Arnie slipped it into his breast pocket. 'Save it for later, then.'

'You do that.'

Arnie turned to face James. 'Who's this one?'

'Sorry,' Alex said, placing a hand on James's shoulder. 'Forgetting my manners. This is James. Al 'Anson's nephew. He's down for the summer.'

Arnie nodded, digested the information. 'You got my money?' he asked Alex.

Alex produced a sealed envelope from his back pocket, handed it over. 'All there. What we agreed.'

Arnie ran a long, grubby fingernail along the envelope's flap and peeped inside. 'Just checking,' he said, resealing it and closing his fist around it. 'Seen them films where it's all torn newspaper inside. Not stupid, you know.'

'There's enough there to stop you fretting about where your next meal's coming from for a long time,' Alex said.

'Don't fret over anything no more,' Arnie said, weighing the envelope in his hand. 'Before this, an' all.' His mouth parted to reveal a jagged grin. James looked away; it was like the 'before' photo from a scare poster in a cosmetic surgeon's waiting room. 'Not you who's the only one with money-making schemes. Got a few of my own.'

'Sure you have,' Alex said, sounding bored. He glanced at James and announced, 'Said we were meeting Plugs and

Michaela in a few minutes, didn't we?' James didn't know what Alex was talking about, had only met Plugs once, hadn't even heard of Michaela. But he nodded anyway, played along. 'Better get going, then,' Alex concluded.

Arnie's hand darted out and snapped like a dog's jaw, latching onto Alex's wrist. 'Don't reckon I'm telling you the truth, do you?'

' 'Course I do, Arnie,' Alex said, slowly unfastening Arnie's hand. 'Bet you've got more schemes up your sleeve than I've had hot dinners.'

Arnie gobbed heavily on the ground between them. A fleck landed on Alex's boot, clung there like cuckoo spit on a leaf. 'Taking the piss now.' His lips curled back over his teeth again and he inserted his finger and thumb into his mouth, pinched at one of his teeth, and jiggled it where it sat loosely in the gum. 'Get these fixed up like a film star. Bright and white and brand new. Soon have plenty of money for that sort of thing.' He waved the envelope in front of Alex's face. 'This is nothing, I'm telling you. Be able to use this to wipe my arse on soon.'

'Yeah?' Alex asked. 'How's that, then? Decided to sell the car park? Or you doubling the rate you charge for mowing people's lawns? That it?'

Arnie shook his head. 'Don't need to. Not now. What I got's worth ten times this patch of dirt and the gardening work put together.' His eyes narrowed. 'Not telling you what, though,' he added quickly. 'You're a sly one.' He smiled. 'That's why I like you. Hate Murphy and them, same as me. But I still ain't telling you where my money's coming from.'

Alex started to turn to go. 'Well, Arnie, I gotta get moving now, but I'll tell you what: you give us a shout when you get your money and you can take me out for a drink. That sound good?'

'You wait,' Arnie shouted. 'You'll see. Who'll be the crazy then, eh? I'll buy you that drink. Just you fucking wait.'

'Too many nights sucking off cider bottles,' Alex commented quietly as they walked away. He laughed. 'Fix his teeth. Apart from what I just gave him, he hasn't got enough to buy a tube of toothpaste.'

They found Dan, sitting on the edge of the stage, wedging the remains of a hot dog into his mouth.

'All right, dog dick,' he said to James with a wink. He wiped his hand across his mouth, smeared mustard over his unshaven jaw. He grinned at Alex. 'The 'Raker's packed out with trendy little hipsters from London. Come all the way down for this. Dad can't believe his luck. 'Specially the way things have been since Dawes got wasted. Might as well be chucking their money at him. Had to clean the till out twice already. Paranoid he's gonna get robbed.'

'Have to get him to have a word with the Town Council for us, give us a medal for services to the local economy,' Alex replied. He lowered his shades and peered into Dan's eyes. 'Wide awake, or d'you need a little kick-start?'

Dan tapped his nostril. 'Been there, done that. Bright-eyed and bushy-tailed.'

Alex replaced his shades and stepped back. 'Good. Need you keeping it together the next couple of hours.'

Dan rolled onto his side, screwed up his face and farted. 'Jesus,' he exclaimed appreciatively, listening to the reverberations echoing off the wooden stage. 'Fuck the DJs. I've got all the tunes we need up my arse. Stick a mike up there and I'll have 'em dancing till dawn.'

'Reckon they might feel ripped off, if that's all they get for their money,' Alex said.

'Yeah, yeah,' Dan said, sliding off the stage to make way for some crew-cut roadie setting up the mikes.

People started arriving about an hour later. An hour after that and a queue was stretching, three bodies thick, a hundred yards past where Murphy and his crew were stationed. James stood next to Alex at the gate, watching the freaked-out procession eagerly swapping cash for licks from fluorescent stamps on the backs of their hands. From behind came the sound of feedback and drums, the agonised wail of the first band's front man. James turned, surveyed the writhing mass of pogoing bodies in front of the stage.

It was shaping up nicely. He watched until Dan returned from the beer tent and handed over bottles of Bud.

'Looks like it's kicked off,' Dan observed.

'Better carry on like that,' Alex said, 'amount of cash we've ploughed into this.'

'Sorted already. Look at them. They fucking love it.'

Alex shook his head. 'This is business, all right? Don't go forgetting it. Right up till that queue's passed through. Fun comes after we've got the money.' He turned to face Dan. 'Stay here and keep an eye on the cash. Ride back with Lennie once they're all through and stash it in your room.'

'Where you gonna be?'

Alex waved his hand vaguely in the direction of the stage. The sunlight was fading now, the electric lights on stage powering up to take its place. The search light scanned the sky. 'Around.' He drained his beer, dropped the bottle on the ground. 'You stick close,' he told James. 'Keep your eyes peeled for Murphy and the squad.'

They reached the beer tent and slipped inside. Bass bumped from the speakers roped over the bar. James followed in Alex's slipstream towards it, nodding hellos at the various people he'd met through Alex and Dan over the preceding weeks, forcing his way past strangers. Somewhere amongst these stunted conversations, he lost track of Alex. One minute he was there, his shoulder pressed against James's, the next James turned and tapped him on the shoulder, only to find that he'd been miraculously transformed into a red-haired girl with a spliff clamped in the crook of her fingers.

'You got anything for me?' she asked him.

She was stunning. He almost wished he did have something to give her, and certainly wished that Alex was still here so that he could be associated with him as the deal went down. Instead, he shrugged apologetically, knew that his reply would almost certainly signify the end of the conversation.

'No,' he said, then added, 'Sorry.'

'Well,' she said, looking vaguely around him, stoned, 'have a suck on this, then.'

He accepted the spliff gratefully, took a couple of hits and handed it back, saying, 'Cheers.'

She threaded it between her lips, took a toke. Her words

came out in a cloud, smoke-signals: 'Anyone dealing round here?'

'Guy called Alex. Wears shades all the time.'

The smoke cleared from her face. 'Yeah? You give us a shout if you find him?'

'Sure,' James said, finding himself smiling back at her as they stared at each other. 'Where will you be?'

'Around. You'll find me . . .'

James finally succeeded in clawing his way to the bar. He stretched up on tip-toe and scanned the crowd for Alex: no joy. No sign of the redhead either. He sighed. All lucked out.

Boom.

He saw her, hovering at the entrance to the tent, t-shirted and tanned, talking to a girl in a tie-dyed top and combat trousers, another girl with hair tied in bunches.

Definitely her. Even at this distance and in spite of the backdrop of dusk, there was no doubt. Short black hair, long eyelashes, mahogany eyes: Suzie. Suddenly, he was glad he'd lost Alex, was pleased that Dan was stuck at the gate, out of sight. He raised a hand, waved, then realised the futility of the action at this distance. He was about to push back through the crowd, surrender his coveted position at the bar, when she changed his mind for him, entered the tent. Her friends hung back. James craned his neck, tracked her movement, unblinking. Once in the crowd, she moved laterally, shifting in and out of his sight, edging along to the side of the tent where it was less frantic. Then her progress became swifter. Ultimate docking point: the far right of the bar. James began to elbow his way across for the interception.

She finally spotted him, apparently oblivious to her presence, nudging his way past a group of people, wading through the mass of arms grasping like tentacles for a grip on the bar. He turned as soon as he reached the bar, swept his gaze deliberately across her without recognition, only to swing it into reverse, settle on her with what he hoped was a look of mild surprise. He projected the pulling paradox: cool but interested. For a second, he thought it was going to backfire and she was going to ignore him, but he risked a smile and, thankfully, she returned the gesture, pushed her way past the bodies huddled between them, and joined him at the bar. He felt her body pressed up close to his by the pressure of the crowd.

'You're sweating like a pig,' she told him.

He wiped his hand across his brow, lowered it and acknowledged the wet varnish with a smile. 'Sumo wrestler in a sauna,' he said, looking round the tent. 'Comes with the territory, I guess.' He noticed her studying his face. Her smile was gone. 'What?' he asked.

She frowned. 'You OK?' There was genuine concern in her voice.

'Sure,' he said.

Her voice sharpened. 'You look wasted: coked.'

The antagonism in her voice jarred his mood. This wasn't the way things were meant to be going. He didn't want her thinking of him this way. Besides, this wasn't the way he was. The coke's half-life had dwindled to the microscopic way back. Just trace elements left. Ammo for a drugs test maybe, but nothing more. No way. And the hash. A couple of drags. A few flecks of red bursting against the whites of his eyes. No big deal, though. No cause for this aggro.

'No,' he said with a shake of his head, 'totally straight.'

She smiled sceptically, said, 'Really.'

He shrugged. 'I'm clean.' He indicated the bar with his thumb. 'Apart from beer.'

'I'll take your word for it.'

But it was obvious that she hadn't. 'You don't believe me, do you?'

'Seen you around with Alex and Dan a lot recently. Like you say, "goes with the territory".'

'And you disapprove?'

'I disapprove.'

He noticed the people behind him starting to get aggravated by his lack of ordering. 'You'll have to tell me about it some time.'

'Yeah, maybe I will.'

'Anyway,' he said, concentrating on projecting some

lightness into his voice, 'back to the beers. Can I get you something?'

'No, it's all right. I'm getting a round in.'

'OK.'

She waved her hand and a barman came over and fixed her drinks.

'You OK with those?' James asked, as she turned to face the crowd, three beer bottles gripped in her hands.

'I'm fine,' she said, and moved away without another word. Blown out.

He watched her drift into the crowd, turned and ordered a double shot of vodka and a bottle of beer, downed the vodka at the bar, moved through the crowd with the beer raised to his lips.

'Where the fuck have you been?' Alex asked, materialising at his side.

'Nowhere,' James said. 'The bar. Just getting served.'

'Come on,' Alex said, pushing his way out of the aggro-zone. 'We've got work to do.'

Alex stationed himself in the corner of the tent. James stood at his side, a sentry, and divided his attention between hawk-eyeing the crowd outside and monitoring Alex's deals. First came faces James recognised, could match to names: Grancombe people. Tried and tested from the right pocket. Local price. Then later, as word spread from pill-popping tongue to pill-popping tongue, outsiders, strangers. Potential garbage from the left pocket. Rip off. Alex was subtle, a card sharp at work, all smiles, palmings and sleights-of-hand. An illusionist. Everyone's best friend and no one's.

'Hello again.'

The redhead was back. Her voice was a shout, like every-one's here, trying not to be buried by the thump-thump of bass.

'He's there,' James said, nodding in Alex's direction. 'Alex. He's got what you want.'

'You gonna introduce me?'

James took her across to Alex and they waited for him to conclude some business with a gang of blokes.

Alex gave her a cursory inspection, asked her, 'What's your flavour?'

She named it and Alex rolled his thumb across his fingers. She pulled some cash from her pocket and he took it, slipped her her change along with three E's from his left pocket.

'Enjoy,' he said, staring back into the crowd, the interview concluded.

The redhead grinned at James, placed one of the pills on her tongue and took a slug from her beer, swallowed. 'You want in?' she asked, holding a second pill up before her like she was presenting him with a flower.

'I—'

She moved her hand forward, so that the tips of her fingers pressed tantalisingly against his lips. 'Open wide.'

'He's already sorted,' Alex interrupted, gently lowering her hand.

She looked between them for a couple of seconds, realised Alex wanted her elsewhere, then, shrugging, muttered, 'Whatever.'

'You were gonna swallow it, weren't you?' Alex asked, once the redhead had faded back into the crowd.

'I don't know.'

'Yeah, you do.'

'It still scares me.'

'But you were gonna do it, anyhow. Temptation's getting the better of you.'

'Yeah,' James admitted, 'I guess so.'

A satisfied grin settled on Alex's face. 'Knew you'd come round to it in the end. Only a matter of time.' Alex lit a cigarette. 'Let's take a break,' he said. 'Return trip to heaven.'

James's heartbeat was stuttering. He took the pill from Alex and stared at it, like he was waiting for it to speak. The tent they'd moved to was smaller than the beer tent, the atmosphere relaxed to the point of being anaesthetic. Slow-beat music dripped from the speakers at the back, where the DJ, head down over the decks, earphone clamped to the side of his head by a sweating palm, concentrated on slowly turning back the record, switching over and catching the break. James knew his world was about to shift shape. He'd soon be stepping through the looking glass into a parallel universe characterised, he hoped, by pleasure. Glazed eyes, slumped bodies, wide smiles, loose limbs. The space ship crew were all about, waiting for him to join their ranks, wanting him to come up – surface alongside them.

'Medication time,' Alex said, dropping a pill. 'Reality cure.'

'It's safe, yeah? All those stories . . . You sure it's safe?'

'It's OK. I'm gonna be here. I'll ride you out. No bad trips. I'll take you through and out the other side. You're gonna love it. Believe me. You're not gonna want to come back.'

'OK,' James said, taking a drink, lubricating his throat. 'Just don't leave me, all right. Not till I'm coping.'

'I'm your guide. I won't leave you till you're there. Howley Holidays Ltd. Come fly with me. Take the trip of a lifetime.'

James placed the pill in his mouth, his tongue hypersensitive, exploring the pill's contours, searching for a taste. He swallowed, and visualised it hitting his stomach; imagined the acid closing in around it, setting to work, breaking it down, preparing to ship it off and distribute it round his body. Embarkation point. He smoked cigarettes, let the music embalm him, monitored his mind and waited.

Time ticked by.

Then rush.

He was smiling, staring at a guy cross-legged on the floor next to him, smiling back. Feel-good factor. These people were friends, wrapped round him like skin.

'You up?'

'Yeah.' James smiled at Alex. A breeze of pleasure stroked over him. 'This is good, Alex. This is so . . .'

'Beautiful,' Alex filled in for him.

James shook his head, ground his cigarette out. 'Thanks. This is so . . . Jesus, this is just so . . . there . . .'

Alex was nodding. 'You got the sensitivity yet? You got the love?'

James's grin was wide, the mouth of a cave. All the smiling people. So much love. 'I got the love. For all these people. I fucking love them all.'

'Wanna put them all in your pocket and take them home.'

'Yeah. All of them. Boys and girls. I don't care. You know what this is?'

Alex was laughing now. 'No, tell me.'

'This is orgasm, man. This is shooting your load. Only it's not stopping. It just keeps on coming. An eternal orgasm.'

'Making love to the world.'

'Yeah, marrying the world. Living with it forever.'

'Come here,' Alex told him.

James leant forward and Alex slid his hand under his shirt, stroked his fingers down his spine. Warm electricity.

'Feels good.'

Alex removed his hand and slumped back against the side of the tent. 'Yeah, but d'you know what's best?'

'What?'

'It's gonna get even better.'

And it did.

Dancing now, his blood turned to mercury.

Quicksilver.

Rush.

Love Alex.

Love Suzie.

Love everyone.

Don't want this to ever end.

It was about two hours later that he first noticed the commotion in the corner of the tent. The E dropped a notch. He'd learnt to control it by now. He could fade it out when he wanted to. Like adjusting volume. He could zoom in and out, focus its intensity like sun through a magnifying glass, fry his brain, or just leave it simmering. Control. Don't you just love it? He could enjoy the ride, or take the wheel, apply the brakes.

Someone was shouting.

The DJ was looking now. A circle of bodies in the corner of the tent. Someone was screaming. The DJ deserted his decks. He crossed the floor, pushed his way through the crowd, his long top trailing behind him. Moses parting the waves. This was bad. Instinctively, James knew something wasn't

219

right. No longer high. Dropping down like falling off a building. Panic setting in. Faces wiped of smiles. He started moving. Slow motion, then faster. The whole crowd was moving, like a quake had occurred, causing the ground to be tilted, and they were suddenly on a slope, gravitating towards the corner of the tent. Helpless.

Voices.

'What's going on?'

'Oh, Jesus.'

The scream: 'Call an —'

Shouting, drowning out the scream. James was at the edge of the circle of bodies now, standing there, focusing inwards at something on the ground, teetering towards it, balancing, trying not to fall in.

Shouting.

The scream again: 'Call an . . .'

James stretched forward, over the assembled heads, and stared down onto the ground. The redhead was lying there, immobile. Same as Dawes. Eyes open. Blank screens with no programme. Shut down. Her face and hair were soaked, like she'd been dragged from the sea drowned. Like Monique. Only this was sweat not sea water. Redhead. Red face. Scalded and burnt. Another girl was crouched next to her. The DJ ducked down, placed his fingers against the redhead's neck, searched for a pulse. Behind him, someone was vomiting, sticking his fingers down his throat in blind panic.

The DJ's mouth opened, mimed beneath the shouting.

The scream exploded from the girl crouched next to the redhead: 'Call an ambulance. She's —'

James fell back. He'd seen the look on the the DJ's face. The ground turned to ice and his feet slid away from beneath him. He collapsed back into the bodies behind him, turned and stumbled, started flailing, drowning in the crowd, thrashing his way out.

He'd seen the look on the DJ's face.

Redhead.

Dead-head.

He'd seen it in her eyes.

CHAPTER FIFTEEN

current

James sat up in the hotel bed, his face flushed and pillow-creased, his clothes pasted like wallpaper to his skin. The redhead's face was with him now, as it had been with him a decade ago. And the guilt and the sickness he'd felt then remained too, as incurable and recurrent as malaria. The redhead's name was Victoria Cooper. She'd been seventeen years old when she'd died.

He looked across the bed where Alan's papers were strewn, crumpled where he'd slept on them. He checked the clock, worked out how much time had passed since he'd fallen asleep. Exhaustion still clung to him. Sleep had gathered like grit in the corners of his eyes, as if they'd seen enough and had resorted to sealing themselves up whilst he'd slept. He examined the clock again. Lucy, David and Becky would be here soon.

So move.

He gathered the papers up, piled them in the cardboard box next to Alan's computer in the corner of the room. The computer, like the papers (mainly short stories predating Monique's death), had revealed little of the direction Alan's life had moved in over the past ten years. Alan had cleaned the computer's hard drive, same as he'd cleaned the house. Nothing but some ancient household accounts on a primitive database remained. Nothing personal. No clue or explanation as to why he'd killed himself. And, strangest of all, no writing. No unfinished masterpiece. Not so much as a short story. It was as if he'd employed all those hours James remembered him being locked away in his study repeatedly pressing the space bar and nothing more.

He walked to the bathroom and stared into the mirror, studied the alterations that time had carved on his face in the intervening years. Not Victoria Cooper, though. She'd never grown old. Just died. Buried by her parents in some grave-yard. He and Dan and Alex had stolen her future, stripped it from her and watched her fade into nothing. He imagined her grave with its attendant bunch of wilting flowers. And there, behind the grave, slouched against the church wall, he saw Alex, cigarette hanging from his lips, the sun bouncing off his shades, smiling, not giving a fuck.

James's phone rang and he went through to the bedroom and answered it.

'Hey, mate,' David's voice came on the phone. 'We've docked in Hicksville and – guess what? – we're lost.'

'Where are you?'

'If I knew that . . .'

'Yeah, yeah . . . just tell me what you can see.'

James could hear the girls chattering in the background. 'Well,' David said, 'I spy with my little eye something large and made of stone and beginning with "C".'

'Church,' James said.

'You've played this game before.'

James gave him instructions on how to get to the hotel, then returned to the bathroom and splashed cold water on his face. Again, the regret hit him over not having told Lucy *no* to coming down here. David he could handle. Becky, too. But not Lucy. Not the way he was feeling now. He tried to picture a moment he'd spent with her, searched his memory for something involving her that would bring him pleasure, make this meeting easier. But there was nothing. All the good times – from meals out to jokes to orgasms – meant nothing now. Suzie's shadow hung over them, robbing them of their light.

He heard a car horn blast three times, walked to the window and looked down. David's car was there, its exhaust steaming into the cold Grancombe air. The back door opened and Lucy stepped out and stretched. She was a good-looking girl. He could still see that in spite of the fact he could no longer find her attractive. Why was that? How could the same person draw him to her one moment, then drive him away the next? How could the poles switch so easily? Becky got out next and the two girls dragged the bags from the boot to the hotel, disappearing from his view. He watched David drive the car round the corner to the small car park at the back.

Enough procrastination. He went over to the desk and turned the laptop off. Smile, he told himself as he walked down the stairs. Don't make this any more painful than it already is.

Lucy and Becky were at the reception desk when he saw them. They were giggling over the hotel literature, waiting for someone to come and book them in. Sisters. And here he was, a crocodile smile on his face, knowing it was only a matter of time before he broke the happy family up. They looked so London, all hip-topped and cool-shoed. A snapshot of Suzie flashed into his mind, with her clothes just plucked from a wardrobe, her face so much more important than what she wore. And then these two – his closest female friend and his girlfriend. They almost seemed like strangers. Part of him wanted to fade away, sneak back up the stairs and wait for them to go away.

'Hi,' he said, reaching them and tapping Lucy on the shoulder. She turned and beamed at him and they hugged. Then they kissed. Her lips felt different to how he remembered them; no longer passionate, just flesh. It was like kissing a relative, devoid of sensuousness.

'Hello, babe,' she said.

He looked into her eyes for a moment and wondered what she saw. He couldn't believe the distance he felt with her standing so close. He released her and turned to Becky instead, 'Mate,' he said. 'So you guys finally made it,' he went on, resorting to banter, feeling like an actor reciting lines. 'Getting country fear yet? Paranoid about the lack of traffic and shops and people?'

Becky grinned. 'I can do country. You just watch. I've got

walking boots and jackets and jumpers. My lungs aren't going to know what's hit them.' With that, she lit a cigarette, adding, 'It's the healthy life for me from now on.'

James could feel Lucy at his shoulder. Timing. It was all about time. Because it *was* over between them. He liked her, couldn't mess her around, pretend that things were just fine when *fine* was the last thing they were. But not now. Not here in front of Becky. He heard the door opening and turned to see David walking over to them. Distraction. Thank God for friends. He brushed past Lucy and shook David's hand.

'Beer,' David said. 'Now. Six hours of driving. Crappy local radio stations. Tape jammed in the machine. I need my sanity restored.'

'I want to see my room,' Becky announced.

'I've booked you a couple of singles,' James told her. 'That OK?' He saw Lucy grinning, watched Becky draw slowly on her cigarette and unsuccessfully attempt to prevent a smile monopolising her face. 'What?' he asked. Lucy just shrugged, continued to grin. 'Well?' he asked Becky.

She nudged David in the ribs. 'Are you going to tell him, or shall I?'

'Ummm,' David began. 'Well, it's like . . .' He glanced at Becky. 'You going to help me out here, or what?'

'Typical bloke,' Becky said, rolling her eyes. She stepped across, so that she stood by his side, and slipped her arm round his waist. David put his arm round her shoulder, squeezed her tight.

James found himself laughing. 'You're kidding?'

'Er, no,' David said, blushing.

'But when? How? Who? Come on, details . . . Who made the move?'

'I don't know,' David said, looking confused. 'I suppose we both did . . .'

'He's being modest,' Becky said. 'He did.'

'My God,' James said. 'David takes a chance. What the hell caused that unlikely event to occur?'

'You,' David said bluntly.

'Details, please,' James prompted.

'That chat we had in T-rooms,' David explained. 'You asking me how come I'd never made a move on Becky. And I came out with all that shit, all those dumb reasons why I hadn't. Well, I ended up thinking about it the next day.' He smiled at Becky. 'And the next . . . and the next . . .'

'Come on,' James said. 'Cut to the chase.'

'He asked her out for dinner,' Lucy filled in.

'What,' James teased, 'as in a date?'

'Not exactly. At least I knew that's what it was, but I didn't —'

Becky pinched David's waist. 'He rang me up and told me he was bored and hungry and asked me to keep him company.'

'Last of the great romantics, huh?' James said.

'And we went out and ate and got drunk and got a cab and went back to Becky's and carried on getting drunk and . . .'

'And the rest is history,' Becky concluded.

'Yeah,' David agreed, 'I suppose it is.' He looked warily at James. 'So, what do you think?'

James suddenly felt a huge surge of affection and placed a hand on each of their shoulders. 'What do I think?' He laughed. 'What a question. I think it's about fucking time, that's what I think.'

And then he turned and looked at Lucy and felt hardly anything at all.

A couple of hours later, James was sitting at the desk in his hotel room. He could hear Lucy singing in the bathroom, accompanied by the occasional swirl of water as she moved in the bath. They'd been for lunch in a new restaurant on the High Street and made their plans for the next few days. Becky had been serious about getting some walking done and had David pegged down for a hike that afternoon. James and Lucy, meanwhile, would get their work out of the way, so they could all relax and enjoy the weekend. Once Lucy had finished getting the road off her skin, they'd head for the graveyard and the cliffs about South Beach, and she could run off a couple of films.

James continued to stare at the screen. The article was just about finished. Before him, the cursor flashed at the end of the word *motive*, inviting him to write more. All his brain kept replying, though, was: *there is no motive*. But he knew that wasn't true. There was always a motive, no matter how random and crazy events initially looked. Take Peter Headley. All those men he'd killed. Different towns, different ways of killing. But Headley had seen the connection between them. He'd *chosen* them. And it would have been the same for whoever was responsible for the killings here.

He typed out the names, dates and places, just as Headley had done before he died:

1. JACK DAWES   1989   Woods/Near Dawes
2. KENNETH TRADER   1989   Woods/Cliff Top
3. DANIEL THOMPSON 1998   Woods/Cliff Top

Then he focused on the screen. Why the gap in the killings? That wasn't how serial killers operated. It was an addiction. That's what the L.A. cop who'd investigated Headley had said. They needed their fix regularly. It wasn't a whim. Not like this pattern. Not something they could take or leave. He picked up the phone, dialled a number.

'Toby Clifford, please. Tell him it's James Sawday.'

'James, mate,' a voice came on the line a few seconds later. Heavy Borders accent; it was Toby's. 'How you doing?'

James had been mates with him at university. They'd worked on the student rag together, and had kept in touch after they'd both moved down to London following graduation. James was C.I.D. – on the fast track, as bright and as sharp as a diamond. As well as being a close friend, he was an invaluable contact. They small-talked for a while, then James got to the point.

'I need to pick your brains.'

'Pick away,' Toby said.

James began to outline the assignment he was working on, as well as his concerns over the gap between the killings. Toby, who knew the case already, cut James off, saying, 'A colleague of mine here, Derek, took the case on a while back – landed it after Trader's death. The guy who was dealing with

it back in the eighties retired a couple of years back. Anyhow,'
he went on, 'he ran through the whole thing from start to
finish, did checks on checks, if you know what I mean . . .'

'And?'

'And nothing. Blank sheet. There haven't been any other
unsolveds which might link up. You know, like has whoever's
responsible been up to this anywhere else – Britain, Europe,
whatever. Nothing. Got Derek's back up good and proper. I
tell you, James: you're right; it doesn't make much sense. But
Derek's a thorough bastard, and if he says there's nothing out
there, then that's how it is. This killer's a one off. Breaks all
the rules. No pattern. Leaves us scuppered.' There was a
pause, then Toby said, 'Derek has got a theory, though.'

'What?'

'That maybe the murders aren't random. Maybe it's not a
psycho like the papers say. That maybe whover did them did
them for rational reasons. Then the gap doesn't matter.'

Which brought James back to motive.

He thanked Toby, arranged to meet up for a drink and
returned his attention to the screen. Dismiss Kenneth Trader.
He knew all about the why and how of Trader's demise. That
left Dawes and Dan. Forster was right: there was nothing
superficial to link them. But that didn't mean there was no
link at all. Just like Headley's victims, they'd been *chosen*. So
what was the choice based on? The answer to that was the
key.

Something was nagging at him. He knew the feeling. He'd
experienced it dozens of times before. There was something
he'd heard, something he'd seen . . . There was something out
there that might make some sense out of all of this. But what?
Maybe Murphy. He'd been skipping in and out of James's
mind since Forster had mentioned his disappearance. Men
like Murphy didn't just vanish. Not unless they had a good
reason to. Sure, he'd disappeared before Dan's death. But that
didn't mean he wasn't responsible. James remembered what
Alex had told him about that dealer who'd disappeared way
back – Paddy somebody – the one who'd crossed Murphy. Of
all the people who'd lived here, Murphy had been the one

James had feared. Just because he'd disappeared didn't mean that he couldn't come back. To get rid of another dealer. Another dealer like Dan who might have had something on him, maybe known the real reason he'd disappeared. Was that what was nagging? So link him to Dawes. Why would he have killed Dawes?

James shook his head. With Dawes dead and Murphy gone, there was no answer to that. Maybe just the way Murphy had wanted it. He pressed the delete key, wiped the names and dates out. Back to the blank screen. Back to what Forster and the police and Dan's parents and Suzie were faced with every day.

'James,' Lucy called, cutting his concentration.

Her voice made him ache. He'd forgotten she was even here. 'What?' he called back.

'Come here a minute.'

He walked through to the bathroom. She was still in the bath, smiling up at him. He felt a fraud, standing there, looking down at her naked body beneath the water. She drew her knees up to her chin, ran her hands down her thighs. He stared at her face, refused to let his eyes wander over her. It felt wrong. It felt – he could hardly believe what he was thinking – unfaithful. Lucy's lips blew out a kiss, but all he felt was the touch of Suzie's on his own. He sat down on the toilet seat and looked down at the white tiles between his feet.

'D'you fancy getting in?' she asked.

Tell her. Tell her now. There's just the two of you. Spit it out.

'Well?' she asked.

'I don't think . . .' His voice faded out.

'What?' Concern clouded her face. 'James?' she asked again. 'Are you OK?'

I'm fine, he wanted to tell her. *But we're not. We're not OK. We're over. Can you hear me? WE'RE OVER.* But she couldn't hear him, because he couldn't speak. Doubt flowed through him like an anaesthetic, weakening his resolve by the second. What if he was wrong about Suzie? What if that had just been a kiss and nothing more? Just flirtation. Harmless. Something only he had given weight to. What then? Lucy and he got on. Who knew where it might go? Maybe nowhere, sure, but maybe it would end in love. Same as with David and Becky. Out of the blue. Just like in songs. So throw it away? On an impulse? On a memory? On someone who might have simply smiled ruefully and forgotten him by the time it had taken him to walk down the steps from Surfers' Turf onto the sand? He wanted to sleep. He wanted to crawl next door and lie alone and wake up to certainty.

'I'm fine,' he told her. 'Just a bit tired.'

'You sure you don't want to get in? It'll do you good, help you relax.'

'No.' He was suffocating. The steam from the bath clogged his lungs. He stood up, swayed uneasily. 'I'm going to get some fresh air,' he said. 'Clear my head. Been staring at that screen too long.'

'OK, babe,' she said, disappointed. 'How long you going to be?'

'I don't know. An hour. No more. I'll go down by the sea.' He managed a smile. 'You finish off in here and then we'll go and get your photos sorted out.'

The wind struck him like a hammer outside. He didn't want to be here. He stood on the steps of the hotel and looked out to sea. Somewhere else. That would be good. Anywhere but here. But even as he thought this, he knew that wasn't the case. This place could be beautiful. It was to David and Becky. He'd seen it in their eyes as they'd headed up the stairs to their bedroom. Just like he'd seen it in Lucy's eyes, as she'd lain there, submerged, wanting him to undress and join her. He swallowed hard, walked on. No point in just standing here. Forget Lucy for now. Suzie, too. Think about something else.

He carried on walking quickly away from the hotel and along the front, pausing only to see that he was out of sight of his window. It was only then he really relaxed, felt safe, hidden, like a kid concealed in a den. He sucked the cold air into his lungs. There was freedom here, away from the others. He walked on. Up ahead was Current, Alex's place. His palace of cool in this quiet backwater of England.

James meant to walk straight on past, but curiosity got the better of him. The unfinished article crept back into his mind. He'd been slack about it, coming down here and sitting on his arse and sweating it out, waiting like he'd used to do at school for the days to be gone. Anywhere else, any other article, and he would have been out there, asking questions, unravelling leads, getting his angle. And, face it, there was no reason not to do that now. Everything was already messed up. Check out his emotions, twisting through his gut like a typhoon, out of his control. And as for his plan of keeping himself to himself . . . He checked out the car park at the side of Current. Alex's car wasn't there. So fuck it. Do your job. Get in there and ask some questions. Find out what the fuck Dan was up to before he got killed.

There were no windows on the building, just a black door set in the centre of the black wall. Glass displays either side of it advertised the events for tonight and tomorrow night. James thought back to the rave up at Eagle's Point. Alex had been right then: give people what they wanted and they'd come and they'd pay. It had happened then, all right, and there was no reason why the same theory shouldn't apply now. In the centre of the door, at head height, there was a black glass view hole. To its left was a buzzer. James glanced round, suddenly fearful of Alex creeping up on him, then got a grip, pressed it and waited for a response.

The door was opened by a girl, pretty in an unhealthy sort of way, round twenty years old, with short hair gelled back over her scalp. Her slim waist showed between her grey top and jeans. Her skin was sallow, like she hadn't slept in weeks, her eyes dull. 'We don't open till seven,' she said flatly. Her accent was sharp, urban, probably London.

James nodded. 'I know.'

She looked James up and down and leant against the doorpost, folded her arms. 'So how come you're here?'

'I'm a friend of Alex's.'

Derision filled her face. 'No, you're not.' James was taken aback. It must have shown in his face, because she laughed, pulled a pack of cigarettes from her pocket and lit one. 'You're lying.'

'Yeah?' he asked. 'You sound fairly sure of yourself.'

'I've never seen you before.'

'So?'

'So, I'm Alex's girlfriend and, if you were a friend of his, I'd know.'

'I'm an old friend,' James said. 'I've been away for a while.'

'How long?'

'Nearly ten years.'

She tried to blow smoke out of her nostrils into his face, but the wind just sucked it up like an extractor fan. She settled for words, 'Sounds like a pretty shit friendship to me.' She brushed her fingers against her bare forearm where goose-pimples stood out like braille. Their message: get inside; it's freezing out here. She glanced behind her, then asked, 'He expecting you?'

'No, I'm just passing through. Thought I'd look him up.'

'Who told you where to find him?'

'I asked in the pub,' James lied. 'The Moonraker.'

'What did they say?'

'That he owned this place, might be here.'

'They don't like him much in there,' she commented, dropping her half-smoked cigarette and staring down. 'D'you mind?' she asked.

He followed her gaze. The cigarette was on the doorstep, next to her bare feet, threatening to roll inside. 'No problem,' he said, grinding the cigarette out with the toe of his foot.

She stepped back inside. 'He's not around at the moment. Back in about an hour. You wanna wait?'

James checked his watch. He'd be long gone by the time Alex returned. 'Thanks. That would be good.' He held out his hand. 'I'm Jimmy, by the way.'

She glanced at his hand, uninterested, turned away. 'T,' she said, 'as in Katie.'

The air inside hung heavy, stale with the stink of stale cigarette smoke and spilt beer. He followed her past the cloakroom and ticket point, down the black-walled corridor and through to the dance floor. It felt illicit, being here. No bouncers. No dealers. No wired kids. Nothing to betray what this place would become in a matter of hours. She reached the main bar and walked round behind it.

'What's your drink?' she asked.

'Whatever's easy.'

She exhaled weightily, stared through the dim lighting across the rows of optics. 'Everything's easy.'

'Vodka.'

She pulled a bottle and two shot glasses from beneath the counter. 'I'm beginning to like you,' she told him, filling the glasses and handing one to him. She knocked her shot back, reloaded the glass. 'You can tell a lot by what a person drinks.'

'Yeah?' James asked, sipping at his glass. 'And what can you tell about me?'

'That you're nervous. That you don't want to look like a wimp. That if I told you to match me shot for shot, you'd do just that. Because you want to stay here. Because there's stuff you want to know.'

James lifted his glass to her in a toast, then downed its contents, clacked it down on the bar and watched her refill it. 'That's a lot to tell. You ever thought of going into the fortune telling business?'

She clinked her glass against his and they drank again. 'Nah,' she said, 'that stuff's for wankers.' She smiled shortly at him. 'Losers who need someone to tell them how to live their lives.'

'Not like you, then?'

'Not like me at all.'

She picked up the bottle and her glass and walked over to a table in an alcove at the side of the room. He went over and joined her, accepted another refill and looked around the club. he had to admit it: he was impressed. Even without music and lights, the place had soul. It was easy to imagine caning a night away in here. He ran his tongue around his mouth, breathed out and smelt the scent of vodka rising to his nostrils. Yeah, this club would be just great, if it wasn't for the tosser who owned it.

'So tell me,' he asked her, 'how long have you been seeing Alex?'

She counted back on her fingers. 'Eight . . . nine months.'

'You from Grancombe?'

Her face scrunched up in distaste. 'Are you kidding me? What – do I look like some country bumpkin?'

'No,' James said truthfully, 'you don't.'

She sat back in her chair. 'I'm from Essex. Came down here on holiday. Met Alex in here.'

'So you stayed?'

'Yeah. And what about you? How d'you know him?'

'I used to live here.'

Her head lolled to one side and she stared at him, hard. 'You don't sound like it.'

'It was just for a year. After I left school. A relative of mine lived here.'

'What was he like?'

'Who?'

'Alex,' she said. 'I don't give a fuck about your relatives.'

James smiled despite himself, then frowned when he remembered what Alex had been like. 'He was a great guy.' James forced out the words. 'The best.'

T pinched at her pale nose. In the dim light, her skin almost glowed. 'You want some Charlie?' she asked.

'No.'

'D'you mind if I do?'

'No. Go ahead.'

She did a couple of lines along the table surface and sat back up, saying, 'That's better. I get tired, you know?'

He smiled sympathetically. 'Has Alex got you working here?'

'Yeah, I work bar. But not for much longer, right. Alex reckons . . .' The rest of her sentence was lost in a mumble as she rubbed the back of her hand across her nose. As she picked up the bottle and poured, he noticed the tiny red blood vessels webbed across the rims of her nostrils.

'You must have known Dan, then,' James said, thinking that now, with her half-cut and half-high, was probably as

233

good a time as any to take the plunge. 'Dan Thompson. He used to work here for Alex, too, didn't he?'

She looked surprised. 'You knew Dan as well?'

'Oh, yeah,' James said. 'Me, Alex and Dan were thick as thieves when we were kids.'

'Right little gang of criminals, I bet.'

'Yeah, that's about the sum of it. I heard they fell out after —'

'Understatement,' she butted in. 'They hated each other.' She shrugged apologetically. 'I'm sorry, you guys being friends and all that when you were younger, but it's true. Alex fired him,' she added. 'A bit before he got wasted up in the woods. Cut his wages off and told him he didn't want him round here no more.' She smiled ruefully. 'Not much of a loss to the business, it has to be said. I never quite worked out what he did, anyhow. Hired muscle, I suppose.' She drummed her fingers on the table, then lit a cigarette. 'Can I trust you, yeah?' she asked, suddenly leaning forward, staring deep into his eyes.

'Of course.'

'I mean with Alex? If I tell you something, d'you promise not to tell him? It's no big deal, but I need to know it won't go any further. Alex gets funny about stuff like that.'

'Stuff like what?'

'Disagreeing with him.' James waited as she inhaled greedily on her cigarette. 'You see, I liked Dan. I thought he was all right. A giggle, yeah?' She stared down at the table. 'OK, so he did too much gear, but it's not exactly the end of the world, is it?'

'No,' James said.

'And he helped Alex set this place up. Once told me it was his money as much as Alex's that paid for the site. Only it all somehow ended up in Alex's name . . . I don't know . . . Alex explained it to me once, but it was kind of complicated.'

'How did Dan take it – when he got fired?'

She shook her head, like there was a mosquito there that only she could hear, and hummed part of a tune. 'I dunno, really. It was weird. He didn't seem to care. Probably too high. Just didn't give a fuck. And that's what pissed Alex off. Dan didn't show him any respect, just kept on coming back here, even after Alex had told him to stay away.' She stubbed out her cigarette, watched the embers glow and die. 'And that was weird, as well . . .'

'What?'

'Well, I mean, you know Alex. He's not exactly the most tolerant guy. Usually, when he tells someone to do something, they'd better bloody do it. Only when Dan didn't, Alex just put up with it. Apart from the night Dan got killed . . .'

'Why? What happened then?'

She looked vague. 'Some argument. In Alex's office at the back. Dan walked in there like he owned the place and Alex sort of freaked. Had Pete – he's one of the bouncers – kick him out the back door. But apart from that, nothing. I tell you, it doesn't make sense.'

'Maybe Alex still felt something for him, despite what he said.'

'Maybe.' She didn't look convinced.

James checked his watch. Lucy would be waiting for him. And then there was Alex. He didn't want to be here when he got back. 'Listen,' he said, standing up. 'Thanks for the drink and the chat, but I've just remembered something I've got to do.'

'What about Alex? I thought you wanted to see him.'

'I'll call back.'

'And it's Jimmy, yeah?'

'Yeah.'

'Jimmy what?'

'Cricket.'

She giggled, suddenly beautiful. 'You're joking?'

'No.' He watched her get to her feet. 'My parents – weird sense of humour.'

They walked to the front door and T opened it. The wind had dropped and James thanked her again as he stepped outside.

'What the fuck are you doing here?'

The voice came from behind James. He turned and saw

Alex walking over from his car. He reached James and said, 'You gone deaf, or what? I said what the fuck are you doing here?'

'Just looking round,' James said, doing just that, checking that Alex's goons from out at Alan's place weren't lurking anywhere. They weren't.

Alex spun round on T. 'You been talking to him?'

'Well, yeah . . . He said he was a friend of yours, so we . . .' Fear rushed her face. 'What? What is it, Alex? What have I done?'

'He's a journalist, you stupid bitch. Doing a piece on Dan getting killed. You been telling him about Dan working here? You been doing that, you dozy fucking tart?'

'Sorry. Alex, I didn't mean . . .' Her voice died in a whisper.

'Get the fuck out of my sight,' Alex spat. Then, to James, 'And you – you just keep your fucking nose out of it, all right? You bring me and my club any bad publicity and . . .' He made a gun out of his fingers, pointed it at James's head and pulled the trigger. 'Got it?' he asked, coldly calm.

It was daylight. It was daylight and Alex was on his own. And there was something in Alex's eyes, something James had never witnessed there before: fear. Alex was afraid. Of James. Of James being here.

'I don't make threats, twat,' Alex told him. 'Just promises. And you know I keep them. And you better remember that.'

James turned and walked. Useless staying here, arguing with Alex when they both knew Alex held all the cards. Besides, he'd got the information he wanted. The nagging feeling had subsided. In its place, his heart pounded, regular, assured. The night of Dan's murder. The row between Alex and Dan. Dan acting as though he owned the place. Against the odds. Because he had something on Alex. Just like Alex had something on James.

He remembered Alex up on the cliff top on that last night in Grancombe. Cold. Assured in what he was doing. No feeling. No remorse. Just pragmatism, plain and simple. Off with the hands. Copy-cat killing. By the book. The axe cracking down on Trader's wrists. Just a job. A butcher cutting chops. He thought back to what he'd typed on the screen, concentrated on the places. Dawes in the woods by his house. Trader by the cliff. Then Dan. Dan by the cliff, too. A copy. Same place. Same mutilations.

Same killer.

Could that be it? Was that the reason for the fear he'd seen in Alex's eyes? It was possible. More than possible. Because he knew Alex. Because he'd seen him lay his hands on Dawes' corpse. Because he'd been there with Trader. Because he knew what Alex was prepared to put himself through to secure his future. If he was a betting man, he'd run with it, stake his life on it. Maybe – he remembered Alex's threat – he already had.

But he wasn't a betting man. He was a journalist, trained to rely on facts, not instinct. And there were doubts. No evidence for a start. Nothing, apart from the argument, to link Alex to Dan's murder. And Alex wasn't stupid. If he had killed Dan, he'd have an alibi. Some thug who'd stand there and robotically state he'd been with Alex the night of the murder. But above all that was Dawes. Alex had been out of the country when that had happened, so he couldn't have done it. And if Alex hadn't done it, then that meant someone else had. And that led to another theory. Two killers. One for Dawes; Alex for Trader and Dan. No serial killer at all. That would explain the gap. That would explain everything. Either that, or he was mistaken, and Alex was innocent.

But Alex had never been innocent, not from from the instant his bloody skull had slid free from his mother's womb.

Later, James was sat, huddled against the wall of St Donal's, his coat collar turned up against the cold. It was strange coming here with Lucy, made it seem less personal, like he was just a tourist stopping to look at the church. He watched her amongst the gravestones, standing one moment, crouching the next, the shutter of her camera snapping up views of Dan's gravestone.

Then he heard footsteps and turned.

'Hello, again.'

It was Suzie. In her hands was a box of flower bulbs and a trowel. He stood and walked over to her, kissed her on the cheek. 'Hi.'

She looked over at Lucy, watched her for a few seconds, then asked, 'That her, then? Your girlfriend?'

'Yeah.'

'She's pretty.'

'Yeah, she is.'

'Dan's gravestone.'

'I know. I'm sorry. Do you want me to tell her to stop?'

She looked at him, her eyes clear. 'No, it's all right. Just doing her job.'

Lucy looked over and waved at them.

'Does she know you used to live here?'

'No one knows. None of my friends.' He frowned. 'I'd like to keep it that way. Everything that happened here that summer. Dawes. The girl at the rave. I've never told anyone.'

'Maybe I'd better go then . . .'

'Yeah, maybe you had.' He watched Lucy sheathing her camera inside its case. Suzie made to leave, but he caught her arm. 'I want to see you.' he said. 'Tomorrow. I want to see you tomorrow.'

'What about her?'

'She won't be here.'

Suzie eyed him sceptically. 'And that makes it all right, does it?'

'I mean I'm going to ask her to leave. I'm going to tell her it's over.'

'Because of me?'

'Yes.'

'But nothing's happened.'

'It has to me.'

'Nothing might happen.' She looked imploringly at him. 'James, we hardly even know each other any more.'

Lucy was walking over towards them now. James released Suzie's arm. 'Will you meet me?' he asked.

'Yes,' she said, unsmiling, then walked away.

James watched Lucy smile at her as they passed one another.

'Who's that?' she asked him when she reached him.

'A local. I was just asking her a few questions.'

'Find out anything useful?'

'I hope so,' he said, turning and walking towards the churchyard gate.

CHAPTER SIXTEEN

fire

The night of the rave, Alex had found James standing by the gates at Eagle's Point, staring at the ambulance as Victoria Cooper's body was stretchered inside.

Alex had silently ushered him away from the gathering crowd and out down the lane. Dan had been sitting behind the wheel of a silver Renault Five with 'Hot Tuna' surf stickers emblazoned across its sides. Neither of them had asked him where he'd got it from.

'We're fucked,' Dan said as they got inside.

'Just drive,' Alex told him.

Dan started the engine. 'Where? We can't go home.'

'Just drive,' Alex repeated, his tone agitated. 'I'll tell you when to stop.'

They pulled into a lay-by about a mile further on, ditched the car next to the deserted picnic tables and litter bins, left the keys in the ignition, the lights on, the doors open, and walked into the undergrowth. They followed the line of the cliff, Alex alert as a pointer. It was only when they reached the top of the steps – the same place they'd stopped to rest on the day of the search party – that Alex broke the silence that had engulfed them and told them to sit down. He placed the wash bag on the ground beside him. James couldn't take his eyes off it, couldn't look Alex in the face.

'What we gonna do?' Dan asked. He sounded desperate, scared.

'We're gonna keep our mouths shut.'

'She's dead,' James said.

'You think I don't fucking know that?' Alex snapped, turning on him. 'You think anyone in this town doesn't fucking know that by now?'

James wasn't interested in debate. The facts were too big, Alex's words too small. Just excuses. Pitiful attempts at self-delusion. 'We can't just sit here. She's dead, for fuck's sake. She's dead and we killed her.'

Alex pulled a half bottle of black rum from his pocket, drank deeply. 'We didn't kill anyone,' he stated. 'It was an accident.'

James wasn't buying it. He'd seen the facts in the flesh of Victoria Cooper's body, as sure as if they'd been branded there. 'The pills killed her. That's what they were all saying. Overdose. I heard them. The paramedics from the ambulance. Said they'd seen the same thing before.'

'They could be wrong,' Dan said. 'She might have just died.'

'Yeah,' James said, 'and we might have just killed her.'

'Murphy's gonna be after us, Alex,' Dan said. 'He's gonna fucking track us down, ice us for keeps.'

'Shut it. Both of you,' Alex said, getting to his feet and pacing around. 'Murphy's got nothing on us. Same as everyone else. They don't know shit.'

'But he knows we deal, Alex,' Dan persisted. 'It was our rave. He'll fucking know it's down to us.'

'What? You reckon I was the only person dealing there? No fucking way. Even if she did OD – and we don't know that – then anyone could have slipped her what did it.'

James screwed the cigarette he'd been about to light up in his fist. 'You did it,' he said. 'I saw you. You sold them to her. Potential garbage from the left. It was you. No one else.'

Alex stood over him with his boots inches from his body. 'And you're the one who told her to buy off me.' His teeth bared like a dog's. 'Remember that.'

James stared into the sky. The search light swept across the stars above Eagle's Point. He wanted out so bad he'd risk jumping off the cliff if he thought he'd stand an infinitesimal

chance of survival. He kept swallowing, his throat heavy with
phlegm. Turn back time. Always the same desire. Doing all
these things that weren't him. Having to deal with the conse-
quences. And the remains of the Ecstasy still in his system, too
strong to be flushed away completely by his panic, lodged
there, inescapable as his guilt . . .

'I remember,' he mumbled.

'Yeah, well you make sure you do. 'Cos if any shit comes
down on me over this, it's coming down on you, as well.
Coming down hard. Crushing you right with me.'

'They're gonna tell him,' Dan said. 'Someone's gonna tell
Murphy it was us.'

'No one'll say shit,' Alex snapped.

'I've seen it, man. I've seen it fucking happen. You remember that school kid who died in Brighton? OD'd in some club
he wasn't even old enough to be in. They nicked the dealer. I
remember his face in the papers, fucking everything. Scape-
goat. They ain't gonna stop till they've got one.'

Alex spoke quickly, logically, like he was giving a lecture,
anticipating, answering objections before they were raised:
'We say nothing, they know nothing. The girl was on her own
when I sold them to her. So people say we were dealing, so
what? We weren't the only ones. We been caught with drugs?
No. People who scored off us, they gonna be reliable wit-
nesses? No. Off their faces, that's why. Our word against
theirs.' Alex walked a couple of paces away and knelt on the
ground, ripped up some turf, and pulled the pills from his
pockets and set about burying them, planting them like seeds.
He tugged the wash bag over and emptied out what was left in
there, too, threw the bag away into the bushes. 'We say nothing
and everything's gonna be OK.'

'It's not right,' James said. 'We killed her.'

'It's too late for a conscience attack now.' Anger burnt in
Alex's voice. 'It was an accident. Not like a fucking murder.
What good's grassing ourselves up gonna do? We'll ride this
out, just like we always have.'

James stood up. 'I don't want any part of this.'

Alex stood staring for a few seconds, concluded, 'Forget it.

You're in this now. Up to your fucking neck. Same as us. You got no choice.'

James walked toward him, Alex rising as he approached.

'I'm going,' James said.

'Going where?'

'Home. I didn't deal. I didn't sell shit. This is nothing to do with me.'

Alex side-stepped into his path. 'You think a judge'll believe you? You never heard of conspiracy?'

'I don't care.'

Alex smiled mockingly. 'Oh, you care, all right, James. That's your problem: you care too much.' He moved aside. 'So, go. Go home and sleep on it. If Murphy lets you sleep, that is. But you'll keep quiet. You're not gonna let yourself be the face in the papers, no matter what you think now. Don't kid yourself: you're no better than me.'

'Fuck you,' James said, pushing past him. 'Fuck you both.'

But Alex had been right. About everything. About keeping quiet. About being too afraid to speak out. About being responsible for what had happened. And about Murphy, too.

James got back to Alan's house and turned in at about the same time the sun was turning out. Murphy showed up about an hour later. James heard the pounding at the door downstairs. He wasn't asleep. Miserable. Coming down. Too much paranoia, too. Slumping into the flatline of reality. Coming down would have been hard enough for the first time anyway, but coupled with what had happened . . . He'd gone so far down, he'd be lucky to ever get up again. The only experience he could relate it to was the night he'd spent after hearing about his parents' death. Sleep deprivation. Total alienation. Thousand yard stare. Adrift in space, spinning further and further away from planet Earth, waiting for the oxygen supplies to run out, knowing that things would never return to the way they'd once been.

Straight down to the police station. Numb head. Dream-state. Entranced. Not happening to him. Someone else. Someone he didn't give a damn about. Some piece of scum. A car-journey where Murphy's vitriol provided the soundtrack, where James said nothing. Same as the last time. Same as Alex knew he would. Seeking sanctuary in silence; safety in denial. Grass on Alex, get busted right with him. Dan down, too. Old enough to go to prison now. All of them. Old enough to be deemed responsible for their own actions.

Face-slap.

'How does it feel to have a death on your conscience?'

'I don't know.'

Face-slap.

'Where's Howley?'

'I don't know.'

Face-slap.

'Where's Thompson?'

'I don't know.'

Face-slap.

'She was her parents' only child.'

Face-slap.

'You've left them with nothing.'

And so it went on, a variation on a simple theme. But here was the sick bit: every slap felt right, felt so deserved that the pain transformed to pleasure, the punishment to reward. Murphy was no longer the animal. Just the zookeeper. James belonged in this cage with him. He needed to be smacked back into civilisation. She was dead. Victoria Cooper's eyes had been closed forever. He might as well have pulled a blade across her throat and watched her bleed. He'd done it. As much as Alex. He'd led her to her killer, watched him pass the poison. He needed to be punished, needed to be tamed.

Face-slap.

Face-slap.

He needed to learn to steer clear of Alex Howley and claim his life back as his own.

James didn't go into Grancombe for two weeks after Murphy let him go. In that time, Alex and Dan called round once. From an upstairs window, James watched them standing by the door waiting for an answer. Alex's shades were in place, as was Dan by Alex's side – somewhere, James suspected, he'd always be. The Spitfire was parked in the yard, showroom-stunning. James wanted to puke at the thought of where the money had come from to pay for it, what it had really cost. He didn't go down to greet them. No point. He already had the answers to the only questions he wanted to hear. The local paper had filled him in on that front. No one had been charged in connection with Victoria Cooper's death. It would go down as death by misadventure. They were all in the clear. Free to carry on with their lives as if nothing had happened.

Only that wasn't what James wanted.

The two-week self-imposed exile gave him time to think, restore order to the anarchy of emotions and thoughts in his mind. Sort out your head first, then think about sorting out your life. What he'd done *was* wrong. There was no escaping that. And what he'd done *was* permanent. No amount of grieving or guilt was going to raise Victoria Cooper from the grave, reverse her metabolism's rare reaction to the combination of Ecstasy and manic exercise. It was too late to fix her body's temperature control system, ice the massive explosion of heat, disintegrate the clotted blood in her arteries and veins, repair the organ and tissue damage that had sent her reeling out of consciousness onto the dance floor.

So, where did that leave him? With the past chiselled in stone, the only hope of redemption lay in the future. That was a story he could write any way he chose. He'd stolen Victoria Cooper's life. The least he could now do was ensure that his own life wasn't wasted as well. Let something good grow out of the bad. Nurture a flower from the grave. Be true to yourself. Be happy. He owed her that. And he owed it to himself, as well.

Once he made this decision – to move forward rather than back – his first thought was to return to London. Get away from Grancombe. Leave it all behind. Make a fresh start. But running away wouldn't solve anything. It was himself he had to face up to; and he'd be there in London, just the same as here. It would be as futile as attempting to outrun his shadow. So, what to do here? No point in staying locked away any more. He'd seen what that had done to Alan. He'd focused so far in on himself that the outside world had effectively ceased to exist. Still bolted inside his study, incommunicado. That wasn't what James wanted. James wanted to be reminded that he was still human. He wanted emotions, warmth. He wanted to feel alive again. He wanted people to look at him and care.

He wanted Suzie to look at him and not turn away.

He left the house on a Wednesday afternoon, walked down to the Surf School on North Beach. It wasn't much to look at: a wooden shed wedged between a fishing shack and an outboard engine repair shop. He ducked through the open doorway and approached the counter. There was a hand bell there, with a piece of paper sellotaped to it which read 'RING FOR SERVICE'. In a back room a radio played. He rang the bell.

Simon appeared at the doorway a few seconds later. 'Hi, James,' he said, rubbing his eyes. 'You been waiting long? I've been sleeping on the job again.'

James had met Simon a few time before. Used to see him at the beach parties. Beach bum incarnate. Owned the Surf School and ran it during the summer. Hibernated during the winter in a nest of hemp, according to Dan.

'How's tricks?' James asked.

'Good, you know. Sun's out. Can't complain. How about you? Didn't see you at the bash on South Beach on Saturday... You been OK? Alex said you'd done a bunk.'

'Just taking some time out.' James coughed, cleared his throat. 'That thing with the girl up at Eagle's Point. Kind of did my head in.'

'Yeah, man,' Simon said, shaking his head and looking down at the counter, 'me too. Crying shame. Only a kid, you know. Fate deals some shitty hands.'

The word *deals* raised a flag in James's mind. 'How's Alex doing?'

'Hard to tell. I think what happened kind of freaked him out, too. 'Specially the heat Murphy brought down on him afterwards. Must have been like crash-landing on the sun.'

'He still dealing?'

'Oh, yeah.' Simon sounded surprised. 'Not like he had shit to do with the kid's death. Down to some outsider, the way I heard it. Some shit-for-brains profiteer coming here and selling dodgy pills. Not Alex's style. Well out of order, Murphy holding him and Dan overnight like that.'

James looked around the walls at the equipment hire prices and posters. 'Suzie working today?'

Simon nodded his head. 'Out with a couple of kids at the moment.' He checked his watch. 'Should be back soon. They only paid for an hour. You want me to let her know you called by?'

James shook his head. 'No, don't worry. I'll wait for her outside.'

He sat on the nearby car park wall and smoked, gazing across the beach, observing the oiled tourists frying up like bacon in a pan. He saw Suzie emerging from the surf about twenty minutes later, sealed in a fluorescent pink wetsuit cut off at the elbows and knees. She heaved the surfboard out of the water and wedged it under her arm, then stretched down and unfastened the cord which linked it to her ankle. A couple of boys in black wetsuits came splashing up to join her and the three of them stood talking for a couple of minutes. The boys laid down their boards on the sand and, standing on them, crouched down and slowly rose to their feet. They practised the exercise a few more times under her gaze, then she left them there and padded up the beach towards the Surf School.

'Suzie,' James called, sliding off the wall, walking across the sand to join her.

She pushed her wet fringe back and rubbed the salt water from her eyes. The quartz from the sand sparkled like diamonds on her cheeks. 'Hi,' she said. 'What are you doing here?'

'Just thought I'd see how you were.'

'Yeah?' She stood the surfboard upright in the sand next to her, rested her elbow on it. 'London get boring, did it?'

'What do you mean?'

'Well, that's where you've been, isn't it? That's what Dan said. Said you skipped back there after Eagle's Point.' She read something in his face. 'He's talking crap as usual, then?'

'Yeah,' James confirmed, 'I haven't been anywhere. Just out at Alan's.'

'Just bored of hanging out with Dan and Alex . . .'

'Something like that.'

She peered at him, interested. 'Can't say I blame you. Never really had you guys down as a natural group.'

When he spoke, he meant it: 'I'm not.'

They looked at one another for a few seconds. A lock of her hair flopped down, curled across her eyebrow. He controlled the urge to reach out and push it back, to touch her skin. He heard laughter and turned to see the two boys walking their boards over.

'I'd better get their boards stashed,' Suzie said. 'Simon's probably ready to go home. Thanks for calling round, though. It's good to know you're still alive.'

James stared awkwardly at the strip of sand which separated them. He could feel the moment slipping away from him. 'Are you finished teaching for the day?'

'Yeah, all done.'

Now. Now or never. 'How about a drink?' he asked, looking up. Her face was neutral. Not pleased, but not horrified either. He pressed on: 'With me. Do you want to come for a drink with me?'

'I can't.'

He'd been half-expecting it, and had his reaction taped already for this eventuality. He even managed a smile. 'Some other time, then,' he said, turning to go.

'Wait.'

He froze for a second, before turning back to face her. 'What?' he asked.

'I've got to do the accounts for Surfers' Turf tonight. They're tough enough without adding alcohol to the equation. But I would like to see you.' The two kids were standing by the door to the Surf School now, watching them intently. One of them giggled, but she ignored him. 'I should be done by half-eight, and it's closed Wednesdays, so why don't you come over then, have a coffee? We can talk.'

His smile was real this time, lasting. 'OK,' he said. 'I'll see you there, then.'

James left the beach and joined the procession of tourists tramping back to their B&Bs with their beer coolers and beach balls. Life was tasting sweet again. He continued up the hill, stopped by the church wall and sat on the grassy verge and had a smoke. Already, the thrill of riding past here in Alex's Spitfire seemed distant, disconnected from himself. Control was possible after all. Not taking the ride. That's all it reduced to in the end. Choice. Making the right decisions. Choosing to live a life you were happy to claim as your own when you woke up in the morning.

He finished his cigarette and turned and looked at the clock on St Donal's tower. Six-thirty. Two hours to go before he met Suzie. There wasn't much point in walking back to Alan's place; he'd hardly have time to rest his legs before it was time to set back out again. He looked across the undulating roofs of Grancombe. Despite his familiarity with the view, he felt alienated. It was like returning to a town you'd once lived in after a long absence. No longer connected to it, no longer part of its fabric. A stranger. James understood why. It was all down to Alex – the fact that James had pulled the ejector switch, jettisoned him from his life. Grancombe had always been tied up with Alex in James's mind, so now that his links with Alex had been severed, so too had his links with the town. Alex had been the lens through which he'd previously looked. Alex had interpreted everything he'd seen. With Alex gone, James might as well have been stepping off the train all over again.

But no matter. He got to his feet, walked towards the High Street. He'd grown since then, no longer needed people like Alex to introduce him to the world. He was capable of doing that himself. He reached the Moonraker and went inside. No need to hide anymore. Fresh start. If Alex and Dan were in here, so what? He'd get by just fine without them.

As it happened, it was quiet. There was no sign of Alex or Dan. Just the usual group of locals lined along the bar stools, staring straight ahead.

'Hello, James,' Johno said, moving across to the corner of the bar as James reached it. 'Boys aren't here, if you're after them.'

'I'm not. Just a pint, thanks.'

Johno moved across to the tap. 'Coming right up.'

'I still can't bloody believe it,' Cliff, a trawler captain at the bar, said loudly. 'I mean, we all know he's a nutter, but not that. Never have had him down for doing that.'

'Say they got all the evidence they need to put the bastard away for life, way I hear it,' Sam, his long-time drinking companion came back. 'Jesus, you gotta be thick, though, haven't you, thinking you can just go selling something like that and no one's gonna go asking any questions.'

Johno came back with James's pint, placed it on a beer mat before him.

James handed him some cash, caught his eye and nodded down the bar. 'What are they on about?'

Johno shot him a world-weary glance. 'Same as everyone's been on about all afternoon: Arnie Oldfield.'

James sucked the froth off the top of his pint, wiped the foam moustache from his upper lip. 'Why, what's he done?'

'Jesus, James, I know you haven't been around much lately, but where've you been? Doing an ostrich down the beach? Burying your head in the sand? I thought everyone in the whole bloody town knew by now.'

James just shrugged. 'So, you going to tell me, or what?'

'Murphy's arrested him.'

James was iced. 'For what happened to that girl on Eagle's Point?'

Johno looked with discomfort down the bar. His son's detention by Murphy was obviously public knowledge which he didn't want raked up again. 'No,' he mumbled to James, 'nothing to do with that. It's Dawes. They've arrested him in connection with Jack Dawes' murder.'

'What happened?'

According to Johno, Arnie Oldfield had been arrested in Andersford the day before and charged just after lunch today. Andrew Rawlings, one of Murphy's boys, had been into the

Moonraker earlier and let slip over a couple of pints the details of what had happened. It would make no difference in the long run. The press were already onto it. Oldfield's photograph would provide the focal point of millions of breakfast tables the following morning. A nation's eyes would focus on Grancombe through the lens of television cameras again.

What had gone down was this: Arnie Oldfield had caught the bus over to Andersford the previous day. Andersford was a market town around forty miles away, renowned throughout the county as a thriving arts and antiques centre. He'd gone into one of the auction houses with a thin rectangular parcel under his arm and demanded to see an art specialist. The receptionist had left him waiting for a while, her suspicions already raised, doubting that such an uncultured scruff could have anything of interest in his possession. But Arnie had waited, sat there silently, staring at her and, once it had become apparent that he wasn't going to give up and go and bother someone else, she'd tried fobbing him off with an office junior. This hadn't worked either and so she'd succumbed to his persistence and persuaded the expert to give him five minutes of her time. Arnie had been shown through to the expert's office. Without being asked or bothering to introduce himself, he'd approached her desk, carefully placed the parcel down. He'd then pulled a penknife from his pocket and cut the red string that bound the parcel, ripped the brown paper free.

And at that precise moment, Arnie Oldfield's life had taken a decided turn for the worse.

'Couldn't have gone to a worse place, see,' Johno explained. 'This expert woman, she was a friend of Jack Dawes. Real fan by all accounts. It was her that was arranging the exhibition for his new collection up in London. Recognised the brush strokes and that straight away. Didn't even need to see his initials down the bottom.'

The painting was of the back of nude woman, crouched in the corner of a room, her face totally obscured by her dark hair. The expert had looked from this to Arnie and back again. Eventually she'd asked him if he knew who it was by, what it was worth. He'd told her, outright: Jack Dawes; deceased;

probably worth a fortune now that he was dead. She'd asked him where he'd got it and he'd told her that that was none of her business. He'd said he wanted cash for it. There and then. No receipts. Simple transaction. If she gave him the money, he'd give her the painting, and then he'd walk away.

'That's what he was on about up at Eagle's Point,' James interrupted.

Johno looked confused. 'Eh?'

'Said he wasn't going to have to worry about money any more. Said he was going to be rich.'

'Yeah, well he couldn't have been more wrong if he'd tried, could he?'

The expert had verbally agreed to what Arnie had said, had suggested a ridiculously high price which all but had Arnie drowning the painting with a slop of saliva. She'd fixed him up with a steaming cup of coffee in his hand, then excused herself from the room on the pretence of going to the bank to withdraw the cash. When the door to the office had opened twenty minutes later and Arnie had turned to observe his fortune-bearer's return, the coffee cup had fallen from his hand and rolled across the antiquated carpet between his feet. A uniformed arm had descended on his shoulder to discourage him from attempting to run.

He'd been nicked. Cold.

'Trouble with being thick, that,' Johno reflected. 'No foresight. Should've seen it coming. Same with the whole plan. Didn't stand a chance of getting away with it the first place, stupid bastard. Wasn't for what he'd done to Jack, I'd even pity him. As it is, I hope they bring back the death penalty, string the bastard up.'

Arnie had protested his innocence there and then and, by all accounts, had stuck to this throughout the long hours of interrogation that followed. His story was weak, though. The police weren't convinced.

'Said he found the painting up in the woods,' Johno said with a sad expression and a shake of his head. 'Just lying there next to a tree. Said he'd been walking back from working Jack's garden. Nearly trod on it. Couldn't believe his luck.'

Johno's eyes locked with James's. '*He* couldn't believe his luck,' he scoffed. 'Problem was, neither could the police.'

The way the police saw it, Arnie's story had fallen down on so many counts that it was practically black and blue. For a start, there was the claim that he'd been working Dawes' garden. Dawes had already been dead a week the day Arnie claimed he'd found the painting. So what had he been doing there? He'd said Jack had treated him well, that his small way of paying him back for his kindness had been to keep the garden how Jack would have wanted it. Fine. Fine and honourable. The clichéd act of a faithful retainer. Only it hadn't fooled anyone for a second. Consistency. That's where Arnie's story had first collapsed. So he'd respected Jack and continuing to work the garden had been his way of mourning. So how come when he'd stumbled across the painting of the nude in the woods (a miracle not even his fertile imagination had been able to explain), he hadn't decided to hand it in to the police? How come he'd decided instead to steal it and try and sell it? *Money*, he'd come back. *Money*. He'd needed the money. *Motive*, they'd come back. *Motive*. They'd needed a motive.

And he'd just handed it to them on a plate.

James was still reeling from the news. 'You don't reckon he killed Dawes, though, do you?' he finally asked.

'Don't matter what I believe. Just the police and judge and jury. Only opinions worth a damn. If it gets that far, that is . . .'

'How do you mean?'

'Andrew Rawlings says they've got their suspicions and that. That assault up on Eagle's Point two years back. Not like he's not capable of doing something like that. But suspicions ain't worth a damn 'less Arnie admits to it. They can bang him up for theft easy enough. After all, he had the keys to Dawes' place and he had the motive, eh? But not murder, I don't reckon. Not without any proper proof.'

'Bad business,' James commented, wondering if word had already reached Alan about this.

'Ain't over yet. The press will have a field day. But it'll be

253

over soon. That's the main thing. Way I see it, it's better to get the bad publicity in at the end of the season, but have the whole matter cleared up for the next. Unsolved murders never do no one or nowhere no good. Business has been bloody terrible since you kids found Jack up there in the woods.' He lowered his voice. 'Some people – and I'm not mentioning no names – been saying it might've been better you never found him at all. Tourists don't like that kind of thing. No one does. But 'specially tourists. Not gonna go bringing your kids down here next year, you think their gonna get their hands cut off. Aye,' he reflected, 'sooner the slate's wiped clean on Jack's behalf, the better for everyone concerned.'

James stayed for another couple of drinks in the Moonraker. The conversation stayed tied to Arnie Oldfield, failing to cut loose as other customers arrived and slid into the debate. James briefly considered phoning Alan. Maybe this was the news that would break him out of his cell, set his spirit free. But half-way to the pay phone at the other end of the bar, he remembered that Alan's phone had been cut off. What did it matter? Alan was probably too far gone now to give a damn. James returned to his drink and, eventually, the hand of the clock above the bar wound down towards half-eight. James finished his pint.

'I'll see you around,' he told Johno.

'Aye,' Johno said, reaching over and taking the empty glass, 'see you soon. You see that son of mine, tell him to get his arse back here. Meant to be helping out this afternoon and ain't shown his face all day.'

I don't give a damn about your son, James thought as he pushed through the door onto the street. *Just your daughter. Just the woman I'm on my way to see.*

As he walked up over Eagle's point and descended the steps the other side which led to South Beach, his feelings towards both siblings intensified. Johno had been right: the season was drawing to an end. And when it finally did end, James's time here would end with it, fade away like a sunset. Not long now, and he'd be climbing onto the train and heading back to London, and then from London onto Edinburgh. The cold of the Scottish winter would kick in and this hot, crazy summer in Grancombe would be consigned to his memory for ever. And already – even though that time hadn't yet come – he had regrets. He'd visited the junction, read the signs on the post: Suzie and sanity to the right; Alex and anarchy to the left. He'd gone left, left himself behind, and only now was he able to see that he'd been wrong, that right had been the right road for him all along.

She was sitting at a table in Surfers' Turf when he reached the door. Low and mournful music drifted through the open windows onto the evening breeze and out across the beach. He stood motionless for a few seconds, watching through the pane of the glass door as she tapped away at a calculator and filled in columns in a book. He felt content, imagined that this was what it must be like to have children, to watch them from a distance, study their movements without inhibition, marvel at the good fortune that had allowed them to be a part of your life. He opened the door and stepped inside.

'Hi,' she said, turning in her seat, smiling. She looked at her watch, then held the calculator up, waggled it at him. 'Time sure flies when you're having fun.'

'Finish off,' he said, heading towards the kitchen. 'Don't mind me, I'll go and fix us a coffee. Milk, sugar?'

'No and no,' she called back. 'Thanks.'

He returned to the table five minutes later and set the two mugs of coffee down next to the closed accounts book.

'Cheers,' he said, raising his mug to his lips and sipping, letting the steam funnel over his face.

She sat back in her chair and stretched. 'Well, I finally did it,' she said, nudging the calculator across the table. 'Been putting it off for weeks. I should feel pleased.'

'But you're not, right?'

'No,' she said, leaning forward and taking a drink. 'I knew this summer was going to be make or break and now I know the result.'

It didn't take much for him to guess which. 'Break?'

She made a gun out of her fingers and fired it at her head. 'You got it.'

'So what next? Close it down till next summer and go back and work at the Moonraker till then?'

Her eyebrows bobbed. 'You've got a good memory.'

'Some days you don't forget.'

She looked puzzled for a moment, then said, 'Of course. That was the day you guys found Jack Dawes.'

'I wasn't talking about that.' He took a deep breath, then thought what the hell. No point being here and biting his tongue. 'I meant you. I meant I remember that day, because it was the day I met you.'

She laughed at him, hid her face behind her mug. 'You don't waste time, do you?' she finally asked. 'Aren't we meant to be at the mild flirting stage now? You know the thing. Boy meets girl. They joke around. They tell each other stories about their lives and see if they find each other interesting. They catch each other staring, because they're staring, too. And when they do, they always look away, maybe even blush a little. Isn't that stuff meant to come first? Before one of them comes out with a line so obvious the other one can't ignore it without blowing the whole thing out?'

He was laughing now, as well. 'OK, you're right. Let's take things back a bit. Wipe what I just said from your mind. But I think we've covered the joking part, so – what was it you said came next? – story-telling?'

'Story-telling,' she said. She stared at him, didn't look away, didn't blush, not even a little. 'Tell me about you and Alex and my brother. Tell me all about that.'

'In at the deep end, then?'

'Twenty-thousand leagues and counting . . .'

'Why that? Out of all the things you could ask, why do you want to know about that?'

'Because one minute you're surgically attached to them, the next you're acting like you'll come out in a rash if you so much as step near them.' She lit a cigarette. 'Now call me stupid, but to me that looks like the result of some pretty major shit.'

'Well,' he said, concentrating, 'where to begin? Not the

beginning. I think you already know about that. You saw me hanging out with them. You've probably got a pretty good idea what we were spending our time doing. So,' he went on, 'I might as well start with the end. I might as well tell you why I'm not hanging round with them anymore . . .'

'Well . . .'

He studied his hands, didn't want to look at her while he spoke. 'It was the girl. Up at Eagle's Point. Victoria Cooper. The girl who died. She changed everything.' He stared at her, briefly considered telling her the truth: that it was Alex who gave Victoria Cooper the killer pill. But he couldn't. What if she hated him for it? What if she hated him for the same reason he hated himself? 'It wasn't that any of us were directly involved with what happened,' he lied. 'It's just that they – that we – were there when it happened. And that if we hadn't fixed the rave up, then she'd still be alive.'

She reached out and laid her hand on his. He looked up and she said, 'You can't blame yourself for what happened. And you can't blame Dan and Alex either. The police let them go. It wasn't their fault.'

'I don't accept that. They deal. Both of them. It could just as easily have been them who sold her the pills.'

She leant forward. 'But it wasn't them, was it?'

'No,' he said quickly. 'Not them.' He breathed deeply, tried to surface, the urge to speak the truth still weighing him down. He blinked heavily. 'But it *could* have been, and I guess that's the point. It could still happen. Who knows? Maybe one day it will. And I don't want to be there when it does. I don't ever want to have to cope with that kind of guilt.'

'Have you told them this?'

He shook his head. 'I don't need to. They already know.'

'And you don't think you could bring them round to your point of view?'

'No.

'Not even Dan?'

'No.' He lit a cigarette. 'It's too late. He's Alex's now. For keeps.'

'He's really pissed off at you.'

257

'Yeah?'

'Yeah.' Her eyes half-closed. 'He would've appreciated you being around when all that stuff with Murphy went down.'

'Murphy had me in, as well. Him and Alex weren't the only ones.'

'I know. I heard. He still took it bad, though.'

'And Alex?' James asked. 'How did he take it?'

'I don't know. I don't talk to him.'

'So why are you blaming me for choosing to do the same?'

She withdrew her hand. 'Because Dan isn't Alex.' She was angry. 'He's my brother. He's different to Alex. Or he would be if he ever got the chance.' She chewed on her lip. 'If you'd been there for him, then maybe he wouldn't have ended up back in Alex's pocket again. Maybe after that girl died, he would have done the same thing as you – the right thing. Maybe he would have walked away.'

'OK,' James said, drawing the conversation to a close, 'I'll talk to him.'

'Thanks, I'd appreciate that.'

They stayed there talking over cigarettes and coffee for another hour or so, reading each other chapter after chapter from their life stories. He heard himself telling her about his parents, keeping nothing back. And he told her about Alan, about the way he'd become. And she told him about herself, about growing up in Grancombe with Dan and her parents. She told him about how Dan had been friends with Alex since they could first talk. She told him that she wished they'd never met. They discussed the future, James going to Edinburgh, his writing, his wish to become a journalist and novelist. And ways to make Surfers' Turf work, so as to travel the world and always have something to come home to. And then he told her about her; about what he thought of her. He told her what he'd wanted to tell her from the first day he'd met her.

'Come here,' she said, getting to her feet and walking round to his side of the table.

He stood and she took his hand, pulling it round her, and leant forward, kissed him. He pressed his waist against hers, breathed her in. Then she pulled back.

She touched her lips briefly against his. 'You're a good kisser, you know.'

Without speaking, he followed her across the room and behind the counter, through the clutter of aluminium surfaces and pots and pans in the kitchen, and into a small room at the back. Surf posters covered the walls. In the corner was a single bunk with a thin mattress on it and a rolled up sleeping bag. On a table next to the bed was a radio. She flicked it on and the music flowed. She sat down on the bed, kicked her shoes off.

'Crash room,' she explained, getting to her feet and pulling her t-shirt over her head. He found himself staring at her flat stomach, at the thin gold ring running through her navel. Then up, settling on her bra. 'I sometimes sleep here when I want to catch some waves before the tourists wake up.' She jerked her jeans down to her thighs, sat back down again and pulled them off. 'So,' she said, sitting back against the wall, her knees tucked under her chin, 'are you going to take your clothes off, or do I have to do it for you?'

James removed his shirt and shoes and socks and sat next to her on the bed. He unbuckled his belt, got to his feet and turned his back on her. He raised his legs one after the other and pulled them free of his jeans. He looked down at his penis poking through the flies of his boxer shorts, suddenly sick with nerves. *You can do this. This is what you want. She needn't ever know.* But it was no good. He sat down on the bed and turned to face her.

'There's something I think I should tell you. And I know it's not what I'm meant to say . . .'

Concern crossed her face. 'What is it?'

He found himself smiling, then pursed his lips together, tried to get a grip. 'I just want to tell you that . . .' He halted, shook his head. 'Sorry,' he said, 'but this is embarrassing . . . I've never done this before. I thought I should warn you. I don't know. . . . You hear stories . . . If it's a disaster, I just want you to know why.' He smiled again. 'I don't want you to think that that's how it'll always be.'

She leant across and kissed his shoulder, ran her lips down his arm.

'Don't worry,' she whispered. 'It's going to be just fine.'

And he believed her.

Her arms disappeared behind her back and she unfastened her bra, pulled the straps down over her arms, and tossed it onto the floor.

'It's all right,' she said. 'You can look. You can touch.'

He moved towards her, slipped his arms around her and pulled her close. He felt her chest dissolve into his and stared into her eyes for a moment, watched them close, then closed his own, found her mouth and slid his tongue inside. Then, movements – rolling down onto the bed. Her face pushing across his, her tongue darting into his ear. The sound of the ocean, released. Her breath brushing against his ear. His fingers being guided over her hip, between her legs, being shown how to move; learning to walk. Her hand sliding under the waistband of his shorts, pulling them down, stripping them off. Him doing the same for her. More movements, gropings, guidings. His frantic fumbling with the condom wrapper. Her moving him inside, both gasping. Then over so quickly. Pulling out, lying back beside her, pulling the condom off and staring at it, marvelling at the sperm that had been inside her only seconds before.

And finally, his arm around her, he slept.

'Wake up.'

He opened his eyes. She was standing up, dressed, her face no longer flushed. 'What?'

'I've got to get back. I promised Dad I'd help him close up tonight. You can stay here if you want . . .'

He sat up, fighting against the drowsiness. 'No. Give me a couple of minutes and I'll walk you back.'

Half-an-hour later, they were standing outside the Moon-raker. On the walk over, they hadn't mentioned what had happened. They had talked about other things instead: Grancombe, Alex and Dan, Arnie Oldfield and Jack Dawes, things that suddenly no longer mattered to James at all. There was only her. And he needed to be sure.

'No regrets, then?' he asked.

She slipped her arms round his waist. 'None.'

'You don't have to say that.' The sound of drunken laughter came from behind the door. 'If you want to leave what's happened tonight as a one-off, then that's fine. I'll understand.'

'Is that what you want?'

'No, you know it's not.' Her eyes fell away from his, causing him to check himself. He couldn't read her yet, in spite of what had happened, wasn't sure whether this meant she was pulling away. 'All I'm saying,' he said, 'is that if you wake up tomorrow morning and never want to set eyes on me again, then that's OK. I won't feel good about it,' he added, 'but I'll accept it for what it is.'

She scrutinised his face, asked, 'This really is all new for you, isn't it?'

'I would've thought that was pretty evident from what happened before . . .'

The corners of her mouth folded into a half-smile. 'I don't mean that. I mean the whole thing. Now. Us standing here talking. You telling me it's all right if I want to bail out and never speak to you again.'

'I don't want to pressure you. I don't want to risk —'

She took his hand in hers, gently applied pressure. 'Relax,' she told him. 'I've already told you I don't regret what happened.' She leant forward and brushed her lips against his. 'I fucked you sober, James. If we'd been wrecked, then maybe you'd be right to worry. Maybe then I'd tell you that I wasn't up for seeing you again. And that's something else you should know about me,' she added. 'If that was what I thought, I'd tell you. Up front. To your face. There wouldn't be any shit about not being able to look you in the eyes.'

The bell for last orders chimed inside.

'I'd better get going,' she said, letting his hand go.

'So, we'll take it from here, then? Just see how things go?'

'Sure. We'll take it from here.'

'I'll call you.'

She reached out and grabbed his belt, pulled him in close to her again, kissing him.

'You'd better,' she said, and opened the pub door and disappeared inside.

He wasn't tired. Might as well have been back on the coke again for all the hope he had of being able to keep his eyes shut tonight. Too many thoughts pummelling his brain, too many possibilities bursting out of his imagination. He walked slowly along the High Street and up the steep winding road to Eagle's Point. Once there, he walked to the edge of the cliff and leant on the railing, stared out across the shimmering moonlit sea. Calm settled on him. He felt cradled, like nothing could touch him. The world had become new. What had gone before had been cancelled out.

He was at peace with himself.

He set off towards South Beach, wanting a long walk home, never wanting this night to break into dawn.

He reached the foot of the steps which led onto South Beach and across the sand past Surfers' Turf. In the distance, at the far side of the beach, he saw flames, a campfire. Alex. His favourite spot. It could only be him. James surveyed the fire's position, remembered sitting there himself. It was thirty yards along the rocks from the steps which led up to the woods at the top of the cliff. He could pass, a shadow, and they'd be none the wiser. He walked on.

And then the shouting stopped him dead.

CHAPTER SEVENTEEN

one

'You're a fucking prick.' David said. His cheeks were flushed with blood, his eyes pinched with disgust. 'You know that, don't you?'

James walked away from him to the window, looked down. Becky was closing the car boot of David's car, the last of their bags now stowed inside. Through the misted, rain-splashed window, he could see Lucy's silhouette inside, her head and shoulders slumped up against the door. A pang of misery stabbed through him. Ditching her like that. No explanation. Nothing. The two of them coming in from dinner last night. Her climbing into bed. Him climbing in beside her. Then silence. His lying on his side as she stroked his back, asked him what was wrong. The calm. The serenity of the moment, with her whispered words and warm body pressed against him. The peace and unity of it all, before he opened his mouth and told her that it couldn't go on any longer.

'I thought you were happy,' David accused.

'I thought I was, too.'

'So what's happened?' David was at his side now, confusion distorting his face. 'Everything seemed fine last night when we went to bed.' He sat down on the window seat. 'You've got to tell me. Tell me what's going on. If you can't tell her why, then at least tell me.'

James rubbed his face with his hands like he was washing it; like he was washing it all away. But when he lowered them, David was still here, still waiting for an explanation. As with

Lucy, though, James had none he could give.

'It's just over, that's all. You know how it is, same as me. Sometimes there isn't an explanation. Sometimes you just know things aren't right and they're going to stay that way. Sometimes it just happens.'

'That's not good enough.' David lit a cigarette. His hand was shaking. This was bad. It had been the same with Becky. He could understand why. The two of them in love, down here for a romantic break – and here James was, screwing it all up, shitting on someone, same as he'd been shitting on people for years. And David had moved on now. He'd got Becky. He'd thought James had had Lucy. He'd thought they'd move on, the four of them, together. 'I know you, James. Don't fucking forget that. And I know Lucy makes you happy.'

'Made,' James said. 'Lucy *made* me happy. Not any more.'

'She loves you. You know that, don't you?'

'Yes.'

'I mean *loves* you, James. For real.'

'I know.'

'And you don't care,' David said flatly. 'Look at you. You couldn't give a shit.'

'Don't you dare to fucking tell me what I feel.' The pain of the previous night flashed back. It had gone on for hours. It was the hardest thing he'd ever had to do. Hurting people. He wasn't good at it. All he ended up doing was hurting himself. But Lucy hadn't deserved that. She'd deserved better. Better than him. Better than being with someone who'd wanted to be with someone else. So *over*. He'd finished it, because he'd known last night, as he still knew now, that to continue would have been so much worse.

But David wasn't being fobbed off. 'Well, something's changed. What is it?' His eyes flared and he asked acidly, 'You meet someone in L.A.? That it? You meet some chick and have a two week fling and reckon that's worth chucking what you've got going with Lucy over?'

'No.' James felt sick. No, it wasn't even a two week fling that had driven him to this. Just a kiss. A kiss and a memory from childhood. Nothing more.

David grimaced, muttering begrudgingly, 'Well, that's something, I suppose.'

'Thanks for taking her back,' James said. 'I know it's cocked things up for you and Becky, having to go home, but thanks . . .'

David doused his cigarette in the ashtray, stood up and shook James's hand. 'Call me when you get back,' he said before going to the door. 'Call me when you feel ready to tell me what the hell's going on.'

James turned to the window and listened to the bedroom door closing behind David. He stayed there, staring, as David got into the car without looking up. So this was it. He was committing. He was making his choice. Now. He could run after them now. He could open the window and shout and what he'd had with Lucy might be his again. But his hands stayed by his side and, as he watched the car pull away from the pavement and disappear up the street, he felt relief. For the first time in his life, he'd shown some courage. He'd made a decision, taken a risk. He thought back to what Suzie had said during their brief encounter in the graveyard yesterday. About the fact that nothing might happen. About hardly even knowing each other any more. He'd see her later today. He just prayed that the moment he did, he'd know that he'd been right and she'd been wrong.

But the time for that wasn't here yet. Still things left to do. He walked away from the window, over to his desk, stared down at his computer. Lucy was gone from his life. And he was determined that soon all the bad baggage from that summer would be gone, as well. It had to be so, if things were going to work out with Suzie. A clean slate. Something on which they could draw. Something on which they could carve out a life together.

If that was what she wanted, too.

He took his jacket, checked his car keys were in his pocket and left the room. As he drove from Grancombe to Alan's house, Alex kicked his way back into his mind. Loathing – that was all James felt. He wondered if it was clouding his judgement, convincing him that Alex had been responsible for Dan's death, as well as Trader's.

But it was a loathing he couldn't shake. It had been with him too long. It had thrown up too many issues of guilt. Like Oldfield. What, he'd wondered down the years, if Oldfield had been guilty of killing Jack Dawes? What if the only reason the police had stopped looking for more evidence to convict him was because of Trader's death?

In sporadic, cold-sweated awakenings down the years, he'd continued to stress over whether he'd been responsible for letting a murderer stay free and perhaps kill again. Until he'd got the job at *Kudos*, that is. *Kudos* with its state-of-the-art research facilities. *Kudos* with its database.

He'd resisted accessing it at first – typing in the word *Grancombe* and seeing what would be dragged up. But it hadn't lasted. One drunken, depressed evening, he'd returned late to the office, booted the system up and run the search. All the articles had been there, all the old names. And Oldfield's had been last of all, a postscript to a story James had hoped had ended. He'd died, cremated in his own house, away from Grancombe, in some seaside town in Norfolk, where no one would have known his name. He'd moved there after Murphy had released him due to lack of evidence. A faulty gas pipe had been to blame. If it hadn't been for the memory of the local journalist who'd penned the piece, Oldfield's connection with Grancombe would have slipped the attention of the world.

The news of Oldfield's death had brought with it relief. If he *had* been the killer, then at least he could kill no more. So, as with Trader, James had tried to forget. But he'd failed, and now he realised that there was to be no forgetting. Only resolution. That was the only way he'd ever be free.

He thought it through. Of the suspects – or, rather, the lack of them – Alex was the prime. Neither Tawnside nor Oldfield could have killed Dan, because both of them had already been dead. And, as James knew only too well, neither of them had killed Trader. That left Dawes. Tawnside had motive, sure. Dawes sleeping with his wife. Infidelity. One of the oldest motives in the book. And Oldfield had had a motive, too:

money. But these weren't the motives of a serial killer. *One-offs*. And, working on that logic, his theory of there being two killers made even more sense. Tawnside or Oldfield – or some unknown third party – had killed Dawes. Alex had killed Trader and copycatted Dawes' murder. And – hey presto – a serial killer had been born. Doing the same with Dan, once he'd become a nuisance, would have been child's play. For someone like Alex, anyway.

Whatever, there was still no proof. And, even he had it, there was nowhere to take it. Not without implicating himself in Trader's death. Not without being found guilty, too. Not without Dan there to take his side in the dock. And then there was Murphy, perhaps lurking in the shadows, watching. Wouldn't he have loved this, watching James twist the blame in on the person who'd once been his best friend?

James checked the yard in front of the barn when he reached the top of Alan's drive: nothing. He parked in front of the house and walked back down. A shining new chain and padlock held the barn door secure. So the dope was still in there. That fucker was still messing with his life. *Nothing you can do about it*, James told himself. So concentrate on the matter at hand. Into the house. Into the basement. Clear out whatever's in there, just like you've done with the rest of Alan's possessions. *Then Alex can use this place for what he wants. You've washed your hands of it. And then you're free. To go and find Suzie. To convince her to leave this place and Alex far behind. To get on with the rest of your life.*

The door of the shed at the back of the house splintered the first time James put the boot in, its rusted lock snapping its screws and falling into the deep, wet grass. He fumbled around in the gloom inside, searching through the damp garden tools. Then he stepped outside into the drizzle. He held the crowbar up and examined it, even managed a smile. And why not? It had been the first bit of luck he'd had in weeks.

Inside, getting the basement door open was tougher than he'd expected. For a start, it wasn't simply a matter of wedging the crowbar into the door-frame next to the lock and hefting the metal free, like in some TV crook drama. Ten minutes of

brute strength and strained grunting got him nowhere. A closer
inspection of the door-frame where the wood had splintered
showed why: the inside frame was metal. A quick visit to the
garden shed and back, and he was hammering at the end of
the crowbar with a mallet, driving it in at an acute angle to the
lock itself. Then – *crack* – the end of the crowbar sheared
through the bolt.

Wiping the slime of sweat from his brow, he tried the
handle: it turned three-quarters round, rattling, the lock
mechanism mangled. One last effort. He twisted it violently,
slammed his shoulder up against the door. The metal shrieked
and he stepped back, threw himself into the side of the door
again. This time, it went. Or rather, he did. Through the open
door and down the stairs, leading with the side of his face and
his forearm, bouncing down the slippery stone steps until he
came to a halt, his body crooked, wedged against the dusty
brickwork.

Looking up the stairs, through the swarm of dust, to the
light in the corridor at the top was like staring out of a dry
well, trapped. With the darkness wrapped round him, claustro-
phobia sent his muscles tightening. The air was cold and wet.
His breathing came heavy, but he refused to panic, scramble
wildly away from the site of his fall. Instead, he gently shifted
his limbs, rolled his neck, waiting for the lance of pain that
would signal a breakage. None came and, aside from an ache
in his rib cage, he decided that whatever damage had occurred
was limited to bruising. He got to his feet and brushed the
dust from his clothes.

He looked around: the light wore thin after a couple of feet
to his left, then all was darkness, as thick and uninviting as
brackish water. He climbed the stairs and found a light switch
by what was left of the door. Looking down, he flicked the
switch and saw dim light spread across the cobbled floor
beneath. It flickered like candlelight. He picked the crowbar
up and walked back down.

Rounding the corner where he'd fallen, he ground to a halt.
There was a door and, for a moment, depression swamped
him, as he thought he was going to have to use the crowbar

yet again. It wasn't necessary, though. The door, though on heavy hinges, swung open, allowing him through to another room, again lit by a flickering bulb. He halted again. The room was vast, the size of half a tennis court. But that wasn't what was responsible for his immobility. It was what stood at the end of the room, against the wall. There, beneath a drape of cobwebs, was a desk. On it were papers, stacked high. It made no sense, Alan working down here, away from the light, locking himself up like a prisoner. James started forward. But that would explain the blank drive of the computer, the absence of work in the papers from upstairs. Alan like some vampire. Working down here. Night after night. His work. Whatever he'd been working on all those years would be here. And maybe – there was a chance – an explanation for why Alan had finally chosen to take his own life.

As he drew close to the desk, his eyes grew accustomed to the strobe effect of the bare light bulb above the desk. Other details stood out – faded newspaper clippings stuck to the brickwork, an unfinished bottle of whisky, a crystal tumbler, a pair of old gardening gloves pegged to a clothes line on the wall, a clutter of dictionaries and reference books amongst the handwritten papers, empty food tins on the floor. There were boxes beneath the desk, crammed full of more papers.

James pulled the wooden chair back and sat down, brushing aside the dust and cobwebs, and picked a piece of paper up at random. Words jumped out at him as the light flickered. They made no sense. Gibberish. Streams of profanities, a madman's mutterings. He tried another piece of paper, and another. But they were all the same. Hate letters. Written to whom? To God? To the wrathful God who'd destroyed Alan's life by taking the woman he loved from him?

James rubbed his eyes, the light and dust and crazy handwriting making them sting. He looked around. Something was propped up against the wall to his right, covered by a sheet, grey and filthy with muck and damp. He reached down, pulled the cloth off. Underneath was a painting. He got to his knees and peered closer. But it was no good. The air down here had done for it. Just a brown surface, like an out-of-focus photograph, and what looked like a human figure. He pulled the frame forward, placed it on the floor. Behind was another frame, this time wrapped tight in a blanket, and behind that another. He gently tugged the first free, undid it. This was better. He could make out the body of a woman, the pose erotic, her legs spread wide, her head tossed back. There was something familiar about her, something he . . .

Oh, Christ.

He let the painting clatter to the floor, jerked the one behind from against the wall. The pulse in his ear beat heavily as he unwrapped the blanketing. Another nude. The same model. Only this time the painting wasn't only of the woman, but the artist. The two of them together, limbs wrapped around one another, an expression of ecstasy clear on each of their faces. And he knew the faces. Hers as well as his.

Alan's wife, Monique.

Jack Dawes, Alan's best friend.

Together.

His guts shuddered and he felt the sweat pouring again from his brow into his eyes. The conversation he'd had with Suzie's father about the painting Oldfield claimed he'd found in the woods came back. The nude woman. The erotic pose. Her face hidden by her hair. Found in the woods between Dawes' home and Alan's. The explanation the police had dismissed, attempting to pin Oldfield for a thief instead. Not believing he'd just stumbled across one of Dawes' paintings out there amongst the trees. Because paintings weren't dropped in woods for other people to find. Because it was ridiculous. Because no one would have done that unless they'd been panicked. Unless they'd been panicked and running through the dark with other paintings and hadn't realised that one had slipped until it was too late to return for it.

James scrabbled to his feet and lunged across the desk, pressing his face up close to the newspaper cuttings. Front page articles. Local and national press. Their pictures were inscrutable. The same went for the small print. But the headlines read true. The death of Jack Dawes. Ritualistic killing. Psychopath strikes. Then Trader. He'd made his way to this gallery, too.

James slumped into the chair. *No. Not Alan.* It could just be research. He grabbed the whisky bottle, twisted the rusted top free and gulped heavily and quickly. Maybe Alan had been planning to write a book about the killings. That's what the articles were for: to keep him focused. Just because they were there didn't mean he'd killed Dawes. But the paintings . . . Monique and Dawes . . . So what? So she used to model for him before she'd died. Big deal. They'd been friends. Alan might not have minded her modelling nude. He'd trusted Dawes. Despite his reputation in the town with other men's wives. He would have trusted Dawes with the woman he held more precious than anything else in his life. He looked down at the painting of Dawes and Monique together. But that? Would he have known about that? He drank again, this time retching, regurgitating the liquid over his lap.

He let the bottle crash to the floor. All circumstantial. Nothing more. Two plus two makes five. He'd been down here too long with this maddening light casting trickery on his mind. He stood. Get out. Just get out. His eyes ran over the desk as he stumbled back. Shouldn't have come down here. Just rantings. He looked at the painting, then started to turn. Mad Alan. Ranting down here in the dark. Doesn't mean anything. Then he saw the gloves on the wall again. Up close this time. In detail. It was like seeing them for the first time. Thin fingers. Collapsed palms.

Not gloves.

Hands.

The hands of an artist.

The hands that had painted and held Monique.

He stumbled back through the swing door to the foot of the stairs. And he breathed. He breathed deep and he thought. In spite of the gloom down here, everything was clear. The sequence of Alan at Dawes' funeral played through his mind. He saw once more Alan's gesture of throwing the keys on top of his friend's grave. The symbol of their trust. And he saw the

anger in Alan's eyes. Only it wasn't anger any more. It was
triumph. And the keys weren't a symbol of trust, but revenge.
And then the view of his mind's eye switched to Alan's own
grave, and zoomed in on the incongruous words his atheist
uncle had chosen after he'd made his decision to die:

Set me as a seal upon thine heart, as a seal upon thine
arm: for love is strong as death; jealously is cruel as the
grave.

And now he was certain. Not circumstantial. The truth. Alan's
confession and suicide note rolled into one, there in black
and white for the whole world to see. Just like the keys at
the funeral, the keys that would have given Alan access to
Dawes' home whenever he wished, to instigate whatever grim
sequence of events he chose and remove whatever evidence,
too.

It was easy to speculate on what might have happened, to
conjure up a chain of events that would fit the blueprint of
evidence to be found in this room. After Monique's death,
Alan would have sought solace with his closest friend,
Jack Dawes. They would have spent time together, drunken
evenings mourning her loss.

And on one of these nights, half a year after Monique's
death, perhaps with Dawes asleep on the sofa, Alan would
have gone wandering through to Dawes' studio, maudlin,
knowing that Monique had modelled for their friend, seeking
a glimpse of the dead woman he still loved. And then he
would have found the paintings. His love, naked and in
another man's arms. Words sprang back at James: Alan's
words as they'd descended the steps onto South Beach the
morning of the search, 'Some things you don't want to know.
Some things it's best you never find out.' Had he been talking
about this?

And next, after Alan had discovered Dawes' secret . . .
what then? Rage? No. There'd been no sign of a struggle.
Calculated, then. Premeditated. Cold revenge. Alan asking
Dawes over to his house, knowing the path he'd take, waiting

there in the darkness of the woods, an axe in his hand and only the whispering of the trees to repeat the tale of what would happen there. Then back to Dawes' house and all its intact domesticity: the smell of simmering stew drifting from the stove; Zack, Dawes' dog, waiting for his master's return. James visualised Zack greeting his master's friend, wagging his tail and following Alan to the studio, watching him remove the evidence of Monique's affair, carry his motive away with him and close the door behind him.

James held a cigarette to his mouth and lit it. Yes, it was easy enough to speculate, but the order of events hardly mattered. Just the players. Just Alan and Dawes. Alone in the woods. The hands on the wall next door told him that as sure as if they were spelling it out for him in sign language. One Killer. One victim. Not Oldfield. Not Tawnside. Not Murphy. The picture – though he was reluctant to even think of the metaphor after what he'd uncovered just now – was almost complete. Alan killed Dawes. Alex killed Trader. Two killers. And only one of them was alive when Dan had been murdered.

Only one.

'Alex,' he said aloud and, in that instant, he was certain. Forget Murphy. Murphy was just another face of fear; another demon from his past he'd failed to outrun – another ghost; nothing more. Alex was the only logical choice. His cigarette fell from between his fingers to the ground. And it was only then that he noticed the light on the bottom of the stairs darkening as a shadow stretched towards him, elongated, and fell across him like a shroud.

'So sorry to disturb you.'

'Alex,' he said again, this time in recognition, as he looked up the steps to see Alex leaning against the broken door frame. He was wearing a t-shirt and unbuttoned shirt, jeans and boots. A cigarette was gripped in one hand, a gym bag in the other.

Alex snorted in derision. 'Look at the fucking state of you.'

And that was all it took. James snapped, a fusewire through which too much current had been fed. He was on his feet and charging up the stairs. Dan's death. Trader's death. All the misery he'd suffered the last ten years channelled into his fists. Gonna get. Gonna get him. 'You fucker,' he bellowed as he covered the last few stairs. 'You killed Dan, you murdering piece of shit.'

And then he stopped still, the muzzle of the pistol Alex held only inches from his face.

'Get your stupid fucking arse back down there.' Alex slammed the bag into James's shoulder, sending him spinning back down the stairs, landing in a battered heap at the bottom.

'Keep moving,' Alex instructed, walking down after him, the gun held straight in front of him.

James raised his hands, backing through the basement and through the swing door, until he reached the desk. He waited, tensed up, a cornered animal. This was bad. Way bad. One route out, Alex blocking it as he checked out the room and swung the partition door closed behind him.

'Always thought your uncle was a bit fucked in the head,' Alex commented, apparently seeing the room as James had at first, not understanding what this place signified. Then he smiled, saying, 'Oh, and thanks, by the way.'

'For what?' James grunted.

'For confirming what I already knew.'

'I don't—'

Alex dropped his bag on the floor, held his hand up to silence James. 'I had a chat with T after your visit. Well,' he reflected, 'I call it a chat, but T would probably call it a beating. Whatever, she let on she'd been stupid enough to tell you about me and Dan having a run-in that night. And what with you being a journalist, and probably giving a shit about Dan's death and all that, I kind of figured out that you might put one and one together and make me.'

'You killed him,' James spat. 'You killed Dan.'

Alex, under the flickering bulb, showed no emotion. 'Correct. Second question: can you possibly guess why?'

'Because he wanted money. Because he said he'd go to the cops about Trader's murder if you didn't pay up. Because he knew I'd back his story up about you doing the killing.'

'Correct again. I never trusted you after that night. Never really trusted Dan either.' He ran his tongue across his lips. 'Should have killed you both a long time ago. Best way to handle pests,' he went on. 'Like rats. Like lice. Like Murphy.'

'Murphy?' The word came out without intonation, like a computer's.

'Oh, yeah. But surely you're not going to begrudge me that one. Not much of a fan yourself, way I remember it.'

'Where?'

'Well, would've been best to do another copycat, I suppose, but there were too many bullets in his fat gut for that.' A note of pride crept into his voice. 'So I took a leaf out of his book. Weighed him down and dumped him like the piece of shit he was into one of the flooded slate mines. Just like Hayworth. Left him to fucking rot.' James opened his mouth, but Alex, as always, seemed one step ahead. 'Made the mistake of getting him on board for shipping the gear in. Stuff in your barn, yeah? Been doing it for years. You should've hung around,' he reflected. 'Might've made some real money. But he got greedy. I pay him to turn a blind eye, do fuck all for his money and he gets greedy on me. Pig through and through, that one. So I had to stop it.' His expression flattened into determination. 'Same as I always do.'

'Listen,' James said, looking around, seeing how hopeless the situation was, spotting the crowbar a foot or so away from him, 'you don't need to do this. I'm not going to say shit. Same as with the dope in the barn. You've already got me. That thing with Trader. Like you said, it was as much me as you. Your word against mine.'

'Uh-huh,' Alex grunted, and from the look on his face James knew this verdict was final, 'but I'm fed up with equality. Look where it got me with Dan. Nah, the sooner you're over the better. Peace of mind, yeah? Like I say, should've done it years ago.'

'And that's it?' James asked. 'You're just going to shoot me?'

Alex laughed, reached down and unzipped the bag. 'Course not, mate. Got to do these things by the book, haven't you?' He pulled out an axe and weighed it in his hand. 'Can't go breaking tradition – yeah? – depriving the press of their copy, letting the police wise up. Wouldn't make sense.' He placed the pistol on the floor, stood back up and kicked it behind him with a flick of his heel. Then he grinned. 'Bet you've never seen a chopper this big, eh, mate?' he asked, holding the axe handle with both hands now, swinging it in slow arcs before him. 'But I'll tell you what: seeing as how we used to be such great pals, I'll make it quick.' He started forward, the axe suddenly above his head. 'Chop-chop, as they used to say . . .'

It was then that James made his move. He slid sideways and, in one fluid move, grabbed the crowbar and sent it spinning through the air. He saw Alex duck, but it wasn't Alex he was aiming for. What he was aiming for, though, he hit. The bulb smashed and the room went black. As Alex swore, James moved silently sideways up against the opposite wall. And then he held his breath, waited, listened to the sound of Alex's own breathing coming strong, coming close.

'You think you're going anywhere?' Alex was shouting. 'You stupid prick,' he continued to mock. 'You stopped doing that the moment you stopped hanging out with me.'

James stretched his arms wide. Rugby field again. He counted Alex's breaths, the swish-swish of the axe slicing through the air, calming himself with their rhythm. Alex was here. Next to him. Now's the time. The tackle of your fucking life. And he acted. He launched himself across the room, keeping low, beneath the blade of the axe.

And contact.

He caught Alex at the waist, kept on running, ploughed him into the opposite wall. Behind him, he heard the axe clash to the ground, and there was no longer darkness.

Only red.

Only the colour of rage.

There were no words in the struggle that followed, none that James heard, anyway. Just the hissing of their breath as he worked his way up Alex's body and pinned him to the floor. And then there was just the sound of his fist smacking against Alex's face, the sound of Alex's skull being repeatedly smashed against the cold stone floor.

And then he realised he was breathing alone.

It was five days later. James was sitting in the garden at the back of Alan's house on an old wicker chair, reading the final part of his article on his laptop:

And the inhabitants of Grancombe had been right to think that the slaughter would continue. This morning, at twelve-fifteen, two days after his BMW was sighted in a nearby car park – and only hours after a warrant had been issued for his arrest in connection with the discovery of a huge drugs cache whose whereabouts was revealed by an anonymous source – the body of Alex Howley was found barely yards from where Jack Dawes was discovered a decade ago. As with Dawes and the victims that have come between, the signature of the killer was the same: a mutilated corpse, with the hands brutally severed by the blows of an axe. And, as with the other victims, the hands have yet to be found.

James closed the laptop, leant forward, and stabbed the poker into the glowing embers of the fire and the charred, hand-written sheets of paper, watching the wind catch the sparks and carry them towards the woods. He stabbed again, pushing what looked like a gardening glove deep into the heart of the fire.

He checked his watch, but there was no need. Plenty of time before he'd have to leave to pick Suzie up. They were going to drive down the coast to a new restaurant for dinner. It was going to be good. Like Grancombe itself, it sounded like it had potential. Sitting back in his chair, relaxing again, he surveyed the land before him: his land. Who could tell? Maybe it was worth giving this place a go after all.

EMLYN REES

The Book of Dead Authors

When acclaimed author Adam Appleton opens the door of his charming Hampstead home to an alluring stranger, he has no idea that he is turning the page on the last short and horribly violent chapter of his life. However, it is merely the exhilarating opening scene in a long and grisly narrative of revenge as one by one famous writers come to sticky and wickedly appropriate ends.

Soon a nation is holding its breath, waiting for the murderer's next bloody instalment, while terrified authors cower in their Soho clubs, hoping against hope that they are not about to feature in this appallingly gripping serial. But the creator of this most unusual murder mystery is no mere hack, and when the final climax comes, it comes with one last terrifying heart-stopping twist . . .

'A wonderfully black piece of gratuitous sex and violence, well plotted . . . in splendidly bad taste'
Evening Standard

'Sex and violence on every page . . . brilliant'
Mail on Sunday

0 7472 5721 3

review

BEN RICHARDS

Don't Step On The Lines

In a flat high above London Kerry can't stop remembering Gary. Marco awaits the pleasures and
temptations of summer in the city...

Kerry, finally taking control of her life, has returned
to college to study English. Marco, friend and flat-
mate, deeply obsessed with sharks, roams the bars
and clubs of London. Drifting in and out of various
jobs, relationships and drugs, he watches Kerry's
progress with a mixture of love and envy.

Then Robin appears. For Kerry, Robin – rich, good-
looking, a fellow student – represents new opportunities and possibilities. For Marco, however, he is
nothing but trouble.

'Scenes of London life sparkle within the narrative...
It's all wonderfully recognisable and realistic, told
with a laddish exuberance at once hilarious and
touching' *Literary Review*

'Kerry is a proper nineties heroine: bright, lovely,
struggling to define her life' *Mail on Sunday*

'Refreshingly unpretentious and very entertaining'
The Times

'The London he sees is vivid and impressive' *TLS*

'A terrific book' *Time Out*

0 7472 5280 7

review